the Flower Power Collection

HarperCollins *Children's Books*

Shrinking Violet first published in Great Britain by Collins in 2002
Passion Flower first published in Great Britain by Collins in 2003
Pumpkin Pie first published in Great Britain by Collins in 2002

First published in this three-in-one edition by HarperCollins *Children's Books* 2006
HarperCollins Children's Books is a division of HarperCollins*Publishers* Ltd,
77-85 Fulham Palace Road, Hammersmith, London W6 8JB

The HarperCollins *Children's Books* website address is
www.harpercollinschildrensbooks.co.uk

1

Text © Jean Ure 2002, 2003, 2002
Illustrations © Karen Donnelly 2002, 2003, 2002

The author and illustrator assert the moral right to be
identified as the author and illustrator of this work.

ISBN-13   978 0 00 720155 6
ISBN-10   0 00 720155 9

Printed and bound in England by
Clays Ltd, St Ives plc

Shrinking Violet

JEAN URE

Illustrated by Karen Donnelly

For my niece, Anna Ure,
and for Susanna Buxton,
who both helped.

I am a twin. Unfortunately! It is not always easy, being a twin. People expect you to:

> look alike
> think alike
> dress alike
> talk alike.

They also expect you to:

> sit together
> walk together
> play together
> and
> LOVE EACH OTHER TO BITS.

Some twins, I suppose, might do all these things. We don't! We try our hardest not to.

My twin is called Lily. I am called Violet.

This is Lily   This is me

Spot the difference! We are *not identical*. If anyone thinks we are, it is because they have not looked properly. "Oh! (they go) They are like two peas in a pod! How ever do you tell them apart?"

LOOK AT THE PICTURES. That is what I say.

Lily says you would have to be blind to mistake her for me. But just to make sure, we always try to wear different clothes. When we can! Like, for instance, Lily will wear black jeans and I will wear red ones. She will wear an orange top and I will wear a white one. We can't do this at school because of the uniform, but most people at school have learnt to tell us apart. They know that Lily is the **LOUD** one and I am the quiet one. It's only, sometimes, new teachers that get us in a muddle. But not for long. If one of us is shrieking, they know at once that it is Lily!

Dad calls her Lily Loudmouth because of all the noise she makes. He claps his hands to his ears and goes, "Here comes Lily Loudmouth!" She loves to dance, and sing along to her favourite music. I do, too, but I only do it when I am at home. Lily does it all over. At home, at school, in the street, in the shopping mall... everywhere! I would be too embarrassed.

Dad teases me and says I am a shrinking violet. Mum says I live too much in Lily's shadow. Lily just says I am a twonk.

Twinkle twonkle, little Vi,
How I really wonder why
Lily's brash and you are shy!

This is a rhyme that I made up, but it is in my Secret Filofax that I keep locked with a key. The key hangs round my neck on a special silver chain. I wouldn't want anyone reading the things that I keep in my Filofax! Also, I *hate* it if people call me Vi. I only did it for the rhyme. Violet is bad enough, but Vi is the pits.

The reason we've got these weird names is that Mum is a huge gardening person and her two most favourite flowers just happen to be the *dear* little shrinking violet and a great big blustering lily thing that is covered in spots and grows about eight feet tall.

How *she* got to be Lily and I got to be Violet was just a mistake. I was supposed to be  Lily! I was born first (by five whole minutes) and L comes before V in the alphabet so Lily was going to be *me*. But what with us being twins, and all babies looking the same anyway, Mum went and got us mixed up. Our nan – Big Nan – had knitted this cute little violet suit for one of us and a sweet little white one for the other, and Mum dressed us in the wrong ones! The only way that she could tell which of us was which when we were first born was by this brown birthmark thingie, in other words *spot*, that Lily has on her bottom, if you will excuse the expression. It is just as well we have now grown up to look so different because who would

8

want to keep gazing at Lily's, pardon me, *bottom* all the time? Ugh! Yuck! What a sight!

On the day of the christening, Mum says she was in such a flap, "I couldn't remember which of you had the spot on her bot!"

Then she laughs like she thinks it's really funny. Imagine! A mum not being able to tell her own babies apart! But I was the one that had to suffer. I mean…*Violet*. It's a granny name. Well past its sell-by date. Lily, I think, is quite cool, though Lily herself disagrees.

"Lily! *Yuck*. It's like skimmed milk… all white and flabby."

Dad once said that we should count our blessings. He said just think how much worse it could have been.

"Imagine if your mum's favourite flowers were nasturtium or geranium!"

Except that then I could have been Geranium, shortened to Gerry, which would be neat, and *she* could have been Nasturtium, shortened to Nasty. Which would suit her!

She's all right really, I suppose. Sometimes she can be quite nice, like when our cat Horatio went missing and I thought we'd never see him again and I cried and cried and couldn't stop. She put her arms round me and said, "Don't cry, Violet! He'll come back." Of course we were only little, then. It's as we've got older that she's got horrid. Mum says ten is a bad age. She says, "When I was young you didn't start throwing tantrums till you were twelve or thirteen. Now it's happening when you're *ten*."

She said it the other day when Lily went into a simply tremendous sulk about not being allowed to go to a party wearing a skirt that didn't even cover her knickers. Mum and Lily are always having battles over stuff that Lily wants to wear and that Mum doesn't think is suitable. The reason I don't have battles isn't that I'm a goody goody, which is what Lily says, it is just that I would be too shy. Like with singing and dancing in Tesco's! She swung upside down on a handrail the other day, in full view of absolutely everyone. I just nearly died! But Lily is a natural show off. She will probably be a movie star when she is older.

Well, anyway, that is about me and Lily. Now a bit about Horatio, that is our cat. Horatio is what Mum calls "a grand old gentleman". He is two years older than Lily and me! Black, with a white bib.

Horatio is a *good* cat. He is a kind cat. Once when I was ill in bed he came and snuggled under the duvet with me and stayed there till I was better. I thought that was so sweet of him! Dad laughs and says, "Don't kid yourself! He just knows when he's on to a good thing." But that isn't true! He didn't go and cuddle with Lily when she was ill. Just with me because he knows how much I love him.

So. That is Horatio. Now Mum and Dad. Dad is a computer person. I am not quite sure what he does exactly, but he goes into his office every day and does it and it seems to make him

happy. Mum is a flower person. She has this flower shop called Flora Green, with a dear little green

van with flowers painted on it. Really cute! Sometimes, if Dad is in a rush, she takes me and Lily to school in it. Lily grumbles that it is seriously uncool, being taken to school in a van, but this is because her best friends that she hangs out with, Sarah in a Whittington and Francine Church, are really posh and would think a van beneath them. I don't care about such things as I don't have any posh friends and so it doesn't bother me. I like Mum's flowery van!

Lily has lots of friends. Sarah and Francine are her best ones, but there is also Ayesha and Haroula and Debbie and Jessica. Lily is tremendously popular.

On account of being silly and shrinking, I am not very good at making friends. I get nervous and blurt out the first thing that comes into my head, which is not always the best thing. Like one day when Ayesha said to me that she was going to go on a diet and lose weight.

"But I'm going to do it sensibly," she said. "Just a bit at a time. I don't want to lose too much all at once."

You will never believe what I said! I said, "No, 'cos that would look silly with a great fat face."

I didn't mean to be rude, or to upset her. It just, like, burst out of me before I could stop it. I couldn't understand why she went off in a huff and wouldn't speak to me, not even when we were put as partners for gym. It was Lily who told me.

"You said she had a great fat face!"

"I didn't!" I said.

"You did, too," said Lily. "You said if she lost too much weight it would look silly with a great fat face!"

"Oh, dear," said Mum.

I was so ashamed! I am always doing this kind of thing. Another thing I do, I drop stuff and smash stuff. Like I dropped Haroula's genuine Victorian glass bubble with a snowstorm inside it that she'd inherited from her great grandmother. It was a family heirloom and I went and dropped it! Fortunately it didn't break, it just rolled over the floor, but a huge *groan* went up, like everyone was thinking, "Trust her!"

Like another time when we'd been told to clear the stuff off our dinner plates into one bin and chuck plastic pots, etc., into another, and I got confused and put it all in the same bin and Lily said, "You would, wouldn't you?"

This is the sort of person I am, and that is why I am not very good at making friends. When I do, it is mostly just one at a time; not hordes, like Lily.

I used to be best friends with a girl called Greta. We did everything together and I really missed her when she went back to America with her mum and dad. We wrote to each other for a while. I quite enjoyed writing letters, but after a bit it sort of faded out. Like I would write a really *long* letter, and Greta would just send back a postcard, and then I would write again and for weeks and weeks she wouldn't bother and then it would be just another card, or maybe an e-mail. *Hi! How R U? NY is fab! Will write soon. Luv & xxx Greta.*

In the end we stopped altogether. I suppose we didn't really have all that much in common is what it came down to. It was all right while we could do things together, but Greta wasn't really a word person. Lots of people aren't. Dad isn't. Lily isn't. Mum isn't. I am the only one in the family!

Anyway, all that was in Year 5. Now we'd moved up to Year 6 and I was sort of going round with this girl called Pandora who is very good-natured and

pretty but quite honestly not the brightest. I am not being horrible here, I am just telling it like it is. She is one of those people, she is so sweet and innocent she would trust just about anybody. Like she would take sweets from strangers and go jumping into cars unless there was someone to watch over her. So I was kind of watching over her because I mean someone had to and I didn't have anyone else. To be friends with, I mean.

Well, apart from this girl called Yvonne that I sometimes hung out with, but she is quite bad-tempered and also bossy, and in spite of being shrinking I don't like people bossing me and pushing me around. Plus sometimes she makes Pandora cry

by saying these really mean things to her, so I only hung with Yvonne on days when Pandora wasn't there or when I was feeling strong enough to stand up to her. We certainly didn't see each other out of school.

I didn't really see anyone out of school. Me and Greta used to meet up sometimes, but now I just did things on my own. Usually on a Saturday I'd go and help Mum in Flora Green. I enjoyed watering all the plants out in the yard, and arranging the cut flowers in their buckets. I didn't even mind stacking flower pots or sweeping the floor. Lily wouldn't be seen dead in there! She would be scared her posh friends might catch sight of her. But most often she was out doing things with them, anyway. They rode their ponies in the park, or went ice skating or slept over at each other's houses. Lily has this really *full* social calendar. Her life is a whirl!

Sometimes I used to wish that my life could be like Lily's. I used to wish it *so much*. Dad always said that I was his little stay-at-home while Lily was Miss Gad About. I always pretended that I thought it was funny and that I didn't mind. I even pretended it to myself.

It is *silly*, pretending things to yourself.

One day near the start of the spring term Lily came home all excited because Sarah's mum, who is something important to do with TV, had said that Sarah could invite some of her friends to visit the set of *Riverside*.

"She said we could go next Saturday, so is that all right, Mum? It is all right, isn't it? Sarah's mum will take us there and bring us back, so can I say I'll go?"

"I don't see why not," said Mum. "Who else is going?"

"Just me and Sarah, and Francie and Hara. Debbie was going to, but she can't."

"So what about Violet?" said Mum.

There was a pause. I felt my cheeks go tingly. I did wish Mum wouldn't!

"She didn't invite Violet," said Lily. "Just me. 'Cos I'm Sarah's friend."

"I wouldn't want to, anyway," I said.

Well, I wouldn't! Not with Lily and her crowd. They're all loud and shrieking, just like Lily. And they don't really like me, they think I'm freaky.

"Wouldn't want to?" said Mum. "But you're such a fan! Even more than Lily is!"

"But she hasn't been *invited*," said Lily. "Not just anyone can go. You have to be *asked*."

"Well, I'm sure Sarah would ask her if she knew what a fan she was. After all, she is your twin!"

Lily set her jaw in that way that she does, like it's made out of cement, or something. I felt myself shrivel. Mum does this to me, sometimes.

She tries to push me in where I'm not wanted. It gets Lily so mad! And it gets me all hot and embarrassed.

"Mum, it's all right," I said. "I've got to help you in the shop."

"You haven't *got* to help me in the shop," said Mum. "I'm very grateful when you do, but it seems a shame to miss out on other things. A visit to *Riverside*! And if Debbie can't go—"

"That isn't any reason for *her* to come."

Mum said, "Lily!"

"Well, it isn't," muttered Lilly. "People don't have to invite her just 'cos they've invited me. Just 'cos we came out the same *egg* doesn't mean we have to do everything together all the time!"

"You don't do anything together any of the time," said Mum. "I just thought, this once—"

"But I don't want to go!" I snatched up Horatio and buried my face in his fur. "Mm… yum yum," I mumbled, nibbling at him with my lips.

"Stinking swizzlesticks, you're disgusting!" said Lily.

She could talk! I've seen her doing things that are far more disgusting than chumbling in Horatio's fur. I've seen her chewing her *toenails*. That is gross!

Later that day I heard Mum and Dad discussing me. They were in the kitchen and didn't know I was there. Well, I wasn't actually *there*, exactly. I mean, I wasn't sitting in a cupboard or anything. What it was, I was outside the door, about to go in, when I heard Mum say "too much in Lily's shadow" and I immediately froze.

I heard Mum say about Lily going off with her friends, and me not going anywhere. Then Dad said, "She's my little shrinking violet," and Mum said, "But she *ought* to have friends!" And then a tap started running, and the sound got blotted out, and next thing I heard was Dad saying something about chat rooms.

"That way, she could meet someone with her own interests… that's what she needs! Someone to share her interests with."

"Not in a chat room," said Mum.

Dad said, "Oh, come on! We'd monitor her."

"*No*," said Mum. "No way!"

She'd read this horror story just a few days ago about a young girl being picked up (in a chat room) by this middle-aged man pretending to be a fifteen-year-old boy. Lily had said boastfully that that could never happen to *her*. She'd soon suss him out! But Mum was now convinced that all chat rooms were full of middle-aged men in mackintoshes (I don't know why she thought they were in mackintoshes), all looking for young girls and pretending to be fifteen years old. She had forbidden Lily to go anywhere near one.

She said to Dad, "If I'm not letting Lily visit one, I'm certainly not letting Violet!"

I wondered if this meant that Mum cared more about me than she did about Lily, or whether it simply meant she thought that I was more stupid than Lily and more likely to be deceived by the men in mackintoshes.

Probably she thought that I was more stupid, although in fact it is Lily who talks to strangers, not me. Lily talks to people everywhere she goes. In the supermarket, in buses, on trains. She just strikes up these conversations. I would be too shy! I was really relieved when Mum stood up to Dad and said *no way*. I didn't want to visit any chat rooms! It would be too much like actually meeting people; I would get tongue-tied and not know what to say.

But then Mum had an even worse idea. Worse even than Dad's!

"Maybe we could find some sort of club."

I thought, No! Please! We'd already tried a club. An after-school club. I'd hated it! Lily had *immediately* made about twenty new friends and I'd just sat in the corner like a droopy pot plant waiting for Mum and Dad to come and pick us up.

"Maybe on her own," said Mum, "without Lily…"

It is true that I tend to get a bit crushed by Lily. She is so loud, and so bouncy! She bursts through doors like she's jet-propelled.

And then it is all shrieking and screeching and stinking swizzlesticks. (Her favourite expression for this term.) It is very difficult, when you are a shrinking kind of person, to have a twin that is so noisy. Everyone expects you to be the same.

Actually, it's funny, but no one ever expects Lily to be like *me*. They all expect me to be like Lily. And I can't be! I've tried. It just doesn't work. Maybe if I was on my own, people wouldn't think it so peculiar if I was a bit quiet. But I still didn't want to join any clubs!

I never got to hear what Dad thought of Mum's suggestion 'cos just as he started to say something there was this loud CRASH, followed by a series of thuds and bangs, like the house was collapsing. All it was, was Lily, coming out of her bedroom and hurtling down the stairs. She always hurtles down the stairs. Dad asked her the other day if wild elephants were after her.

"Mum!" She went shrieking past me, into the kitchen. "I've been trying to find something to wear on Saturday and I can't! I haven't got anything!

Mum, I need something new! I've got to have something new! 'Cos it's *Riverside*, Mum. There might be actors! I've got to, Mum!"

She goes on like this all the time. Like, if she's already been seen wearing something, she can't possibly be seen in it again. To be seen in it again would be *death*. It's what happens when you lead a mad social life.

Under cover of all the shrieking I slid into the kitchen and helped myself to a bowl of cereal, which is what I'd been going there for in the first place. I stood by the sink, munching it, while Mum and Lily got into one of their shouting matches about how many clothes a person of ten years old actually needs.

Lily yelled, "Enough so your friends don't keep seeing you in the same old thing all the time!" To which Mum retorted, "What utter rubbish!" and told Lily that she was:

a) too obsessed with the way she looked
b) in danger of becoming shallow-minded and
c) *spoilt*.

Lily screeched that Mum was mean as could be. "You don't understand what you're doing to me! You're ruining my life!"

This is nothing new. Dad once counted up and said that on average Lily accused Mum of ruining her life at least three times a week. Sometimes I feel like telling Lily that *she* is ruining *my* life. If she weren't so shrieky, I might not be so shrinky. Though I suppose it is not really fair to blame Lily.

At least it got Mum off the subject of clubs. By the time she and Lily had finished yelling at each other, Mum was all hot and bothered. She said she was going to go and soak in the bath and calm herself with thoughts of grass and trees and flowers.

"And not of spoilt selfish brats!"

So that was all right. But I kept thinking about it, especially when Saturday came and Lily went swaggering off (in new jeans and a new top, which were in fact *mine*). I would have loved more than anything to visit the set of *Riverside*! But you can't barge your way in where you're not wanted. Sarah was Lily's friend, not mine. I would only be a drag.

I spent most of that day helping Mum in Flora Green, but somehow it wasn't as much fun as usual. I kept thinking of Lily, on the set of *Riverside*. She might even get to see Tony! (Tony is my A1 favourite character. I once wrote him a fan letter and he sent me a signed photo, which I have on my wall.)

Lily doesn't have one because she never wrote to him. She doesn't even specially like *Riverside*.

When we got home that evening, Lily was already there. She'd just been dropped off by Sarah and her mum.

"Well? So how was it?" said Mum.

Lily said that it was "totally and utterly brilliant".

"You know the Green, where Nick and Tina live? Where all the little houses are? They're not real! I always thought they were real. But it's just the front bits. Like you can open the gate and go up the path, but when you open the door there's nothing on the other side! It's absolutely amazing! And there's all these girls going round with clipboards and stuff. They're called PAs." She looked at me. "I don't expect you know what a PA is, do you?"

I shook my head.

"It's a *production assistant*," said Lily, all self-important. "They help the producer. Like Sarah's mum's got one called Lisa. She looks like a model! She told me all what they do. It's what I'm going to be when I grow up. I've decided… I'm going to be a PA!"

She strutted off round the room, holding her imaginary clipboard and an imaginary something else which she kept looking at, and frowning at, and clicking.

"This is a *stop watch*," she said. "I'm timing things. It's very important to know how long a scene will take. You have to know *exactly*, down to the last second. It's for programme planning, and fitting in the commercials."

She couldn't stop talking about it. She went on and on, all through tea. Suddenly she was like this huge fan.

"And hey, guess what?" she said, jabbing me in the ribs. "I saw your boyfriend!"

My heart went CLUNK, right down to my shoes.

"You saw Tony?" I said.

I hated her. I hated her!

"Yes," said Lily. "He was acting a scene with Mara Banks, and when he came off he *smiled* at me."

I double hated her. I *triple* hated her. I would have liked to murder her!

Instead, I raced upstairs to my room and kissed my photo of Tony and burst into tears. Why did Lily always, *always* get to have all the fun? It wasn't fair!

Why couldn't I be the one who rushed around shrieking and being popular and have zillions of friends?

I once read somewhere that if you're shy it just means you're not interested in other people. You're only interested in *you*. But that wasn't true! I was interested in people. I just didn't know how to talk to them.

I could talk in my head. I could say lots of things in my head! And I could say them in letters, as well. I used to write pages and pages to Greta, when she first went to America. Maybe – sudden brilliant idea! – maybe I could find a *pen pal*?

This thought was so exciting that I immediately snatched up the latest copy of **Go Girl**, which is the magazine that I like best because it once had Tony as its centrefold. (I made a poster of him and it is on my wall with his photo.)

Hurriedly, I scrabbled through the pages till I came to the one where people advertise for pen pals. There were simply loads! I'd never bothered to look at it properly before. I'd never even thought of having a pen pal!

The first one I read, which was no. 364, said,

✉ *Hi to all you cool cats out there! I'm Cindy. I'm ten years old and I love to party. My fave bands are Boyzone, Steps and Five. Please write to me!*

I didn't think, probably, that Cindy would find me very interesting. Not if she loved to party. I quickly moved on to the next one.

✉ *Hi, my name is Danni and I am cool! My hobbies are singing, dancing and listening to music. I am 12 years old.*

I gulped. Danni was cool! She wouldn't want to be my pen pal.

The next one said, ✉ *Hi! My name is Pippa. I'm ten years old and I just love to meet people. My nickname is Giggler!*

The next one said, ✉ *Hi, I'm Shelby. I'm 11 years old and I love parties, dancing and having a good time.*

I'm Tara, I'm Sam, I'm Linzi. I love to party, I love to dance, I love to meet people.

After a while I began to get a bit depressed, as quite honestly I couldn't see any of these cool, fun-loving people wanting to correspond with a person like me. They would soon start thinking, "Oh, this girl is not cool, she is a dead bore, I shall have to stop writing to her." I wondered if maybe I could advertise for a pen pal myself, and if I did, what would I put?

✉ *Hi, my name is Violet. I am ten years old and I like reading, writing letters and making up stories. I am a huge fan of the soaps and my fave character is Tony, from Riverside.*

I knew what Lily would say: BIG TURN OFF.

I was just starting to despair when I came to Pen Pal no. 372:

✉ *Hi! I'm Katie. I'm ten years old and I love to draw and do puzzles. I also like to tell jokes and play with my cats, Bella and Bertie. Please write to me, I would truly love to have a pen pal.*

When I saw that my heart started beating really fast. Katie sounded just like me!

I was so excited I grabbed a pen and wrote to her straight away.

Dear Katie,

Hi, my name is Violet! I like reading, writing letters and making up poems. I also like drawing (though I am not very good at it) and doing puzzles.

I have a cat called Horatio and I love to cuddle him, especially in bed. I used to play games with him but he is a bit too old for that now.

I am the same age as you (but will be eleven in April).

I am enclosing a photograph so you

can see what I look like. I would love
to have one of you, and to be your
pen pal if you would like me to.
Please write back!
  Yours sincerely,
  Violet Alexander.

PS   PLEASE WRITE SOON!

Mrs Frost's class

It was the only photograph I had. Well, the only
recent one. It was all our class at school, with me at
one end and Lily at the other. (We always keep as far
away from each other as possible when our photos
are taken.)

Mum had got spare copies, like for some weird reason she always does. I can't think why as they are always foul. But the only other one I had was when I was nine and looking really goofy, so I put in the school one and hoped she wouldn't notice that there was any resemblance between Lily and me.

It was only after I'd addressed the letter (to Go Girl, Pen Pals no. 372) and gone over the road to the post box that I thought what I could have done. I could have cut Lily out! I could have taken the scissors and simply *removed* her. I wished that I had! But it was too late, now. The letter had gone.

On Sunday I heard Lily on the telephone, telling Debbie all about her visit to *Riverside.*

"You know the Green, where Nick and Tina live? Where all the little houses are?"

She told her about the little houses not being real. She told her about the girls with the clipboards. She told her about Tony, acting in a scene with Mara Banks. She told her about Tony smiling at her.

"At *me*! Not the others. Just me! I know it was me 'cos the others were all looking the other way."

Later in the day, Big Nan rang up and Lily rushed to the phone before anyone else could get there and told Big Nan about it, too.

"You know the Green, where Nick and Tina live? Where all the little houses are?"

I had to listen to it all over again. Well, I suppose I didn't *have* to, exactly, but it was kind of hard to avoid it. Lily's voice is like a really loud car horn.

On Monday, at school, she told all the rest of the class. Nina and Lucy and Jamila. Justine and Kelly and Meena. They listened, open-mouthed. Even Pandora and Yvonne hovered on the fringes, drinking it all in.

"And then, guess what?" Lily did this little showing-off twirl. "He *smiled* at me! Tony… he *smiled* at me!"

Meena squealed and clasped her hands. Lucy went "*To*nee!" Jamila fell into a pretend swoon. Kelly Stevens gave a loud screech and staggered backwards into Justine Bickerstaff. They then clutched each other

32

and started moaning, like they were in pain. Even Pandora squeaked, *"To*nee!" and made her eyes go all big.

"Soaps are *dross*," said Yvonne.

I was glad there was someone that wasn't impressed, though I knew it was only 'cos Yvonne was jealous. She hates it if she's not the centre of attention. (She hardly ever is, which is maybe why she is so bad-tempered all the time.)

I try very hard *not* to be jealous as it is such a horrid feeling, you get all twisted up inside and it gives you a headache and makes you sick. Well, it does me. I once got so twisted up when we had a birthday party and I thought Lily was getting all the attention (which she was) that I had to go to the bathroom and put my head in the toilet and throw up. That is so disgusting! I didn't want it happening while I was at school, so I did this little hum to myself – "Ho di ha di ho!" – and went over to my desk, where I started arranging all my felt tips in order of colour. *Pink* ones, *orange* ones, *red* ones…

I WAS NOT GOING TO BE JEALOUS.

Yellow ones, *green* ones –

Ho di ha di ho! *Blue* ones, *mauve* ones –

"Violet?" Pandora prodded at me. "Isn't Tony the one you like?"

I made a mumbling sound.

"*Isn't* he?"

The trouble with Pandora is that once she's started there's no way of stopping her. She's a bit like Horatio when he decides that he wants something. Usually food, in his case. He'll just keep on and on nagging at you until he gets it.

Like he'll spread himself out across your homework that you're trying to do, or walk about yowling and winding himself round your feet. Pandora just prods and pokes and keeps asking the same question over and over.

"*Isn't* he? The one that you like?"

Ho di ha di ho! Black ones, brown ones –

"*Yes.*"

Gold ones, silver ones –

"Wouldn't you have liked to meet him?"

"*Yes*!" I slammed down my desk lid. I'm not usually impatient with Pandora, but I was really trying *so* hard. I didn't want to be sick!

Lily's voice came clanging across the room.

"…going to be a PA when I leave school."

"What's a PA?" said Pandora.

I said, "Pompous airbag!" and fortunately at that moment the door opened and Mrs Frost, our teacher, came in.

At first break the airbag was still telling everyone who would listen how she had been smiled at. I kept as far away as possible. I could see that even Sarah and Francine were getting a bit sick of it. The thing with Lily is, she just never knows when to stop.

Me and her went home together at the end of school. We don't always. Sometimes Mum picks us up, sometimes Dad, sometimes we get the bus and sometimes the airbag goes back with one of her friends. Today we went on the bus together and she started off all over again about Tony and how he had smiled at her – "At *me!*" – but I just took a book out of my bag and sat there pretending to read it. Not that it stopped her, but at least I was able to make like I wasn't listening. Which in fact I wasn't, as far as I could help it. I mean, bits of it kept breaking through but mainly what I was doing was wondering when I would hear from Katie and whether she would want to be my pen pal...

I'd posted the letter on Saturday, but I knew the postman wouldn't have come and taken it away until today. But I'd made sure to put a first-class stamp on it, so by tomorrow it would be with the magazine, and if they sent it on straight away it could be with Katie by Wednesday, and if she wrote back *immediately* – which was what I would do – then on Friday morning I could have a letter!

The post comes really late in our house. It comes after we've left, so that all of Friday I was, like, counting the hours, waiting for the moment when I could get back home and find out if my letter had arrived!

It hadn't. All there was, was a bill for Dad and a seed catalogue for Mum.

It didn't come Saturday, it didn't come Monday, it didn't come Tuesday. By Wednesday I was feeling quite despondent. I kept trying to remember what I'd written. If I'd written anything that might have put her off. I wished I'd kept a copy! Maybe I shouldn't have said about being eleven in April; maybe that had been too much like boasting. Or maybe I'd just sounded totally dim and boring.

Maybe she'd had so many thousands of replies she'd simply picked out the ones that sounded like they'd be most fun. Maybe she hated *Riverside*. Maybe I should have mentioned that my favourite band is Flying High, except that Lily says it is a nerd's band and anyway not many people have heard of it.

Maybe she'd taken one look at my photograph and thought, "Puke! Pur*lease*!"

Maybe I was doomed to just never have a real proper friend ever, and that was all there was to it.

And then I got home on Wednesday, and there it was, waiting for me… my letter!

Lily said, "Who does *she* know that writes letters?"

"None of your business," I said.

"Who's it from?"

"Not telling!"

I turned the envelope over in my hands. It was pink and smelled of fruit and had two little furry cat stickers in one corner.

"Aren't you going to open it?" said Lily.

"Not right now," I said.

"Why not?"

"Because I don't want to!"

"So w—"

"Lily, just leave Violet alone," said Mum. "Letters are personal! How would you like it if she pried into yours?"

Lily tossed her head. "Wouldn't ever have one! Don't know anyone who still writes them!"

She can say what she likes. I enjoy having letters! I like seeing my name on the front of the envelope and

I like looking at the stamps and studying the postmark and trying to guess who could have sent it. (Though I have so few that I almost always know!) I could guess that this was from Katie by the little cat stickers; and anyway, who else would be writing to me?

I waited till we'd finished tea then I rushed upstairs to my room and tore open the envelope. I'd gone all trembly because I had this fear she might be going to say, "Thank you for writing to me but I'm afraid I have found someone else to be my pen pal." Someone who sounded like more fun!

It is terrible to have so little confidence, but it is what happens when you are one half of a twin and the other half keeps telling you that you are a nerdy party pooper. I tell her that she is a noisy windbag, but being a noisy windbag is not necessarily such a bad thing to be. Being a party pooper is the *worst*.

I slid the letter out of the envelope r-e-a-l-l-y s-l-o-w-l-y. It was quite thick. It was three pages! I couldn't believe it!

The first thing I saw was the address, which was in London. I would rather it had been somewhere miles away, such as for instance the Outer Hebrides, as all I wanted was a pen pal. I didn't want to *meet* her! But I thought that I would read the letter first and worry about other things later.

Hi, Violet!

This is Katie, writing back to you. I was really pleased to get your letter! It came just this morning, so here I am replying IMMEDIATELY.

I would love it if we could be pen pals! You sound incredibly interesting and exactly the sort of person I have dreamt of writing to. I hope I sound like the sort of person you have dreamt of writing to!

I will tell you about myself, and then you can decide. I live with my mum, whose name is Clare. I don't have any brothers or sisters but I do have two cats. They are:

Bertie, who is small and stripy
Bella, who is small and black.

Bertie is full of fun! The other night while we were asleep he stole a toilet roll from out of the bathroom and carried it all the way downstairs, then chewed it to pieces and spat out the bits. When we woke in the morning it looked like confetti! We thought someone had got married!

Bella is a sweetheart. She is very round and cuddly. She just loves her grub! Mum says she cannot decide whether she should be called Belle of the Ball or Bella the Ball!

Please tell me about your cat Horatio. I would love to see a picture of him!!

Thank you for sending me your photo. I am sending you one of me. I hope it will not put you off!!!

I noticed in yours that there was another girl at the end of the row that looked just like you! Is she your sister? Are you twins? I would love to be a twin! I think it would be so neat for there to be two of you and no one knowing which was which. I said this to Mum and she said you could get up to all kinds of mischief. But she also said, maybe it would not be quite as much fun as I seem to think. Is it???

Tell me about your mum and dad. My mum is a teacher, she teaches violin and piano. She does it partly in a school (not my one!) and partly at home. When she is teaching violin the house is full of unearthly screechings and scrapings and sometimes my cat Bella sits outside the door and joins in. She thinks she is a violin!

I love to draw! I am not very musical but I think when I grow up I will be an artist of some kind. What will you be?

Underneath your photo it says "Mrs Frost's class". But I counted up and there are only fourteen people! We have twenty-eight in my class. I go to St Saviour's Juniors. Where do you go?

I hope you don't think I am being too nosy but it is just because I am so interested. Whatever you want to know about me, you can ask!

I had better stop now in case I am
boring you. Please, please, PLEASE,
write back! If you would still like to be
my pen pal, that is.
Lots of luv
From
Katie Saunders XXX

PS   Where does an elf go to get fit?
To an elf farm! Ha ha!

The minute I'd finished reading the letter I
went hurtling back downstairs, thump thud bang!
I sounded like Lily.

"Mum!" I cried. "I've got a pen friend!"

"Really?" said Mum. "That's wonderful!
Where did you find her?"

"If it is a her," said Dad.

"*Dad*! Of course it is," I said. I wouldn't want
to write to a boy! "Her name's Katie and she's the
same age as me and she has two cats and her mum
teaches the piano and she advertised in **Go Girl**
for someone to be her pen pal!"

"So you wrote to her?" said Mum. "That's
very enterprising! Can I have a read, or is it private?"

I hesitated. "You can read this first one," I said. "But after that they'll be private!"

I thought that in future letters we would probably share all kinds of secrets that I certainly wouldn't want Mum reading! But there wasn't anything secret yet, and I was just so bursting with pride. Katie found me interesting! Katie wanted us to be pen pals! I thought if Mum read her letter it would make her happy and she would stop worrying quite so much about me living in Lily's shadow.

I was right. It worked!

"She sounds lovely," said Mum. "I think that was such an excellent idea, Violet! Finding yourself a pen friend. I see she lives with her mum... I wonder what happened to her dad?"

I said that I had wondered that, too. "Maybe they're divorced?" I said. Lots of girls at school have mums and dads who are divorced.

Mum agreed that this was possible. "But you'd better not ask her," she warned. "It might be something she doesn't want to talk about. Wait till she feels ready to tell you."

"Yes, I was going to," I said. I am not like Lily! Lily always goes rushing in with both feet. "Where is your dad?" is probably the very *first* question she'd ask. I try to consider other people's feelings, 'cos I know how I would feel – which just makes it all the worse when I go and say stupid things like I did to Ayesha about her face.

Mum folded the letter and handed it back to me. "It's nice she lives so near," she said. "When you get to know each other better, you'll be able to meet."

I said, "Mm!" Doing my best to sound enthusiastic.

"In fact," said Mum, "why don't y—"

"Look!" I waved the envelope in the air. Quickly, quickly, before Mum could get carried away and start arranging things. "She's sent me a photo! D'you want to see it?"

I was just handing the photograph to Mum when Lily came crashing into the room. Needless to say, she had to come bundling over to take a look.

"Who's that?" she said.

I told her that it was a picture of my pen pal. "Katie."

"Hm!" Lily studied it, critically. "Her nose is like a *blob*."

"I think she looks rather cute," said Mum. "Like a little pixie!"

Lily said, "*Pixie*," in tones of deepest scorn.

"Munch munch munch," said Dad, pretending to nibble a carrot.

Lily flushed bright scarlet. Our front teeth are just the tiniest bit rabbity, so that we have to wear a brace. Lily really hates it! She is really self-conscious about it.

"Well, I'm sorry, but people who live in glass houses," said Dad.

Angrily, Lily said, "What's that s'pposed to mean?"

"It means," said Mum, "that we do not mock the way other people look unless we want to be mocked in return. What are you doing down here, anyway? I thought you were going to have a bath?"

"Am! Don't want anything!" shouted Lily; and she slammed out of the room and went thudding back up the stairs.

"That girl!" said Mum.

I pointed out that it was all right for Mum, she was only her mother. "I'm her *twin*!"

I decided that I would write back to Katie straight away and tell her that being a twin was not always as much fun as you might think.

Hi, Katie!

Thank you for writing to me so quickly. And for writing such a lovely long letter. I am so glad you want to be my pen pal! I am writing back at once as I know what it is like when you are waiting and waiting for something to come, and thinking that it never will and worrying to yourself in case you have said something to upset the person.

First of all I will try to answer your questions! The girl at the end of the row that you thought looked like me is my sister, Lily. We are twins but NOT IDENTICAL. In fact we are just about as different as two people can be! You mum is right, it is not always fun to be a twin, although sometimes of course it can be. Like for instance if you dress the same and pretend to people that you are each other. We used to do this quite a lot when we were little but we don't do it so often now as we are so completely different that it probably wouldn't work. And anyway Lily wouldn't want people to think that she was me and I wouldn't want them to think that I was her. No way!

What I would really, really like would be if it was just me on my own, but if Mum was to have another baby I would love a little brother! But this unfortunately is not very likely to happen as Mum says two children are quite enough for one family what with the world being over-populated and people starving, etc., and in any case they are both so busy they probably wouldn't have time for one. A baby, I mean.

You asked me to tell you about my mum and dad. My mum is called Emma and my dad is called Steve. They both work all the time, which is why they are too busy to have another baby. (Plus over-population, etc.) Dad does things with computers and Mum has a flower shop, where sometimes I help on a Saturday. Lily doesn't help. She has lots of posh friends and thinks it is beneath her to have a mum who works in a shop, even if the shop is her own one. You can see it is true that we are not at all alike.

Another thing you ask is what I will be when I grow up. I haven't yet decided! But it will not be anything to do with computers, I don't think. Maybe I could be a flower artist and make flower arrangements for weddings and parties, etc. But if I cannot do that (as I may not be artistic enough) then perhaps I will be something to do with writing. I really love to write stories! But I cannot do the pictures to go with them. You are so lucky that you can draw! I wish wish WISH that I could. All I can do is stick figures.

I expect you will say that this is utterly pathetic and the sort of

stuff you would
do in Reception,
but it is just one
of those things. I
can see pictures
in my head, but
when I pick up my
pen my hand won't do what I want
it to. This is probably something
that you will not understand, as I
expect when you pick up a pen it
does exactly what you tell it to.

It would be just SO brilliant if I
could write stories and you could
illustrate them! But only if you
want to, of course. You might not
want to. You would most probably
be too busy doing drawings of
your own.

I just loved the pictures you did
of your cats! It is so nice that
you are a cat person. One of my
nans has a cat allergy, which
means that whenever she comes
to stay poor Horatio is banished.

He has to go to a cattery for what Mum calls "a little holiday". But I am sure he hates it and thinks we have abandoned him. He probably wonders what he has done wrong when in fact he hasn't done anything. It is just my nan, wheezing and sneezing and complaining of cat hair on the furniture.

My school is called Lavendar House. It is very titchy and tiny. We have sixteen people in my class but on the day when the photograph was taken two of them were away. It is all girls. No boys! Do you have boys at your school? Most people do. Sometimes I wish that we had but on the other hand they can be a pain. A girl called Francine Church had some at her birthday party last term and they ruined everything by rushing about, shouting and showing off and spoiling all our games.

Do you have a uniform at your school? We have to wear:

       Mauve blouses
       Purple skirts
       Brown shoes
       Plum—coloured coats
       and BERETS! (also plum
       coloured)

It is so naff! Some rude boys in our road call us the Plum Puddings. Dad calls us the Lavendar Hill mob, which is the name of an old movie that he loves.

Do you like to watch TV? I don't watch a lot, except for wild life programmes (where I always make ready to shut my eyes TIGHT if there is any killing as it upsets me to see animals torn to pieces) and also the soaps, which I am a big fan of, and especially Riverside. Do you watch Riverside? If so, who is your favourite character? Mine is

Tony. Last year I wrote him a letter and he wrote back and sent me a signed photograph.

"To Violet xxx Tony". It is on my bedroom wall, right opposite my bed, where I can see it first thing when I wake up in the morning. As you will probably guess, I am in love!!!

Besotted, is what my dad calls it. He loves to tease me, and I always go bright scarlet! It is for this reason that when I watch Riverside I like it best if my dad is not there. Otherwise I spend the whole time all boiled up like a beetroot!

You know I said I don't like to see animals torn to pieces? It is one of my things and is why I am against fox hunting. I have a badge that says BAN BLOOD SPORTS. I got it off an animal stall at a summer fete and I signed a petition to the Government asking them to get it stopped.

I hope you are not a hunting person but if you are then I am sorry but I have to say what is the truth even if it makes you decide that you don't want to be my pen pal after all. I will understand if you don't only it is something I feel quite strongly about. I just felt that I had to say it. I hope you will not be offended as I don't mean to be rude or anything.

I must go now as Lily has just got out of the bath and Mum is yelling at me that it is my turn. What time do you have to go to bed? I have to go at nine thirty in the week and half-past ten on Fridays and Saturdays. It is too early, if you ask me, but Mum says I will thank her for it when I am older. She says if you don't get enough sleep you start to LOOK YOUR AGE. I don't know about you but I would quite like to look my age. One of

Mum's friends the other day asked me when my birthday was. She said, "And how old will you be? Ten?" It is so insulting!

I do hope you will write back to me and not be angry at what I said about fox hunting. But please don't feel you have to do it immediately! (Though it would be lovely if you did.) I am sure you are very busy, especially if you have lots of homework. We have OCEANS. I don't really mind, except if it takes too long when I would rather be writing to you!

Love from your pen pal,
Violet
xxxxxxxx

PS   Someone told me this joke at school the other day.

Question: What is green and slithers and goes "hith"?
Answer: A thnake with a lithp!

PPS   Here is a photo of my
cat Horatio: You can keep it if
you like.

I posted the letter on my
way to school next day. The
very minute that it plopped
into the box I started to
worry! Dad says I am a
regular worry guts and
I know that he is
right. I don't only
make mountains out of
molehills, I make them out of
microdots! I just can't seem to help it.

These are some of the things I worried about:

1. Fox hunting. Why did I have to go and
mention it??? It is true that it is something I feel
strongly about, but it is not the only thing. I feel
strongly about lots of things! For instance: people
starving, and babies dying of AIDS, and global
warming, and land mines. To name just a few. I
didn't go and mention them! Now I had probably
upset her and wouldn't ever hear from her again.

2. The second thing was saying I'd gone to Francine's party when I hadn't. Not that I'd actually *said* that I'd gone, just made it read like I had. Telling her about the boys and how they'd ruined things, rushing around shouting and spoiling all our games. I was just repeating what Lily had said. She was the one that had gone to the party, not me! Why had I done it???

3. The third thing was saying how we had to wear those hideous berets and how our school uniform was naff. But I like our school uniform! Lily's the one that thinks it's naff.

I suppose I was trying to be cool. Which is truly pathetic! But going on about fox hunting, that was really *dumb*. There's a girl at school, Justine Bickerstaff, that in the hunting season she gets on her horse and gallops madly about the countryside with packs of hounds. She has even done this *revolting* thing called cubbing, where they tear dear little sweet innocent fox cubs to pieces. I hate that! I hate that so much. But Justine gets into this simply mega-rage if anyone ever says about banning blood sports. For all I knew, Katie could be the same. And I had gone and lectured her and now I had probably RUINED EVERYTHING.

I was just so relieved when I got her next letter. All that worrying, all for nothing! (It usually is, but I still do it.) I knew as soon as Mum handed me the envelope that things were all right. Instead of the little furry cat stickers there was one that said, STOP HUNTING WITH HOUNDS. So I hadn't upset or offended her! She was on my side. Hooray!

"Is that from the Blob?" said Lily. "Are you going to open it this time?"

I said, "No. I like to read my letters in private."

Lily tossed her head and said, "Letters! You're so uncool. Why don't you e-mail?"

"You could, you know," said Dad.

He's always trying to get me on the computer. I am not terribly awfully into them, to be honest. Lily is.

She is on it the whole time, whizzing about doing things, sending e-mails to all her friends. She sees them all day and e-mails them all night! When she is not text-messaging on her moby.

"Think about it," said Dad. "It would be far more fun than scribbling on bits of paper!"

"But *she* might read them," I said.

"Me?" Lily gave a hoot of laughter. "Who'd want to read what you and the Blob have to say to each other?"

Dad said, "Violet, I give you my word, nobody but nobody would read your e-mails. They would be for your eyes only."

That's what he *says*. But I bet she'd still find a way!

"Why not ask?" said Dad. "Ask her if she'd like to."

I said that I would, 'cos I like to make him happy and it is true that most people seem to prefer sending e-mails to writing real letters. Maybe if I'd e-mailed Greta we would still be in touch.

As soon as tea was over, I rushed upstairs to my room. (Mum calls it my *burrow*.) I tore open the envelope and a whole wodge of paper fell out. Which is far more fun than e-mails, if you ask me!

Hi, Violet!

Don't worry, you have not offended me! I HATE people that kill foxes. So does my mum. We have both filled in petitions against it. If I see a badge I will buy one and wear it.

I laughed over your snake joke! Here is one for you. A joke, I mean. Not a snake joke. (It is a knock-knock joke.)

Knock knock!

Who's there?

Ivor.

Ivor who?

Ivor let me in or I'll break the door down!

Har har!

Your school uniform doesn't sound naff, it sounds fabbo! I love berets! Ours is just green. Green everything!

It makes us look like gooseberries.

And yes, we do have boys. Yeeurgh!

You are so lucky, not having them. They are such a nuisance. Well, I think they are.

What will happen when you change schools? Where will you go? I will probably go to Friars Stile, which is just down the road. Mum doesn't really want me to, she says it is too big and too rough, but all my friends would be going there. Will you be able to stay with your friends? Do you have lots of them? Do you like to party?

I laughed when you said about boys rushing round shouting! This is what they do ALL THE TIME. Susanna, one of my friends at school, is having her birthday party next week but she is not going to invite any. Boys, I mean! She is just inviting girls from our class. It will be such fun! I would go to parties non-stop if I could. I will tell you all about it in my next letter!

You asked if I like to watch TV. The answer is... yes! But I like to draw and paint and read books as well. Riverside is my ace fave soap, and I think Tony is gorge! Even Mum says he is a hunk. I am so envious of you, having him on your wall! Do you kiss him goodnight before you go to bed? I would!

I am sorry it is not fun to be a twin. Mum said, "I told you so!" She also said what nice names you have. Lily and Violet. She says, "I hope they are not shortened to Lil or Vi, as this would be a shame." Are they???

I am a bit like you, I would love it if Mum would have another baby but I don't think she will as the only man friend she has is rather old and I cannot see that they would ever get married. He is called Arthur and has grey hair but is very nice. He is like a granddad. Mum enjoys going to the theatre with him, and sometimes we all visit places in his car.

You know you said that you and your sister are not identical? I have looked VERY HARD under a magnifying glass, and I don't see how anyone could tell you apart! I hope you are not cross with me for saying this. I can quite understand that you are two different people, for instance your sister will not help your mum in her shop because of her posh friends. Whereas you do not mind about such things. Do the posh friends go to your school? Is it a posh sort of school?

I hope you don't think I am prying or being nosy. Like I said before, you can ask me ANYTHING. I will not mind!

Bertie has just been chasing his cat nip toy. He is so sweet! He jumps in the air and claps his paws.

I am glad you like my drawings, and I do understand what you say about your hand not doing what you want it to. It is the same with me and singing. I can hear all the notes as clear as can be in my head but then when I open my mouth they just come out all wrong. Mum says I sound like a lovesick hen! She has to put her hands over her ears.

Here is a game. Close your eyes and do a scribble on a piece of paper, then send it to me and I will make a picture of it. Like this:

This is GENUINE. I closed my eyes and did the scribble, then I traced it (so you could see what it looked like) and then I made the picture. I play this game all the time, but it would be ever so much more fun to play it with someone else. It doesn't matter if you can't draw! Anyone can play the scribble game.

I'll do one for you, if you like.

You don't have to make a picture if you don't want to! But if you do then I'll make one as well and we can compare them. It will be interesting to see what different things we make! But only if you want to. I'm going to trace the scribble right now.

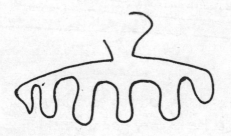

I've traced it. Now I'm going to put this letter in an envelope and tomorrow

on her way to work Mum will post it.
Write soon!
  Luv and kisses
  From
  Katie

PS   I have drawn a maze for you!
See if you can find your way in.

PPS   Thank you for your photo of
Horatio. He is very handsome! I am
going to put him in a frame next to my
ones of Bella and Bertie.

After I'd read Katie's letter I was glad that I'd told her about Francine's party. Even if I hadn't been there! I mean, I hadn't actually told a lie. Not straight out. But Katie was starting to sound a whole lot more cool than I'd thought she was going to be. Nobody who thought it would be fun to party non-stop would want to go on writing to a nerdy stay-at-home, which is what Lily calls me. (When she's not calling me a twonk, or a party pooper.) I really wanted Katie to go on writing! I loved the jokes that she told and the little drawings that she did and the way she played with her cats and the games that she invented. Surely it wouldn't matter if I just pretended once or twice? It wasn't like we were going to be meeting-up-and-getting-together sort of friends. Just pen pals!

I spent ages trying to turn her scribble into a picture. I think perhaps I cheated as I made lots of copies on Dad's photocopier so's I could have lots of goes. I didn't want her to think I was *completely* useless. Although I am! Lily can draw quite well. It is so unfair because she doesn't even enjoy it, particularly. She would rather do graphics on the computer. On the other hand she is not much good at writing. She can't spell for toffee and her essays are only ever about one page long, and that is using

65

REALLY BIG TYPE. Mine are sometimes five pages, or even six! Mrs Frost writes little notes at the end like "Very inventive use of language!" or "You have a good imagination, Violet." She has never said that about Lily!

But Lily could have done cleverer things with Katie's scribble. If she could be bothered, which most likely she wouldn't. This is the best that I could do:

A sort of… *thing*. But I did the maze all right!

I showed Katie's drawing of Bertie playing with his cat nip toy to Mum. I didn't show her the letter because by now things had started to become a bit private, but I wanted her to see Bertie.

"He's so cute," I said, "isn't he?"

"Like a little stripy tiger," said Mum. "She's very good at drawing, isn't she?"

"Yes, and she just loves Bella and Bertie," I said. "She plays with them all the time. Specially Bertie. He's really mischievous!"

"Like Horatio used to be," said Mum.

I said that I couldn't remember Horatio ever playing, but Mum said that was because he was two years old when I was born.

"Cats don't stay kittenish very long."

"I suppose," I said, trying to sound casual, "we couldn't have one, could we?"

"One what?" said Mum.

I said, "A kitten!"

Mum laughed. "Is that what all this has been leading up to?"

"Mum! No!" I said. I put on this very hurt and surprised expression. "I just suddenly thought it would be fun."

"Just suddenly?" said Mum.

"Well... fairly suddenly." Like immediately after reading Katie's letter! "Mum, please!" I said. "Couldn't we?"

Sometimes, if I really beg and plead, I can get round Mum. Lily says I am a right creep. She says I play at being little shrinky winky Violet and Mummy's girly. Lily would rather rant and roar and yell that Mum is ruining her life. Sometimes Mum gives in, just for the sake of peace and quiet, like sometimes she gives in to me because I have asked *nicely*. Sometimes! Not always. This was one of those times when she didn't.

She said that Horatio was too old to cope with a kitten. It wouldn't be fair on him.

"Why don't you ask Katie if you can go over and play with hers?"

"Mum, we're *pen* pals," I said.

"So? That's no reason you shouldn't get to meet each other!"

I said, "But then we wouldn't be pen pals."

"Of course you would!" said Mum. "There's nothing to stop you being both."

I didn't want to be both! I just wanted to be pen pals. I almost began to wish that I'd never told Mum about Katie. I only did it 'cos I thought it would please her. Now she was going to start nagging at me to do something I didn't want to do. She was going to ruin everything!

"All right, all right," said Mum. "Calm down! No one's going to force you."

"I just want to write letters," I said.

Mum said in that case, writing letters was all I need do.

"Whatever makes you happy."

And then she hugged me and said, "Cheer up! No one's having a go at you!"

I wondered to myself whether Katie's mum nagged her to do things. I thought probably not. Katie wasn't shy! She went to parties and had lots of friends. I wished I could think of something interesting and exciting to tell her, to stop her getting bored with me. But I don't ever do anything interesting or exciting! Not what other people would think was interesting or exciting. It was Lily that did things. Like going to visit the set of *Riverside*. That was interesting. And exciting! And I'd heard all about it in the hugest detail...

Dear Katie,

Hi! I have something very exciting to report. I went with my friend Sarah and her mum to visit the set of Riverside!!! It was just fantastic!

You will never guess what happened! Tony was there and he smiled at me!!! I thought I would just die! He is every bit as gorgeous in real life as he is on the screen. Sarah was SO jealous,

'cos she likes him, too. It was a
moment I shall treasure for always.

How was your party that you were
going to? The one without boys? I am
dying to hear about it! I want to know
everything you did.

Now I am reading through your
letter to see what questions you ask.
By the way I don't think you're prying
or being nosy! I think it is only natural
to want to know each other.

Please tell your mum that Lily and
me get mega-mad if anyone dares to
shorten us to Lil or Vi! We think that
Lily and Violet are quite bad enough.
It is because of them being my mum's
favourite flowers. I mean, that is why
we are called them. But we think they
are HIDEOUS!

I am really surprised that you like
our school uniform! Personally I would
rather be a gooseberry than a plum
pudding, but I am stuck with being a
pudding until Year 12, when I will
probably go to sixth form college as

there is no sixth form at our school. I
told you it is very titchy and tiny.
(Though you can stay there until you
are sixteen.) I don't think it is posh,
exactly, even though there are some
posh people that go there. But most of
us are just ordinary. At the moment I
think it is nice that there are no boys,
however Mum says this may change as
I get older. I don't think so!!!

And now... ssh! I do kiss Tony
every night. But don't tell anyone!
Not even Lily knows. She would laugh
at me if she did.

I am not cross with you for saying
that we look the same. Lots of people
think this. Usually it is because they
do not look properly. I know you said
that you looked with a magnifying
glass, but the photograph I sent you
was taken last term. We have
changed A LOT since then. And when
two people are very different I think
it has to show in their faces even if
they did come from the same egg.

I hope it does not embarrass you, me saying about eggs. It is only biology. But I once said it to this girl Pandora that is in my class and she turned very red and said that I was rude to talk about such things. But she is a very odd sort of girl.

You are not the only one who cannot sing. Nor can I! I cannot sing and I cannot draw. I think it is so annoying when you cannot do things that you would like to be able to do. When I sing my dad says I sound like a toad with tonsillitis. Could you draw a picture of that? Then I would be able to show it to my dad and he would laugh.

I want to ask you something. Do you let your mum read your letters? I don't let anyone read mine, except just your first one I let my mum see. But not now! Now they are STRICTLY PRIVATE, even though Lily would just love to get her hands on them. But I won't let her. Don't worry!

Oh, I have just remembered. Dad says, why don't we e-mail, instead of writing letters? He says it would be more fun. Do you think that it would? If you would like to e-mail, then we can do it. I don't mind.

I made a picture out of the scribble, but I'm afraid it is not very good.

Thank you very much for the maze, which I managed to find my way into. I don't mean to boast, but it was quite easy. Can you do another one and make it more difficult?

I have a game for you! Guess what musical instruments these are:

      Teful
      Tigura
      Novili
      Glube

I have just made this up!

Do you like playing word games? I can think of loads more! Sometimes what I do, like when I am travelling on the bus for example, I look at the

advertisements and I find a word
and I see how many other words I
can make from it. Like yesterday me
and Lily had to go to school by
ourselves because of Mum and Dad
being too busy and there was this
huge traffic jam and Lily got all
twitchy and impatient but I just sat
there making up words.

The word I made them from was
INSURE. Sitting on the bus I only
made up nine, but that was in my
head. I have just done it again and
this time I have made up twelve! If
you like, I will tell you what they are.
I will do it at the end of this letter.
It is just a game, but it is quite fun.

Next week my class is going to
visit the British Museum. After we
have been there we are going to
write stories about mummies.
Egyptian ones, I mean! I am really
looking forward to it!

Please write back soon and do
another maze. I hope I have not

upset you by saying the one you
sent was easy. It wasn't as easy as
all that! I think you are very clever,
being able to draw mazes.

That has made me think of a joke:
I am totally a—MAZED.

Ho ho! Must go!

Lots of luv

Violet xxx

PS   TOP SECRET!
These are the words I made but DO
NOT READ THEM until you have
seen how many you can make! By
order!!!

Ire rue rise run ruin rein
rinse sure sin sun sue nurse

I expect you may be able to find
more.

PPS   I think it is cool to have a
'granddad' called Arthur. I have only
one granddad. He is called James.
He is my mum's dad. Going now.
        Byeee!

I put in the bit about granddads in the hope that maybe next time Katie would tell me about her dad. I still didn't like to ask. I know she said "Ask me anything. I don't mind," but I remembered when Kelly Stevens' mum and dad split up. Kelly was in tears for weeks. I didn't like the thought of Katie being in tears. Her photo made her look so bright and perky! She looked like a really happy sort of person.

On Tuesday we went to the British Museum. The whole class, with Mrs Frost and another teacher, Miss Adams, to keep us in order. Some of us need keeping in order! Lily and her friends just behave *so* badly. Even on the tube they couldn't keep quiet but shriek and giggle and swing to and fro on the handrails. Lily kicked someone and had to apologise, and Sarah almost fell into the lap of a man that was reading his newspaper. She went, "Oops! Sorry!" and giggled. She didn't

seem at all embarrassed. I would have been! I would just have died.

Miss Adams told them to calm down. She said, "Lily! Sarah! Please!" But nobody ever takes any notice of Miss Adams. She is one of those teachers, she just has no idea how to control us. Not like Mrs Frost. She can be quite fierce! But Mrs Frost was way down the far end and couldn't see what was going on. By the time we got out at Tottenham Court Road, Lily and Sarah were giggling and shrieking at just about everything.

"Ooh! Look. Panties!" shrieked Sarah, as we went up the escalator, past all the adverts. Lily screeched.

"*Panties*!" she went.

I don't know what they found so funny about it. I mean, everyone has to wear them, even the Queen. (Unless they're a nudist, which I personally wouldn't want to be as I would almost certainly break out into goose pimples.)

"Pantyhose!"

"Chest hair!"

"Ooh, look, there's a naughty one!"

They giggled and shrieked all the way up the escalator. By the time we reached the museum they were totally hyper. Mrs Frost spoke to them, quite sternly. She said that unless they pulled themselves together and stopped acting like five year olds she would send them straight back to school with Miss Adams.

So then they went a bit quiet and crept round on exaggerated tiptoe, silently pointing at things and pulling faces. Every now and again Mrs Frost would check them out. She'd shoot them one of her dagger glances and they would stare soulfully back with these hurt expressions on their faces. Lily can look just *so* angelic when she wants to.

I walked round with Pandora. I would rather not have walked with her as I was trying to make mental notes of everything I saw so that I could report back to Katie next time I wrote. It is very difficult to make mental notes when someone is constantly wittering at you, but Pandora is a person that just kind of *sticks*. Unless you are rude there is no getting rid of her. I didn't want to be rude as she is very easily hurt, she crumples at the least little thing, so I did my best to shut out her wittering and hoped that I would remember a few interesting things to tell Katie. She was going to tell me about her party, so I had to have something to tell her in return!

It was the mummies we all wanted to see. They were quite spooky! I'd seen mummies before, of course, on television and in books. But never in the f-f-f-flesh!

Not that mummies have flesh, really. Not that you can see. They are all done up in bandages. You can only imagine what lurks beneath…

Fortunately they are all kept in glass cases, otherwise I would probably have had visions of them getting out and walking round the museum at dead of night, like in a film I once saw. I was only quite little and I had to keep hiding my head in a cushion. Mum said afterwards that I shouldn't have watched it. I do have this rather over-active imagination.

Lily doesn't have any imagination *at all*. To her a mummy is just a dead guy. This is what she yelled – "Dead guys!" – as she went shrieking off with Sarah across the polished floor. Pandora clutched at my sleeve and said, "Are they really dead?"

"Well, they're not *alive*," I said.

"But are they real people?"

I told her that they had been, once; a long time ago.

"So if you took the bandages off… what would they be like?"

"Just sort of… *skin*," I said. "All dried and withered. 'Cos there's nothing inside them. It's all been taken out. All their organs," I said. "Their intestines, and their livers, and their lungs… they used to take them out and put them in special jars."

Pandora's lip quivered. "While they were still alive?"

I said, "No! When they were dead."

We'd already done all this at school, but Pandora's a bit slow at taking things in. She always has to be told several times over. It is no use being impatient with her. Something happened when she was born and made her not quite right. Maybe for all I know something happened when I was born and made me not quite right. Maybe that is why I am a shrinking violet and it is not my fault any more than it is Pandora's fault that she keeps asking stupid questions all the time.

While we were talking, Lily and Sarah had been racing excitedly from mummy to mummy. All of a sudden, Sarah shrieked, "Hey, look at this one! Who does he remind you of?" Naturally we all went running over to look.

"It's Mr Spooner!" cried Lily. "What is he doing here?"

We all collapsed! We just couldn't help it. Poor Mr Spooner! He is one of our teachers at school.

"Mr Spooner," said Pandora, gazing at the mummy.

Just then, Mrs Frost came over to see what we were giggling at. She must have heard what Pandora said! I could see her lips start to

twitch, as if she would have liked to giggle, too. I mean, that mummy really did look like Mr Spooner! But of course, being a teacher, she couldn't let herself.

We all stopped giggling except for Pandora, who had only just started. The rest of us made like we were sucking on lemons. Disgraceful! Quite disgraceful!

Mrs Frost shook her head. "Without any doubt," she says, "you are far and away the worst bunch I have ever had to deal with!"

After that we all went for snacks in the cafeteria then back to the station to catch the train home. And I've gone and forgotten every single mental note that I made! All I can think of to tell Katie is Mrs Frost saying we're the worst bunch she's ever had to deal with...

Good morning! This is me. Katie!

How are you? I think your scribble picture was really good! Some people that in the past I have tried to play it with, they have just had no imagination at all. It is no fun when people have no imagination.

The maze that I sent you was one I did in a hurry as I wanted you to have it. I have done another one that is more difficult. I like drawing mazes. It is something I have only just started doing. I didn't mind you saying the first one was too easy, though a maze doesn't always have to be difficult. There are some that are just pretty. My one wasn't but that was because I didn't have time.

I loved hearing about your visit to Riverside. I am just SOOOO envious! If I was smiled at by Tony I think I would swoooooooon. I would never recover! I knew about the little houses not being real because I read about it somewhere but I would still very much like to go and see them. If I didn't swooooon!

I told Mum about you not liking to be called Lil or Vi. She says she is glad. But we don't know why you don't like your names! Mum says they are charming and unusual. I think Violet is nice as I just happen to love violets. They are so sweet and dainty! I don't like Lily so much. (But don't tell her I said so!!!) I think lilies are a bit too pale and droopy. They smell nice, of course. But so do violets! Plus you can have violet chocolates. I never heard of lily chocolates!

Here is you and your sister:

It didn't embarrass me, you saying how you both came out of the same egg. We have already done this at school, so it is something I know about. How silly of that girl Pandora to go red! As you say, it is only biology. She must be really weird. There is a girl in my class that is weird. She is called Shayna and she eats flowers! Our teacher once told us that you could eat nasturshums (?) and so now she eats every flower she comes across. Nothing is safe from her! Last week there was a bowl of hyercinths (?) in the hall and she picked off the top and devoured it! Mrs Glover (our teacher) says that she will make herself ill, but still she goes on doing it. Mum thinks that maybe she is feeling neglected and it is her way of drawing attention to herself. I think she is just loopy.

I have drawn a picture for your dad of you being a toad. I will cut it out and stick it on NOW.

I agree it is sad when you cannot do things that you would like to do. It is very frustrating. Especially when there are people that can do them that don't particularly want to. Then you think to yourself that they do not know how lucky they are and that life is so unfair. Only I try

not to think that too often as it is
what Mum calls COUNTER PRODUCTIVE.
Meaning: it doesn't get you anywhere! It
just makes you bitter and unsatisfied.

No, I don't show Mum your letters!!!
No way!!! I tell her things that I think
will interest her and that I think you will
not mind if I tell her, like for instance
about you being a twin. That sort of
thing. But nothing private!

I do like to play word games, even
though I am better at the drawing ones.
I worked out all the musical
instruments! I will draw them for you.

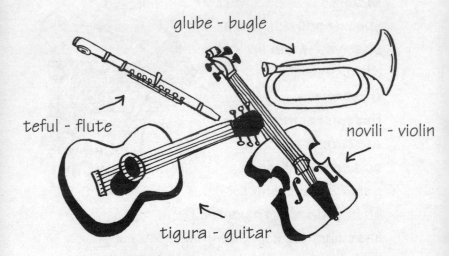

glube - bugle

teful - flute

novili - violin

tigura - guitar

But I could only make seven words out of that word you gave me. The ones I didn't get were: ire, rue, rein, sue, rinse. I asked Mum if she could do it and she got the same as you! She says you must be very good at English. I am afraid you will think I am rather ignorant as I had never heard of the word ire! Please don't be shocked. I have heard of it now and I will remember it.

Mum told me what it meant. She said it is another word for RAGE, which is what I felt last week at school when a stupid boy called Rory McArthur bashed out at another boy (Kevin Halliwell, who is his Dire Enemy) and got my friend Yasmin instead. He got her on the ear and made her cry. I know he wasn't aiming at her, but I still felt ire. He is such a clumsy boy, and so aggressive. Poor Yasmin had to go to the rest room and lie down. Rory got a good telling off. But he will just go and do it over again. There is nothing that can stop him. He and Kevin have this hate thing, and anyone that gets in the way, well that is just too bad. BOYS. puke!

We are on half-term! Are you? If so, are you doing anything exciting? I am just staying home with Mum but we are playing lots of games and having fun.

Oh, you asked me about e-mails! I am afraid we do not have a computer. I am really sorry about this, Mum says we will have to get one some time but not just yet as she has too many bills to pay. I expect Arthur would get one for us if Mum told him I wanted one, but Mum always says she is not going to SPONGE. In other words, we must make do and be independent. I know she is right and I am not complaining. But meanwhile we will have to be pen pals by snail mail, if this is all right with you?

I hope you will not mind. There are a lot of things that other people have that we do not. For instance, a video. For instance, a microwave. For instance, a dishwasher. A girl at school called Carrie Francis once asked me how we survive. She says it must be like living in the

1940s house that they showed last year on TV. Did you watch it? I was like GLUED to the set, it was so fascinating. Seeing how people lived! But Carrie is just stupid to say that me and Mum live like that. We don't! We have central heating and a television and a washing machine, just like everyone else. We are not primitive! That girl really gets on my nerves at times.

Now for the exciting bit! I have been keeping it till last. THE PARTY!

It was the hugest fun! It was held in a hall, and there was this DJ called Ryan who organised everything and did Prince Charles impressions. He looked just like him! It was really funny.

There were thirty of us in all. NO BOYS. Carrie Francis arrived wearing a tall white floppy hat with a smile on it. She kept batting her eyelashes at the DJ, trying to make him fancy her. (Which he clearly didn't!) Susanna, the one that was having the party, said she was way over the top. In the end Susanna's mum had to step in and tell her to calm down.

You will want to know what we did. Well, we danced a lot! The bands we danced to were S Club 7 and Steps. (Two of my favourites!) He also played "Sex Bomb" by Tom Jones, which Susanna's dad didn't approve of! Susanna says he is not very cool. But anyway there was nothing he could do to stop it!

As well as dancing there were also lots of songs that you do the actions to, such as "Superman" and "Macarena" by Los Delrio. We also had a limbo contest using the DJ's microphone stand, plus a game where there were three teams and we had to pass a balloon over, then under, from person to person. Phew! I think that DJ wanted to tire us out. Which if he did he certainly managed it, as by the end even Carrie Francis had stopped batting her eyelashes. Oh, and her tall floppy hat wasn't tall any more! She took it off and put it on a chair while we were doing the limbo and a girl called Abbie that is rather BIG, went and sat on it and squashed it flat. So now it was a squashed floppy hat! It looked ridiculous. Well, it looked ridiculous to begin with, but after Abbie had sat on it it looked even more ridiculous. I expect it was a bit mean of me but when I told Mum about it afterwards I giggled. I said, "It looked like a hat that's had too much to drink!" But it serves her right for saying me and Mum live like they did in the 1940s.

Anyway, that is all about the party. I hope you enjoyed it. Now I want to hear about your visit to the British Museum! And see how quickly you can get into my maze.

Loadsa luv,
Katie.

PS   Here
is another joke.
What do sea
monsters eat?
Fish and ships!

Ho ho!

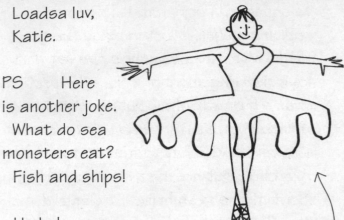

Here is my drawing
from the scribble.

Hi, Katie!

You sound like you had really good
fun at the party! My friend Sarah
had a DJ last year but I don't think
it was the same one. I cannot
remember his name, but he didn't look
like Prince Charles! I would remember
if he had.

Our visit to the British Museum was
totally brilliant! We saw all these
ancient old mummies wrapped up in
bandages. Quite s-s-s-scary! But

very interesting, of course. Now we have to write our mummy stories. Lily says she is going to write one about a mummy that starts pouring "fountains of blood" out of his eyes. It is a mad mummy! Somehow or other it gets hold of a chain saw and starts running all about the museum sawing people in half. She says there are going to be "arms and legs chopped off and intestines spilling out". You might think this shows what a great imagination she has, but in fact it was in a film we once saw, so all she is really doing is just copying.

My story is going to be about a sad mummy. He is a mummy who is suddenly brought back to life and can't understand where he is, or why he is shut up in a glass case with everybody staring at him. He misses his wife and children! He doesn't realise that he has been dead for thousands of years. I will have to work out a happy ending, though, as I wouldn't want him to suffer for all eternity.

I must tell you that it was really funny, while we were at the museum. For starters, me and Sarah got a bit hyper on the train going there. We couldn't stop giggling! We giggled at just about everything. Mrs Frost told us to behave ourselves or she would send us back to school, so that quietened us down a bit until we got to the museum and then, oh dear! We discovered a mummy that looked exactly like this really nerdy teacher that we have called Mr Spooner. He is very dry and withered, like a piece of old twig. Or like a mummy! If you wrapped him in bandages, you wouldn't be able to tell the difference. It was Sarah that saw him first. She showed him to me, and before I could stop myself I had cried, "Mr Spooner! What is he doing here?" Everyone just collapsed into mad giggles. Even Mrs Frost nearly laughed, I saw her lips twitch! She told us that we were the very worst bunch she had ever had to deal with.

I hope she doesn't put it in my report!

We are just having half-term now. A week after everyone else! I don't know why we always seem to have different holidays from other schools. I am not doing anything special. Lily has gone away with one of her posh friends to a cottage they have. They are going to ride ponies and go to gymkhanas, and be all hectic. I could have gone if I had wanted, but I decided I would rather just stay at home. I have lots of things to do. Such as:

Sticking things in my scrapbook
Sorting photographs
Helping mum in Flora Green
Writing to you!

Please don't worry about not having a computer. I would rather

write real letters and don't mind if
it is snail mail. I think that girl that
you told me about, Carrie Francis,
was extremely rude to say how did
you survive.

Your maze that you sent me was
HEAPS harder than the first one. I
had to start it three times before I
could find the way in. It was a really
good one and I wish I could do one
for you but I have tried and I can't.
So here is another word game. Can
you find which flowers these are:

Uptil Sore Drogmail
Foglevox Shopytalun

I think the last one is quite
difficult!

Next weekend we are going to
visit Little Nan and Popsy. (Popsy is
what we call my granddad James.) It
is Little Nan's birthday. She will be
the big six—oh. Sixty! All the family
are going to be there. All my aunties
and uncles and cousins. I will tell you
about it.

I have been trying to think of a joke but I can't so here are some book titles I have made up.

DOG'S DINNER by Nora Bone
HOLE IN THE BUCKET by Lee King
HOW TO GET RICH by Robin Banks
(this one is my favourite!)

Now I have to go because Mum is calling that tea is ready.
Bye for now!
xxxxxxxx Violet

PS   The Lily that Lily is named after is not a droopy one but a big spotty thing about 5 metres tall!

Friday morning, Lily came home from visiting Francine. Just in time for us all to go down to Nan and Popsy's. Mum and Dad were both taking the day off work. Daphne, who looks after the shop when Mum is not there, was left in charge of Flora Green. I worried that without me and Mum she wouldn't be able to manage, as weekends are really busy, but Mum told me to just relax and enjoy myself.

"Talk about an old head on young shoulders," she said.

"She just has a strongly developed sense of duty," said Dad, as we piled into the car. "Which is more than I can say for some people," he added, glancing over his shoulder at Lily.

Lily was in a sulk. Francine's mum had brought her home, but Francine's mum was then driving back down to the country because tomorrow there was some big horsy show or something that Francine was taking part in and Lily was dead resentful.

"*I* could have taken part! I could have ridden Cobbie! Francie said I could. She was going to let me borrow him! I don't see why I had to come to Nan's birthday. I went last year! Why do I have to come again?"

Mum said, "Because it's a family thing and Nan's going to be sixty and she would be very disappointed if you weren't there."

"But all we do is play stupid games! That's all we ever do. I could have been riding Cobbie! I bet I'd have got a rosette!"

She went on and on about it. She said it was all right for me: "She *likes* playing stupid games."

I do like playing games, it is true, and so does Lily when she's actually there. But she'd had such a good time with Francine I could sort of sympathise with her. She'd been riding every day. She'd helped out at the stables; she'd gone to a Pony Club meet; she'd made heaps of new friends; she'd taken Cobbie over a jump that nobody else had been able to manage; she'd only come off once – "And even then I remembered to hang on to the reins!" – and now she was thinking that instead of becoming a PA when she grew up she would enter the horsy world and ride for Britain in the Olympics.

She told us all this in the car as we drove to Nan's. Nobody else got a word in edgeways! It's always the same when Lily gets obsessed. Like the time she was going to be an ice skater, and the time she was going to be a pop star. I think to be fair to her she probably *will* be something. I mean something with a great big capital S. It just depends which particular enthusiasm she's got going when it comes time to leave school.

"Francie's mum says I have a really good seat!" bawled Lily, bouncing up and down in the back of the car and making me feel sick. "She says I can ride Cobbie whenever I want. She says I can go down there again at Easter if I like. She says I could even go h—"

Lily stopped.

"Go what?" I said.

"Oh!" Lily waved a hand. "Just… you know!"

"*Go what?*" I screeched it at her. Lily cringed back against the seat. "*Go hunting?*"

"I didn't say that," said Lily.

"You were going to!"

"I was not!"

"You were too!"

"I was *n*—"

"Lily and Violet!" Mum turned in her seat and thundered it at us. "Stop that! Right this minute! I don't want to hear another word. Have you got that? Not another word!"

Lily and I glared at each other. We sat the rest of the way in simmering silence. A few minutes ago I'd been half wishing that I'd told Katie it was me going to stay with Francine. I would have had so much to report! The only reason I hadn't, really, was 'cos she was just staying at home with her mum and I wouldn't have wanted it to seem like I was boasting or anything. Now I was glad! Katie felt the same way I did about fox hunting. I'd always thought Lily did, too, but she obviously didn't. Because she *had* been going to say fox hunting! She was a TURNCOAT.

I think she must have felt a bit ashamed of herself 'cos she was nice as pie to me all weekend, and when we went to bed that first night she whispered, "You know I wouldn't really go hunting." I was glad that she wouldn't but I did think she should have said something to Francine and her mum. I'd said something to Katie! And that was *before* I knew she was on my side. She might not have been. She might have got into a huff and never written to me again. So I just, like, grunted at Lily and pulled the duvet over my head and pretended to go to sleep. I didn't want to hear any more about her and her horsy friends!

When we got home on Sunday I looked eagerly at the front door mat to see if there was a letter for me, but there wasn't. Lily said, "Are you expecting something from the Blob? Don't tell me you're still *snail* mailing?"

"She hasn't got a computer," I said. "I did ask her!" I said this for Dad's benefit. "I said we could e-mail but she said her mum's got a lot of bills to pay and they can't afford a computer just at the moment."

Lily looked at me like she wasn't hearing right. "Can't afford a *computer*?"

"She hasn't got a dad," I said.

"Why not? Where is he?"

"I don't know. She hasn't told me."

"You mean, you haven't asked? I would ask!"

"That would be a personal question," I said. "You can't ask people personal questions. Her mum and dad might be divorced."

"So what? Lots of people's mums and dads are divorced. Francie's mum and dad are divorced. She doesn't care who knows. I'd say straight out," boasted Lily. "Are your mum and dad divorced? That's what I'd say. It's nothing to be ashamed of. I mean, it's nothing odd. Not like not having a computer. That is just so weird! How do they live?"

"They live just the same as anybody else," I said, crossly.

Lily looked over at Dad and made her eyes go big. I know she was expecting him to be on her side, what with him being a computer person and all, but Dad just laughed and said, "You could do with a spell on a desert island, my girl!"

Hooray! That told her.

Hi, Katie,

I know it's not my turn to write but I wanted to tell you about my ace weekend with my nan and granddad.

Nan had a birthday cake with SIXTY CANDLES on it. Truly! She counted them. It was a VERY BIG cake! It took her several goes to blow out all the candles. In the end we had to help her!

What made it such fun was that all the family came and we played games. All the family is: aunties and uncles (two of each); my great aunt (Nan's sister); my cousins (six in all).

Two of my cousins are boys, but they are quite nice. This is because they are still little*!!!* One of them is seven and the other is five. They have not yet had time to grow horrible... Of my four girl cousins my favourite is Stephanie as she is like us and hates fox hunting. Stephanie is twelve. You would get on with her!

The games that we played were:

Miming

20 Questions

Charades

How does it resemble me?

This last was particularly funny! How it is played is that one person has to go out of the room and all the rest think of an object. The person then comes back and goes round in a circle asking "How does it resemble me?" and trying to guess what it is. It was SO hilarious! When my nan went out of the room the object chosen was: a flower pot. Well, she came back and started to ask questions, and when she got to my granddad and said, "How does it resemble me?" you will never guess what he replied! Very solemnly he said, "It has a hole in its bottom." Nan looked quite shocked for a moment so that I felt sure she was going to tell him off for being rude, but in the end she couldn't help laughing, and so then we all did.

Charades was also fun. In case you don't know it, this is where you divide into teams and each team chooses a word and breaks it down into syllables. You then act out each syllable and people have to work out what the word is.

I was in a team with Stephanie, Uncle Dave, my dad and my great aunt Annie. Our word was AEROBICS. (Air-o-bix.) When we did the first syllable Aunt Annie pretended to be an opera singer (singing an AIR). She dressed up

in a big lacy tablecloth and put a
lamp—shade on her head! She is a
very dignified sort of person — she
is a head teacher!!! — and it was
just hilarious. I couldn't help
wondering what the children at her
school would think if they could see
her!

It was a really great weekend.
Even Lily enjoyed it, though she was
moaning like crazy on the way there
as she didn't want to leave her
friend Francine and miss out on
riding a pony called Cobbie in a
gymkhana.

What sort of things do you do
when you go and visit your nan?
Where does your nan live? Mine
lives in St Alban's, which is not so
very far away.

Tomorrow we go back to school.
WOE. I don't really mind though it
would be far more fun just to go on
playing charades and seeing my Aunt
Annie in a lampshade! Her school had

already been on half-term. We were a whole week later than everyone else but we break up a week earlier. On the other hand we do LOADS of homework and we start at half-past eight every morning and don't finish until half-past four, which I think is quite a LONG DAY.

Please write soon!
Lots of love
from your friend
Violet xxx

PS   This is a joke my Uncle Dave told me. How do you make a sausage roll? Push it!

PPS   Did you manage to work out all the flower words?

Hi, Violet!

Sorry I haven't written for ages. Almost ten days! I expect you will have been wondering what has happened and whether you have said something to offend me, which is what I would most probably be wondering if you didn't write back to me like almost IMMEDIATELY.

I have been in bed, boo hoo! I have had this really bad cold and couldn't go to school, which I absolutely hate. There are some people that think it is fun, not having to go to school, but I am not one of them! It is just so boring, lying in bed, even though Mum stayed home to keep me company. I kept thinking all the time of what was going on at school without me, and wanting so much to write to you but I just felt too woozy. Like my head was full of fog. I did try starting a letter but my hand went like all across the page so that you wouldn't have been able to read it anyway! It was, like, all sh-sh-shivery and sh-sh-shaky. Like a g-g-g-ghost.

I am not yet back at school so I am going to write you this really LONG letter. Be warned!!!

I did your flower arrangements. (Mum says it is called ANAGRAMS, when you mix up the letters of a word.)

Uptil (tulip)

Sore (rose)

Drogmail (marigold)

Foglevox (foxglove)

Shopytalun (polyanthus)

Marigold and polyanthus were really difficult! Especially as polyanthus is one I hadn't heard of... Mum had to help me with that one! I expect you know all about flowers because of your mum.

The flowers were in your first letter, which I expect by now you will have forgotten what you wrote. I will have to remind you!

I keep all of your letters. Do you keep mine? While I was in bed I read through all of yours and I just felt so happy that we are pen pals!

Mum says that the lily that Lily is named after is probably a TIGER lily. A tiger lily would look like this:

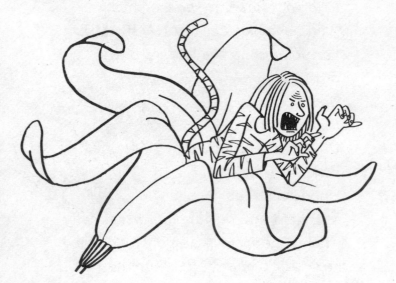

I still like violets best!

I couldn't help laughing about your visit to the British Museum and seeing a mummy that looked like one of your teachers! I have done a strip cartoon of it. I will stick it on Now.

Next week, me and Mum are doing a sponsored walk for the Cats' Protection League. We got Bella and Bertie from them and so that is why we always support them. These are the people I have been sponsored by:

The lady who lives upstairs, Mrs Cathcart. (She is old but very nice.

Sometimes if I am at home when Mum is at school I go upstairs and watch TV with her.)

Our next door neighbours (both sides).

The lady in the newspaper shop.

The whole of my class at school!

If I walk right round (five miles) I will make… £52!!! I am really looking forward to it.

I am glad you enjoyed your nan's birthday party. It sounded like fun. I specially liked Auntie Annie in the lampshade!

I told Mum about your granddad saying to your nan that "It has a hole in its bottom". Mum thought it was very funny! Mrs Cathcart came down on Sunday afternoon for tea and we played the game of "How does it resemble me?" but we didn't have a flower pot! Mrs Cathcart is too old and might have been upset.

You asked me what we do when we visit my nan and where she lives. She lives in Yorkshire but we don't ever visit her. She won't have anything to do with us, except just at Christmas and on my birthday she sends me a present and I write to thank her, but that is all. She doesn't want to see us or even for me to ring her up. This is because she thinks we are beneath her. She was my dad's mum, and she was very angry when he and Mum got married.

Unfortunately she is the only nan I have as Mum was brought up in a children's home and has no family. She and Dad were so happy together! There is a photo of them holding hands and looking all smoochy into each other's eyes. But my dad died when I was only three and so I never really knew him and I have never met my nan at all as she cut us off and retired to live in her dark and spooky house and never see the light of day. Dad was her only child so perhaps when he died it unhinged her mind, but Mum says she is a very proud and unforgiving woman and so I cannot really feel too sorry for her. Mum is the one I feel sorry for. I think it is so unkind, the way she has been treated.

You are lucky to have a mum AND a dad AND a sister (even if it is not always fun) AND two nans and a granddad. I am not being jealous when I say this but I would like to at least have a nan. Mum says Mrs Cathcart is "as good as" but Mrs Cathcart has children of her own and always goes off at Christmas to stay with them. So then I am completely nan-less! It is just Mum and me. Even Arthur has a family.

I hope this letter doesn't sound too glum and gloomy. It is not meant to. But you did ask! About my nan, I mean. I am not feeling sorry for myself, I am just telling you how it is.

The reason you have half-term at a different time from everyone else is because you go to a posh school and posh schools do everything differently from everyone else! I expect you have to be quite rich to go to your school. I don't mind if you are rich! My nan is rich. Mum says she has more money than she knows what to do with. Mrs Cathcart says, "It is a pity she doesn't spend some of it on her granddaughter," but Mum says, "We can do without her charity."

I have not yet done another maze, but here is a joke! I just made it up.

Question: What kind of robbery is the easiest?

Answer: a safe robbery!

I think that is quite good.

And now I must tell you something. I have had this totally brilliant and earth shattering idea! You know in one of your letters you said how it would be great if you could write stories and I could do pictures to go with them? Well, we could do a magazine! Like Go Girl, only we could make it funny. You could do the writing bits and I could do the drawings. Do you think this is a good idea? We could have problem pages and letters pages and short stories and poems and articles. And then when we had done it you could maybe make copies on your computer and I would do a cover for it. Say if you want to! You don't have to. I mean, like if you're too busy or anything. Or if you think it would just be a drag. But if you would like to you could send me something next time you write and I would do the pictures straight away.

I hope this letter is not so long that you have stopped reading it! I must close now as my hand is beginning to ache. I suppose that would be one good thing about having a computer. Mum says maybe next year. I will keep my fingers crossed!

Lots of luv from
Katie xxxxxxxxxx

I told Mum about Katie's dad, and about her nan being too proud and unforgiving to have anything to do with Katie and her mum. (I didn't tell Lily as she was still calling Katie the Blob and so I  didn't think she deserved to be told. Plus she would probably only say something stupid and annoying.)

"It's so sad, isn't it?" I said to Mum.

Mum agreed that it was. "But it's nice that she's told you. She obviously felt ready for it. And it explains why she's always seemed so close to her mum, if there's only the two of them."

"At least she has Arthur and Mrs Cathcart," I said. "I know it's not the same, but it's better than nothing."

I was so excited by Katie's idea of writing stories and poems for our own magazine. It is just exactly the sort of thing that I really love to do! I sat down immediately and wrote a poem and sent it to her.

Dear Katie,

I will write a proper letter soon. I love the idea of doing a magazine! Here is a poem I have written for it.
  xxx Violet

PS   What shall we call it? The magazine, I mean.

POEM

I'M HAVING A VERY BAD HAIR DAY,
MY HAIR SIMPLY LOOKS SUCH A SIGHT!
IT STICKS UP IN SPOKES, ALL OVER THE
PLACE,
IT WON'T DO ANYTHING RIGHT!

OH, WHAT CAN I DO WITH MY HORRIBLE HAIR,
HOW CAN I MAKE IT BEHAVE?
I'M OFF TO A PARTY TOMORROW,
IT'S GOING TO BE QUITE A BIG RAVE!

HOW CAN I GO WITH MY HAIR IN THIS STATE?
IT IS SUCH A TERRIBLE MESS!
AND TO THINK THAT I'VE BOUGHT SOME NEW
  SHOES,
AND A HUGELY EXPENSIVE NEW DRESS!

I KNOW WHAT I'LL DO! I'VE GOT A GOOD
PLAN.
I WON'T GO AND SULK IN MY BED.
I'LL INVENT A NEW FASHION, I'LL BE REALLY
  COOL,
I'LL JUST WEAR A CAT ON MY HEAD!

Dear Violet,

Your poem is really funny! It made me laugh. I have tried to draw some funny pictures for it. I hope you like them.
xxx Katie

PS   How about GIRLZONE (Girls' Own... Girlzone! Geddit?) But you can suggest something else if you prefer.

Hi, Katie!

The pictures are ace! And I think GIRLZONE is cool. Now I have made up some problems for a problem page. I will type them out on the computer and send them with this letter. But I have not done the answers as I think it would be better if you did those.

Your last letter that you wrote me was not in the least glum and gloomy though I am sorry if I upset you by asking about your nan. I know that I am very lucky to have a family even if I do sometimes complain about my sister. She is quite a tiresome sort of person, but in future I will try to complain a bit less and just put up with her.

It is true you have to pay to go to my school, but we are not rich!!! Mum said to Lily just the other day that "We are not made of money". This was because Lily was nagging about these new riding boots she wants.

She says her old ones are naff, and she can't be seen in them. She has to have SPECIAL ones like her friend Francine has. So Mum told her she couldn't and Lily got into one of her sulks and that was when Mum snapped we weren't made of money.

I have asked Mum if we can sponsor you for your walk! She says that we can and we would like to give you a pound for every mile. Just let me know how many you do! We got Horatio from a lady that comes into Mum's shop, but if ever we get another cat we will go to the Cats' Protection League. That is a promise!

I look forward to hearing your answers to my problems!

Luv and kisses (lots of them!)
From
Violet

PS   I keep all your letters, too! In a special box with a LOCK.

Dear Katie,

My sister has such a big head that if I walk behind her no one can see me. What do you think I should do? Please help! – *Norah Nobody.*

Dear Katie,

I have a confession to make… I am frightened of my own shadow. This is so pathetic! How can I cure myself? – *Scaredy Cat.*

Dear Katie,

When I go to parties I stand in the corner and nobody talks to me. How can I make myself more noticeable? – *Mouse.*

Ever since the incident with the riding boots, Mum and Lily had been on *really* bad terms. Lily, as usual, said that Mum was ruining her life, because how could she hope to be a top class rider and ride for Britain if she didn't have the proper riding boots. Mum said the riding boots she had were perfectly adequate and that Lily was a spoilt brat.

She said, "Sometimes I wonder why your dad and I bother! We work our fingers to the bone, all the hours God sends, and what for? Just so that you can go to your snotty little school and mix with your snotty little friends and be thoroughly grasping and disagreeable!"

Wow!

She said she had a good mind to take Lily away from Lavendar House and send her to the local comprehensive.

"Why just me?" said Lily. "What about little Shrinky Winky? Of course, *she* couldn't go to the comprehensive, could she? She's too *delicate*. She'd get *crushed*."

"I could go there!" I said. Though as a matter of fact I am the reason that Mum and Dad work their fingers to the bone and send us to our snotty little school. (Which is quite nice, really.) It is because of me being a shrinking violet and Mum being scared that I couldn't cope. Which maybe I couldn't.

The thought of being with *boys*, and lots of tough kids, is scary. It wouldn't scare Lily. She'd be all right! She'd be one of the tough kids.

But she was really resentful.

"Why just *me*? Why is it always *me*?"

"Because Violet doesn't constantly make demands," said Mum.

"No, 'cos she never does anything!" screeched Lily. "She just sits upstairs writing letters to the Blob!"

"I'm not just writing letters," I said. "We're doing a magazine. We're going to call it GIRLZONE... Girls' Own. Geddit?"

Lily said, "Hey! That's quite cool," in tones of some surprise. She then got a bit sidetracked, wanting to know when the magazine was going to be finished and what sort of things were going to be in it and whether we were going to have any articles about horses.

"'Cos if you like, I could do one for you."

I said that I would ask Katie, though to be honest I didn't really think we wanted anything about horses, I mean it wasn't a *horsy* mag, and I definitely didn't think I wanted Lily interfering.

"Well, just let me know," said Lily. "I could do you a really good article about riding boots."

She looked at Mum quite boldly as she said this. Mum snapped, "I don't wish to hear another word!

If you want to go down to Francine's again at Easter, my girl, you had just better watch your step!"

So after that, Lily started being all polite. Unnaturally polite. Like everything was *please* and *thank you* and could I *possibly*. And always with this big bright beam to show how charming she was being. Sickening, really.

One day she came home from school and said that Debbie's dad was going to take Debbie into town on Saturday and they were going to go on the London Eye and Debbie had asked Lily if she'd like to go with them.

"Of course I said I'd have to ask my mum," gushed Lily, beaming away as hard as she could.

"You can go on the Eye," said Mum. "I have no objections to that."

"Oh, how darling!" cried Lily.

Mum gave her this long look, then slowly shook her head.

"*She* could come, if she wanted," said Lily. "I don't s'ppose Debbie would mind."

"Violet? Would you like to?" said Mum.

I would have done, quite. But I just knew that Lily was only saying it to get in Mum's good books. She didn't really want me.

"Just say," said Lily. "You've only got to say."

"'S all right," I said. "I've got things to do."

"Violet? Are you sure?" said Mum.

"I've got to write a short story," I said.

"Oh! Well." Lily tossed her head. "If you'd rather write a *short* story—"

"I've got to," I said. "I promised Katie."

I went upstairs to my bedroom, thinking that I would do it straight away, but I couldn't even get started! I kept thinking how I could have written a story about someone going on the London Eye, and wishing that I'd said I'd go. It would have been something to tell Katie! I am so *stupid* at times. I really annoy myself.

Dear Violet,

I have answered all your problems! I have done some pictures to go with them.

I thought that we could also, maybe, have some funny articles. But only if you feel like doing them. If you are not too busy with all your homework! I told Mum about your homework. She said, "And a good thing too!" She really approves of your school! Ours doesn't really have homework too much, but I do lots of things with Mum, such as working out problems and reading books together. We do that quite often.

Hey, guess what? I have been invited to THREE PARTIES! Two are people in my class and one is a girl that lives over the road. I am really excited and wondering what to wear. Mum says we will go into town at the weekend and buy something. She has promised that I will get to choose! I said, "Can I choose whatever I like?" She said, "Anything so long as it is decent." That means anything! 'cos I wouldn't want not to be decent, would you?

What I would really really REALLY like is this fab top I saw someone wearing, white with gold fringes, and these really swanky jeans with a sparkly belt. Oh, and some zip-up trainers! Pink ones. That is what I would REALLY like. I will tell you if I get them!!!

Must dash.

Oodles of love!

xxx Katie

PTO FOR PROBLEM PAGE.

[ANSWERS]

Dear Norah,

Do not despair! The solution is simple. FIND YOURSELF A PIN. A quick sharp JAB will soon deflate your sister's head.

Good luck!

Dear Scaredy Cat,

There are several things you can try. First off you could avoid going out on days when there is sunshine, then there would not be any shadow for you to be scared of. However, this may not always be convenient. How about suddenly spinning round and shouting "Boo!" very loudly and fiercely? That would see it off!

Alternatively you could try saying "Hi!" It might turn out to be friendly. You never know!

Dear Mouse,

Learn some kind of social skill. For instance you could:

Walk on your hands. But do make sure you are wearing clean knickers without any holes!

Juggle with plates. Though maybe oranges would be safer, just to begin with.

Belch in time to God Save the Queen. This would soon get people's attention!

Try any of these and before you know it everyone will be desperate to talk to you!

Dear Katie,

I thought your answers to my problems were really funny! I love the idea of belching in time to God Save the Queen. I have tried doing it but I can't belch! Lily can. She does it all the time and says it is quite easy. She has tried to teach me but all I do is gulp down air and make myself ill. Lily says I am useless. She says I have no social skills at all.

When are your parties that you are going to? I don't know whether Lily and me will have a party this year. Last year when we had one Lily got hyper and threw Ribena all over the wall and trod on a glass and smashed the banisters. How she smashed the banisters, she was pretending to ride a horse. She was going "Giddyap, giddyap," and kicking at the banister rails. Mum and Dad were just so furious with her! Mum said she was a vandal and Dad said she ought to live in a hole at the bottom of the garden. So I don't know whether we will have one this year. But I want to hear all about your ones!

My news is that I am going to go on the London Eye. I think this will be quite exciting! I am going with a friend from school called Debbie. Her dad is taking us. I just hope I don't get sick, which is what I usually do. Like one time when Dad took us on a Giant Octopus where you sat in this little pod thing at the end of a long arm, and the arm went up in the air like a big wheel and at the same time the little pod thing whizzed round and round incredibly fast. It made me feel sick as sick! I just couldn't wait to get off. And then when I did, you'll never guess what ...

I instantly threw up all over Lily! Boy, was she ever mad! But the Eye moves really s... l... o... w... l... y, so that you hardly even notice, so maybe I will be all right. I would not like to throw up over Debbie's dad!

Here is a pattern I have done for Girlzone.

How to sew yourself a groovy cushion cover:

What you will need:
One of your dad's shirts (if he will let you have one. If not, see if he has put one out for rags. Do not use one of his best ones!!!)
Needle and thread
Stuff for filling

What to do:
1. Lay the shirt flat.
2. Chop off the top bit, from underneath the arms. Chuck this bit away.

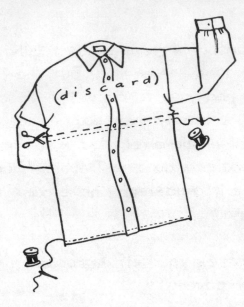

(discard)

3. Take the bit that's left and turn
it inside out.
4. Sew the two sides together.
5. Open the buttons and turn it
back the right way.
6. Stuff with rags or cotton wool.
7. Hide a dog's squeaky toy inside
and do up the buttons.

You now have a groovy cushion that
will make a loud squeeeeeek! when
anyone sits on it. Fun for parties!
I have not tried this out as I am not

very good at sewing, but I think it
would be quite easy.

Anyway, we can use it if you
want. We don't have to.

Please tell me about your parties.
Did you get your top that you wanted?
And your jeans and the trainers?

Luv from Violet xxxxxxxxxx

PS   Next I am going to do a
short story!

Hiya, Violet! Groovy cushion
cover!

Here is Lily riding
the banisters.
Will write soon.

xxx Katie

Dear Katie,

Here is a short story. Hope you like it.
Luv Violet

PS   What happened about your sponsored walk? How many miles did you do? Tell me and we will send you the money!

BETSY BURP, by Violet Alexander

A story in 4 parts

Part 1
Once upon a time there were two sisters. One of them was called Nasturtium, the other was called Geranium. Nasturtium was known as Nasty, while Geranium was known as Gerry.

Nasty was quite nasty. She could often be really mean to her sister.

Gerry was quite merry! At least, she was when Nasty wasn't being nasty to her.

One day when the girls came home from school their mother said, "Guess what? I have just seen a notice in the Radio Times about a singing contest. It is going to be on television, in front of millions of viewers! The viewers will vote who is the winner, and they will be given a contract with a big record company and become famous overnight. Gerry, you have a nice loud voice! Why don't you enter the contest?"

"I will!" cried Gerry. "What a cool idea! I will sing my favourite song and perhaps I will win and become famous!"

Nasty sniffed and said, "Dream on!"

She was just jealous because her mum had not said that she had a nice loud voice. Nasty did have a loud voice, as a matter of fact, but it wasn't very nice. Whenever she started to sing people would stuff their fingers in their ears and go "Ow!" and "Ouch!" and "This is so painful!"

But Nasty was of the opinion she had a perfectly wonderful voice. Far better than her sister's.

"I will go in for the contest as well," she thought. "But I will not tell her."

Part 2

The day of the singing contest arrived. Gerry was so nervous she didn't want to eat anything, but her mum said she must or she would feel faint.

"Nasty," she said, "go and make your sister a sandwich."

"Oh, if I must," said Nasty.

Nasty made the sandwich out of hard-boiled eggs, all mashed up with salt and pepper, oil of cloves, mustard, soya sauce, tomato ketchup, and... garlic! Six whole cloves of it. Yeeeeurgh!

"Tee hee!" thought Nasty. "This sandwich will make her puke, for sure!"

But Gerry was in such a state she didn't even notice.

"Is it all right?" said Nasty.

"Yes. Thank you. It is very yummy," said Gerry, wondering why Nasty was suddenly being so nice to her.

After she had eaten the sandwich, Gerry and her mum left for the TV studio. On the way there Gerry came over a bit peculiar, but she thought that it was just nerves.

"Once I start to sing," she thought, "I will feel better."

She was going to sing her favourite song, Love ya, baby! These were the words:

Love ya, baby!
I sure do.
Don't want her.
Just want you!
Trust me, babe!
It's me 'n you.

She had sat up all night learning them.

When they reached the studio there were dozens of really cool kids there, all hoping to become famous. They took one look at Gerry (who by now had turned quite green thanks to the mustard, oil of cloves, soya sauce, tomato ketchup and garlic sandwich) and curled their lips.

"Look at her!" they went. "What chance does she think she stands?"

"None!" came a voice from the doorway.

Gerry turned, with a gasp. It was Nasty! What was she doing there?

Part 3

"Ha, ha," sneered Nasty. "You didn't expect me, did you?"

Gerry shook her head. She was beginning to feel very odd and weird.

"The minute you left I jumped into a cab and followed you," said Nasty. "My voice is far louder than yours! I will be the pop star, not you!"

Gerry opened her mouth to say something, but all that came out was a big... BURP! Ugh, phew! The smell of garlic was so strong that Gerry's poor mum instantly passed out with the stench.

"Tee hee!" giggled Nasty. "That will teach her a lesson!"

Nasty could not forgive her mum for putting Gerry in for the contest instead of her.

Gerry turned to her sister. She opened her mouth – and another burp came out. Yeeeeeeurgh!!! It was even stinkier than the first one. Nasty promptly joined her mum on the floor. She was out for the count!

And now all the other contestants were plopping down. All those really cool kids that had curled their lips! They were dropping like flies. The smell was too much!

Very soon, Gerry was the only one left...

Part 4

Gerry felt a whole lot better, now that she was getting rid of some of the garlic fumes. But she still couldn't stop burping! How could she sing Love ya, baby! if she was burping all the time?

The answer was – she couldn't! She had to think quickly. There were millions of viewers out there, waiting to be entertained. And all the other contestants were flat on the floor. It was up to Gerry!

So guess what she did? She burped her way through three whole verses of God Save the Queen! (She only knew the words to the first verse, but it didn't really matter as she wasn't singing them.)

Burp burp burp BURP burp burp
Burp burp burp BURP burp burp
Burp burp burp burp.

Nobody had ever heard anything like it! The clapometers went mad! And of course Gerry won the contest, because who else was there?

Now she is famous. She has changed her name to Betsy Burp, and even has her own backing group... Betsy Burp and the Belchers!

THE END

Dear Katie,

I hope you liked my short story that I sent you last week. Maybe you have not had time to read it yet. I expect you are very busy going to parties.

I have been on the London Eye! I was not sick as it really does go slowly so that you hardly know you are moving. The view is amazing, you can see all over London.

Well, that is all for now. Please write back soon!

xxx Violet

PS   You never said how many miles you walked but here is a cheque for the cats.

Dear Violet,

I am sorry I have not written sooner. I read "Betsy Burp" at once and it is brilliant! I nearly died laughing, and so did Mum. We think you are so clever to be able to write like that. I will do some drawings as soon as I can but I may not be able to do them for a little while. But I will do them! This is a PROMISE.

My big big huge GINORMOUS news is that I may be coming to your school in September!!! My gran has said that she will pay for me! You will probably wonder how this can have happened when I told you that my gran is proud and unforgiving and will have nothing to do with us. Well, she has changed her mind! It is so amazing! This is how it happened.

Mum picked up the phone and there she was, at the other end of it. Shock horror and wonders will never cease!!! She asked Mum if she could speak to ME. I was quite nervous, to tell you the truth. I am not usually a nervous sort of person, but I couldn't think what I would say to her. I felt that I hated her because of the way she has treated Mum, but at the same time she is my gran and I have always wanted to have a gran. So I picked up the receiver and said "Hallo?" in what I hoped was a NONDESCRIPT way, like not cross, exactly, but not friendly, either, in case she was going to say something mean about Mum, but she didn't. You'll never guess what she did... she APOLOGISED!!!

She said that she was really sorry about not speaking to us all these years. She said, "I'm just a stupid stiff-necked old woman and you must try to forgive me." So I did, which I hope you won't think was weak of me but she is my gran and she did say sorry. To me AND to Mum. I think this may be because she is growing old and is feeling all alone in the world. She says that now we have "broken the ice" we must behave like a real family before it is too late and so she is going to come and visit with us, and then later on we are going to go and visit with her. I will tell you all about it!

After she had finished speaking to me she spoke to Mum. They were on the phone for simply ages. I heard Mum telling her all about your school and how lovely it is, and my gran said it sounded just the place for me. She said that she would get in touch immediately, and she did. The very same day! They said they have some girls that are leaving at the end of this term and they think that they will be able to take me!

I am so excited! It will be such fun! I do hope we will be in the same class, then we can sit together and do things together and be best friends. If you would like to, that is. Mum says you probably already have best friends and I mustn't push myself in, so please say if you have and I will understand. We can just go on being pen pals if you would rather. It will still be fun. I can't wait for September!!!

Lots and loads of love
from your pen pal, Katie

PS   Thank you very much for the cheque for the cats. Please say thank you to your mum.

PPS   Mum is typing this letter for me on her typewriter. I am dictating it to her! This is so it can be done quickly. Also it will be easier to read!

I was thrown into deadly panic when I got Katie's letter. I know I should have been happy for her about her gran, but all I could think of was *me*. My stomach went blurp! and my heart went *thunk*. I was filled with a bottomless pit of total despair. I knew that if I told Mum – "Katie's coming to my school!" – she would say, "Oh, isn't that lovely?" But it wouldn't be lovely! It would be a disaster! She would discover how dim and nerdy I was and how it was Lily and not me that went to parties and had been on the Eye and had best friends. She would utterly despise me and never want to talk to me again. She might even team up with Lily! I didn't think I could bear it if she did that.

I had to write to her *immediately*.

Dear Katie,

I am really happy that you liked my story. I will look forward to seeing the pictures but I quite understand if you are too busy at the moment.

I was surprised to hear about your gran paying for you to come to my school! I don't think you would like my school very much. For a start (I may have told you this before) it is absolutely TITCHY. We don't even have our own playing field, and for swimming we have to go to the local baths. Also there is no sixth form. I think maybe your gran does not realise this and if she did she would not want to send you there.

Mum said about it the other day that it was "a snotty little school". I think if you are used to going to a real school you would find it rather piddling. It is not really posh. I mean it is not where members of the Royal

Family would go. It is just three ancient houses knocked together, and the teachers are quite ancient also. Like some of them have been here since practically Victorian times, I would think. They are not in the least
bit cool!

Another thing is that there are of course no boys, which is quite nice at the moment as I am not into boys but I cannot help feeling that later on, when you are say twelve or thirteen, you might wish that there were otherwise how will you ever get to know about them?

I do not want to put you off or anything but your gran might not know what it is like and then she would feel that she had wasted her money and you would be disappointed and wish you had gone to a proper school. I thought I should tell you. It is only fair. We can still go on being pen pals!

Please write as soon as you are
not too busy.
   With luv and xxx
   Violet

PS   Have you been to any of
your parties yet?

Every day when I came home from school I
looked for letters on the mat, but all there ever was
was stuff for Mum and Dad. Nothing at all for me.
One day there was even a letter for *Lily*.

"Mine!" She snatched it from me. "Stinking
swizzlesticks! Snail mail!"

All it was was a form for her to fill in if she
wanted to take part in some boring gymkhana. Not a
real letter at all. I'd hoped so much that it might be
for me.

"Hey! What's happened to the Blob?" said Lily.
"Why don't you ever hear from her any more?"

There are times when me and Lily can almost
seem to read each other's minds. I suppose it's what
comes from being part of the same egg, even though
we are now completely different.

"You haven't had any snaily mail in ages," said Lily. "You used to practically write whole *books*." Lily folded up her letter and carefully slotted it back in its envelope. I watched her, jealously. "I suppose you've got bored. You wouldn't get bored if you e-mailed."

"I told you," I said. "She hasn't got a computer."

"Oh!" Lily clapped a hand to her mouth. "Sorry! I was forgetting."

And then she gave this silly snigger and said, "You could always try smoke signals!"

"Lily, leave Violet alone," said Mum.

"I'm not *touching* her," said Lily. "I'm just trying to be helpful, is all."

Huh! Like she would know how.

Dear Katie,

It seems ages since I heard from you. I hope I didn't upset you by saying about my school and how I didn't think you'd like it. I didn't mean to!

148

Here is a joke:

What do birds eat for their
breakfast?
Tweet—a—bix and shredded tweet!

Hope to hear from you soon
xxx Violet

"Still no letter from Katie?" said Mum.

I made a mumbling sound.

"Why don't you try ringing her?"

"Don't know her number," I said.

"You could look her up in the telephone directory.
Why don't you give it a go? Go and get the book,"
said Mum, "and we'll look her up!"

"I don't want to," I said.

"Why not? You haven't quarrelled, have you?"

I shook my head.

"Well, go on, then! Go and get the phone book."

"*I DON'T WANT TO!*"

I yelled it at Mum and rushed from the room. I'm
not like Lily, I don't very often yell at Mum, but I
hate it when she tries to force me to do things. Like
when she tries to force me into going places with

Lily, when I just know that Lily doesn't want me to. I really hate it when she does that.

All the same, it did worry me that I hadn't heard from Katie for so long. I was really scared that I had upset her.

Friday was the end of term and we were let out early. Lily went off with Francine, so I thought I would have to go to Flora Green by myself to pick up Mum, but instead I found that she was waiting for me outside school. I was quite surprised.

"Mum!" I said. "What are you doing?"

"Jump in," said Mum. "I left work early. Listen, I had a telephone call today... at the shop. It was Katie's mum."

"K-Katie's m-*mum*?" I said; and my blood went all to water and my knees went wobbly. Why would Katie's *mum* be ringing?

"The reason you haven't heard from Katie," said Mum, "is that she's been in hospital. Don't look so alarmed! She's had to have an operation, but she's going to be all right."

I swallowed. "What s-sort of operation?"

"Well, it seems she's had a weak heart for a very long time—"

"*Katie?*"

150

I couldn't believe it! In her letters she had always sounded so full of life and energy. I had really admired her for it. I had envied her! How could *Katie* have a weak heart?

Mum explained that it was something she'd been born with and that it had just been getting worse and worse until in the end an operation had been necessary.

"But she's come through it and she's going to be fine. Her mum says she's fretting because she hasn't been able to write to you. She says having you as a pen pal has made all the difference to her these last few months, when she's been so ill. Now she's worried in case you think she doesn't want to be her friend any more. So what we've arranged—"

"W–what?" I said.

"We're going to go over there tomorrow, so that you can pay her a visit. OK?"

"No!" I didn't want to! I didn't want to!

"Violet, she's your friend!" said Mum. "And she's in hospital. It's what you do when your friends are in hospital… you go and visit them. Try to cheer them up."

"I could send her a card," I said. "A funny one!"

"She doesn't want a funny card, she wants a visit. She wants to *see* you. So we're going over there," said Mum. "Tomorrow afternoon."

"But what about the shop?" I wailed.

"Don't worry about the shop," said Mum. "The shop can take care of itself."

"But it's busy on a Saturday!"

"Violet," said Mum. She pulled the car up at some traffic lights. "Katie is your *friend*. You owe her this! Oh! And something you didn't tell me," she said, as the lights changed, "I gather she's going to Lavendar House in September. That will be fun! Won't it? The two of you together. That will really be something to look forward to!"

All that night I stayed awake, worrying. Worrying is a thing that I do quite often. I don't think Lily has ever worried about anything in the whole of her life. I wish I could be more like her!

No, I don't; not really. I just wish I could be a little bit less like me!

Well, sometimes I do.

You'll never believe it, but when we set out next day Lily actually clamoured to come with us.

"I want to see the Blob! I could cheer her up. *She* won't cheer her up! She'll just make her miserable. Oh, Mum, please! Let me come to the hospital with you!"

But Mum wouldn't let her. Thank goodness!

"Katie is Violet's friend," she said, "not yours."

I couldn't help wondering whether she would still want to be, once she'd discovered the truth…

Saturday

Dear Violet,

I was so ☺ to see you today! It was quite a surprise – Mum didn't tell me you were coming so I was truly amazed when the door opened and you walked in. You were just how I imagined you from your letters! I wonder if I was how you imagined me? I don't expect I was, but I hope I didn't come as a huge disappointment. I really really REALLY loved meeting you! I felt very ☺ when you had to go. Please come again soon!

I was deathly ashamed when your mum said about me doing that sponsored walk for the cats and Mum said, "Oh, it was so sad, she was too ill to do it." I felt so dreadful! Like a thief, or a cheat. I should have told you. I don't know why I didn't! I meant to, but then you sent the money and I was just so pleased that I gave it to Mum for the cats and I didn't tell her that I hadn't told you and now she says it was very wrong of me as it was getting money under false pretences and I must ask you if you would like it back. She says we will send you a cheque AT ONCE. She also says that I must apologise to your mum, so please will you say to her that I apologise? I see now that it was a very bad thing to do. I just so much wanted to help the poor cats!

Next week I am going to be back home and I will draw some pictures for "Betsy Burp" which I LOVE! I will send them to you as soon as I have done them.

Please say if you would like the cat

money back and say sorry for me to
your mum.

  Love and lots of xxxxxx
  From Katie

Saturday (same day as Katie wrote to me!)

Dear Katie,

We have just got back after seeing
you. I was really shocked when Mum
told me yesterday about you being ill
and having to have an operation. I
have never known anyone before
that has had to have one. I think it
must be very scary. I would be
scared!

  But I expect you are a lot braver
than me. Like Lily. She is brave. She
would not be scared by anything! If
you had told me I would have sent
you a card. I would have sent LOTS
of cards. One a day! With messages
and jokes to cheer you up. But I can

understand why you didn't. It was probably something you didn't want to think about. If I was going to have an operation I would do my best to pretend it wasn't happening. I am glad it is all over and that you are now better.

I was quite scared of meeting you. I am afraid I am a bit of a scaredy cat about all kinds of things. What I was scared of was that I would not be able to think of anything to say, which is this thing that happens when I meet people for the first time, and especially if they have had an operation and might still be feeling poorly so you are not sure how to behave. I hope I did not seem too stupid.

You know when our mums were talking and your mum was saying about how you couldn't do things and it was so frustrating for you, and my mum said how I COULD do things but I wouldn't, such as for example

going into town with Lily and her
friend Debbie and going on the
London Eye? I could tell that you
were really surprised when she said
this. I could tell that your mum was
surprised, too. I am sorry I told you
that I went on the Eye when it was
Lily that did. I expect now you will
think I am totally mad.

Mum says why doesn't she take
you and me on the Eye some time?
She says to ask if you would like to
do this. (As soon as you are well
enough.) I would like it, but I will
understand if you would rather not.
I am really sorry that I told you a
lie.

I hope you will still want to write
to me. I promise I will not tell you
any more lies about things that I
have done that I have not really
done.

With love from
Violet

Hi, Violet,

I just got your letter. Did you get mine? Mum says they must have "crossed in the post".

I was not scared of having an operation as they put you to sleep and so you know nothing about it. I am more scared when I go to the dentist and they stick needles in you. I hate it when they stick needles in you! I go AAAh and OOOh and OUCH! Mum says I am a real baby.

I am sorry if I did not tell you. Mum says I should have done (as you are my friend) but if I had said at the beginning that I could not do things I thought maybe you would say to yourself this girl is no fun, I do not want to write to her. So that is why I didn't tell you. But I am very sorry.

I suppose I was a LITTLE bit surprised when your mum said about it being Lily that went on the Eye and not you, but it really doesn't matter. I don't think you are mad. But if you are, then I am too, 'cos I told you that I went to Susanna's party and danced and did the limbo contest and played games, and I didn't. I went to the party but mostly all I did was just sit and watch. Next time I go I will be able to join in! But it wasn't quite the truth, what I told you, so I am glad you pretended you had gone on the Eye as now that makes us equal!

I would love to go with you and your mum! Mum says not this week but maybe next, if that would be convenient for you.

Now there is something I have to ask you. It is about your school. I know you said you weren't trying to put me off but then Mum said about you probably already having best friends, like Sarah that you mentioned, and I thought maybe you might not want me coming there. I am sorry, it is too late for me to go anywhere else as my nan has already fixed it all up, but I just wanted to say that I will not try to come between you and Sarah. We do not have to sit together or do things together if you would rather not. I hope this makes it all right.

Write soon!

xxx Katie

PS   Here are the pictures I have done for "Betsy Burp and the Belchers".

Dear Katie,

Thank you for your letter saying that you were 😊 to see me. I was 😊 to see you! I am glad Mum made me go. I didn't want to at first because of being such a scaredy cat but I am going to try and be braver in future.

This morning I got your second letter that you wrote! Mum says next week would be fine for going on the Eye. If you still want to come, that is.

The reason for me saying if you still want to come is because you may not want to when I have told you something. This is what I have to tell you. Sarah that I talked about is not my friend, she is Lily's. Lily has loads of friends. It is Lily who races about going to parties. I am more like the girl in our problem page. I expect when you come to our school it will be Lily you will want to be friends with, not me. I am not being self-pitying, but I thought I should tell you. I would not like you to come to our school and think that you have to be my friend if you don't want to. That is all.

It was very silly of me to tell you lies. It is not the same as you saying you played games at the party. It must have been so sad for you when you couldn't, but I am just stupid.

I am very sorry I have said that I have done things when I haven't. Please tell me if you would like to come on the Eye. Lily says it is fun. But I will understand if you don't.
xxx Violet

PS   You can come on the Eye without having to be my friend at school. You can still be friends with Lily.

"Did you ask Katie?" said Mum, next morning.
"About what?" I said.
"About coming on the Eye," said Mum.
"Yes, I asked her," I said.
"And what did she say?"
"She said…" I crossed my fingers behind my back.
"She'll let me know. She's got to ask her mum."

"Maybe I'll give her mum a ring."

"No!" I screeched it. Mum looked at me in surprise.

"Why not? We ought to get it organised. I'll have to arrange things at the shop."

"But she hasn't *said*. We have to wait till she *says*."

"Why? Why can't I just ask her mum?"

"Because she might not want to!"

I yelled it at the top of my voice and rushed from the room. Mum was doing it again! Trying to push me. She didn't know that I'd told all those stupid lies. She didn't know that I'd been found out and that most probably Katie wouldn't ever want to speak to me again. *I* wouldn't want to speak to me again. Not if I'd been lied to.

I'd just reached the top of the stairs when I heard the telephone start to ring.

I'd just reached my bedroom when Mum called to me.

"Violet! It's for you."

"M-me?" I peered over the banisters.

163

"It's Katie."

Katie! Ringing to say she didn't want to come on the Eye. That she didn't ever want to speak to me again.

"Well, hurry up!" said Mum. "Don't keep her waiting."

Reluctantly, I trailed back down the stairs. Mum handed me the receiver.

"It's all right," she said. "I won't listen!"

I waited till Mum had left the room.

"H-hallo?" I said.

"Violet?" said Katie.

"Y-yes."

"This is Katie."

"K-Katie," I said.

"Hi!"

"H-hi."

There was a pause; then Katie giggled.

"I thought you said you were going to try and be braver!"

I curled my toes. "I am!"

"Sounds like it," she said. "This is only *me*. Not a man-eating tiger! Did you like my pictures for Betsy Burp? You didn't say! Does that mean you didn't like them?"

"No," I said. "I loved them!"

"Well, I hope you did 'cos I've done some more! And why are you trying to stop me coming on the Eye?"

I said, "I'm not trying to s-stop you!"

"Just as well," said Katie, "'cos I'm coming! My mum's going to ring yours and we're going to arrange a day. And stop trying to push me off on Lily! I don't want to be friends with Lily. All her friends are posh. That's what you said."

"Yes," I said. "They are."

"Well, I'm not," said Katie, "so I don't s'ppose she'd want to be friends with me anyway. And listen! I've got some more ideas for Girlzone. I thought we could have interviews with celebs. First I could be one, then you could be one, and we could ask each other questions. Like what is your star sign and what is your favourite TV programme and stuff like that. Who would you want to be? I'm going to be a pop star. Listen! This is me singing."

A horrible slurpy sound came oozing down the telephone at me.

"What do you think?"

I couldn't tell if she was being serious, or not.

"Think it'll make the Top Ten?"

I decided to be brave, and take a chance.

"Not drooling like that!" I said.

"New kind of music... drooly music. I'll be a drooler!"

"You'll be Adrooler?"

"Adroola the Drooler!"

I giggled.

"You'll have to write me some drooly songs to sing."

"They won't just be drooly," I said, "they'll be truly drooly!"

Lily had just come into the room. She gave me this irritated look.

"What's going on?"

She wasn't used to me having private conversations on the telephone. She was the one that was supposed to do all the talking!

"Who is it?" she hissed. "Is it the Blob?"

"No," I said. "It's Adroola."

"Who's Adroola?"

"Adroola the Drooler. She's a pop star. Listen!"

I held out the receiver. Katie's voice came drooling down the line. Rather disgusting, actually. It sounded like someone belching into a bowl of syrup.

"Have you gone mad?" said Lily.

I shouted, "Yes! Raving!"

and danced about in front of her with my eyes crossed and one hand held up like a claw. Lily stared at me, with her mouth gaping open.

"Raving! Raving! *Bluurgh!*"

"Mum! She's gone completely mad!" wailed Lily.

"Has she?" said Mum. "Well, I shouldn't worry about it. She seems quite happy."

"But people might think I'm mad!" said Lily. "They might think she's me!"

It is true that just lately people do seem to have started getting us more muddled up than they used to. Even, sometimes, people at school. I can't think why, since we are not in the least bit alike. Lily will tell you that I am completely mad. It is since knowing Katie. She gets you that way! She is so bright and bubbly, she makes me bright and bubbly, too.

It is such fun to have a friend! We do all kinds of things together. I've slept over at Katie's place, she's slept over at mine. (Lily was excluded. But I might let her in on it next time. If she behaves herself!)

What else have we done? We've been shopping together. Lots of times! We really enjoy shopping. We've been on the Eye. At last – and for real! Not just in my imagination. We've been ice skating! (Katie's mum took us.) Oh, and we've written loads more for Girlzone. We did the celebs, and we did a quiz, and we did a special interview with Adroola. Our latest thing, the thing we're working on at the moment, is Makeover of the Month. We're going to have Befores and Afters. Like this:

These are true photographs! We did all the make-up and stuff in my room, with the door barricaded so that Lily couldn't get in. She was practically foaming at the mouth! She knew something was going on, she just didn't know what. Hah! That makes a change. But I don't see why I should let her in on all my secrets.

I have lots of secrets, these days. I share them with Katie. Natch! Most of them are private giggle material, just between her and me. We go round the playground, arm in arm, giggling away together. Sometimes we giggle so much we give ourselves a stitch. People look at us as if we have taken leave of our senses. But do we care?

NO WAY!

Passion Flower

PASSION

JEAN URE

Illustrated by Karen Donnelly

for Samantha and Stephanie Bond

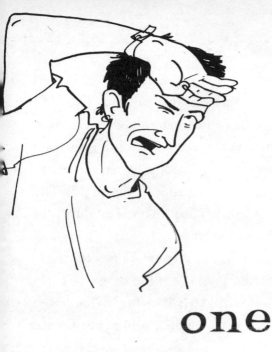

one

OF COURSE, MUM shouldn't have thrown the frying pan at Dad. Especially as it was full of oil, ready for frying. On the other hand, it wasn't as if it was hot. And it didn't even hit him. Mum is such a lousy shot! In any case, Dad deserved it.

Needless to say, the Afterthought didn't agree with me; she always took Dad's side. But I really didn't see what excuses could be made for him this time. Mum had been scrimping and saving for months to buy herself a new cooker. She had been ever so looking forward to it! It was really mean of Dad to go and gamble all the money away at the race track. I said this to the Afterthought, but she just said that it wasn't Dad's fault if his horse had come in last, and that if Mum didn't want him to spend the money why didn't she keep it in a separate account? I said, "Because they're *married*. Being married is about *sharing*." The Afterthought said in that case, Mum oughtn't to complain.

"Dad was only trying to make some money for us!"

I said, "He never makes money at the races."

"He does, too!" said the Afterthought. "What about that time he took us all out to dinner at that posh place and got champagne?"

"*Once*," I said. "He did it *once*. And anyway, Mum didn't want champagne."

"No, she wanted something boring, like a new cooker," said the Afterthought.

I have to admit that a new cooker would not come high on my list of priorities, but we are all different, and if Mum wanted a cooker I thought she ought to be allowed to have one. As she pointed out to Dad just before she threw the frying pan, she was the one who did all the cooking.

"You never lift a finger!"

"Why should he?" whined the Afterthought, when we were talking about it later. "Cooking's a woman's job!"

174

She doesn't really think that; she was only saying it to stick up for Dad. She was the most terrible daddy's girl.

Dad always hated it when Mum got mad at him. He would rush out and do these awful things that upset her, then grow all crestfallen and sorry for himself. That used to make Mum madder than ever! But somehow or other Dad always managed to get round her. He always promised that he wouldn't ever do it again. And Mum always believed him… until that day when he gambled away the money for her new cooker. That was what made her finally crack. She really blew her top!

"How am I expected to provide for a family of four on this clapped-out piece of junk?" screamed Mum.

I remember we all turned to look at the piece of junk. Half the burners had rotted away; one didn't work at all. The oven was unreliable. It kept burning things to crisps. Really annoying! Mum was absolutely right. But it didn't help when Dad, with a boyish grin at me and the Afterthought, suggested that we should all live on takeaways.

"Suit me! Wouldn't it suit you, girls?"

The Afterthought cried, "Yesss!"

Mum snapped, "Don't avoid the issue!" The issue being, I suppose, that Dad had gone and wasted all Mum's hard-earned money on a horse named Toasted Tea Cake that hadn't even reached the finishing point.

"Daniel Rose, you knew I was saving up for a new cooker!" screeched Mum.

That was when she reached for the frying pan. Dad backed away, holding his hands out in front of him.

"You can have a new cooker! You can have one! We'll go out tomorrow and we'll get you one... heavens alive, woman! Haven't you ever heard of credit?"

That was when Mum *threw* the frying pan. We didn't buy things on credit any more; not since the car and the video got repossessed. We didn't even have a store card. Mum never did anything by halves. I guess I have to admit that she sometimes went to extremes. But it was Dad who pushed her! She'd probably have been quite normal if it hadn't been for him.

I don't know whether Dad was always the way he was. I mean, like, when he and Mum first met. I think from what Mum says he was just easygoing and fun. Dad *was* fun! He was more fun than Mum, but then it was Mum who had to look after us and provide for us and keep things going. Dad was really a bit of a walking disaster. He liked to say he was a free spirit, by which he meant that he couldn't be tied down to a regular job the same as other people, which meant he sometimes earned money but more often didn't, which meant it was all left to Mum, which was why she got so mad when he did some of the things that he did. Not just losing money on what he called "the gee-gees", but suddenly taking it into his head to go out and buy stuff that Mum said we couldn't afford and didn't need. Like, for instance, the time he came home with a camcorder. The camcorder was brilliant! Me and the Afterthought both sulked like crazy when it had to go back. And then there was the trampoline. That was pretty good, too! At least, it would have been if we'd had anywhere to put it. We tried it in the garden but our garden is about the size of a tea tray and the Afterthought bounced too high and fell into a prickly bush and screamed the place down. Mum said she could have poked an eye out, so that was the end of the trampoline.

These are just a few of the other things I remember Dad buying:

* a night owl light, so you could see in the dark (except that we never got around to using it as it came without batteries and Dad lost interest. Anything that came without batteries ended up in a drawer, forgotten).

* a microdot sleeping bag, in case one of us ever wanted to go off to camp. (The Afterthought tried sleeping out in the garden one night but got scared after

she'd been there about five minutes and had to come back indoors.)

* a digital car compass, which didn't work.

* an inflatable neck pillow, for Mum to use in the car. (It was supposed to give off soothing scents, only Mum said they made her feel sick. Even I thought that was a bit mean, after Dad had got it specially for her.)

* a digital watch camera (sent back before we could use it).

* a digital voice recorder (also sent back, more is the pity). and

* a special finger mouse for Dad's new laptop, which he said he needed for his work, whatever that was.

To be honest, I was never quite sure what work Dad actually did. When people at school asked me, like my best friend Vix Stephenson, I couldn't think what to say. Once when we were about ten Vix told me she had heard her mum saying that "What Stephanie's dad does is a total mystery." Vix asked me what it meant. Very quickly, I said, "It means that what he does is top secret." Vix's eyes grew wide.

"You mean, like… he's a spy, or something?"

I said, "Sort of."

"You mean he works for *MI5*?"

"I can't tell you," I said. "It's confidential."

It was so confidential I'm not sure that even Mum knew. 'Cos one time when I asked her she said, in this weary voice, that my guess was as good as hers. I said, "Mum, he's not a... a *criminal*, is he?"

It was something that had been worrying me. I had these visions of Dad climbing up drainpipes and going through windows and helping himself to stuff from people's houses. Tellies and videos and jewellery, and stuff. I didn't imagine him holding up petrol stations or anything like that; I didn't think he would ever be violent. Mum was the violent one, if anyone was! She was the one who threw things. But I was really scared that he might be a thief. I was quite relieved when Mum gave this short laugh and said, "Nothing so energetic! You have to have staying power for that... you have to be *organised*. That's the last thing you could accuse your dad of!" She said that Dad was an "opportunist".

"He just goes along for the ride."

I said, "You mean, he gets on trains without a ticket?"

"Something like that," said Mum.

"Oh, well! That's not so bad," I said.

"It's not so good, either," said Mum.

She sounded very bitter. I didn't like it when Mum sounded bitter. This was my dad she was talking about! My dad, who bought us trampolines and camcorders. Mum never bought us anything like that. I was still only little when we had this conversation, when I got worried in case Dad was a criminal; I mean, I was still at Juniors. I was in Year 8 by the time Mum threw the frying pan. I still loved Dad, I still hated it when Mum got bitter, but I was beginning to understand why she did. There were moments when I felt really sorry for Mum. She tried so hard! And just as she thought she'd got everything back on track, like paying off the arrears on the gas bill, or saving up for a new cooker, Dad would go and blow it all. He didn't mean to! It was like he just couldn't stop himself.

The day after Mum threw the frying pan, Dad left home. The Afterthought said that Mum got rid of him, and I think for once she may have been right. Mum was certainly very fed up. She said that Dad spending her cooker money was the last straw.

I don't think that she and Dad had a row; at any rate, I never heard any sounds of shouting. I think she simply told him to go, and he went. He was there when we left for school in the morning – and gone by the time we got back. Mum sat us down at the kitchen table and broke the news to us.

"Your dad and I have decided to live apart. You'll still see him – he's still your dad – but we're just not going to be living together any more. It's best for all of us."

Well! Mum may have thought it was best, but me and the Afterthought were stunned. How could Dad leave us, just like that? Without any warning? Without even saying goodbye?

"It was Mum," sobbed the Afterthought. "She threw him out!"

That was what Dad said, too, when he rang us later that same evening. He said, "Well, kids —" we were both listening in, me on the extension "– it looks like this is it for your poor old dad. Given my marching orders! Seems I've upset her Royal Highness just once too often. Now she won't have me in the house any more."

Dad was trying to make light of it, 'cos that was Dad. He was always joking and fooling around, he never took anything seriously. But I could tell he was quite shaken. I don't think he ever dreamt that Mum would really throw him out. Always, in the past, he'd managed to get round her. They'd kiss and make up, and Mum would end up laughing, in spite of herself, and saying that Dad was shameless. But not this time! This time, he'd really blown it.

"She's had enough of me," said Dad. "She doesn't love me any more."

"Dad, I'm sure she does!" I said.

"She doesn't, Steph. She told me… *Daniel Rose, I've had it with you. You get out of my life once and for all.* Those were her words. That's what she said to me. *I've had it with you.*"

Oh, Dad, I thought, stop! I can't bear it!

"She's a cow!" shrieked the Afterthought, all shrill.

"No, Sam. Never say that about your mum. She's had a lot to put up with."

"So have you!" shrieked the Afterthought.

"Ah, well… I've probably deserved it," said Dad. He was being ever so meek about it all. Taking the blame, not letting us say anything bad about Mum. Meek wasn't like my dad! But that, somehow, just made it all the worse, what she'd done to him.

"Dad, what are you going to do?" I said.

"I don't know, Steph, and that's a fact. I'm a bit shaken up just at the moment. Got to get my act together."

"Shall I try asking Mum if she'll let you come back?"

"Better hadn't. Only set her off again."

"But you don't *want* to go, do you, Dad?"

"*Want* to? What do you think?" said Dad. "Go and leave my two girls? It's breaking my heart, Pusskin!"

He had me crying, in the end. If he'd been spitting blood, like Mum, I wouldn't have felt quite so bad about it. I mean, I'd still have felt utterly miserable at the thought of him not being with us, but at least I'd have understood that he and Mum just couldn't go on living together any more. But Dad still thought Mum was the bee's knees! It's what he'd always called her: the bee's knees. *He* wasn't the one that wanted to break up. It was Mum who was ruining everything.

"Couldn't you just give him one last chance?" I begged.

"Stephanie, I have lost count of all the last chances I've given that man," said Mum. "I'm sorry, but enough is enough. He has turned my life into turmoil!"

It is very upsetting, when one of your parents suddenly isn't there any more; it's like a big black hole. The poor old Afterthought took it very hard. She went into a crying fit that lasted for days, and when she couldn't cry any more she started on the sulks. No one can sulk like the Afterthought! Mum tried everything she

knew. She coaxed and cajoled, she cuddled and kissed – as best she could, with the Afterthought fighting her off – until in the end she lost patience and snapped, "It hasn't been easy for me, you know, all these years!" The Afterthought just went on sulking.

Mum said, "Stephanie, for goodness' sake talk to her! We can't carry on like this."

I tried, but the Afterthought said she wasn't going to forgive Mum, *ever*. She said if she couldn't be with Dad, her life wasn't worth living.

"Why couldn't I go with him?"

I suggested this to Mum, but Mum tightened her lips and said, "No way! Your father wouldn't even be capable of looking after a pot plant."

"It's not up to her!" screamed the Afterthought. "It's up to me! I'm old enough! I can choose who I want to be with!"

But when she asked Dad, the next time he rang us, Dad said that much as he would love to have the Afterthought with him – "and your sister, too!" – it just wasn't possible right at this moment.

"He's got to get settled," said the Afterthought. "As soon as he's settled, I can go and live with him!"

"Over my dead body," said Mum.

"I can!" screeched the Afterthought. "I'm old enough! You can't stop me! As soon as he's settled!"

Even I knew that the chances of Dad getting settled were about zilch; Dad just wasn't a settling kind of person. But it seemed to make the Afterthought happy. She seemed to think she'd scored over Mum. Whenever Mum did anything to annoy her she'd shriek, "It won't be like this when I go and live with Dad!" Or if Mum wouldn't let her have something she wanted, it was, "Dad would let me!" There was, like, this permanent feud between the Afterthought and Mum.

Her name isn't really the Afterthought, by the way. Not that I expect anyone ever thought it was. Even flaky people like Dad don't christen their children with names like Afterthought, and anyway, Mum would never have let him. Her name is actually Samantha; but I once asked Mum and Dad why they'd waited four years between us, instead of having us quickly, one after the other, so that we'd be nearer the same age and could be friends and do things together and talk the same language (instead of one of us being almost grown up and the other a *child*, and quite a tiresome one, at that). Mum said it was because they hadn't really been going to have any more kids. She said, "Sam was an afterthought." Dad at once added, "But a very nice afterthought! We wouldn't want to be without her."

Oh, no? Well, I suppose we wouldn't. She's all right, really; just a bit young. Hopefully she'll grow out of it. Anyway, that was when me and Dad started calling her the Afterthought. Just as a joke, to begin with, but then it sort of stuck. Mum never called her that. The Afterthought said she wouldn't want her to.

"It's Dad's name for me!"

I wasn't sure how I felt when Dad left home. I mean, like, once I'd got over the first horrible shock. I did miss him terribly, but I also had some sympathy with Mum. Mum and me had done some talking, and I could see that Dad had really made things impossible for her. So that while feeling sorry for poor old Dad, thrown out on his ear, I did on the whole tend to side with Mum. Like I would always stick up for her when the Afterthought accused her of turning Dad out on to the street – 'cos Dad had told us that he had nowhere to go and might have to live in a shop doorway. To which Mum just said, "Huh! A likely tale. He'll always land on his feet." The Afterthought said that Mum was cruel, and I suppose she did sound a bit hard, but I still stuck up for her. Then one day, when Dad had been gone for about two weeks, I told Vix about it, because, I mean, she was my best friend, and she had to know, you can't keep things from your best friend, and Vix said, "It's horrid when people's mum and dad split up, but I'm sure it's all for the best. My mum's always said she doesn't know how your mum put up with it for so long."

I froze when she said this. I said, "Put up with *what*?"

"Well… your dad," said Vix. "You know?" She muttered it, apologetically. "The things he did."

I said, "How do you know what things he did?"

Vix said she'd heard her mum talking about it.

I said, "How did *she* know?"

"Your mum told her," said Vix.

Suddenly, that made me lose all sympathy with Mum. Talking about Dad to other people! To *strangers*. Well, outsiders. I thought that was so disloyal!

"Steph, I'm sorry," said Vix.

I told her that it wasn't her fault. It was Mum's fault, if anyone's. How could she do such a thing?

"Dad wasn't as bad as all that," I said. "He never did anything on purpose to hurt her! He *loved* her."

Vix looked at me, pityingly.

"Well, but he did!" I said. "He couldn't help it if he wasn't very good at earning money… money just didn't mean anything to him."

"I suppose that's why he spent it," said Vix.

187

She wasn't being sarcastic; she was genuinely trying to help.

"He spent it because he wanted Mum to have nice things," I said. "Not stupid, boring things like cookers!"

"But perhaps she wanted stupid boring things," said Vix.

"Well, she did," I said, "but Dad wasn't to know! I mean, he *did* know, but – he kept forgetting. He'd see something he thought she'd like, and he couldn't resist getting it for her. And then she'd say it was a waste of money, or stupid, or useless, or she'd make him take it back... poor Dad! He was only trying to make her happy."

"This is it," said Vix.

What did she mean, *this is it*?

"It's what people do," said Vix. "When they're married... they try to make each other happy, but sometimes it doesn't always work and they just make each other miserable, and – and they only get happy when they're not living together any more. Maybe," she added.

Mum ought to have been happier, now she'd got rid of Dad and could save up for new cookers without any fear of him gambling her money away on horses that didn't reach the finishing point. You'd have *thought* she'd be happier. Instead, she just got crabbier and crabbier, even worse than she'd been before, when Dad was turning her life into turmoil. At least, that's how it seemed to me and the Afterthought. She wouldn't let us do things, she wouldn't let us have things, she wouldn't let us buy the clothes we wanted, we couldn't even *read* what we wanted.

"This magazine is disgusting!" cried Mum, slapping down my latest copy of *Babe*. *Babe* just happened, at the time, to be my favourite teen mag. I've grown out of it now; but at the age of thirteen there were things I desperately needed to know, and *Babe* was where I found out about them.

I mean, you have to find out *somewhere*. You can't go through life being ignorant.

I tried explaining this to Mum but she had frothed herself up into one of her states and wouldn't listen.

"*DO BLOKES PREFER BOOBS OR BUMS?* At *your* age?"

"Mum," I said, "I need to know!"

"You'll find out quite soon enough," said Mum, "without resorting to this kind of trash... what, for heaven's sake, is *Daddy drool* supposed to mean?"

Again, I tried explaining: "It means when people fancy your dad." But again she wouldn't listen.

"This is just so cheap! It is just so *tacky*! Where did you get it from?"

I said, "The newsagent."

"Mr Patel? I'm surprised he'd sell you such a thing!"

"Mum, *everybody* reads it," I said.

"Does Victoria read it?" said Mum.

I said, "No, she reads one that's even worse." I giggled. "Then we swop!"

It was a mistake to giggle. Mum immediately thought that I was cheeking her. Plus she'd actually gone and opened the mag and her eye had fallen on a rather *cheeky* article (ha ha, that is a joke!) about male bums. Shock, horror! Did she think I'd never seen one before???

"For crying out loud!" Mum glared at the offending article, bug-eyed. Maybe *she'd* never seen one before… "What is this? Teenage porn?"

I said, "Mum, it's just facts of life."

"So is sewage," said Mum.

Was she saying male bums were *sewage*? No! She'd flicked over the page and seen something else.

Something I'd been really looking
forward to reading!

"This is unbelievable," said Mum.
"Selling this stuff to thirteen-year-old
girls! I'm going to have a word with
Mr Patel."

"Mum! No!" I shrieked.

I wasn't worried about Mr Patel, I was worried about
Babe. How was I going to learn things if he wasn't
allowed to sell it to me any more?

"Stephanie, I don't want this kind of filth in the
house," said Mum. "Do you understand?"

I sulkily said yes, while thinking to myself that I bet
Dad wouldn't have minded. Mum had just got *so crabby*.

"She's an old cow," said the Afterthought.

Mum and the Afterthought were finding it really
difficult to get along; they rowed even worse than Mum
and me. The Afterthought wanted a kitten. A girl in her
class had a cat that was going to have some, and the
Afterthought had conceived this passion. (Conceived!

 Ha! What would Mum say to *that*?)
Every day the Afterthought nagged and
begged and howled and pleaded; and
every day Mum very firmly said *no*.
She said she was sorry, but she had quite
enough to cope with without having an
animal to look after.

"Kittens grow into cats, and cats need feeding, cats need injections, cats cost money... I'm sorry, Sam! It's just not the right moment. Maybe in a few months."

"That'll be too late!" wailed the Afterthought. "All the kittens will be gone!"

"There'll be more," said Mum.

"Not from Sukey. They won't be *Sukey's* kittens. I want one of Sukey's! She's so sweet. Dad would let me!" roared the Afterthought.

"Very possibly, but your dad doesn't happen to be here," said Mum.

"No! Because you got rid of him! *I want my kitten!*" bellowed the Afterthought.

It ended up, as it always did, with Mum losing patience and the Afterthought going off into one of her tantrums. I told Vix that life at home had become impossible. Vix said, "Yes, for me, too! Specially after your mum talked to my mum about teenage filth and now my mum says I'm not to buy that sort of thing any more!" I stared at her, appalled.

"What right have they got," I said, "to talk about us behind our backs?"

The weeks dragged on, with things just going from bad to worse. Mum got crabbier and crabbier. She got specially crabby on days when we had

192

telephone calls from Dad. He rang us, like, about once every two weeks, and the Afterthought always snatched up the phone and grizzled into it.

"Dad, it's horrible here! When are you going to get settled?"

I tried to be a *little* bit more discreet, because I could see that probably it was a bit irritating for Mum. I mean, she was doing her best. Dad was now living down south, in Brighton. He said that he missed us and would love to have us with him, but he wasn't quite settled enough; not just yet.

"Soon, I hope!"

Triumphantly, the Afterthought relayed this to Mum. "Soon Dad's going to be settled, and then we can go and live with him!"

I knew that Mum would never let us, and in any case I wasn't really sure that I'd want to. Not permanently, I mean. I loved Dad to bits, because he wasn't ever crabby like Mum, I couldn't remember Dad telling us off for anything, ever; but I couldn't imagine actually leaving Mum, no matter how impossible she was being. And she *was* being. Running off to Vix's mum like that! Interfering with Vix's life, as well as mine. I didn't think she ought to have done that; it could have caused great problems between me and Vix. Fortunately Vix

193

understood that it wasn't my fault. As she said, "You can't control how your mum behaves." But Vix's mum had been quite put out to discover that her angelic daughter was reading about s.e.x. and gazing at pictures of male bums. It's what comes of living in a grungy old place way out in the sticks where nothing ever happens and s.e.x. is something you are not supposed to have heard of, let alone think about. Vix agreed with me that in Brighton people probably thought about it all the time, even thirteen-year-old girls, and no one turned a hair.

I said to Mum, "When I am *fourteen,*" (which I was going to be quite soon), "can I think about it then?"

"You can think about it all you like," said Mum. "I just don't want you reading about it in trashy magazines. That's all!"

It was shortly after my fourteenth birthday that Mum finally went and flipped. I'd been trying ever so hard to make allowances for her. I'd discussed it with Vix and we had agreed that it was probably something to do with her age. Vix said, "Women get really odd when they reach a certain age. How old *is* your mum?"

I said, "She's only thirty-six." I mean, pretty old, but not actually decrepit.

"Old enough," said Vix. "She's probably getting broody."

I said, "Getting *what*?"

"Broody. You know?"

"I thought that was something to do with chickens," I said.

"Chickens and women… it makes them desperate."

"Desperate for what?"

"Having babies while they still can."

"But she's had babies!" I said.

"Doesn't make any difference," said Vix. "Don't worry! She'll grow out of it."

"Yes, but *when*?" I wailed.

"Dunno." Vix wrinkled her nose. "When she's about … fifty, maybe?"

I thought that fifty was a long time to wait for Mum to stop being desperate, but in the meanwhile, in the interests of peaceful living, I would do my best to humour her. I would no longer read nasty magazines full of s.e.x., at any rate, not while I was indoors, and I would no longer nag her for new clothes except when I really, really needed them, and I would make my bed and I would tidy my bedroom and I would help with the washing up, and do all those things that she was always on at me to do. So I did. *For an entire whole week*. And then she went and flipped! All because I'd been to a party and got home about *two seconds* later than she'd said. Plus I'd just happened to be brought back by this boy that for some reason she'd taken exception to and told me not to see any more, only I hadn't realised that she meant it. I mean, how was I to know that she'd meant it?

"What did you think I meant?" said Mum, all cold and brittle, like an icicle. "I told you I didn't want you seeing him any more!"

"But why not?" I said. "What's the matter with him?"

"Stephanie, we have already been through all this," said Mum.

"But it doesn't make any sense! He's just a boy, the same as any other boy. It's not like he's on drugs, or anything."

Well, he wasn't; not as far as I knew. It's stupid to think that just because someone has a nose stud and tattoos he's doing drugs. Mum was just so prejudiced! But I suppose I shouldn't have tried arguing with her; I can see, now, that that was a bit ill-judged. Mum went up like a light. She went *incandescent.* Fire practically spurted out of her nostrils. I couldn't ever remember seeing her that mad. And at *me*! Who'd tried her best to make allowances! It didn't help that the Afterthought was there, leaning over the banisters. The Afterthought never can manage to keep her mouth shut. She had to go starting on about kittens again.

"Dad would have let me have one! You never let us have anything! You're just a misery! You aren't any *fun*!"

She said afterwards that she thought she was coming to my aid. She thought she was being supportive.

"Showing that I was on your side!"

All it did, of course, was make matters worse. Mum just suddenly snapped. She raised two clenched fists to heaven and demanded to know what she had done to get lumbered with two such beastly brats.

"Thoroughly unpleasant! Totally ungrateful! Utterly selfish! Well, that's it. I've had it! I'm sick to death of the pair of you! As far as I'm concerned, your father can have you, and welcome. I've done my stint. From now on, you can be his responsibility!"

Wow. I think even the Afterthought was a bit taken aback.

two

"I HAVE SPENT sixteen years of my life," said Mum, "coping with your dad. Sixteen years of clearing up his messes, getting us out of the trouble that he's got us into. If it weren't for me, God alone knows where this family would be! Out on the streets, with a begging bowl. Well, I've had it, do you hear? I have *had it*. I cannot take any more! Do I make myself plain?"

Me and the Afterthought, shocked into silence, just stared woodenly.

"Do I make myself plain?" bellowed Mum.

"Y-yes!" I snapped to attention. "Absolutely!"

"Good. Then you will understand why it is that I am

198

relinquishing all responsibility. Because if I am asked to cope just one minute longer –" Mum's voice rose to a piercing shriek "– with your tempers and your tantrums and your utter – your utter—"

We waited.

"Your utter *selfishness*," screamed Mum, "I shall end up in a lunatic asylum! Have you got that?"

I nodded.

"I said, *have you got that*?" bawled Mum.

"Got it," I said.

"Got it," muttered the Afterthought.

"Right! Just so long as you have. I want there to be no misunderstandings. Now, get off to bed, the pair of you!"

Me and the Afterthought both scuttled into our bedrooms and stayed there. I wondered gloomily if Mum was having a nervous breakdown, and if so, whether it was my fault. All I'd done was just go to a party! I lay awake the rest of the night thinking that if Mum ended up in a lunatic asylum, I would be the one that put her there, but when I told Vix about it next day Vix said that me going to the party was probably just the last straw. She said that her mum had said that my mum had been under pressure for far too long.

"She's probably cracking up," said Vix.

Honestly! Vix may be my best and oldest friend, but I can't help feeling she doesn't always stop and think before she opens her mouth. *Cracking up*. What a thing to say! It worried me almost sick. I crept round Mum like a little mouse, hardly daring even to breathe for fear of upsetting her. I had these visions of her suddenly tearing off all her clothes and running naked into the street and having to be locked up. The Afterthought, being almost totally insensitive where other people's feelings are concerned, just carried on the same as usual, except that she didn't actually whinge quite as much. Instead of whining about cornflakes for breakfast instead of sugar puffs, for instance, she simply rolled her eyes and made huffing sounds; instead of screaming that "Dad would let me!" when Mum refused to let her sit up  till midnight watching telly, she just did this angry scoffing thing, like "Khuurgh!" and walloped out of the room, slamming the door behind her.

I, in the meantime, was on eggshells, waiting for Mum to tear her clothes off. In fact she didn't. After her one manic outburst, she became deadly cool and calm, which was quite frightening in itself as I felt that underneath *things were bubbling*. Like it would take just one little incident and that would be it: clothes off, running naked. Or, alternatively, tearing out her hair in great chunks, which is what I'd read somewhere that people did when they were having breakdowns.

I told the Afterthought to stop being so horrible. "You don't want Mum to end up in a lunatic asylum, do you?" The Afterthought just tossed her head and said she couldn't care less.

"I hate her! I'll always hate her! She sent my dad away!"

"*Your* dad? He's my dad, too!" I said.

"I'm the one that loves him best! You can have *her*," said the Afterthought. "She's your favourite!"

One week later, term came to an end. *The very next day*, Mum got rid of us. Well, that was what it seemed like. Like she just couldn't wait to be free. She'd made us pack all our stuff the night before, but she couldn't actually ship us off until after lunch as Dad said he had to work. Mum said, "On a *Saturday*?" She was fuming! Now she'd made up her mind to dump us, she wanted us to go *now*, at once, immediately. The Afterthought would have liked to go now, at once, immediately, too. She was jigging with impatience the whole morning. I sort of wanted to go – I mean, I was really looking forward to seeing Dad again – but I still couldn't quite believe that Mum was doing this to us.

As we piled into the car with all our gear, I said, "It's just for the summer holidays, right?"

Well, it had to be! I mean, what about clothes? What about school?

"I wouldn't want to miss any school," I said.

"Really?" said Mum. "I never heard that one before!"

OK, I knew she was still mad at us, but I didn't see there was any need for sarcasm. I said, "Well, but anyway, you'll be back long before then!"

Mum had announced that she was flying off to Spain to stay with an old school friend who owned a nightclub. She'd said she was going to "live it up". It worried me because I didn't think of Mum as a living-it-up kind of person. I couldn't imagine her drinking and dancing and lying about on the beach.

How would she cope? It just wasn't *Mum*.

"You'll have to be back," I said.

"Will I?" said Mum. "Why?"

Why? What kind of a question was that?

"You have to *work*," I said.

Mum had this job in the customer service department of one of the big stores in the centre of Nottingham. She had responsibilities. She couldn't just disappear for months!

"Actually," said Mum, "I don't have to work… I jacked it in. I've left."

I said, *"What?"*

"I've left," said Mum. "I gave in my notice."

"Gave in your *notice?*" I was aghast. Mum couldn't do that!

"You can't!" I bleated.

"I have," said Mum. "I gave it in last week… I'm unemployed!"

I shrieked, *"Mum!"*

"What's the problem?" said Mum. "It never seemed to bother you when your dad was unemployed."

"That was because he couldn't be tied down," said the Afterthought, in angry tones.

"Well, I've decided… neither can I!" Mum giggled. I don't think I'd ever heard Mum giggle before. "Two can play at being free spirits."

"But what will we live on?" I wailed.

"Ah!" said Mum. "That's the question… what will we live on? Worrying, isn't it? Maybe your dad will provide."

I glanced at the Afterthought. Her lip was quivering. She wanted to be with Dad OK, but only so long as Mum was still there, in the background, like a kind of safety net. We couldn't have two parents being free spirits!

203

"As a matter of fact," said Mum, "I'm thinking of going in with Romy."

I said, "*Romy?*"

"Yes!" said Mum. "Why not? Do you have some objection?"

"You're not going to *marry* him?" I said.

"Did I say I was going to marry him?"

I said, "N-no. But—"

"She couldn't, anyway!" shrilled the Afterthought. "She's still married to Dad!"

Yes, I thought, but for how long? I remembered when Vix's mum and dad split up. Vix had been *so sure* they would never get divorced, but now her dad was married to someone else and had a new baby. I didn't want that happening with my mum and dad! And the thought of having Je*rome* as a stepfather... yeeurgh! He has ginger hairs up his nose.

"Don't get yourselves in a lather," said Mum. "It's purely a business arrangement." Dreamily, she added, "I've always been interested in antiques."

"Romy doesn't sell antiques!" said the Afterthought, scornfully. "He sells junk. Dad says so!"

I said, "Shut up, you idiot!" But the damage had been done. We drove the rest of the way to the station in a very frosty silence. Mum parked the car in frosty silence. We marched across the forecourt with our bags and our backpacks in the same frosty silence. I thought, this is horrible! We weren't going to see Mum again for weeks and weeks. I didn't want to leave her all hurt and angry. Mum obviously felt the same, for she suddenly hugged me and said, "Look after yourself! Take care of your sister."

I promised that I would. The prospect didn't exactly thrill me, since quite honestly the Afterthought, in those days, was nothing but one big pain. She really *was* a beastly brat. But Mum was going off to Spain, and I was starting to miss her already, and I desperately, desperately didn't want us to part on bad terms. So I said, "I'll take care of her, Mum!" and Mum gave me a quick smile and a kiss and I felt better than I had in a long time. She then turned to the Afterthought and said, "Sam?" in this pleading kind of voice, which personally I didn't think she should have used. I mean, the Afterthought was behaving like total scum. For a moment I thought the horrible brat was going to stalk off without saying goodbye, but then, in grumpy fashion, she offered her cheek for a kiss.

We settled ourselves on the train, with various magazines that Mum had bought for us (*Babe*, unfortunately, not being one of them).

"Mum," I said, "you will be all right, won't you?"

"I'll be fine," said Mum. "Don't you worry about me! You just concentrate on having a good time, because that's what I'm going to do. And you, Sam, I want you to behave yourself! Do what your sister tells you and don't give her any trouble."

I smirked: the Afterthought pulled a face. As the train pulled out, Mum called after us: "Enjoy yourselves! Have fun. I'm sure you will!"

"I'm going to have *lots* of fun," boasted the Afterthought. "It's always fun with Dad!" She then added, "And you needn't think you're going to boss me around!"

"You've got to do what I tell you," I said. "Mum said so."

"Mum won't be there! So sah sah sah!"

The Afterthought pulled a face and stuck out her tongue. *So* childish. I turned to look out of the window.

Why was it, I thought, that our family always seemed to be at war? Mum and Dad, me and the Afterthought…

"It's like the Wars of the Roses," I said.

"What is?" said the Afterthought.

"Us! Fighting! The Wars of the Roses." Personally I thought this was rather clever, but the Afterthought didn't seem to get it. She just scowled and said, "It's Mum's fault."

She really had it in for Mum. She wouldn't hear a word against Dad, but everything that Mum did was wrong. Even now, when we weren't going to be seeing her for months. Poor old Mum!

Actually I couldn't help feeling that Mum and the Afterthought were quite alike. Neither of them ever did anything by halves. They were both so *extreme*. I like to think I am a bit more flexible, like Dad. Only more organised, naturally!

I tried to organise the Afterthought, on our trip down to London. It was quite a long journey, nearly two hours, so Mum had given us food packs in case we got hungry. I told the Afterthought she wasn't to start eating until we were halfway there, but she said she would eat when she wanted, and she broke open her pack right there and then and had scoffed the lot by the time we reached Bedford.

"You're not going to have any of mine," I said.

"Don't want any of yours," said the Afterthought. "We'll be in London soon and Dad will take us for tea."

This was what he had promised. He was going to be there at St Pancras station to meet us, and we were all going to go and have tea before we got on the train to Brighton. I had never made such a long train journey all by myself before. It was quite a responsibility, what with having to keep an eye on the Afterthought and make sure she didn't wander off and get lost, or lock herself in the toilet, or something equally stupid. But I didn't really mind. Now that we were on our way, I found I was quite excited at the prospect of staying with Dad. I'd never been to Brighton. I'd only been to London once, and that was a school trip, when we went to visit a museum. School trips are fun, and better than being in school, but you are still watched all the time and never allowed to go off and do your own thing, in case, I suppose, you get abducted or find a boy and run away with him. *I wish!*

I didn't think that Dad

would watch us; he is not at all a mother hen type. And Brighton sounded like a really wild and wicked kind of place! Vix had informed me excitedly that "things happen in Brighton". When I asked her what things, she didn't seem too sure, but she said that it was "a hub". Nottingham isn't a hub; well, I don't think it is. And *outside* of Nottingham is like living in limbo. Just nothing ever happens at all. Vix had made me promise to send her postcards every week and to email her if I met any boys. I intended to! Meet boys, that is. Mum, meanwhile, said that Brighton was "just the sort of place I would expect your dad to end up in." She said that it was cheap, squalid and tacky. Sounded good to me!

Just after we left Bedford (and the Afterthought finished off her supply of food) my mobile rang. It was Mum, checking that we were still on the train and hadn't got off at the wrong station or fallen out of the window, though as a matter of fact the windows were sealed, so that even the Afterthought couldn't have fallen out.

"Stephie?" said Mum. "Everything OK?"

I said, "Yes, fine, Mum. The Afterthought's eaten all her food."

"Well, that's all right," said Mum. "I'm sure your dad will get her some more. Don't forget to give him the cheque. Tell him it's got to last you."

209

I said, "Yes, Mum."

"Tell him it's for you and Sam. For your personal spending."

"*Yes*, Mum."

"I don't want him using it for himself."

"*No*, Mum." We had already been through all this! Plus I had heard Mum telling Dad on the phone.

"Oh, and Stephanie," she said.

"Yes, Mum?"

"I want you to ring me when you've arrived."

"What, in London?" I said.

"No! In Brighton. When you get to your dad's place. All right?"

I said, "Yes, Mum." I thought, "Mum's getting cold feet!" She'd gone and packed us off and now she was starting to do her mumsy thing, worrying in case something happened. I said, "We're only going to *Brighton*, Mum! Not Siberia."

"Yes, well, just look after your sister," said Mum.

"I've got to *look after you*," I said to the Afterthought.

"I don't want to be looked after," said the Afterthought.

We reached London nearly ten minutes late, so I expected Dad to already be there, waiting for us. But he wasn't! We stood at the barrier, looking all around, and he just wasn't there.

"Maybe he's gone to the loo," said the Afterthought, doing her best to sound brave.

"Mm," I said. "Maybe."

Or maybe we were looking in the wrong place. Maybe when Dad had said he'd meet us at St Pancras, he'd meant... *outside*. So we went and looked outside, but he wasn't there, either, so then we went back to where the train had come in. Still no sign of Dad.

"He must have been held up," I said. "We'd better just wait."

"Ring him!" said the Afterthought. "Ring him, Stephie, *now*!"

"Oh! Yes, I could, couldn't I?" I said. I called up Dad's number, but nothing happened. "He must have switched his phone off," I said.

"Why would he do that?" said the Afterthought, fretfully.

"I don't know! Maybe he's... in a tunnel, or something, and it's not working."

The Afterthought was already sucking her thumb and looking tearful. I thought that if Dad hadn't arrived by four o'clock I would have to ring Mum. Ringing Mum was the last thing I wanted to do! She would instantly start fretting and fuming and saying how Dad couldn't be trusted and she should never have let us go.

211

She might even tell us to jump on the first train home. How could I face Vix if I ended up back in Nottingham without having gone anywhere?

I was still dithering when my own phone rang, and there was Dad on the other end. Relief! I squealed, "Dad!" and the Afterthought immediately attempted to snatch the phone away from me. I kept her off with my elbow.

"Stephie?" said Dad. "That you?"

I said, "Yes, we're at St Pancras. I tried to call you but I couldn't get through!"

"No, I know," said Dad. "The thing's stopped working, I think it needs a new battery. Now listen, honeysuckle, you're going to have to make your own way down to Brighton. I've been a bit tied up, business-wise, and I couldn't get away. I'll meet you at Brighton, instead. OK?"

I gulped and said, "Y-yes, I s-suppose. But I don't know how to get there!"

"Not to worry," said Dad. "I'll give you directions."

Dad told me that we had to *turn left* out of St Pancras and follow the signs to the *Thameslink*. Then all we had to do was get on a train that said Brighton.

"Nothing to it! Think you can manage?"

What I actually thought was *no*! But I said yes because it didn't seem like I had any alternative. I mean, if I had said no, what was Dad supposed to do about it?

"He could have come and fetched us," whimpered the Afterthought.

"That would take for ever," I said. "Just stop being such a baby! There's nothing to it."

It was, however, quite scary. There were so many people about! All going places. All in such a *rush*. Also, just at first I couldn't see any signs that said Thameslink, and then when I did I couldn't make out which road we had to go down and had to ask someone. That was quite scary in itself because St Pancras station is right next door to King's Cross, and I had heard bad things about King's Cross. I had heard it was where all the prostitutes were, and the drug dealers, and the child molesters. I mean, they probably didn't come out until late at night, under cover of darkness, but you just never know. I didn't want us being abducted! Fortunately the person I spoke to (while I held tightly on to the Afterthought's hand in case they tried to snatch her) didn't seem to be any of those things, but just told us which road to take and went on her way.

I said, "Phew!" and tried to unhook myself from the Afterthought's hand, which had become rather hot and clammy, but the Afterthought went on clutching like mad.

"I don't like this place!" she said.

I said, "Neither do I, that's why we're getting out of it. Just come *on*!" And I dragged her all the way down the road until we came to the Thameslink station where an Underground man (he was wearing uniform, so I knew he was all right) told us which platform to go to. I felt quite pleased with myself. I felt quite proud! Dad had trusted me to get us on the right train, and I had. Mum wouldn't have trusted me. She still treated me as if I were about ten years old. (Not letting me read my magazine!) Dad was prepared to treat me like I was almost grown up. He knew I could handle it. I liked that!

Now that I had got us safely under way and hadn't let her be abducted, the Afterthought had gone all bumptious and full of herself again. She went off to the buffet car and came back with a fizzy drink which she slurped noisily and disgustingly through a straw. It really got on my nerves. I was trying to behave like a civilised human being, for heaven's sake! I was trying to have a bit of *style*. I didn't need this underage mutant showing me up. I tried telling her to suck *quietly*, but she immediately started slurping worse than ever. I mean, she did it quite deliberately. Defying me.

"Did you know," I said, "that your teeth have gone all purple?"

"So what?" said the Afterthought.

"So they'll probably stay like it... you'll probably be stained for life!"

I thought it might at least shut her up, but she just pulled her lips into this hideous grimace and started chittering like a monkey. *Well* over the top. In the end I moved to the other side of the carriage and let her get on with it. At least I didn't have to hold her horrible sticky hand any more.

Dad was waiting for us when we got to Brighton. I was so pleased to see him! He was looking just *fan*tastic.

He had this deep, dark tan, and his hair had grown quite long. Dad's hair is very black, and curly. It suited him long! I could suddenly understand how Mum had fallen for him, all those years ago. I could understand how it was that he could always get round her, and make her believe that this time things were going to be different, that he had mended his ways, he was going to behave himself. Dad wasn't capable of behaving himself! Once when Mum was in a good mood, I remember she said that he was "a lovable rogue". (More often, of course, she was in a bad mood, and threw things.)

"Dad!" I galloped up the platform towards him.

"Girls!" Dad threw open his arms and we both hurled ourselves into them. "Oh, girls!" cried Dad. "I've missed you!"

I thought, this is going to be the best holiday *ever*.

three

THE FIRST THING we did was go back to Dad's place to dump our bags. Very earnestly, with her hand tucked into Dad's, the Afterthought said, "I'm glad you didn't have to go and live in a cardboard box. I was really worried about that."

Dad said, "Were you, poppet? That's sweet of you. I bet your mum wasn't!"

"I think she was," I said.

"She wasn't!" said the Afterthought. "She didn't care!"

I said, "She did! But she thought you'd be all right, because she said you always landed on your feet."

"Oh, did she?" said Dad. "And I suppose she thinks that you don't have to work, to land on your feet. I suppose she thinks it just happens?"

I didn't know what to say to that.

"Why are we talking about Mum?" shrilled the Afterthought.

"Good question," said Dad. "Your mum's gone off to Spain to enjoy herself, we'll enjoy ourselves in Brighton. Let's get shot of these bags, then we can go out and paint the town!"

Dad was living in a tiny little narrow street near to the station. The houses were little and narrow, too. All tastefully painted in pinks and lemons and greens, with their doors opening right on to the pavement.

"Oh! They're so *sweet*," crooned the Afterthought. "Like little dolls' houses!"

"Better than a cardboard box, eh?" said Dad.

Better than the house we had at home! Our house at home was on an estate that belonged to the Council, and wasn't very nice. I mean, it was actually quite ugly. Mum had always hated it. Dad's house was palest pink with red shutters at the windows and a red front door. Really pretty!

"Dad, did you *buy* it?" I said.

"No way!" Dad chuckled. "You know me... not the sort to get tied down! No, I just rent it. A bit of it. This bit!"

He led us down some steps, to a little dark door. The door opened on to an underground room. Dad lived in the basement!

"Basements are fun," said Dad. "You can look through the window and see people's legs."

"You can see their knickers!" cried the Afterthought.

"You can't," I said. "And if you could, you shouldn't look." I felt that *someone* had to control her; I owed it to Mum.

The Afterthought just scrunched up her face and went skipping away after Dad into the back room.

"This is where you two will sleep... you don't mind sharing a bed, do you?"

"Sharing with her? She snores!" shrieked the Afterthought.

"I do not," I said, angrily. And if me and the Afterthought were sleeping in the back, where was Dad going to sleep?

The basement only had two rooms, plus an outside loo. It didn't even have a proper kitchen; just a curtained-off corner with a sink and a stove. And no bath! What did we do when we wanted a bath?

Dad said he had an arrangement with the woman who owned the house. "Baths once a week! No problem."

"But where are you going to *sleep*?" I said.

"Don't you worry about me," said Dad. "I'll be OK on the sofa."

"Just stop fussing," said the Afterthought. "You sound like Mum!"

"Now, now!" said Dad. "Enough of that. How about we hit town?"

The Afterthought wanted to go and have the tea that Dad had promised us, so we walked down the hill to the town centre and there was the sea, all greeny-grey and heaving. The Afterthought immediately screamed that she wanted to go on the beach! She wanted to paddle! She wanted to collect shells! Dad said she couldn't just at the moment as the tide was coming in, fast.

"You could go on the pier, if you like."

"Yes!" cried the Afterthought. "Go on the pier!"

I said, "What about tea?" but she wasn't bothered about tea any more. The pier was far more exciting!

Actually, it was. The pier was brilliant! First off you came to a great cavern full of slot machines that you could gamble on. Dad went and changed some money and gave us a bag each of coins to play with. The Afterthought rushed shrieking from game to game, losing all her money (though she did win a bead necklace and a butterfly hair clip). I tried to be a bit more scientific about it, and study the form first. Studying the form is what Dad did with the gee-gees. He used to find out how many races the horses had run, and how many times they had been placed (come first, second or third). The way I did it with the slot machines, I stood watching people, seeing how much money they put in and what they got back – if anything. If it looked like a good bet, then I would have a go. Dad laughed and said I was following in his footsteps. I felt like I was at one of the

casinos in Las Vegas! I still didn't win anything, though, not even a butterfly hair clip, so I don't think I will follow in Dad's footsteps. It was quite fun, but I don't like losing money! I suppose I am a bit like Mum that way.

After the slot machines we walked on, along the pier, past rows of little shops selling souvenirs. I bought a stick of Brighton rock to send to Vix, and the Afterthought clamoured for a cuddly toy from a Hurlaball stall, so Dad said he'd have a shot and hurled three balls and won a white rabbit for her. We would both have liked to have tattoos done – "Semi-permanent. Guaranteed six weeks!" – but unfortunately the stall was closed. However, as Dad pointed out, we could always come back another day. We were there for the whole summer!

On our way to the end of the pier we passed a stall that was making doughnuts, and all stopped to have one. Dad said, "It's a hungry business, having fun!" While we were eating our doughnuts a most extraordinary bird came walking past. It was the size of a chicken, with huge webbed feet that plopped and plapped. I threw it a piece of doughnut, and the Afterthought cried, "Dad! Look! A goose!"

Dad said, "That's not a goose, you goose! It's a seagull."

222

I couldn't really say anything, since I had thought it was a goose, as well. I had no idea that seagulls were so huge!

"Eat up," said Dad. "There's more delights waiting for us."

We hurried on, through another casino – even more crowded and even noisier than the first one. Mum would have hated it! – and finally came out at the far end of the pier. This was where all the rides were. There were so many of them, all crammed into this one small space, that we hardly knew which to try first. The Afterthought wanted to go on the Crazy Mouse and the Waltzer. I fancied the Turbo Coaster, Dad fancied the Dodgems. There was also something called the Sizzler Twist, which was awesome!

"Oh, and look, look!" cried the Afterthought. "Dad, look! Bumper Boats! Oh, look! Helter Skelter!"

"*Be*lter Skelter," I said, but the Afterthought was well hyped and didn't even hear me.

In the end we tried all of them, one after another. Dad shrieked with everybody else on the Sizzler Twist!

The Afterthought then caught sight of a
Funny Foto booth, where you stuck
your face into a hole and had your
photo taken as either a fat lady in

a skimpy
bathing
costume or a

skinny man in voluminous trunks.
She dragged Dad over there, while I
stood and watched. I didn't think I
wanted my photo taken as a fat lady!

While I was waiting, a couple of girls came strolling
past. They looked at Dad and the Afterthought's faces
peering through the holes and sniggered. I don't think
they realised that they belonged to my dad and my sister.
Dad then appeared from behind the skinny man figure,
and I could see these two girls sort of… giving him the
once-over. It was quite strange, watching girls not much
older than me eyeing my dad! As they went on their way
one of them said, "Cool!" and I couldn't help giggling.

"What was that all about?" said Dad.

By now I was giggling so much I could hardly speak.
I said, "D-Daddy drool!"

"*Daddy* drool?"

I had to explain it to him. Dad did laugh!

He said, "Where did you get that ridiculous
expression from?"

"From this magazine," I said. "One that Mum won't let me read any more."

"I'm not surprised," said Dad.

"She won't let us do *anything* any more," said the Afterthought. "She won't let me have my kitten!"

"Oh, for goodness' sakc! Don't start," I said.

We were having such a great time! I didn't want the Afterthought going and ruining it by being mean about Mum.

Fortunately, Dad was already leading us back through the second lot of slot machines, where the music was so loud you could hardly hear yourself speak. *Definitely* not Mum's scene!

We retraced our steps, past the rock shop and the doughnuts and the semi-permanent tattoos, with the Afterthought clutching her rabbit and me clutching my stick of rock.

"Hang about!" said Dad. "This isn't fair… I must get something for Steph! What shall I get you? What would you like? How about a bit of Flower Power?"

Flower Power was a stall where you had to fire rubber suction darts at a big dartboard, which instead of being covered in numbers was covered in pictures. Top prize was a vanity case full of make-up. Wouldn't I have loved that! But I don't think darts was Dad's game as all he won was a flower. It was a very pretty flower, made of silk, with red petals and beautiful blue frondy bits, so I was quite pleased with it. I think I would have been pleased with anything that Dad had won! The man who owned the stall said it was a passion flower. Dad fixed it in my hair, and gave me a big kiss.

"That's what you are," he said. "My passion flower!"

I blushed like crazy, but I thought that I would keep my flower for ever. I said, "Thanks, Dad! It's gorgeous!"

Needless to say, the Afterthought wanted to be a flower, too, so Dad had another go, but this time all he won was a common or garden tulip, a vulgar yellow thing, all stiff and starchy. You can't very well wear a tulip in your hair! And you can't say to someone that they are your tulip. Not without it sounding totally ridiculous. I was so glad that I was a passion flower!

By now it was quite late and Dad decided we should go and eat. We left the pier and walked along the front, and it was so exciting because the lights were all twinkling, and everywhere you looked there were people enjoying themselves, and all around was the sound of music being played. Loudly, in some cases! I thought that Brighton was promising to be every bit as wild and wicked as I had hoped it would be.

We went into a restaurant and Dad asked us what we wanted to eat. The Afterthought immediately said, "Fish and chips!"

"*Sam*." I looked at her, reproachfully. "You know we don't eat animals any more!"

"Fish aren't animals," said the Afterthought.

"They are!" I said. "We had all this out with Mum!" We'd discussed it in great detail, only a few weeks ago. Mum had said that now she didn't have Dad to cater for, she was going to follow her conscience and become a veggie. She said that she wouldn't dictate to me and the Afterthought, we would have to follow *our* consciences, but she said she would like us to go away and think about it. So we both thought about it, and for once we'd been in total agreement with Mum. Eating animals was *cruel*. We had agreed that in future we weren't going to do it. And now here was the Afterthought prepared to go back on her word at the very first opportunity!

"Fish are *fish*," said the Afterthought.

"Yes, and they suffocate!" I said. "When they're taken out of the water they can't breathe. They flop, and gasp, and—"

"Just shut up!" screeched the Afterthought.

"But you *agreed*," I said. "You agreed that it was cruel!"

227

The Afterthought stuck out her lower lip, which is this thing she does when she's sulking. I turned to Dad.

"We talked about it," I said. "We had this long discussion! We said we were going to be veggies."

"Oh, stuff that!" said Dad. "Another of your Mum's crazy ideas."

"Dad," I said, "it's not crazy! Fish can *feel*. They *suffocate*."

"Everyone's looking at us," said the Afterthought.

"Not surprised," said Dad. "This does happen to be a seafood restaurant!"

I felt my cheeks grow red. I hate being the centre of attention! Unless, of course, it's for a good reason. I mean a *nice* reason. But this wasn't.

"Oh, now, come on, Passion Flower!" Dad blew me a kiss across the table. "What the eye doesn't see, the heart can't grieve over. Your mum won't know."

Yes, I thought; but that would be disloyal. I mean, we'd agreed!

"I'm going to have cod," said Dad. "What about you, Face Ache?"

The Afterthought giggled, and said that she would have cod, too.

"Passion Flower?"

I sighed. There really wasn't anything else on the menu. The only dish that wasn't fish was garlic mushrooms, which I can't stand. I suppose I could just have had chips and bread and butter. I thought afterwards that that was what I should have done, but instead I weakly gave in and ate fish, which I regret to say I greatly enjoyed, though I paid the price later, when we got home and I found a worried message from Mum on my moby. I had not only eaten poor suffocated fish, I had also forgotten to ring her, so now I had *two* things to feel guilty about. I called her back at once and said that I was sorry.

"There's just been so much going on!"

"Oh, I'm sure," said Mum.

"I'm sorry, Mum! Really! Do you want to speak to Dad?"

"Only if I must," said Mum.

I looked across at Dad. "Do you want to speak to Mum?"

"Do I have to?" said Dad.

Honestly! It's a real puzzle, sometimes, knowing what to do about parents. They can just make life *so* difficult!

four

ON SUNDAY WE went down to the beach. Brighton
beach is full of pebbles, so that you can't walk on it in
bare feet but can only hobble and hop, going Ow! Ouch!
Ooch! as you do so. Dad said that we had better buy
some flip flops for ourselves. He said, "I'll pay for them.
I'm quite flush at the moment." And then he winked and
patted his pocket and said, "Money! What's it for, eh? If
not for spending?" My feelings *exactly*! Dad and I do
agree about quite a lot of things.

The Afterthought and I both had our swimming
cozzies on under our clothes, but the water was too cold
for swimming so in the end we just paddled. Quite

childish, really! But Dad paddled with us, and when we'd had enough paddling he taught us how to skim stones across the surface of the waves. I discovered that I was quite good at it. Dad cried, "Way to go! That's my girl!" and I felt myself glowing. The Afterthought scowled, and threw as hard as she could, but all her stones just sank.

While we were there, the tide started going out, leaving a beach that looked quite grey and dismal. I looked hopefully for rock pools, but there didn't seem to be any; just endless pebbles and damp sand. I remembered once when we'd gone on holiday to Cornwall and found lots of baby crabs, the size of 5p pieces, and tiny little transparent prawns, all squiggling and squirming.

"Do you remember?" I said to the Afterthought. "We wanted to take some back for Mum to cook."

"They wouldn't have made much of a meal!" chuckled Dad.

"Anyway, it would have been a horrid thing to do," I said.

"No, it wouldn't!" yelled the Afterthought. "We could have had prawn cocktails!"

She had cheered up now that I wasn't beating her at stone skimming. She'd found some seaweed to pop, which seemed to amuse her, and had started making a collection of interesting shells which she said she was going to "do things with".

After a bit it clouded over. Dad said it looked like rain and we'd better decamp, so we put our shoes on and scrabbled back up the beach and sat snugly in a café on the front and watched as the rain lashed down. The Afterthought clamoured to go on the pier again, but Dad said we could do that tomorrow. He said he'd got a better idea for the afternoon.

"I thought we might go to Hastings and look at Battle Abbey."

Me and the Afterthought must have registered total moronic blankness, because Dad had to explain. "1066? Battle of Hastings? William the Conqueror?"

"Oh!" I said. "King Harold!" Importantly, to the Afterthought, I added, "He was the one that got an arrow through his eye."

Even the Afterthought had heard of King Harold. At least, I suppose she had. I had certainly heard of him when I was her age but I don't know what they're teaching ten year olds these days.

"Are we agreed?" said Dad. "Go to Hastings?"

"How do we get there?" I asked, as we squelched our way home through the rain.

"Drive! It's only just along the coast."

"You've got a *car*?" I said. He'd left our one for Mum to use. Mum had said – a bit sniffily, I'd thought – that from now on he would have to learn to rely on his legs. *If* he still knew how to put one foot in front of the other. "Which I doubt."

Dad was famous for going everywhere by car! Even just over the road to post a letter.

"There she is." Dad pointed, proudly, as we turned into his road. "Vintage motor, that is!"

I looked at it, dubiously. It was what I would have called an old banger, only I didn't say so as Dad was obviously pleased with it. But I didn't think Mum would be too happy at the thought of him taking us anywhere in it. It had great rust patches all over, and holes, and one of the bumpers was half-hanging off.

"Old Rover," said Dad. He patted it affectionately. "They don't make 'em like that any more!"

"Dad, it's *beautiful*," crooned the Afterthought. Honestly! There were times when she could be such a creep.

233

As we were going down the basement steps, a woman came out of the front door above us. At first all I could see were a pair of red strappy sandals which made me positively ooze with envy. They were the sort of sandals that I'd always desperately wanted to buy and which Mum would never let me.

"All that money for a few strips of leather? Totally impractical! Wouldn't last five minutes."

Above the sandals were legs that seemed to go on for ever – and ever – and ever. Like *really long*! They finally disappeared into a mini skirt. Well, more of a micro skirt, really. Mum would have had a fit if I'd gone out in a skirt like that! The woman who was wearing it was actually too old, I would have said, to be showing all her legs (not to mention half her bum). I mean, she was about Mum's age, but just quite *incredibly* cool, with this long honey blonde hair and gorgeous golden tan. Dead cool!

She called out to Dad, "Hi, Daniel!" Even her voice was sexy. Very low and husky, like her throat was full of gravel. Or maybe she just smoked. Dad said, "Hi, Shell! Girls, this is my landlady, Shelley Devine. Shell, these are my two girls… this is Passion Flower, this is my little Afterthought."

I said hallo and shook hands, in a proper grown-up manner, but the Afterthought turned shy and hid behind Dad. She is so weird! Ms Devine got into a little red sports car that was parked next to Dad's old banger. As she drove off, Dad thumped on the roof and Ms Levine stuck her hand out of the window and gave a wave.

"That's quite a woman!" said Dad.

"I bet if *she* walked past the window we'd be able to see *her* knickers," said the Afterthought. "If she wears any," she added.

Honestly! I was shocked. I mean, this child was *ten years old*. I would never have dreamt of saying a thing like that at ten years old! I think Dad was a bit shocked, too; or at any rate, somewhat taken aback. He said, "All right, Face Ache! That will be quite enough of that."

"Some people don't, you know," hissed the Afterthought, as Dad opened the front door. "Wear any knickers, I mean."

"Look, just button it!" I said. Mum wouldn't have let her talk like that, and I didn't think I should, either. "Don't be so disgusting!"

"I'm not being," said the Afterthought. "I just—"

"Well, don't! Shut up, or I'll tell Dad."

She pulled a face at that, but at least it kept her quiet.

After we'd changed our clothes and dried ourselves off we piled into the banger. I let the Afterthought sit in front with Dad, as it meant so much to her, but then I got worried because there wasn't any seat belt. Mum would never forgive me if we had a crash and the Afterthought went through the windscreen. I said, "Dad, it's against the law!"

"Not in this car," said Dad, cheerfully. "This car was built in the days before seat belts."

It didn't stop me worrying. The Afterthought could still go through the windscreen.

Fortunately she didn't. We got there unscathed! Dad didn't even have to swear at anyone, which is what Mum complained he usually did.

Battle Abbey was really quite interesting, as old monuments go. I am not really an old monument sort of person, I am more into modern stuff, but I thought it would be a good thing to tell our history teacher about when I went back to school. She hadn't been best pleased with me last term. She had told me that I obviously had "no feel for the historical perspective", whatever that was supposed to be. It's possible she was referring to the fact that my last three pieces of homework had come back marked C-, but that was because it was all

boring stuff about wars and politics. I am not into wars and politics. I am into *people*. Like I once read somewhere that James I used to go to the toilet just anywhere he felt like going. Behind pillars, behind curtains, in the middle of the floor if no one was watching. Truly gross! But that is the kind of thing I find interesting.

I suppose poor old Harold being shot in the eye is quite interesting, although somewhat bloody.

After we'd done the Abbey, and I'd bought some more postcards, we got back into the banger and banged our way back to Brighton. We didn't eat out that night but bought pizzas and took them home with us. I chose a Margherita. Cheese and tomato: *no meat*. Dad and the Afterthought both had ones covered all over with bits of dead flesh. Ham and salami and pepperoni. I was cross with the Afterthought, because this time there wasn't any excuse, and I lectured her about it all the time we were eating. The Afterthought said I was a nag. She said, "Dad! Tell her to stop. I can eat whatever I like!"

"She can, you know," said Dad.

I said, "But Dad, we gave Mum our word! It's a matter of principle. Mum feels really strongly about it."

Dad pulled a henpecked face and said, "Tell me something I don't know! I lived with it for nearly seventeen years. The thing is, Honeybun, your mum may be an admirable woman – she *is* an admirable woman! –

but she gets these bees in her bonnet. If she wants to live on nut loaves and lettuce leaves, that's up to her. But she's got no right to impose it on you."

I pointed out, in fairness to Mum, that she wasn't imposing, that me and the Afterthought had decided for ourselves; but the Afterthought, guzzling pizza as fast as she could go, and spraying disgusting gobbets of food all about the table, screamed that she had changed her mind.

"I can change my mind if I want! Can't I, Dad? I can change my mind!"

"You most certainly can," said Dad.

"*See?*" The Afterthought stuck out her scummy pizza-covered tongue and gave me this look of evil triumph. "You can't tell me what to do!"

I decided that from now on I would simply wash my hands of her.

"I'm going to go and write my postcards," I said. I'd got one for Vix, one for Mum, and one for Gran, Mum's mum, who is very old and lives in a home. "Is it OK if I give Vix your email address?" I said to Dad.

Dad said, "Sorry, kiddo! I don't have one any more. Got rid of the computer. It had to go."

The Afterthought cried, "*Dad!*"

"Needs must," said Dad. "When a man is cruelly turned out of his home without a penny to his name, he has to raise money as best he can. It's no big deal! Who needs possessions, anyway?"

I thought, I do! I like possessions. I love all my ornaments and my trinkets and what Mum calls my bits and pieces. Not to mention *clothes*. I would have wardrobes full, if I could! I said this to Dad, but he just laughed and told me that it was nothing but useless clutter.

"You think it's important, but it isn't. What's important is being able to throw everything you own into a couple of carrier bags. That way, you can be ready to get up and go at a moment's notice. Clutter just holds you back."

Dad certainly didn't have any clutter. He'd taken almost nothing with him when he left home, and he didn't seem to have bought anything since. I couldn't live like that! I don't want to get up and go at a moment's notice. I like to take stay put. I suppose I am not very adventurous.

I wrote my postcard to Vix:

Brighton is wicked! Yesterday I gambled on the slot machines, but didn't win anything, but Dad won a passion flower for me. It is very beautiful. Haven't met any boys yet!!! Will look for some tomorrow.
 xxx Steph.

Then I wrote to Gran, printing it in my best handwriting as her eyesight is not too good:

DEAR GRAN, WE ARE STAYING WITH DAD IN BRIGHTON. IT IS VERY NICE HERE. YESTERDAY THE WEATHER WAS GOOD BUT TODAY IT IS WET. WE HAVE BEEN TO SEE WHERE THEY FOUGHT THE BATTLE OF HASTINGS. IT WAS VERY INTERESTING. LOVE FROM STEPHANIE.

Lastly I wrote to Mum:

Dear Mum, I am sorry I forgot to ring you. I would ring you in Spain if I knew the number. I cannot email you even if I had your email address as Dad has had to sell his computer. Today we went to Hastings to see where Harold was shot in the eye. It was very educational. Lots of love from Stephanie.

In spite of my resolve to wash my hands of the Afterthought, I still got stuck with her next day as Dad said he had things to do.

"Like work, you know? Keep the wolf from the door."

I was a bit surprised by this, as I was not used to Dad working, though of course he had on occasion. I asked him whether it was in an office, which seemed to amuse him.

"Me? In an office? That'll be the day!"

"So what sort of work is it?" I said. I wasn't being nosy, I just wanted to be able to tell Mum: Dad's got a proper job! But I don't think it was a proper job; not exactly. Well, not a being there-every-day-from-nine-till-five sort of job. Dad just said that he had "this nice little number going", and he winked as he said it, which made me think perhaps I'd better not ask any more questions. Just in case. Not that I thought it would be anything *illegal,* but maybe something it would be better for us not to know about, like – well! I couldn't actually think of anything. At least Dad was earning money; that was all that mattered. (I decided, though, that I wouldn't mention it to Mum. Not unless she asked.)

I was really pleased that Dad had found himself a job. What I wasn't so pleased about was the prospect of having to cart the Afterthought round with me wherever I went. I'd been kind of hoping that she might go off somewhere with Dad and leave me to my own devices.

How could I look for boys with a whiny ten year old clinging to me?

"Wouldn't you rather go with Dad?" I said.

But Dad didn't think that was such a good idea, and neither did the Afterthought.

"I want to go on the pier!" she said.

So off we trolled to the pier, with our pockets full of money. (I'd given Mum's cheque to Dad, to put in the bank, and he'd said to go to him whenever we needed anything.)

"I don't think we ought to gamble again," I said. I braced myself for a load of bad mouth along the lines of "I can do what I like! You can't order me about!" but to my surprise the Afterthought agreed. She said, "No, 'cos when you gamble you lose all your money."

I was so knocked out that I asked her what she *did* want to do. She said she wanted to get a printed T-shirt and be tattooed. I said, "Right! Let's do it."

I got a blue T-shirt with *PASSION FLOWER* printed on it. The Afterthought got a red one with *My dad's mad and bad*. She said it was something she'd read somewhere and she thought it was funny. I suppose it was, quite.

"Let's put them on!" she said, so we both dived into the Ladies and did a quick change. After that we went to the tattoo place, which was now open, and got ourselves tattooed. I asked for a passion flower to be put on my

arm, but the woman who did the tattoos couldn't find a picture one so she did a different sort of flower, red, like I wanted. I wasn't quite sure what it was, but it was pretty and I was pleased with it. The Afterthought was *sickening*. She got a heart with the words *I love my dad*. Truly disgusting and yucky! I didn't say so, however, as we were getting along really well and I didn't want to ruin things.

I asked her what she would like to do next. I could have thought of a zillion things that *I* would have liked to do, such as going round the shops, but I didn't mind humouring her, just so long as she behaved herself. "Do you want to stay on the pier or go somewhere else?"

The Afterthought said she wanted to stay on the pier. "I want something to eat! I'm starving."

I was quite hungry myself. Dad didn't really have very much to offer in the way of food; all we'd had for breakfast was a plate of soggy cereal and a piece of shrivelled toast. The Afterthought said there was "a dear little café" near where we had come in, so we turned and started walking back towards it. I held my arm out in front of me, admiring my tattoo. I giggled.

"Just as well they wear off… Mum would have a fit!"

"Don't see why," said the Afterthought. "It's not like a *real* tattoo… I wish I could have a real tattoo! I bet Dad would let me."

I thought that Dad just might. "Don't you dare ask him!" I said.

"Why not?"

"'Cos Mum wouldn't like it."

"Mum wouldn't see it!"

"She could hardly miss it," I said. "Unless you had it done somewhere stupid, like your bottom."

"I'd have it done *here*." The Afterthought tapped the side of her nose. "I'd start a new fashion… I'd have a nose tattoo! And she still wouldn't see it, 'cos we're not going to go back. So there!"

I stopped. "What do you mean, we're not going back?"

"We're not going back!"

I said, "Of course we're going back. Don't be silly! We're only here for the holidays."

"That's what you think," said the Afterthought.

I said, "That's what I *know*."

"Well, you know wrong! She doesn't want us back. Dad said. She told him he could have us, and welcome. So that's it! We're staying with Dad."

"That is such rubbish," I said. How could we stay with Dad? It was great being with him for a short time, but Dad couldn't look after us. He didn't have the room!

He didn't have a kitchen, he didn't have a bathroom, he didn't have anywhere to keep food. We couldn't stay with Dad! Trust the Afterthought to get it wrong.

"Mum just meant *for the summer*," I said. "He was welcome to us *for the summer*. While she had a break, 'cos we'd been mean to her."

"We weren't mean to her!" shrilled the Afterthought. "She was mean to us! She was mean to *Dad*. Throwing him out like that!"

There was no denying that Mum had been quite hard on Dad.

"You're always on her side," grumbled the Afterthought.

"Oh, shut up!" I said. We'd been getting on *so* well. I'd almost been quite fond of her, just for a few minutes. Why did she always have to go and ruin everything?

We found the dear little café and sat at a table outside, eating doughnuts and drinking milk shakes. Probably fattening, but who cared? We were on holiday!

While we were sitting there, I noticed this boy that kept glancing at me from the doorway of a slot machine place. He was with two other boys, but they were busy at a machine, pulling levers and pressing buttons. The one who kept glancing at me seemed more interested in – well, in *me*! I edged my chair round ever so slightly so that he would get a better view of my profile. I don't mean to boast, but I am quite proud of my profile. You know how with some people, movie stars, for instance, they can look fab full face? But then they turn their heads and you suddenly see that they have pointy noses or double chins and look quite ordinary. Even, in some cases, plain. A great disappointment! Especially if you have been thinking to yourself that this is my dream guy and then you see their nose all beaky or their chin sagging down like a waterlogged sock. I mean, talk about *disillusion*.

I have studied myself long and hard in Mum's dressing table mirror, which is one of those with wings on either side, and I feel reasonably confident that my profile would live up to expectations. Assuming, that is, that you had looked at me full face and liked what you saw. I am not being vain here! I think it is important to know these things about yourself; it can save a lot of heartache.

It can also save a lot of heartache if you don't have beastly ten-year-old brats dragging round with you, clocking everything with their beady little eyes and shrieking out their vulgar comments.

"Why do you keep staring at that boy?" demanded the Afterthought, in these loud clanging tones that everybody within a ten-mile radius could probably have heard.

I said, "Which boy? I'm not staring."

"Yes, you are! You're *ogling*."

What kind of word is that for a ten year old to use?

"I suppose you fancy him," she said.

I tossed my head. "You can suppose what you like."

Usually when I toss my head, my hair goes swirling round. But I'd forgotten – I'd tied it in bunches. Reluctantly, I decided that it would look a bit too obvious if I pulled it loose. A pity! My hair is black, like Dad's, and quite thick. Vix once said it was sexy!!! I suppose that really *is* boasting, though I'm only repeating what she said.

"Do you think he's good-looking?" said the Afterthought.

I did, as a matter of fact, but I wasn't giving her the satisfaction of knowing.

"Do you?" I said.

"No," said the Afterthought. "He's got silly hair! He's *ugly*."

I felt like bashing her. He wasn't ugly! And his hair wasn't silly, he'd had it dyed blond and gelled it so it was all gorgeously stiff and spiky. The Afterthought just had no sense of style at all.

"Looks like a hedgehog," she said. "Oh, gobbets! He's coming over… he's going to talk to you! *Yuck!*" She hung her head over the side of the table and pretended – noisily – to throw up.

"Why don't you go back home?" I said.

"Don't want to go back home," said the Afterthought.

"Well, then! Go and buy yourself a funny hat, or jump off the end of the pier, or something."

"No." She settled herself back on her chair. "I want to stay here and see what happens."

Spiky Hair was making his way towards us. The Afterthought was right. He was going to talk!

"Hi," he said.

I said, "Hi," and blushed furiously into my milk shake.

"Love the T-shirt! Is that your name? Passion Flower?"

"No, her name's *Stephanie*," said the Afterthought. "Who're you?"

Spiky Hair grinned. "I'm Zed. Who are you?"

"I'm Samantha and I'm staying," said the Afterthought.

"Quite right," said Zed. "Who knows what I might get up to?"

The Afterthought made a hrrumphing noise and twizzled her straw in her milk shake.

"She your chaperone?" said Zed.

"No," I said, "she's my sister and I'm stuck with her."

"Know the feeling," said Zed. "I've got one at home. A right pain."

"You can say that again," I said.

The Afterthought made another hrrumphing noise.

"Elephants run in the family?" said Zed.

Hah! That got her. She hates being made fun of. Crossly, she shoved her chair back.

"I'm going to feed the seagulls. Don't be all day!"

Zed promptly sat himself down next to me. "Why not?" he said. "In a hurry?"

I shook my head.

"Here on holiday?"

"We're here for the whole of the summer," I said. I didn't want him to think we were just, like, day trippers. "We're staying with our dad." And then I got brave and said, "How about you?"

"Me? I'm a denizen! I live here."

"You *live* here?"

"People do. You'd be surprised!"

"I wouldn't," I said, "'cos my dad does." But I did think Zed was lucky!

"So where d'you live, then?"

I pulled a face. "Nottingham."

"With your mum?"

"Yes. They're separated."

"Mine, too. We have something in common!" He grinned at me. I grinned back. "We both live with our mums, and we both have little bratty sisters... d'you ever manage to get out without her?"

I said, "At home, I do. At home we have practically nothing whatsoever to do with each other. It's difficult, here."

"How about in the evening?"

"Oh! Well – yes." Was he asking me out??? "I guess in the evening she could stay with Dad." I couldn't be expected to keep an eye on her *all* the time.

"There's a gang of us meet up in the Bluebell Caff. Just a bit further along from the pier." He pointed. "Feel like coming along? Eight o'clock?"

I nodded, breathlessly. Zed said, "Great. See you there!"

It was at that moment that my little bratty sister came wandering back. She watched jealously as Zed returned to his mates.

"See you where?" she said.

I said, "None of your business. I have a date!"

And I bought another postcard, to send to Vix.

Have met a Gorgeous Guy!
We're seeing each other tonight.
Will tell more later! xxx Steph.

five

"I SUPPOSE I have to ask where you're going," said Dad. "And what time you're going to be back... that's what your mum would do, isn't it?"

"She's going on a date," said the Afterthought. "With a *hedgehog*!"

"Really? That's novel," said Dad. "Where does one hang out, with a hedgehog?"

Glaring at the stupid Afterthought, who vulgarly stuck her tongue out, I told Dad that we were "just meeting up in a café."

"OK," said Dad. "You know the rules. Home by... what shall we say? Ten? Does that sound about right?"

"Mum wouldn't let her stay out that late," said the Afterthought.

"She would, too!" I said.

"Not with a boy you don't even know," said the Afterthought.

"So how do I *get* to know him?" I said. "If I'm not allowed to go out with him?"

"Good question," said Dad. "How old is he?"

I thought probably he had to be sixteen. Even, maybe, seventeen. But it seemed safer to say, "About my age?"

"More like *twenty*," said the Afterthought.

"Dad, he isn't!" I cried.

"OK, OK," said Dad. "I believe you. Just behave yourself – and make sure you've got your phone with you. There!" He sat back, beaming. "I reckon that's my parental duty taken care of."

The Afterthought sucked in her breath and slowly shook her head, like some cranky old woman. I really couldn't understand what her problem was; I'd have thought she'd be pleased to be left on her own with Dad. She just didn't like me having fun was what it was. She'd been behaving like the worst kind of spoilt brat ever since Mum and Dad split up. Mum said she was insecure and we must make allowances, and I did try, but what about *me?* I was insecure, too!

"I bet he does drugs," said the Afterthought.

"He doesn't!" I shrieked.

"Bet he does!"

If the Afterthought had said something like that in front of Mum, Mum would have gone half demented. It would have been, like, full-scale panic and Stephanie-I-don't-want-you-going-out-with-that-boy! Dad – dear old Dad! – just snapped open another can of lager and said, "Why do you bet? What do you know about it?"

"She doesn't know anything!" I said. "She's all mouth!"

"Well, just watch it," said Dad. "Just don't do anything I wouldn't."

I sent the Afterthought a look of triumph and shot out of the door before she could think of any other objections to raise. Nasty little troll! I was just glad Dad didn't take her seriously. Not that anyone could, though that wouldn't have stopped Mum. But Mum wasn't here. I was *free*!

I rushed off, down to the seafront. Only my second day in Brighton, and already I'd got myself a date! Vix would be *soooo* envious.

I was wearing my new passion flower T-shirt and my denim shorts with the flip flops Dad had bought me. I didn't think I would need a jacket as it was really hot and anyway I didn't want to spoil my outfit. I guess what I really mean is, I didn't want to cover up my tattoo!

Zed was already there, in the café, waiting for me. I was quite relieved to see him as you are always a bit

worried – well, I am always a bit worried – that maybe people won't turn up. That is, *boys*, when they ask you out. This happened once to Vix, and it really upset her. It took her ages to get her confidence back.

Zed waved when he saw me. "Hi, Passion Flower!" It killed me, the way he called me that. So much more romantic than Stephanie!

The others who were with him all turned to look. There were two boys, that Zed introduced as Chaz and Nick, and two girls, Paige and Frankie. Paige and Frankie were truly cool. They both looked like top fashion models and about eighteen years old, though it turned out they were only just starting Year 12 so they couldn't have been. They were still older than me, but I hoped perhaps they wouldn't realise as I do look quite mature for my age. At least, that is what I have been told. It is horrid if everyone knows how young you are as they immediately start treating you like a child, and it makes you feel really inferior. I discovered that all five of them lived in Brighton and went to the same posh school, the

Academy. That was the way they referred to it, just "the Academy", like everyone would automatically know what it was, like Eton or Harrow or somewhere. I knew it had to be posh as they all spoke in these voices like the Queen. What Dad calls "fraffly". Paige asked me what my accent was. I didn't even know I had an accent! Paige said that she collected them – accents, that is. Zed told me that she was going to be an actress and needed to be able to speak in different kinds of voices.

"Like wotcha, cock! Cor blimey, mite!"

I think he was pretending to be Cockney. Paige shrieked, "Zed, don't! That is ex*cru*ciating!"

All five of them then started putting on different accents and shrieking loudly at the tops of their voices. They didn't seem to mind that people were looking at them.

"So what *is* yours?" said Paige, when they had simmered down.

"It isn't anything," I said. "It's just ordinary."

They found that really funny. Paige shrieked, "Just ordinary!" and they all fell about.

"It's Sherwood Forest, isn't it, Passion?" Zed put his arm round my shoulders and hugged me to him. "'Er do come from Robin 'ood territory, don't 'ee, lass?"

"Oh, Zed! Muzzle it!" said Paige.

Chaz told me not to worry. "You don't really sound like that. It's just Zed and his cloth ears."

"This is the guy," said Nick, "who thought Chopin's

256

Funeral March was the Wedding March... tum-tum-ti-*tum*, tum-ti-tum-ti-tum-ti-tum."

Everyone screeched, and so I screeched, too, though to be honest I didn't really know whether the tum-ti-tums were supposed to be the funeral thingie or the wedding thingie.

I was beginning to feel a bit out of my depth and was quite glad when Zed decided that it was time to move on.

"Let's take Passion on the pier! Show her the attractions."

Me and Zed led the way – with Zed holding my hand. I couldn't wait to write and tell Vix! – and the others ambling along behind. As far as I could make out, Chaz and Paige were an item, and Nick and Frankie. I wondered if I might be going to become an item with Zed... I'd never been an item with anyone before. Not properly. I'd once gone out with a boy in my class, Jimmy

Hedges, for almost a term, but the whole time I'd been going with him I'd been sighing over another boy, Chris Whitwood, who was in Year 10. I'd thought Chris was the dog's dinner. Now he just seemed like… rubbish!

Being on the pier with Zed was utterly, totally different from being on the pier with the Afterthought. Even from being on the pier with Dad, though we did lots of the same things. We screamed on the Sizzler Twist and clutched each other on the Turbo Coaster and giggled on the Crazy Mouse (which was really for little kids). We also went on the Dodgems, where the boys had a great time deliberately bumping into each other. The man in charge grew really angry and threatened to switch off the power if they didn't stop it. As we got out, he shook his fist and yelled, "You poxy kids!"

I said, "What is he so cross about?"

Zed explained that he didn't like us bashing up his cars.

I said, "But I thought that was the whole point of it?"

"Yeah, I guess that's why they're called Dodgems," said Frankie.

I blushed; I'd never thought of the name as having any sort of meaning. I could see that it was stupid of me, but there wasn't any need for her to use that sarcastic tone of voice. I had the feeling Frankie didn't like me very much, though I couldn't imagine why. I thought maybe she secretly fancied Zed, and was jealous of me.

 She gave me this *filthy* look when I
started shivering, and Zed took off
his jacket and put it round me. She
really didn't like that!

"You wouldn't be much good on
the nudie beach," said Zed. "You'd
have goose pimples all over!"

"W-what n-nudie beach?" I said.

"Ours, of course! Don't you
know about it? We're famous for our nudie beach!
People come from miles, just to see the sights."

"Yeah, and what sights!" said Nick.

He and Zed then began to act out all the sights that
could be seen on the nudist beach. Paige and Frankie
joined in, and within minutes they were all doubled over,
screaming with laughter. I was laughing, too, but was

259

more embarrassed than anything. I could feel myself starting to grow gently warm and pink. Please, no! I thought. But once you start, you just can't stop. The more I tried to fight it, the worse it became, until warm turned to hot and pink turned to red and before I knew it I was lit up like a beacon. Like a big human blood orange. Being embarrassed by s.e.x. is *so* belittling! So horribly *young*.

"Oh, poor Passion!" cried Frankie. "We've made her blush!"

"That's because she's a nice girl," said Zed. "Unlike some of us."

PASSION

"Speak for yourself," said Frankie.

"You're just a tart," said Zed. "C'm 'ere, Passion! Let me give you a hug… I *like* nice girls!"

"Drop dead," said Frankie. And then she smiled sweetly at me and said, "I suppose you don't have nudists in Nottingham?"

I wished I could have thought of some smart remark, but of course I couldn't. I never can. Vix can! I just go all dumb and stupid.

"You lot naff off," said Zed. "Me and Passion want some quiet time."

The others drifted away, and Zed and I were left on our own. I thought he might try what Mum would call "funny stuff", and I was sort of a bit apprehensive, not knowing whether I could handle it, and a bit tingly, half hoping that he would, but in fact he didn't, he just walked me back home (though still keeping his arm round me). He said that he was going to be in Switzerland for the whole of the next four weeks, staying with his dad, and when he told me that my heart went *thunk*, because I thought it meant I would never see him again, but he said that he wanted to, and he took my phone number so that he could call me as soon as he got back. I couldn't help wondering whether he was just saying it, or if he really would. (I also wondered how I was going to survive for a whole month without him.)

"You don't think I mean it, do you?" he said. Help! He'd read my thoughts! "You think it's something I say to all the girls. But it's not! I really, really want to see you again."

He said it like he truly meant it. He really did want to see me again! I knew that Vix would warn me not to get excited. Not to count on it. She still hadn't properly got her confidence back after her bad experience. Boys weren't to be trusted! They'd tell you one thing, then do another. I knew all that. I knew that I wasn't cool like Paige and Frankie, that I didn't go to a posh school or have rich parents. I knew that Zed could quite easily meet up with some gorgeous girl on the plane on the way back from Switzerland and forget all about me. I knew, I knew! But I could dream, couldn't I?

It was gone half-past ten when I got back indoors. Dad didn't say a word! I don't think he even noticed. I mean, he noticed that I was back, but I don't think he realised what the time was. Or maybe he did, and he simply wasn't bothered. Mum would have been practically foaming at the mouth!

The Afterthought, thank goodness, was asleep, and I slid into bed really *sloooowly* so as not to wake her, but at breakfast next morning she started up.

"You didn't get in at ten o'clock! I know, 'cos I stayed awake!"

I said, "If you'd had a periscope and shoved it out the window you'd have seen that I was standing right outside."

"Doing what?" said the Afterthought.

I said, "None of your business!"

"Smooching, I bet! With the Hedgehog. I told Mum you'd gone out with a hedgehog."

"You told *Mum*?"

"When she rang."

"When did she ring?"

"Last night, after you'd gone."

"Checking to make sure I wasn't letting you starve," said Dad. "OK, girls!" He pushed back his chair. "I'm off. Got things to do. I'll see you later. Be good!"

"What shall *we* do?" said the Afterthought, as the door closed behind Dad.

I felt like saying, "You do what you want, I'll do what I want," but I knew that I couldn't. I'd promised Mum I'd look after her.

"What would you like to do?" I said.

"Go on the beach and find shells!"

"Wouldn't you rather do something more adventurous?"

"Like what?"

"I don't know! Like… go and see the nudist beach?"

"I don't want to see a nudist beach. I want to find shells!"

"The nudist beach would be more fun."

"I'm not taking my *clothes* off!" roared the Afterthought.

"I don't mean take your clothes off, I mean look at the other people with *their* clothes off."

"No! I don't want to. I want to find shells!"

I gave in. "Oh, all right," I said. Zed wasn't around, so we might just as well go and find her stupid shells as anything else. "I must buy another postcard for Vix."

"Why?" The Afterthought looked at me, slyly. "I s'ppose you're going to boast about the Hedgehog!"

I wondered to myself if I had been that tiresome when I was ten years old. I didn't think you had to be; I mean, just because you were ten years old. I knew some ten year olds who were actually quite nice. Vix's little brother, for instance. He was really cute! I thought, "Trust me to get lumbered with a bratty one." I was still trying to come up with some kind of crushing retort when there was a knock at the door and when I went to open it Ms Devine, Dad's landlady, was standing there.

"Hallo!" she said. "Stephanie, isn't it? Is your dad in?"

I said, "No, he's just left. He's gone to work."

"Work?" said Ms Devine. She sounded surprised, as if she didn't expect Dad to work. That made me think that she must know Dad quite well.

"He's got this little number," I said.

"Really? Well! I wonder if you could give him a message for me? Just whisper the word *rent* in his ear. Could you do that?"

"Rent," I said.

"He'll understand," said Ms Devine. "Just tell him… Shell said, rent."

We watched as Ms Devine's legs went back up the basement steps.

"She didn't sound cross," I said.

"Why should she sound cross?" said the Afterthought.

I wasn't sure; it was just that I was used to people sounding cross with Dad. I gave him the message when he got back that afternoon. Dad said, "Oh, yes! Don't worry about it. I have it in hand. What say we go up the road for a Chinese?"

"What, now?" I said.

"Why not now?" said Dad.

I said, "It's only five o'clock!"

"So what?" said Dad. "There's no law says you can't eat at five o'clock, is there? I don't know about you, but I eat when I'm hungry!"

It was one of the *best* things about being with Dad: there wasn't any routine. There weren't any set rules. We had meals at all odd times, just whenever Dad decided we should. Sometimes we had takeaways, sometimes we went out and sometimes we made do with stuff out of a tin. We got up when we liked, and watched telly when we liked, and went to bed when we liked. We never knew when Dad was going to be home or when he was going to be out. When he was home we all did things together, like maybe we'd mosey into town (Dad's way of putting it!) or jump in the car and go for a drive.

One day we went to see the Royal Pavilion, near the seafront. The Royal Pavilion is very historical, being built for George IV. It is full of many beautiful and precious objects. From the outside it looks like white onions shining in the sun. Well, I thought it looked like white onions. The Afterthought said it was more like meringues, and promptly decided that she had to eat meringues *immediately*, so we all rushed madly around in search of a tea shop, ending up in this big hotel on the seafront, feeling very grand.

This was the sort of thing that happened when you were with Dad. One day it would be spaghetti hoops out of a tin, the next it would be meringues, with tea in china tea cups, in a posh hotel. You just never knew.

When Dad wasn't home we were left to our own devices and could do pretty well whatever we liked. No one to fuss and bother over us! No one to huff and puff when we forgot to phone, or didn't arrive back when we were supposed to. Mum would have had fifty fits, but Mum wasn't there, she was living it up in Spain. She'd sent us a postcard saying, *Dear Both, I am having a wonderful time, I hope you are. Be good! Love, Mum.* Nothing about missing us, or looking forward to having us back. None of her little mumsy frets about whether we were eating properly, whether the Afterthought was behaving herself, whether I was keeping an eye on her. She was just busy enjoying herself. So after that I stopped feeling guilty when the Afterthought stayed up till the small hours and Dad let her watch unsuitable programmes on the telly and we both stuffed ourselves with junk food day after day. We could do what we liked!

The only thing I didn't like was having to lug the Afterthought with me wherever I went. Occasionally, as we searched for shells, or played the slot machines, or wandered along the seafront nibbling candy floss or eating ice creams, I'd catch sight of Zed's friends, either all four of them together or in ones and twos. They'd wave at me and say hallo, but they never asked me to join them. I felt sure this was because I had my little bratty sister with me. I asked her one day if she wouldn't rather I left her at home.

"What for?" she said, instantly suspicious.

"Well! I don't know... wouldn't you like to do things with your shells? Or watch telly, or something?"

"You just want to get rid of me," she said. "But you can't, 'cos you promised Mum! You told her you'd look after me."

"I'm trying to," I said. "That's why I thought maybe you'd rather stay at home. I don't want you to wear yourself out," I said.

The Afterthought said she wasn't wearing herself out, she liked going on the pier, and going on the beach, and paddling in the sea.

"Anyway," she said, "I'm not allowed to stay home by myself. You know Mum wouldn't let me."

Since when had that ever bothered her?

"Let's go and look round the shops," she said. "Let's buy things!"

"We can't," I said, "we haven't any money." I'd asked Dad for some, but he'd forgotten to go to the bank and until he did we only had enough for the odd ice cream or bottle of Coke.

"We can still go and *look*," said the Afterthought.

As we were wandering round the shops, we bumped into Paige, and another girl. One I hadn't seen before. Paige was quite friendly. She said, "Hi, Passion Flower!" It was the only name she knew me by. I would have liked it to stay that way, but my dear little sister immediately had to go and pipe up.

"Her name's not Passion Flower, it's Stephanie!"

Paige could obviously see me squirming, and took pity on me. She said, "If I were called Stephanie, *I'd* change it to Passion Flower. This is Marie-Claire, by the way. She's our exchange. *Elle ne parle pas beaucoup d'anglais*, do you?" Marie-Claire giggled and shook her head. "*Et moi*," said Paige, "*ne parle pas hardly any français du tout*. I suppose you don't, do you, Passion?"

"Only *un peu*," I said. "*Un très peu.*"

"Anything would be a help," said Paige. "Frankie speaks it OK, but she's not here. She's gone off to the Algarve for a fortnight. The boys are away, as well, so I'm all on my ownsome. I'm taking Marie-Claire to see the Pavilion. Feel like joining us?"

I was all ready to leap at the chance when *she* had to go and pipe up again. "We've already been to the Pavilion!"

"Yes, and you thought it was boring, so you might just as well *shove off*," I said, "and do something else!" I gave her a push. "We don't need you hanging around whining."

I know it was rather harsh of me, and that I wasn't making allowances, but she was *such* a nuisance.

"I'm going with Paige," I said. "You go and do your own thing."

"You can't go!" shrilled the Afterthought. "It costs money to get into the Pavilion! You haven't got any!"

"I have," said Paige.

"So naff off," I said; and I gave the Afterthought another push. A bit harder, this time. "Go on! Hop it!" And then I remembered, and tossed the front door key at her. "Go home and do your shells! I'll see you later."

"Will she be OK?" said Paige.

"She knows where we live," I said. I had had just about enough of my whiny little sister. Mum was off enjoying herself and obviously couldn't care less, so why should I?

I stayed out most of the day. After we'd been to the Pavilion we went on a little train that ran along the seafront, which was quite fun – though it would have been more fun if Zed had been there! But then everything would have been more fun if Zed had been there. Feeling rather bold, I said, "What about the nudist beach?"

"*Boring,*" said Paige. She turned to Marie-Claire. "You don't want to voir people sans clothes, do you?"

Marie-Claire giggled and said, "Sans clothes? Ah, mais non!"

"Me neither," said Paige. "Let's go back home and get something to eat. Come on, Passion! You, too."

Paige lived in a house a bit like the one that belonged to Ms Devine. It was all furnished with beautiful delicate antiques – little spindly chairs that looked as if they would collapse if you were gross enough to sit on them, and sofas covered in wonderful satiny stuff, and tiny little round tables standing on one leg.

Paige seemed to take it all for granted. She led us down some indoor stairs to the basement, which was about the same size as Dad's but had been turned into one big room with a counter running down the middle. On one side of the counter was a kitchen that Mum would have died for. It was the sort of kitchen you see in glossy magazines at the dentist's, with rows of shiny pots and pans, and strings of garlic hanging from the ceiling, and this vast great stove with double ovens. I tried not to let my mouth hang open, as I didn't want to look like a yokel, but I was distinctly gob-smacked. I asked Paige if Zed lived in a house like hers, and she laughed and said, "Zed! His place makes this look like a cupboard." So then I was even more gob-smacked and wondered what he saw in me and whether he really would ring me when he got back.

It was half-past four when I arrived home. I banged at the door, and Dad let me in.

"Where's your sister?" he said.

I said, "Isn't she here?" and my heart did this great walloping *thump* almost into my throat.

"She's not here," said Dad. "I thought she was with you?"

"She was," I said, "but I – I sent her back."

Dad looked grave. It takes a *lot* to make Dad look grave. "When was this?" he said.

"I don't know! About... eleven o'clock?"

"For heaven's sake, Stephanie! That's over five hours ago. Where can she have got to?"

six

Dad went rushing up the basement steps and out into the street, as if perhaps the Afterthought might have been following without me noticing. I raced after him.

"You're telling me," said Dad, "you haven't seen her since *this morning*?"

"I s-sent her back home," I stammered. "I g-gave her the key!"

"Not good enough," said Dad. "Not good enough! Totally irresponsible! Where's she likely to be? Think! Where do you usually go?"

I said, "The p-pier?" It was the only place I could think of. The Afterthought loved the pier. She was pier-crazy. She'd told me only the other day she would like to live on it, in a little booth like the one where the woman did the tattoos.

"We'd better go and look for her," said Dad. "Come on! Both of us! Two pairs of eyes are better than one."

We jumped into the car and roared off towards the seafront. Dad told me again that I had behaved totally irresponsibly. I felt like saying that so had he and Mum, what with Mum running off to Spain and leaving us with someone who couldn't even look after a pot plant. I mean, she *knew* what Dad was like, it wasn't fair expecting me to cope all by myself. Dad didn't have any right to heap all the blame on me! The only reason I didn't say it was that I was too worried about the Afterthought.

We reached the pier, and Dad dropped me off.

"You go and see if you can find her in there, I'll drive along the front. I'll meet you back here."

It wasn't easy, searching for the Afterthought on a crowded pier, but I did my best. I searched *all* through the slot machine rooms, both of them, squirming and burrowing amongst the bodies. I checked all the rides, I checked the tattoo booth and the cafés, I even went into the Ladies and called out, "Samanth*aa*?" but she wasn't anywhere to be found and I was getting really scared.

Dad was waiting for me in the car. I went tearing over, hoping and praying that I would see the

Afterthought beaming up at me, or even scowling up at me, I wouldn't have minded! But Dad was on his own.

"No luck?" he said. "Are you sure you looked all over?"

"Dad, I looked *everywhere*," I said. "She's not there!"

"OK, hop in. We'd better drive round a bit. Keep your eyes peeled."

We drove slowly round the streets, me with my head hanging out of the window. A couple of times I saw girls that looked a bit like the Afterthought, and my heart leapt, but as soon as we got close I could see that it wasn't her.

"I just don't know what possessed you," said Dad. "Leaving a ten year old on her own!"

"I told her to go back home," I wailed.

"Stephanie, she's *ten years old*. What were you thinking of?"

What I'd been thinking of was me. Having some time to myself, for a change, without the Afterthought tagging on and ruining things.

"I can't cart her round with me everywhere I go!" I said.

"Well, I can't be expected to take her with me," said Dad. "I've got work to do. Are you keeping your eyes open?"

274

Resentfully I snapped, "*Yes!*"

I hung my head back out of the window. Already I was beginning to have scary pictures of the Afterthought on the evening news, and to hear the voice of the announcer saying how police were gravely concerned for the safety of a ten-year-old schoolgirl, Samantha Rose, who had disappeared while staying with her father and sister in Brighton. The Afterthought had been told repeatedly, we had *both* been told repeatedly, never to talk to strangers, never to get into a car with anyone we didn't know. Not even if it was anyone we did know, unless we knew them really well. We had had it drummed into us by Mum. Every time we went anywhere, it was, "Just remember, d—"

"*Don't talk to strangers!*" We'd chant it in unison. "*Don't get into cars!*" It had become like a sort of joke. "Mum!" we'd go. "Stop fussing!"

I knew that the Afterthought wouldn't normally do anything silly. I mean, she wasn't daft. But if she'd been in one of her moods, there was no telling what she might get up to. I imagined her marching down to the pier, angry and defiant, thinking to herself that if I was having fun, she was going to have fun, too. I imagined someone watching her, seeing that she was on her own. Offering to buy her an ice cream, or take her on the turbo coaster, and the Afterthought, thinking she would show me, going off with them, all innocent and trusting, and—

"Stephanie?" said Dad.

"W-what?" I smeared the back of my hand across my eyes.

"You OK?" said Dad.

No! I wasn't OK! My little sister had gone missing and it was all my fault.

"We'll just do one final check at home," said Dad, "see if she's turned up, then we—"

He stopped, as the car began to judder and ground to a halt.

"What is it?" I said. "What's the matter?"

Dad banged his fist down, hard, on the steering wheel.

"We're out of gas, is what's the matter!"

"Oh, Dad!" I said.

"Don't you *Oh Dad* me! I didn't know we were going to have to drive halfway round town looking for your sister. Well, that's it! No car."

"There was a petrol station just a little way back," I said. "We could—"

"Could what?" said Dad. "Fill her up? What with? Air?"

I bit my lip.

"I didn't bring any money," said Dad. "Unless you've got any?"

But I hadn't; not enough for petrol. Not even enough to just get us back home.

"W-what shall we d-do?" I said.

"Walk," said Dad. "Come on! Shake a leg."

Dad set off really fast, with me trotting beside him.

"If she's not th-there," I said, "do we g-go to the police?"

Dad frowned. "We'll keep our options open."

"But, *Dad*—"

"I said we'd keep our options open."

"But, D—"

"Stephanie! Just remember, you're the one who's caused all this."

I was starting to cry again. "M-maybe we should r-ring Mum," I said. "She'd know what to do!"

"Your mother's the last person we want to bring in," said Dad. "Oh, now, come on, Passion Flower!" He slowed up, to put an arm round me. "You've got to have a bit more backbone than this. She'll show! She's probably pottering about on the beach. We didn't look on the beach, did we?"

Through sniffles, I said, "The t-tide was in."

"Well. OK! So—" Dad waved a hand. Even he was starting to sound a bit uncertain.

"Dad, we've got to go to the police!" I said.

"All right, all right! We'll go to the police. Let's get home first."

You will never believe it! We had just arrived back, and gone down the basement steps, when my dear little sister comes skipping out of nowhere, her face one big beam from ear to ear, going, "Dad, Dad! A lady up the road has got some kittens. She said I could have one! Oh, Dad, *can* I? Please, Dad, say I can! *Please!*"

All my instant relief turned to absolute fury. "Where have you been?" I shrieked.

"Up the road! To see the kittens! Dad, they are so *sweet*."

"There you are," said Dad. "I told you, didn't I? All that fuss! I said she'd show up."

"But where have you *been*?" I screamed it at her, really loud. "I told you to come home!"

"I did," she said. "But then I got bored, so I went for a walk, and I met this lady, and she was getting out of her car and she dropped her shopping and all these tins of cat food went rolling about, so I helped her pick them up and she said she'd got this cat that had had kittens and would I like to see them? So I said yes, and I went in with her and—"

"You went indoors? With a total stranger? Are you *mad*?" I said. "She might have kidnapped you!"

"What would she want to do that for?" said the Afterthought. "She's got kittens! There are two black

278

ones and a ginger one and the *dearest* little fluffy one, and she said if I wanted one I could have one, like, *now*, immediately, 'cos they're ready to leave their mum, so please, Dad, *can* I? Please?"

"Don't let her!" I said. "She doesn't deserve one!"

"I do! Don't be horrible!"

"You don't," I said, "and I'm not being. You deserve to be smacked. We've been looking all over for you!"

"And there I was, just up the road," said the Afterthought, as if that made it all right. "Were you worried about me?"

"Yes, we were!" I snapped. "Though goodness knows why."

"You shouldn't have left me on my own," said the Afterthought. "You're supposed to be looking after me. Anything could have happened! I could have got lost, I could have got run over, I could have been *abducted*."

"I wish you had!" I snarled.

"Girls, girls!" Dad held up a hand. "Don't let's fall out. All's well that ends well. I'll tell you what… let's go and fill up the jam jar then drive out somewhere for a meal."

"I thought you didn't have any money?" I said.

"Money? I've got loads of money! I've got a whole wad." Dad winked. "Close your eyes, both of you."

Obediently, we closed them. I heard Dad's footsteps moving across the room.

"OK! You can look... *now*!"

We looked. I think my mouth fell open. Dad had a whole fistful of notes!

"See? I told you I'd been working!"

"It looks like you've won the lottery," squealed the Afterthought.

"I wish!" said Dad. "But I'm not complaining. So come on, let's go!"

All the way back to the car, the Afterthought kept on about her kittens. Dad said that we would discuss it over dinner.

"One tiny little kitten," said the Afterthought, as she and I sat in the car while Dad set off for the petrol station with the spare can from the boot. Empty, needless to say. I couldn't help thinking that if it had been Mum, the spare can would have had petrol in it. But if it had been Mum, we'd probably never have needed to use the spare can in the first place.

"He's all little and tiny," crooned the Afterthought.

"Kittens usually are," I said.

"Yes, but he's like a little mini one."

"In that case," I said, "there's probably something wrong with him."

"There isn't! Don't be so horrid!"

"Well, but look, what's the point?" I said. "You know Mum won't let you keep it."

"I told you, we're not going back to Mum!"

It worried me when she said that. I knew it was nonsense, but it still worried me.

Dad drove us all the way to Lewes, where he said there was a nice little pub. We sat outside, in the garden, and the Afterthought ate scampi and chips, which made my mouth water, only I wasn't sure whether scampi counted as animal so to be on the safe side I had a baked potato filled with coleslaw, which in truth was rather boring. But sometimes you have to make sacrifices, for the good of your soul. I just wished Mum could have been there, to see me. *And* to see the Afterthought.

She was still carrying on about her kitten. In the end – of course! – Dad said she could have it. The Afterthought was always able to get round Dad. Mum once said, "If that child asked you for an elephant, you'd go out and buy her one."

I'm not sure he'd have bought an elephant for me, but then I would never have asked.

When he said she could have her kitten, the Afterthought flew round the table and hugged him.

"Darling Dad! Sweet Dad!"

Yuck yuck *yuck*. But Dad seemed to like it. He promised that we would ring the cat lady as soon as we got home. The Afterthought flashed me this look of triumph.

"Mum will never let her keep it," I said. I knew this wouldn't make an atom of difference, but I just wanted to hear what Dad had to say.

Dad didn't say anything: the Afterthought got in first.

"It's nothing to do with Mum! Mum won't know anything about it!"

"She will if you try taking it home."

"We're not going home! Are we, Dad? We're not going home! We're staying with you."

"Would you rather stay with me?" said Dad.

"*Yes!* 'Cos you give me kittens!"

"Stephie? How about you?"

"I – don't know," I said. "How would we live? And what about school?"

"Who cares about school?" scoffed the Afterthought.

"I do!" I said. "I've got friends."

"Only Vix!"

"She's my *best* friend. I've got others!"

"Mum doesn't want us back, anyway," said the Afterthought.

"Dad!" I appealed to him. "That's not true, is it? It's not true! Tell her!"

"There, there." Dad patted my hand. "Don't get in a lather. It may never happen."

I said, "What? What may never happen?"

"Anything," said Dad. "The end of the world, little green men from Mars… just take life as it comes. That's my motto."

"Mum still won't let her keep the kitten," I said.

"Stephanie, you worry too much," said Dad. "It ain't worth it. It'll all come out in the wash."

There were times when I really couldn't understand what Dad was talking about. It was one of the things that used to get Mum so mad at him. She called it "evading the issue".

"Can't give a straight answer to a straight question!"

The minute we got home, the Afterthought insisted that Dad rang about the kitten.

"Don't forget, it's the fluffy one… I want the fluffy one!"

She got the fluffy one.

I have to say, he was really cute! Like a little black furry imp, skittering about the place. The Afterthought couldn't think what to call him, so Dad suggested Titch.

"Yes," crowed the Afterthought, "'cos he's titchy!"

I said, "What happens if he grows big? He might grow enormous!"

"In that case," said Dad, "it will be funny… *Titchy, Titchy, Titchy*! And then this monstrous great bruiser of a cat lumbers up."

"He's not going to be a bruiser," said the Afterthought. "He's going to stay as a titch!"

Having a kitten really transformed the Afterthought. I suddenly realised, it was months since I'd seen her happy and laughing. Ever since Dad left home, she'd been just about as mean as she could be. She'd been really hateful to Mum. Looking back I could see that I hadn't behaved all that well, but the Afterthought had deliberately gone out of her way to be hurtful. I could understand why Mum had packed us off. I would have packed us off. But now she had Titch, the Afterthought was all smiles. She told me that I could share him.

"He'll be my cat, but you can cuddle him. If you want to."

Anyone would have wanted to! He was just so adorable. I didn't say any more about Mum not letting us keep him; I thought that even Mum, once she saw him, would be unable to resist. I still couldn't really believe what the Afterthought had said, about us not going back, but I did ask Dad if I could telephone Mum and find out when she was expecting us.

"Best not," said Dad. "She gave me strict instructions… *only call if there's an emergency*."

"But you have got a number for her?" I said.

"I've got a number," said Dad. "But it would be as much as my life's worth to let you use it! You know how your mum terrifies me."

"Oh, Dad!" I said. "She doesn't!"

"Are you kidding?" said Dad. "She could even frazzle me down a phone line!"

He was making like it was a big joke, but he wouldn't let me have the number. He said Mum really had told him that she didn't want to be disturbed.

"But how are we to know if she's all right?" I wailed.

"She'll be all right," said Dad. "Don't you worry about your mum. She's one tough cookie!"

A few days later, we had a postcard from her.

Dear Girls. Sun, sand and sangria! Total bliss. Why didn't I do it before??? Hope your dad's coping. Hope you're having fun. Lots of love, Mum

I pored over it, reading and re-reading it. Mum was happy. Yeah! She was enjoying herself. Good! She sent her love. *Lots* of love. That meant she wasn't mad at us any more. But she still didn't say she was missing us, or was looking forward to having us back. It really was a bit worrying.

As well as a card from Mum, I had one from Vix, who had gone on a camping holiday to France with her mum and her little brother.

Hi, Steph! We just arrived last night so I haven't had time to check out the boy situation. I will report! Has Zed come back yet? Has he rung you? I hope you won't be too upset if he doesn't, you know what boys are like. But if he does you must be cool! Whatever you do, don't show him that you are pleased or he will think you are too easy. Anyway, that is my advice. xxx Vix

It was now almost a month since Zed had gone to Switzerland. I'd been counting the days, secretly marking them off on the wall of the toilet, down low where it couldn't be seen. I did it like people in prison do, if they are in solitary confinement:

1/ 2/ 3/ 4/ 5/

I couldn't tick them off on the calendar, or the Afterthought would have noticed. I didn't want her making any of her silly remarks.

I knew the exact day when Zed would be back. I spent the whole of it in a state of jitters, waiting for him to ring. He didn't! I thought perhaps he was suffering from jet lag (from Switzerland?) or that he hadn't arrived home until late. He would ring tomorrow! Maybe. Or maybe not. I couldn't help drooping, just a little. I knew that Vix was bitter, on account of her bad experience, but a month is a terribly long time! I didn't really think, probably, that Zed would remember me. I mean, there wasn't any reason why he should, it is not as if I am anything special. I know I am quite prettyish and look mature for my age, but a boy like Zed could get any girl he wanted. He could get rich girls, cool girls, girls who really were sixteen. Not just pretending!

These were the things I told myself, to stop from being disappointed. If I had bumped into Paige or any of the others I might even have been brave enough to ask them, "Is Zed back yet?" But I hadn't seen any of them since the day the Afterthought gave us such a fright. We hadn't really been out all that much, which was partly because it had been raining rather a lot, and partly because we didn't have any money. Dad had peeled some notes off his wad and given them to us, but we had spent all that and now Dad said he was "a bit skint" until something else turned up. In other words, he didn't have any money, either! I couldn't help wondering what had happened to all the rest of the wad, but I didn't like to ask in case he thought I was nagging. (Which was what he used to accuse Mum of doing.)

Now that she had her kitten, the Afterthought didn't mind staying in. Sometimes Dad was home, but most often it was just me and the Afterthought by ourselves. When we weren't playing with Titch, I helped the Afterthought do things with her shells. She was sorting them into different shapes and sizes, and then painting them with nail polish in all different colours. I'm not sure what she was doing it for, but it kept her happy. I didn't really mind. At least we were friends again.

It was the day after Zed was due back, when we were in the middle of shell painting, when my mobile rang. It rang and rang, and I couldn't find it! I was racing round the room in total panic, trying to trace the sound, when the Afterthought calmly picked up a cushion, and there it was. I shrieked, "Gimme, gimme!" but she danced away, out of reach, behind the 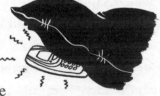 sofa. In this very posh voice she said, "This is the Rose residence. How may I help you?" And then she pulled a face and said, "It's W."

I said, "What?"

"W," said the Afterthought. "P. Q. *Zed*. The alphabet person. Your beloved… it's all right! I've pressed the secrecy button, he can't hear."

I snatched the phone from her and dashed into the bedroom. *Cool.* I had to be *cool.*

"Hi," I drawled, doing my best to sound like Paige and Frankie.

Zed said, "Hi, Passion!" Was he *laughing*? I went hot all over. Don't say that stupid child hadn't pressed the secrecy button after all! "Have you missed me?"

I knew Vix would tell me to say no, but I'd gone and said yes before I could stop myself. Zed said, "Good! I wanted you to. Hey, listen! There's a party on Saturday. Feel like coming?"

Vix would have been so cross with me! I forgot all about cool. I even think I might have *gushed.* Yuck! I can't stand people who gush. But being invited to a party by this totally gorgeous male! I couldn't wait to write a postcard...

Before I could do that, however, I had to ask Dad whether it was OK for me to go. I knew if it had been Mum the answer would have been a big firm NO. She would have reminded me that I was only fourteen – *just* fourteen. She would have pointed out that I didn't really know Zed properly. She would have said that in any case he was too old for me. (She only liked me to go out with boys my own age. Anything over fifteen and she freaked.) Mum would also have wanted to know where the party was at, and if I'd said "Haywards Heath" that would have been it. The final nail in the coffin. *No way!*

When I said Haywards Heath to Dad he just said, "Oh, that's all right! Twenty minutes on the train. No problem."

I almost jumped in the air and clapped my hands. Three cheers for Dad! Dad *trusted* me. That was the difference between him and Mum: Mum treated me like a child.

"Don't you want to know what time she's going to be back?" said the Afterthought. She didn't say it to be mean; more like she was actually trying to be helpful. Trying to remind Dad of his responsibilities.

Dad said, "Yes! Absolutely right. What time are you going to be back?"

I hesitated.

"What time would your mother say?"

Mum wouldn't have let me go in the first place; but if she *had* let me go, she'd have told me to be back at some absurd sort of hour, like half-past nine.

"How about midnight?" said Dad. "That sound about right? For a party?"

The Afterthought looked at me, wide-eyed. I gulped and said, "Y-yes! Midnight sounds fine."

I couldn't believe it! *Midnight.* I flew at Dad and kissed him.

"That is just so brilliant!" I said.

Dad looked pleased. "You're welcome. Just have a good time.

I intended to!

seven

I COULDN'T THINK what to wear for the party. It was obviously important. Very important! Not to say, *crucial,* if I wanted Zed to stay interested in me. But I'd only brought a few clothes with me, and now I didn't have any money to buy more. I tried asking Dad, but he shook his head, regretfully, and said, "Sorry, kiddo! Funds are a bit short right now."

For several minutes I felt quite cross and resentful, wondering what had happened to the cheque that Mum had given us. I knew what had happened! Dad had gone and spent it. He had spent *our money*, just as he had spent Mum's.

But then I remembered how he had taken us on the pier that first day, and given us change for the machines, and how he had bought us our flip flops and paid for our tattoos and our T-shirts; and all the times he had taken us out to dinner, and the trips to Lewes and to Hastings, and the Afterthought's kitten; and I reminded myself, also, that if it had been *Mum* who was in charge of us, I wouldn't be going to the party anyway. So then I stopped being resentful and decided to make the best of things.

The Afterthought helped me. Now that she had Titch, and was happy again, she was really eager to make up and be friends. We laid out all my clothes on the bed, trying to decide which were most suitable for a party. The Afterthought picked up my one and only dress, bright pink, with a halter top. Greatly loved by Mum! I was quite fond of it, too.

"You think I should wear that?" I said.

"It's what makes you look prettiest," said the Afterthought. "But it also makes you look *young*."

"Forget it!" I waved the dress back on to the bed. No way did I want to look young! "What about that?" I pointed to a top that I particularly liked as I thought it flattered me. "Could I wear that?"

"Mm…" The Afterthought studied it, through half-closed eyes. "That would be OK."

"What shall I wear with it? Shorts?" No! Zed had already seen me in my shorts. "These!" A pair of Capris

– well, that's what the girl in the shop said they were. Trousers that came to just below the knee. I'd seen Frankie wearing some a bit like them, so I knew they were OK. Frankie's had been flowery. Mine were white, like the top, with red embroidery and red fringes. I held them up against me and gave a little twirl. "What do you think?"

"Shorts are best for showing off your legs," said the Afterthought. "But trousers are more sophisticated."

I settled for the trousers, with my flip-flops since my only sandals were too infantile for words, and as the Afterthought said, "You can't wear trainers. Not if you're going to be dancing." She then had a brilliant idea for what she called "an assessory". (I didn't tell her that the word was *accessory*. It didn't seem fair, when she was trying so hard to help.) She suggested that I should use some of her bottles of nail polish to paint my nails all different colours.

"Would that look good?" I said, doubtfully.

The Afterthought said it would be the height of fashion, she had seen it in a magazine, so I took her at her word and gave myself two nails blood red, one green, one gold, and a silver thumb!

"See? I told you!" said the Afterthought. "That looks fab. And look, look!" She snatched up my silk flower, the one Dad had won on the pier, and thrust it at me. "You could put this in your hair!"

It was strange, the Afterthought had absolutely *no* sense of style when it came to herself, but she could choose stuff for me OK.

"What are you going to wear on top?" she said. "Your denim jacket?"

It was all I had, and it was quite old and tatty, but the Afterthought said that denim was meant to be old and tatty. She said, "It would look really sad if it was new. Like you'd gone out and bought it specially."

Oh, wise Afterthought! I hugged her and said, "From now on, you will always be my fashion consultant."

I was meeting Zed and the others in the Bluebell Café, so Dad said he and the Afterthought would give me a lift down to the front.

"It's all right," he said, "I won't get out of the car and shame you. I'm sure you wouldn't want to be seen with a tatty old dad! Incidentally, you're looking very chic, if I may say so."

I was glad Dad thought I looked chic. I just hoped Zed did, too!

He was there in the café, with Paige and the other three. He was even more gorgeous than I remembered him! His hair was still blond, but now he had a deep golden tan to go with it.

"Yo, Passion!" He reached out a hand to pull me down beside him. I did so want to be cool and elegant! Instead, to my shame, I went and tripped over the leg of someone's chair and practically fell on top of him. Everybody thought it highly amusing, except for me. I, of course, turned bright red like a pillar box.

"Somebody's eager!" cried Nick.

"Somebody happens to have *missed* me," said Zed. "Isn't that right, Passion?"

"Don't be so big-headed!" Paige aimed a smack at him with a menu. "Boys!" she said. "Think they're God's gift!"

"We are," said Zed. "What would you do without us?"

"Get on very nicely, thank you," said Paige.

I felt that it was time to make a contribution, other than tripping over chair legs. Brightly I said, "What time does the party start?"

"Any time," said Frankie. "Just whenever we care to turn up."

"We'll be leaving in a few minutes," said Nick.

"Why, anyway?" said Frankie. "Do you have to go to bed early?"

She really *didn't* like me. But Zed did! That was all that mattered.

"So whose party is it?" I said, determined not to be squashed.

"Yes! Whose party is it?" said Zed.

"I don't know," said Chaz. "I thought you knew?"

"I don't know," said Zed.

"Well, somebody must! Whose party is it?"

In bored tones, Frankie said, "It's a friend of Gary Meldrum."

"Who's Gary Meldrum?" said Zed.

"I dunno," said Chaz. "I thought you knew?"

"I don't know!" said Zed.

"Oh, shut up!" said Paige. "You know perfectly well who he is. He was in Year 12. Don't take any notice of them, Passion. They are quite *stupid*."

When we walked up to the station, Zed held my hand all the way. Paige and Chaz held hands, too, but I noticed that Nick and Frankie didn't. That just made me think all over again that Frankie secretly fancied Zed and was jealous of me. I knew she was jealous of me because she actually tried to get rid of me! As we reached the station, she suddenly said, "Are you sure you're old enough to come to this party?"

"Of course she's old enough!" said Zed. "What kind of question is that?"

"She doesn't look old enough to me," said Frankie.

Zed said, "How old are you, Passion?"

I was so glad I hadn't worn the pink dress! Boldly I said, "I'm sixteen. Just," I added. I thought it made it sound more like the truth if I said "just", though I could tell from the way Frankie tossed her head that she didn't believe me. Zed did. He told Frankie to stop behaving like a mother hen.

"Come on, Pash! I'll get your ticket."

I suppose, really, what with equality of the sexes and all that, I should have said that I would get my own, but I didn't because I knew that Zed probably had loads more money than I did, and if I'd had to buy my own ticket it would have left me with about 2p in my purse. Which is always a bit scary.

We got to the party at eight o'clock, but we only stayed for an hour because Zed and Chaz decided it was boring and wanted to move on. I didn't find it boring! I thought it was fun. But it seemed there wasn't enough happening. Zed said, "This is not where it's at."

"So where shall we go?" said Frankie.

Chaz said he knew of something in Croydon. "We could try that."

"Let's do it!" said Zed.

I was a bit alarmed as I didn't know where Croydon was, but Zed assured me it was only a short train journey.

"Are you certain that you want to come?" said Frankie.

Zed said, "Of course she wants to come!"

"You mean, *you* want her to come."

"It's not a question of what I want," said Zed.

Paige said, "Oh, no? Since when?"

"We ought to put her on the train back," said Frankie.

Honestly! The cheek of it. Like it was up to her to decide my life for me.

"I'm coming," I said. "I want to go to a party!"

Frankie didn't say any more; just shrugged her shoulders. I felt triumphant. I had won! Zed paid for my ticket again and we all got on a train for Croydon. The journey was longer than the one from Brighton to Haywards Heath had been, so that it was nearly ten o'clock when we arrived. I thought, "I'll never be home by midnight!" but it was too late, now, to start worrying. It would have been altogether too babyish to have gone home.

I never did find out whose party it was. I'm not sure any of the others knew, either, except perhaps Chaz, who was the one who had suggested it. It was held in someone's flat, on the ground floor of a big old house, and by the time we turned up it had really got going. Lots of noise, lots of people, and music loud enough to blow your brain. Just the sort of party I would normally have loved! But right from the word go I had this feeling I had made a mistake. Frankie was right: I shouldn't have come! For starters, everybody was heaps older than I was. There wasn't a single person there who looked to be under eighteen. Most of them looked like they were in their twenties. It was difficult to find anything to drink that wasn't alcoholic, and I just knew that people were smoking stuff they shouldn't, and that some were doing worse than just smoking. I am not a prude! I am a very broad-minded sort of person. I believe that everybody should be allowed to do their own thing. But I didn't feel I was ready for this!

I didn't think that Zed was ready for it, either, in spite of being seventeen and going to a posh school. He started drinking almost immediately and just didn't stop, and although he wasn't drunk, exactly – at least, not falling-over sort of drunk – he became really silly so that I couldn't get any sense out of him. I asked him when we were going to go home, and he said, "Who knows? Today, tomorrow? This time next week? Maybe never!"

"It's getting really late," I said. "It's nearly half-past eleven."

Zed said, "Shock horror! Half-past eleven… soon 'twill be the witching hour! Ghoulies and ghosties and long-leggety beasties, and things that go bump in the night! Have a drinkie. Make you feel better."

He held out his glass, but I pushed it away.

"I think we ought to go," I said.

"Don't want to go," said Zed. "Having fun. Drink up and don't be such a misery!"

This time he actually tried to force the glass between my lips, and when I shoved it away it spilt all down his

front. Zed said, "Look what you've done! What a waste of good booze. Now I shall have to go and get some more."

He went weaving off, across the room. I didn't know whether to go after him or not. I didn't know what to do! I was starting to feel quite frightened. How was I ever going to get home? I looked round for the others, but they didn't seem to be there. Icy bullets went zapping down my spine. Suppose they had already left? I would be on my own with Zed! And Zed had gone silly, with too much drink. He wasn't going to take me home. Why had I ever come???

I'd come because I'd resented being pushed around by Frankie. Because I didn't want Zed thinking I was just a little kid. And now I was frightened and wished I wasn't here!

I suddenly became aware that someone was looming over me. A tall skinny man with a straggly beard. I'd already noticed him across the room, looking at me.

"Hallo!" he said. "What are you doing here?"

I felt sure there ought to be some witty kind of response to this question, but I couldn't think of one. I couldn't think of *any* kind of response. I was just, like, frozen.

"All on your own?" said Skinny. He leant over, and the beard waggled at me. I hate beards! "Been abandoned?"

I shook my head, very frenziedly, to and fro.

"No?" Skinny studied me, and waggled his beard again. He seemed friendly enough, but you can't trust men with beards. I knew this, because Vix had told me so. She had read it somewhere. (They grow beards to *hide* things.) "You looked a bit lost," he said, "that's all. I take it you belong to someone? Are you here with your mum and dad?"

Heavens! He thought I was a child. He was checking whether I would be missed if he made off with me. I gasped, "No, I'm – with my boyfriend. He's—" I flapped a hand in the direction in which I had seen Zed disappearing. "He's over there! I've got to... get him!"

I shot off across the room. I expect it probably sounds quite pathetic, but I was really scared. I wasn't scared that the skinny beard man was actually going to make off with me, because if he tried it I would scream the place down. *Someone* would notice. Wouldn't they? They couldn't all be drunk! I mean, some of them had to stay sober so they could drive home.

If they were going home. If it wasn't the sort of party where they all crashed out and didn't come to until the following day. I think that's what I was really scared of. Having to spend the night with all these druggy people! I was sure most of them were on something. Ecstasy or something. Zed could be, for all I knew. Boys from posh schools were always being busted for drugs. He was probably zonked out of his skull right now. If only Frankie hadn't been so unpleasant! If she'd just taken me to one side and said, "Look, Passion, you can't fool me! I know you're only fourteen. You really don't want to come to this party." Well, I might just have listened. Instead, she'd sneered and jeered and tried to make me feel stupid. It was her fault!

I knew it wasn't, really. But I was just so frightened! I was thinking of all the movies I'd seen (movies that Mum hadn't wanted me to watch but Dad had always let me) where innocent young girls had drugs pumped into

them and became helpless addicts living on the street, or died hideous contorted deaths, rolling their eyes and frothing at the mouth.

I blundered through a press of bodies and into the hall. I'd got to get away! I'd got to get back home! Someone grabbed me by the arm and I let out a yell.

"Passion?" It was Chaz. Chaz and the others! "Where's Zed? We're leaving."

The minute he said that, my heart stopped hammering, the bullets stopped pounding. Great waves of relief washed over me. I said, apologetically, that I wasn't sure where Zed was.

"I think he went to find some more booze."

"Oh, God!" said Chaz. Paige rolled her eyes.

"You stay here," said Nick. "We'll go and find him."

"Well, just hurry!" said Frankie. "We don't want to miss the last train."

Nervously, I said, "W-when *is* the last train?"

"Twenty-five after midnight," said Frankie. "Way past your bedtime," she added.

Paige said, "Shut up, Frankie!"

"Well, she shouldn't have come. *I'm* not taking responsibility for her. It's up to Zed."

"Zed couldn't take responsibility for a paper bag," said Paige.

Like Dad, I thought. Zed was just a younger version of Dad! He was doing to me what Dad had done to Mum. All of their married lives Dad had behaved irresponsibly; Mum had never been able to rely on him. He'd spent money they didn't have, he'd made promises he didn't keep, he'd just always, always let her down. The same as Zed had done to me!

I wondered miserably if it were true, what Vix had once

told me (something she'd read in a magazine) that girls often fell for boys who reminded them of their dads. It certainly seemed to be what I'd done. Well! I'd learnt my lesson. Next time I would make sure I chose someone solid and boring and responsible. I didn't want this happening again! Chaz and Nick came back, dragging Zed with them. Zed cried, "Hi! There's Passion!" and launched himself in my direction but fell headlong before he could reach me. Nick grabbed him just in time. "Passion, Passion!" cried Zed. "Where have you been all this time?"

It was quite embarrassing. I don't think I will ever take up drink.

We got to the station just two minutes before the train was due. It didn't get in to Brighton until gone one o'clock! I'd never in my life been out so late all by myself. Without Mum or Dad, that is. Paige said, "Don't you think you ought to ring someone and tell them you're on your way?"

I tried ringing Dad, but there wasn't any reply. I knew what had happened: Dad hadn't re-charged his mobile. He'd got a new battery for it, but he didn't always remember that it needed re-charging.

"No one there?" said Paige, sounding surprised.

I explained about Dad forgetting to re-charge.

"Don't you have a land line?" said Frankie.

I thought she said *landmine*. Bewildered, I said, "What's a landmine?"

Zed chortled. "Something you tread on and it blows you to smithereens!"

No one took any notice of him. Frankie, speaking very slowly and deliberately, as if I were half-witted, said, "*Land LINE.*"

"An ordinary phone," said Paige.

"Oh! No, we don't have one of those," I said.

So then they all looked at me like I was some kind of alien. All except Zed, who was still sniggering to himself.

Suddenly, more than anything else on earth, I wanted to be home. *Really* home. Back in Nottingham, with Mum! I didn't care if Nottingham was dull and boring. I didn't care if Mum fretted and fussed and treated me like a child. I wanted to be treated like a child! I wanted to be fussed over! I would have given anything to hear Mum laying down her rules and regulations. *Don't talk to strangers. Don't get into cars... don't go off to wild parties with boys you don't know!*

I had thought I was so grown up. I had tried so hard to be cool and mature. All I'd succeeded in doing was frightening myself.

I felt ashamed, afterwards. When I looked back on it I felt that I'd behaved like a stupid baby. After all, what had happened? Nothing! No one had tried to abduct me, or have their way with me, or force me into taking drugs. There was a girl in my class at school, Rhiannon

O'Donnell, who went to parties like that all the time. Or so she claimed. Maybe she did. She'd started going with boys when she was only eleven. I hadn't gone out with a boy till I was thirteen! I decided, sadly, that in spite of *looking* mature I was obviously extremely young for my age. Vix, too! Because when I told her about the party she said that she couldn't have handled it, either. She said it was nice that we could admit these things to each other.

"Instead of just boasting, you know?"

I wished Vix could have been there with me, on the train that night. I wouldn't have felt so alone and so insecure. I knew that I was a nuisance, and that the others felt responsible for me. Not Zed, who was the one who had brought me. Zed was well out of it. But Paige and the two boys. Paige said they couldn't let me go home on my own, and Chaz and Nick agreed. Frankie just pulled a face. I knew what *she* was thinking… *I told you so*! I was grateful to Paige as I would have been really nervous of walking home by myself.

It was gone quarter-past one when I arrived back. I thought for sure Dad would be worried about me. Even Dad! I imagined him trying to ring me and discovering that his mobile wasn't charged. I braced myself for angry cries of "Stephanie! What time of night do you call this?" Instead, I found Dad slumped on the sofa, fast asleep, with the telly still blasting away. I wondered whether to simply turn it off and creep past into the

bedroom, but before I could do so Dad suddenly opened his eyes and said, "Steph? That you? I must have drifted off!" Then he sat up and stretched and said, "Had a good evening?"

I don't think he even noticed what time it was.

eight

"Hey! Stephanie!" The Afterthought shot up the bed and pummelled me into wakefulness. I opened a reluctant eye.

"Wozza time?"

"Nearly seven o'clock!"

"Too early! Go back to sleep."

"I can't, I'm awake!"

"Well, I'm not. Leave me alone!" I punched, irritably, at the pillow. "I didn't get to bed till half-past one."

"I know. I tried waiting up for you, but I fell asleep – and that was after *midnight*!" The Afterthought bounced, and my head went bang, thud, wallop. "I want to hear about the party! Tell me about the party! Was it good?"

I grunted.

"What did you do? Did you dance? Did the Alphabet person kiss you? Did you enjoy it?"

I said, "Yes, it was fun." And then I, too, catapulted up the bed. "Actually," I said, "it was horrid! I wished I hadn't gone."

The Afterthought stared at me, her eyes wide. "Why? What was horrid about it?"

"Everything! The people – Zed. He got *drunk*. And I'm sure there were drugs. It was scary, 'cos they were all heaps older than me, and –" I hugged my knees to my chest "– we didn't stay at the first party, we went on to another one in Croydon, and Zed wouldn't come home, and—"

"Where's Croydon?" said the Afterthought.

"I don't know! Somewhere. On the train. Miles away. And I didn't have my ticket, Zed had it, and I didn't know how to get to the station, and it was really late and I thought Dad would be so worried."

"Dad never worries," said the Afterthought. "Mum would have done."

"Mum would never have let me go in the first place," I said.

"No."

We fell silent, thinking about it. The Afterthought sat back on her heels, looking like a little plump elf in her nightie. For some reason, I don't know why, I suddenly felt fond of her.

"I don't think I *ought* to have gone," I said. "I don't think Dad should have let me."

The Afterthought put her thumb in her mouth and sucked at it.

I said, "Dad lets us do all kinds of things he shouldn't."

"Like what?" said the Afterthought, through a mouthful of thumb.

"Like watching stuff on telly that Mum would say wasn't suitable. Like eating junk food every day. Like driving in the front seat of the car without a seat belt!"

"Mm. But it is *nice* being here with Dad," said the Afterthought. She scrambled out of bed, scooped up Titch from a pile of clothes, and jumped back into bed again. Titch immediately started purring, and kneading with his claws. "If we hadn't come to stay with Dad,"  said the Afterthought, "we wouldn't have had a kitten."

"Would you still like to stay with him all the time?" I said.

The Afterthought considered the question, her head to one side. "*Most* of the time," she said.

"What's that mean?"

"It means I'd stay with Dad in the holidays, 'cos it's more fun with Dad, but I'd stay with Mum during term."

"Then you'd be with Mum longer than you would with Dad," I said.

The Afterthought frowned. "Maybe Mum could come and live in Brighton. That'd be best! Then we could live with either of them, depending how we felt."

"So if we felt like having a good time we'd stay with Dad, and if we felt like being looked after we'd go and stay with Mum."

"Something like that," said the Afterthought. "But Mum would have to come and live in Brighton. We couldn't keep going up to Nottingham."

I said, "Why don't you dream that Dad might win the lottery while you're about it?"

"'Cos he says the chances of winning the lottery are even worse than... something to do with horse racing that I couldn't understand," said the Afterthought.

"Yes," I said, "and the chances of Mum coming to live in Brighton are about nine million to one, so you can forget that idea!"

"In that case, I'll stay with Dad," said the Afterthought; but she didn't sound quite as bullish about it as she had before. I felt she was just saying it.

I wondered what *I* was going to say to Vix, about the party. Unfortunately I had already sent her a card telling her that I was going, otherwise I would probably just have said nothing at all. I knew she wouldn't forget about it as I'd made this really big thing of it. I suppose

I'd boasted, just a little. *Zed has asked me to a party!*
She'd be breathlessly waiting to hear what it was like.

I didn't want to lie to her and say it had been brilliant,
because if you lie to your best friend it is almost like lying
to yourself; and besides, I had this feeling that once I was
back home – because we *were* going back home. We had
to! – I might want to talk about it with her. On the other
hand, I didn't want to admit that I had been a baby and a
scaredy cat and a total wimp as I thought she might meet
up with Anje or Heidi (our other two friends from school)
and just casually mention that "Poor old Steph's been to a
horrible druggy party and frightened herself!" and then it
would be all round everywhere in next to no time 'cos Anje
and Heidi are two of the biggest goss-mongers around. I
wouldn't want people like Rhiannon getting to hear of it!

In the end, I just sort of fluffed.

Hi, Vix! I guess you'll be panting to
hear all about the party, but there's
TOO MUCH TO WRITE on a postcard so
you'll just have to contain yourself!
Will tell all when I am back. Loadsaluv,
Steph.

I also did a postcard for Mum.

Dear Mum, I went to a party Saturday night with this boy I met on the pier. (It is all right, he goes to a POSH SCHOOL.) Dad said I was to be home by midnight but we left the first party and went on to another, so I didn't quite make it!!! It was gone one o'clock when I got in, I know you wouldn't approve, but I came home with other people so I was quite safe. Please don't worry! xxx Stephanie

I suppose I was being a bit sneaky, telling Mum all about the party and about not getting home till one o'clock. I didn't want to get Dad into trouble – though I thought it probably wouldn't matter, now that he and Mum were separated. After all, Mum couldn't do anything to him. She couldn't throw any more frying pans – but I did want Mum to get rattled. I wanted her to fly into one of her panics and snatch up the phone and ring me and say, "Stephanie! I'm catching the first plane back. I want you and your sister to come home *immediately*!"

I wasn't certain how long it took a postcard to get to Spain. A day or two, maybe? I imagined that Mum would probably ring on either Wednesday or Thursday, and I thought that I would keep my mobile with me at all times and make sure (unlike Dad) that the battery was always charged.

Monday morning, Zed rang. He said, "Hi, Passion! Enjoy the party?" Just as if nothing had ever happened! As if he had never had too much to drink and got silly and refused to take me home. But I am such a coward, I didn't say anything. I just meekly mumbled, "Yeah, it was great." The Afterthought, who was sitting on the floor nearby, playing with Titch, looked at me and pulled a face. I pulled one back and whisked myself away into the bedroom. When I came out, a few minutes later, the Afterthought said, "Are you going to see him again?"

I didn't tell her to mind her own business. She wasn't being nosy; it was just sisterly concern. I said, "No. I told him we'd got to go somewhere with Dad."

"Suppose he sees you?" said the Afterthought.

"He won't," I said.

"He might, if we go into town."

"So we won't go into town! We'll stop indoors."

"But there's no food," wailed the Afterthought.

I said in that case we would sneak out and buy some and bring it back with us. The Afterthought liked that idea. She said she didn't particularly want to go out, anyway, because of Titch.

"He'd get lonely, by himself."

I pointed out that people left cats by themselves all

the time, but the Afterthought said not when they were just tiny kittens.

"I wouldn't mind if he had a catty friend... we ought to have got two!"

"You'll be lucky if Mum lets you keep *one*," I said.

"Not going back to Mum," muttered the Afterthought.

I did wish she would stop saying it! It was starting to make me nervous. It worried me that it was such ages since Mum had last rung. It worried me that she'd told Dad she only wanted to be contacted in emergencies. If only I'd asked her about it, last time we'd spoken! But I'd been too busy telling her about all the things we were doing. The Afterthought was convinced that Mum had washed her hands of us.

"She doesn't want us any more! She's given us to Dad."

But I still refused to believe it. Mum wouldn't do such a thing! She just needed a break, without having to consider other people for once in her life. By the end of the holiday she'd be back to normal. At least, that was what I told myself. But every time the Afterthought muttered about "not going back", little niggling doubts began worming their way in.

The one time I'd tried asking Dad, he'd just told me that I worried too much; there didn't seem much point asking him again. Also, I think perhaps I was a bit scared of what he might say, I mean, in case things might have changed. I thought what he would *probably* say would be, "Hang loose, Honeybun! Don't get yourself in a lather." But suppose he didn't? Suppose he said the Afterthought was right? I couldn't cope with that! I didn't want to know.

So I told the Afterthought to just shut up – which somewhat to my surprise she did, which was a bit worrying in itself – and dragged her off down the road to the little shop on the corner, where we stocked up with a day's food.

Coca Cola, Pot Noodles, cheese and onion crisps, Mars bars, Smarties, two apples, a pint of milk and a tin of kitten food.

I got the apples because I felt guilty about not eating our five portions of fresh fruit and vegetables a day, like you're supposed to. Mum always made sure that we did, but since coming to Brighton we'd eaten hardly any fresh fruit or veg at all. It had been nothing but fish and chips and takeaways.

On our way back to Dad's basement we bumped into Ms Devine. She didn't seem as friendly as she had before. She asked me, quite coldly, where Dad was. I said that he was out working.

"Working where, exactly?" said Ms Devine.

I said I didn't know. "He didn't tell us."

"No!" She gave a little snicker, but not like she was amused. "I'm sure he didn't!"

"Would you like me to give him a message?" I said.

"What a good idea! Why not? Just tell him, when he gets back from doing whatever it is he's doing, that my patience is running out. OK?"

I said, "Your patience is running out."

"Right! My patience is running out. He'll understand."

"I don't think I like that lady," said the Afterthought, as Ms Devine went on her way.

I said that when we had first met her I had wondered if she might perhaps be Dad's girlfriend, but now I didn't think she was.

"She might have been," said the Afterthought. "And then Dad might have decided he didn't want her any more, and that's what's made her angry."

I said, "Mm... maybe." But I had a feeling it was something more than that.

319

When Dad came home that afternoon, I gave him Ms Devine's message.

"Wretched woman," said Dad. He didn't sound particularly bothered.

"Have you thrown her over?" said the Afterthought.

"Have I what?" said Dad.

"Thrown her over... you know! Junked her. Given her the elbow... *jilted* her."

I have no idea how the Afterthought knows these expressions. Dad gave a loud barking laugh and said, "What on earth makes you think that?"

"She sounds like she's mad at you," said the Afterthought.

"Oh! Well." Dad shrugged.

I said, "Did you ever pay her the rent that she wanted?"

"Not yet," said Dad. "I haven't had a chance, she's been away."

"I think she's there now," I said. I'd heard her playing music earlier on. "Maybe if you gave her the rent it would make her happy."

"Oh, she can wait!" said Dad. "She's not short of a bob or two. Let's go out and eat, I've had a hard day."

It seemed that Dad was back in the money, which meant he *must* have been working. I tried asking him where, so that I could tell Ms Devine if she stopped us again, but he just waved a hand and said, "Here and there, round and about... where shall we go for dinner?"

*　*　*

We all stayed home next day. I was still scared to go out
in case I bumped into Zed, Dad said he didn't have any
more work to do just at the moment, and the
Afterthought was worried about Titch. She said that he
had to have his injections. The lady up the road had said
he had to. If he didn't have his injections, he would catch
some horrible disease and die.

"We've got to get them done, Dad!"

Dad said we would get them done later, when he had
a bit more money.

"But he'll catch something!" wailed the Afterthought.

"He won't catch anything," said Dad. "How can he
catch anything when he doesn't go out? Where's he
going to catch it from?"

That reminded me of something else. "He needs more
litter," I said. "His litter tray's practically empty."

"Yes, and he needs more food, as well," said the
Afterthought.

I was beginning to see what Mum meant, about looking
after a cat. Titch was only tiny, but he had to eat every day,
and he had to have litter, and sooner or later, when he was
bigger, he *would* have to have his injections.

Dad grumbled, but he agreed that I could go up the
road and get some cat food. He said, however, that litter
was a luxury, and we should go into the garden and dig
up some earth.

"While I'm getting the cat food," I said, "should I get something for us?"

Dad said yes, but not to go mad. He gave me a £5 note and told me to "spend it sensibly".

"Dinner *and* lunch?" I said. "Or are we going out again?"

"Just get what you can," said Dad. "See how far you can stretch it."

Well! Quite honestly, £5 doesn't stretch all that far. In fact it stretches hardly any way at all. I had to keep adding up in my head as I went round the shelves. One tin of kitten food, one loaf of bread – tin of baked beans – apples! Tomato soup. Cheese. Crisps. Phew! I even got 2p change!

I went racing home with my bag of groceries, thinking that I had done really well and that Mum would have been proud of me. I had managed to buy enough food for three people, not to mention a kitten, and it was *all healthy*.

"Look!" I laid it out, on the table. Dad just grunted. I thought that he seemed preoccupied, like his thoughts were elsewhere. "We can have baked beans for lunch, with apples. Then crisps in the afternoon, if we get hungry. Then for dinner we can have soup followed by bread and cheese." I sat back, triumphantly.

"It's all *veggie*," said the Afterthought.

"Yes, it is," I said. "So what?"

"Why couldn't you have got a TV dinner, or something?"

"'Cos TV dinners cost more and in any case they're *junk*," I said.

"So's crisps," said the Afterthought. "Mum wouldn't let us eat crisps all the time! We had crisps yesterday."

"Well, you have to eat *something*," I said. It was difficult trying to plan a balanced diet without any proper cooking facilities.

"Could have got frankfurters," said the Afterthought.

I said, "Frankfurters are dead pig. You want to eat dead pig?"

She sniffed.

"Just shut up whingeing," I said.

"Could have got sardines!"

"Could have got all sorts of things if we could *cook*!"

Still she went on whingeing. "I don't like baked beans. I don't like tomato soup. Why can't we go out again? Dad, let's go out again!"

"Not tonight," said Dad. "we're staying in tonight."

"We could go on the pier, we could go to that place we went to before, we c—"

"I said, not tonight," said Dad. "We're staying in tonight."

"Couldn't we even get a takeaway?"

"Samantha, I am not made of money," said Dad.

The Afterthought subsided. She went off, muttering to herself, to open a tin for Titch. Titch pranced after her, his tail in the air. He was happy, at any rate. I did think it rather odd that Dad should have enough money to take us out for a meal one day, and the next day claim to be broke. Well, "not made of money". He had obviously been made of money yesterday. What had happened to it all? I thought perhaps he was saving it to give to Ms Devine; it was the only thing that made any sense. But then, at six o'clock, just as I was thinking we ought to eat our soup and bread and cheese, there was a knock at the door and Dad went, like, help, help, hide me! and fled into the bedroom.

"If that's her from upstairs," he said, "tell her I'm out. Tell her I won't be back till late. Tell her I'll pay her the rent tomorrow morning!"

He grabbed the Afterthought and pulled her in with him; in case, I suppose, she gave the game away. Feeling distinctly nervous, I opened the door. Ms Devine was standing there. She looked pretty angry.

"I should like to speak to your father," she said.

"I'm s-sorry." I gulped down a golf ball that seemed to have lodged in my throat. "He's not here."

"Where is he? Do you know?"

I said, "N-no. I'm s-sorry, I don't."

"When is he coming back?"

I gulped at a second golf ball. I am not actually terribly good at telling lies. It's not so much that I think it's wrong, though of course it *is* wrong – well, usually. It's just that I get all embarrassed and tongue-tied. I would be absolutely useless if I ever had to take a lie detector test.

"He won't be b-back till l-l-late," I said. "But he s-said to t-tell you… he'll pay you the rent tomorrow!"

"Oh. Will he?" She was peering past my shoulder, trying to see if she could catch me out.

"He will!" I said. "He will! Tomorrow m-morning. He said!"

"He'd better," said Ms Devine. "*Or else!* Just make sure he gets the message."

With that, she swished back up the steps. I could tell that she had "had it up to here", as Mum would say. Meaning, if she'd had a frying pan to hand, she would most probably have thrown it. Dad gets you like that. I shouldn't be surprised if there aren't people all over England that would like to throw frying pans at him. Except why stop at England? People all over the *world*. All wanting to throw frying pans. I would quite like to have thrown one myself, if there had been one around, though I think, probably, I was more anxious than cross. Dad had gone and upset Ms Devine! He obviously owed her loads and loads of rent, and didn't have enough money to pay it. I had visions of the police coming round and arresting him. Of me and the Afterthought – and Titch – being thrown on to the street, without any money to get back home.

"Dad!" I rushed across to the bedroom. "That was Ms Devine! She said to tell you that you'd better pay the rent, or—"

"Or what?" squeaked the Afterthought.

"Or else!" I said.

"Or else?" The Afterthought's voice had gone all quavery. "What does she mean?"

"She means she's going to kick up," said Dad. "The woman is a menace! She obviously has a very small, grasping mind. Well, there's only one thing for it... the time has come to move on. Don't worry!" He held up a hand. "I've been expecting it. I have it all under control. Everything taken care of, no need to panic. Life's a big adventure, eh?"

He grinned, and chucked me under the chin. I smiled, uncertainly.

"Are we going somewhere?" said the Afterthought.

"Later," said Dad. "When it's dark. Let's eat first. Come along, mother!" He pushed me back into the other room. "Where's our din-dins?"

I remember that evening as being very strange. After
we'd eaten dinner, we all settled down to watch
television, like nothing was any different from usual. I
kept trying to find out from Dad what he was planning
to do, where he was planning to take us, but he just
shook his head and said, "It'll all work out, don't worry."
But I couldn't help worrying! At one point Dad said,
"You did bring your passports, didn't you?"

"Dad, we're not going *abroad*?" I said. He'd
originally told us to bring them in case we might make a
trip over to France. Mum had said, "You'll be lucky!"
and up until now Dad hadn't mentioned anything more
about it. "We're not going to France?" I said.

"Oh, just a day trip, maybe," said Dad. "I don't know,
I haven't decided. But we've got to get out of here!"

"Because of her upstairs?" said the Afterthought.

"Not just her," said Dad. "She's nothing. She's rubbish! I can handle her. But there are... other people. Bad people. People that have got it in for me."

"You mean, like they're... after you?" I quavered.

"After me," said Dad. "Yes! But don't worry! They'll never find us. I've got it all in hand. Big adventure, eh?"

This time, I only managed half a smile, just crimping my mouth at the corners. I wished I could ring Mum! I asked Dad again for her number, but he said, "Stephanie, for heaven's sake! Now is not the time."

"Dad, *please*," I said.

"Stephanie, did you hear what I said? *Now is not the time!*"

"But, D—"

"*STEPHANIE!*"

Dad never shouted at us. Never. So I knew at once that this was serious. It made me even more desperate to ring Mum, but I didn't dare ask him again.

"Steph, I'm sorry," said Dad. "I didn't mean to be cross, sweetheart! But you must understand that there's a time and place for everything, and now is quite definitely not the time to go bothering your mum. What could she do, over there in Spain? You'd just worry her half out of her mind. No! Let's get ourselves settled first."

"Settled w-where?" I said.

Dad tapped a finger to the side of his nose. "Secret venue. Trust me! I've got it all worked out."

Far from making me feel better, this just made me feel worse. Since when did Dad ever have anything *all worked out*?

"When are we going?" said the Afterthought.

"When I say and not before," said Dad. "The less you know, the better."

"Why?" said the Afterthought.

"Because I say so, that's why!"

"Is it so we won't be able to tell them anything if they catch us?"

"If who catch us?" I said.

"The people that are after us!"

"No one's after you," said Dad. "It's me they've got it in for, not you. Now just sit down and keep quiet. Read a book, or something. Watch the telly!"

We watched television right through till nearly midnight. The Afterthought had long since fallen asleep, curled into a corner of the sofa with Titch. I was too worried to sleep. I didn't quite know what was going on, but whatever it was, I knew it wasn't anything good. When Dad said people were after him, I didn't think he meant people with frying pans, and I didn't think they were after him simply because he had got up their noses. I remembered the day he had shown us his wad, a great fistful of money. I couldn't help wondering where it had all come from – and where it had all gone. I didn't think Dad would have stolen it; I didn't think he was a thief.

But it was very peculiar how he could have all that money one day, and none the next. What could he be doing with it?

And then I thought of Mum's cooker money, and the way Dad had lost it all on the horses. I thought of the time he had taken us out for a champagne dinner, when he had *won* money on the horses. And I knew, I just knew, with horrible certainty, that Dad hadn't been going to work all those times, he'd been going to the race track, or to the betting office, and now he had done something really stupid and upset some really bad people, and they were coming after him, and we were all in danger. Big adventure, eh? But I don't think I'm a very adventurous sort of person, because all I wanted was to be back at home with Mum, safe and sound in Nottingham.

At midnight, Dad switched off the telly and said, "Right, girls! This is it… time to go. Wake up, sleeping beauty!"

He told us both to pack all our stuff and make ready to leave. The Afterthought was worried about Titch.

"He hasn't got a carrying case!"

Dad said not to bother about a carrying case, just put him in the car and keep an eye on him, but the Afterthought wouldn't. She said it wasn't safe, he could escape and get run over. Dad made impatient clicking noises with his tongue, but the Afterthought can be stubborn. When she digs her heels in, there's no moving her. Dad knew this. He said, "Oh, for God's sake!" and snatched up a cardboard box that we had once brought groceries home in. "Punch some holes in this and shove him inside. And be quick about it!"

But the Afterthought wouldn't be hurried; not where her precious kitten was concerned. I can't say I blame her. I helped her make some air holes, and settle Titch inside, and then we bound it round with a belt to make it secure. Dad, who was fretting and fuming at the door, said, "All right, all right, that'll do! Let's get moving."

He told us to go up the steps "like little mice" and open the car "as quiet as can be". He practically threw us into the back, all higgledy-piggledy with our bags and packages. He said we'd stop when we got out of town and transfer stuff to the boot.

"There's no time right now. We have to get away!"

"We're not going to run out of petrol, are we?" I said.

"No, we're not," said Dad. "Don't be cheeky!"

I wasn't being; I was genuinely frightened. I imagined all the bad people coming after us in fast cars, with guns, and us suddenly grinding to a halt as we had before. But this time, it seemed, Dad was prepared. He had obviously been planning his getaway and had filled up the tank in readiness.

"I told you … trust me! I know what I'm doing."

I wished I could believe him. I wished I could speak to Mum! But I couldn't, and there was nothing I could do.

We drove and drove, all through the night. The Afterthought went to sleep again, and after a bit I slept, too. I'd meant to stay awake and watch where we were going, but  in the end I couldn't stop my eyes from closing. When I opened them again, it was just getting light.

"Are we here?" said the Afterthought.

"We're here," said Dad. "Now, I want you to be very quiet or we'll wake people up. Just remember, it's still early. OK?"

We nodded.

"OK! Grab your stuff and let's get you indoors."

We staggered out of the car and followed Dad up some steps to a block of flats. I wanted to ask where we were, but I didn't get a chance. Dad had pressed the intercom and a man's voice was crackling at us. "Daniel? That you?"

"Yeah, it's me," said Dad.

There was the sound of a buzzer, and Dad pushed the door open and shepherded us through, into an entrance hall. There was a lift, but Dad took us up the stairs. At the top of the first flight a man was waiting for us. I have tried and tried to remember what he looked like, but I only just saw him the once; and, besides, everything was so weird and confusing, and I was still half asleep from the drive.

The man asked Dad if everything had gone OK, and Dad said yes, fine. He said he would just get me and the Afterthought bedded down, then go and see to the car, but the man said to give him the keys and *he* would see to it. I don't know what he meant by "see to it", but it didn't seem to be there any more after that. Not as far as I could tell, though I really couldn't tell very much.

We didn't go out again for the next few days.

nine

WE LIVED IN this one room. It was a bedroom, and at least it had a double bed, which was something to be thankful for. Me and the Afterthought shared the bed; I don't know where Dad slept, but I think it was on the sofa, outside, because once when I went to the bathroom I saw the cushions all rumpled, and a dent in one of them like a head had been lying there.

The only times Dad would let us leave the bedroom were if we needed to go to the loo, and then we had to ask him first. I think he wanted to make sure that we didn't bump into anyone. We weren't ever allowed into the rest of the flat – in case, I suppose, we poked around and saw something we shouldn't, like a name and address, or telephone number, or something – so we never got to see the man again. The one who'd met us on the stairs.

Dad said, "Trust me! It's for your own good."

At night he locked us in. It was so embarrassing, he gave us a *bucket*. He tried making jokes about it.

"Slopping out, that's what they call it in the nick… pretend you're making a movie! You're a couple of bank robbers, and you've been banged up. Prison movie! Right?"

I said, "Right!" and tried to smile. But it wasn't funny. We felt we really *were* in prison.

"Oh, come on, now, cheer up!" said Dad. "It's not as bad as all that. It's not like you're in for a ten-year stretch… with time off for good behaviour, you'll be out before you know it. Couple of days! Three at the most. Surely you can manage that for your old dad?"

Actually, it was five days. Five whole days, shut up in one room! Apart from a big dramatic scene – Don't look! And *don't listen*! – every time she had to use the bucket, the Afterthought coped with it better than I did. She said she didn't mind where she was, so long as she was with Dad.

"After all, I've got Titch," she said.

At least Dad got Titch some proper cat litter. *That* was a relief. But I discovered that I suffer from this thing where I don't like to be locked up. I know now how animals must feel in zoos. I think zoos are just so *cruel*. I won't ever go to one again. Not unless the animals are allowed to roam about. I couldn't roam anywhere, and I began to have these nightmares that Dad had gone mad and we would be kept locked up for ever.

We weren't even supposed to look out of the windows in case somebody saw us. I tried, once, just lifting up the edge of the blind, and the Afterthought nearly went berserk. She yelled at me to "Get away, get away!" She thought the bad guys might be out there, watching.

"How would they know who we were?" I said.

The Afterthought said they would know because they would have cased the joint. (She picks up this sort of language. She is like a magpie.) She said they would have spied on us in Brighton. They would know that we belonged to Dad, and they would guess that if we were here, Dad would also be here, and then they would come and get him. She was really quite scared, so after that I didn't try looking out of the window any more. Partly because I didn't want to upset the Afterthought, and partly because – well, because I thought she just *could* be right. I didn't want anything happening to Dad.

"What's out there, anyway?" said the Afterthought.

I said, "Nothing very much. Just garages."

Dad did his best to keep us occupied. We had a television, and we played lots of games, like going through the alphabet with pop stars, movie stars, TV programmes. We played card games – Dad taught us how to play poker! – and pencil and paper games, and Scrabble and Monopoly, on a very old Monopoly board that was falling to pieces. Dad also brought us books and

magazines – including the one that Mum wouldn't let me read. I asked him to get it for me, not thinking that he would, but he didn't seem to see anything wrong with it, or maybe he just picked it off the shelf without really looking. The only thing was, I couldn't enjoy it properly. I opened it up, looking forward to a good wallow, and all I could think of was... Mum! How I was deliberately going behind her back. Reading stuff she didn't approve of. I mean, like, normally it wouldn't have bothered me, I'd have thought "Sah, sah, and sucks to Mum!" But now it just seemed like I was being disloyal.

The day after we arrived I tried ringing home on my mobile, but there wasn't any reply and I couldn't leave a message as we didn't have an answer phone. (We do now.) I then tried Vix, but she obviously wasn't back from holiday yet. I left a bit of a message, just saying that we weren't in Brighton any more and I'd ring her later, or she could ring me when she got back, but it wasn't the same as actually talking to her. I needed to talk to someone!

"There's nobody around," I said. I collapsed, dispiritedly, on to the bed. "I can't get anyone!"

"You shouldn't be phoning people, anyway," said the Afterthought. "The line could be bugged. They could be *listening*."

By "they" she meant the bad guys. The Afterthought had become obsessed by bad guys. At night she was terrified of going to sleep in case they broke into the flat with machine guns. I told her there was no way anyone could have bugged my mobile. I mean, there probably was, because what do I know about these things? But I didn't want her totally freaking out. I said that just ringing Mum or Vix couldn't do any harm.

"It could if they traced the call," said the Afterthought.

"Not if I only speak for a few seconds," I said. "They wouldn't be able to trace it." I had seen enough police series to know that much.

The Afterthought still wasn't convinced. "They'd know who you were calling! They might go and get Mum and beat her up."

I said, "What would they do that for?"

"To find out where Dad is!"

"But she wouldn't know where Dad is! *We* don't even know where we are."

The Afterthought sucked at her thumb. "She might go to the police."

I had already thought of that. Maybe, at the back of my mind, it was what I was hoping for. I wouldn't do it myself, because that would be betraying Dad; it could get him into a whole lot of trouble. I still didn't know what he'd done, exactly, or where he'd got his money from, but I had this uneasy feeling that it might be something not quite legal. I wouldn't want to be the one who got him into trouble! I didn't care how oddly he was behaving, he was still my dad, and I still loved him. But if Mum were to ring the police – well! There wasn't much I could do about that.

"Do you honestly think she would?" I said.

"Yes! 'Cos if you told her we weren't in Brighton any more she'd want to know where we'd gone, and if you said you didn't know she'd get really mad and tell the police that they'd got to find us, and then Dad would get into trouble *big* time for running away without paying the rent!"

"That would be better than the bad guys getting him," I said.

"It wouldn't, 'cos they'd put him in prison!"

"But at least he'd be safe," I said.

"He wouldn't!" The Afterthought shook her head, violently. "They could still get at him! They could get at him in prison, it's what they do!" I wasn't the only one who'd seen police series. The Afterthought knew all about bad guys and what they got up to. "I don't think you ought to ring *anybody*," she said.

As it happened, I didn't have the chance. Next time I tried (shut away in the bathroom, where no one could hear me) I discovered that I had run out of credit. And I didn't have another phone card! That is the trouble with mobiles; they can let you down. I once saw this movie where some poor woman was having her house broken into by a gang and she was shut in the loo trying to ring for help and she couldn't because her phone was dead. Really scary.

I was starting to get a bit scared, too. There were moments when I actually, almost, felt really *frightened*.

It wasn't so much the thought of the bad guys, nor did I truly believe that Dad had gone mad, but I was desperately worried about how we were ever going to get home, especially now I didn't have my phone. I asked Dad next day, without too much hope, if I could get my credit topped up. He said, "Why? Who do you want to call?"

The Afterthought said, "She's trying to ring Mum! I told her not to. I told her it wasn't safe!"

"I'm afraid Sam's right," said Dad. "I'm sorry, poppet! I know it's not easy for you, cooped up here, but it won't be for much longer. Promise! Just give it another forty-eight hours, and we'll be out."

"Are we going back to Brighton?" said the Afterthought.

"Not on your life! We're going somewhere far more exciting than Brighton."

"Where are we going?" I said.

"Would you believe, the South of France?" said Dad. He announced it with a big happy grin. I stared at him, in dismay.

"The South of *France*?" I said.

"Nice, to be exact," said Dad. "You've heard of Nice?" I nodded. "You'll love it down there!"

"But… what about Mum?" I said.

"Stephie, love, face it," said Dad. "You're with me, now. Your mum—" he waved a hand. "It's not that she doesn't love you any more, but – well! She feels it's time to make a new life for herself."

There was this moment of absolute silence. I think even the Afterthought was a bit stunned. She didn't even try saying *I told you so*.

"You mean…" I could feel my voice starting to crack. "You mean, she *really* doesn't want us back?"

"Oh, I'm sure! For holidays," said Dad.

"N-not to s-stay?"

"Well, yes, like you've stayed with me."

"But not to *live*?"

"See, it's like this," said Dad. "Your mum feels she's done her stint. Now it's my turn. That's all right, isn't it? It's not so bad, being with your dad?"

Stupidly, I said, "But what about s-school?"

"Find you a new one. Go to a French one!"

"But I don't speak French!"

"Soon learn," said Dad. "You'll probably learn faster than me. Now, come on, cheer up! Happy face! It'll be fun! Life's a big adventure, eh? Sam wants to come with me, don't you? She loves her old dad!"

"Don't you at least think we ought to – to ring Mum and ask her?" I said.

"I've already asked her," said Dad. "She's given us her blessing."

I was, like, gob-smacked. I couldn't believe it! I couldn't believe that even Dad would do such a thing. He had gone behind my back! Spoken to Mum without telling me! Why hadn't he let *me* speak to her?

"When did you do it?" I said.

"Oh! A few days ago. Just before we left Brighton."

"Why didn't you tell us?" I screamed.

"Sorry, poppet! Didn't mean to upset you."

Dad reached out to give me a hug, but I wriggled away from him. I didn't feel like being hugged. I felt hurt, and angry, and betrayed. He was treating us the same way he'd treated Mum all those years, making decisions without consulting her, doing things he knew she wouldn't approve of. Then saying sorry and expecting to be forgiven.

"Stephie, Stephie! Don't be cross." Just like with Mum! "My main concern," said Dad, "was to get you girls safely away. We were in a lot of danger, you know. I couldn't bear it if anything had happened to you!"

I thought to myself that if Dad was so worried about me and the Afterthought, he shouldn't have got mixed up with the bad guys in the first place.

"Now she hates me," said Dad.

"I don't hate you," I said. "But I don't want to go to France!"

"Ah, Steph, you'll love it once you're there!"

"You will," said the Afterthought. Her hand stole into mine. "You will, Steph! Honest!"

The Afterthought seemed to be OK with the idea now that she had had time to get used to it. Me, I was sunk in gloom. It is really upsetting to be told that your mum doesn't want you any more. I knew we had both been mean to her, but I had never, ever thought she would get rid of us. I didn't want to go to France! I didn't want to go to a French school, I didn't want to speak French. I wanted to go home, to my mum! And there was something I didn't understand. If Dad hadn't had the money to pay Ms Devine her rent, how come he had the money to take us all to Nice? If he really *did* have the money to take us to Nice.

I put this to him, and he laughed. "I've got money! You surely don't think I'd be irresponsible enough to let you join me on my travels if I didn't have the means to look after you?"

I knew what Mum would say. But Mum wasn't there. She didn't care!

"If you've got money," I said – I said it quite carefully, not wanting Dad to think I was having a go at him – "couldn't you have paid Ms Devine her rent?"

"Oh, look, just forget about Ms Devine!" Dad sprang

up and began pacing the room. "She's loaded, she doesn't need it. You don't want to waste your time feeling sorry for people like her. As far as they're concerned, we're just scum. They wouldn't give us the snot out their noses! I've had to work hard for this lot."

 Dad patted a hand on a case that he had brought with him. One of those smooth, flat sort of ones that people snap open in movies to reveal bundles of notes. Did Dad's contain bundles of notes?

"I've put my life on the line for this! Why should I give any to the likes of her?"

"She was hateful, anyway," said the Afterthought. "She didn't deserve it!"

"Precisely," said Dad. "So don't let's shed any more crocodile tears for Ms Devine. I have you two girls to care for. You're far more important to me than she is!"

I still felt that it was wrong of Dad not to pay her the money, but I didn't try arguing. Dad hated being argued with; he always said it was a form of nagging. Mum used to argue all the time. It was one of Dad's worst accusations, to say that either of us was "starting to get like your mum". Not that he ever really said it to the Afterthought. She didn't argue. She thought whatever Dad did had got to be OK.

"Ms Devine's got a *whole house*," she said, as we lay in bed that night. "Dad hasn't got anything!"

"Still doesn't make it right," I muttered.

"Oh, stop sounding like Mum!" said the Afterthought. She'd picked it up from Dad; she knew he used it as an insult.

"At least Mum doesn't run away without paying people what she owes them," I said.

"Mum doesn't need to! She's got things. She's got a house, she's got a job, sh—"

"Yes, and how is Dad going to look after us when he hasn't got *anything*?" I said. "He hasn't got a house, he hasn't got a job... how's he going to earn money?"

"Dad can earn money," said the Afterthought.

"He can *get* money," I said.

"It's the same thing!"

"It's not," I said. It wasn't the same thing at all. I thought of the case he had showed us. The flat case with the snap locks, like you see on the movies. I sat up, and crawled to the end of the bed.

"What are you doing?" said the Afterthought.

The case was sitting there, on top of the dressing table. I reached out for it.

"That's Dad's!" shrilled the Afterthought.

Yes, it was – and I wanted to find out what was inside it. But I couldn't! It wouldn't open; it had one of those special combination locks. It did feel quite heavy, though. How much money could you get in a case like that? Hundreds? Thousands?

"Stephanie, put it back!" said the Afterthought. "It's nothing to do with us."

I had the feeling that in spite of her bravado, the Afterthought was actually a bit nervous. She really didn't want to know what was in the case.

"I think Dad got this from gambling," I said.

"So what?" said the Afterthought. "People are allowed to gamble!"

"Yes, but it's not the same as earning it… it's not like doing a proper job. And why are we having to run away?"

"Because of the bad guys!"

"But why? What do they want? Why are they after us? Because it's their money, maybe. Because Dad—" I didn't want to say because Dad had stolen it from them; I refused to think my dad was a thief. But perhaps… perhaps he had been too clever for them?

"I'm going to sleep," said the Afterthought. She scooped up Titch, and put him into bed. "I don't want to talk about it!"

I didn't want to talk about it, either, but I felt that I had to say *something*. To Dad, I mean. I wasn't brave enough to ask him where the money had come from, but I did think I needed to know what was going to happen to us once it had run out.

"Quite right!" said Dad. He had brought in our breakfast tray next morning, plus a little saucer of cat food for Titch. "A sensible question. I'm glad you asked it! I did tell you, didn't I, that I wouldn't take you with me if I couldn't provide for you?"

"Dad, you're not going to – to *gamble*?" I whispered.

Dad laughed; this big hearty laugh. "Oh, Stephie, Stephie, you grow more like your mum every day! No, I'm not going to gamble – at least, not for a living. I might have a little flutter on the gee-gees just now and again. You wouldn't begrudge me that, would you?"

Numbly, I shook my head.

"That's all right, then! I couldn't lead a totally joyless existence. Got to have a bit of fun, eh?"

He winked at the Afterthought, who beamed and nodded.

"Good! Right. Now, you'll be happy to hear –" Dad rubbed his hands together "– that today is the day... we're up and off! So, it's a question of finishing your breakfast, getting yourselves packed, and we'll be on our way."

The Afterthought instantly began cramming food into her mouth as fast as she could go. Dad, amused, said, "No need to choke yourself!"

He still hadn't answered my question.

"Dad," I said.

"Mm?"

I took a deep breath. "What *are* you going to do?"

"What am I going to do? I'll tell you what I'm going to do! First off, I'm going to find us somewhere to stay, and then I'm going to pay a visit to an old chum who runs a casino."

"Casino like on the pier?" said the Afterthought.

"Casino like in Las Vegas," said Dad. "Bright lights, diamond tiaras – and money, money, money!"

"I thought you said you weren't going to gamble!" I cried.

"*I'm* not going to gamble," said Dad. "Other people are. Your dad's going to be a—"

I thought he said "croopyer", but have since discovered it's spelt *croupier*. It's one of those people that stand at gaming tables with a sort of rake thing, raking in the money and pushing little piles of it back to you if you've hit the winning number.

"What do you think of that?" said Dad.

He sounded so proud of himself! He'd got a real job to go to – or would have, once he'd seen his friend.

"Don't worry! It's there, waiting for me."

"See? I told you," said the Afterthought, as we packed up our stuff yet again. "I told you Dad would take care of us!"

And then it came time to leave. I grabbed our bags, while the Afterthought cradled Titch, in his makeshift carry box.

"Oh – um – Sam," said Dad. "I meant to say, earlier… you'd better leave Titch here."

Leave Titch? The Afterthought froze. I could see Dad knew at once he was treading dangerously. No power on earth would separate the Afterthought from her beloved kitten.

"He'll be looked after," pleaded Dad; but the Afterthought just clutched at her box, standing stock-still and mutinous in the middle of the room.

"All right, all right, bung him in the car! But get a move on."

Dad was starting to grow edgy, like he thought the bad guys might jump him if we didn't leave immediately. We bundled ourselves downstairs and into a green car parked out front. It wasn't the car Dad had had before. The Afterthought squeaked, "Oh! It's different."

"I thought Stephanie would like seat belts," said Dad. "Come on, in you get! Quick, quick!"

I wondered if we were going to drive all the way down to the south of France. I thought that Mum wouldn't be very happy about it. She always used to say that Dad was a menace on the roads because a) he drove too fast and b) he never took any notice of road signs. Dad used to say that Mum was even more of a menace.

"Crawling along at 30mph, holding up the flow of traffic… it's people like you that cause accidents!"

As usual, the Afterthought always sided with Dad. She liked going at 60mph and shooting the lights. I guess I am a bit more of a wimp. Nervously I said, "Dad, are we *driving* to Nice?" I was quite relieved when Dad said we were getting a plane.

I still didn't know where we were, but after a while I began to see signs that said Luton and I guessed that we were heading for Luton Airport. We had been there once before, when we had gone on holiday. I couldn't decide whether I was scared or excited. I think I still couldn't quite believe that it was happening.

"Dad," I said, "couldn't we *please* ring Mum before we leave? *Please*, Dad? *Please*?"

"Stephanie, I told you, we'll ring her when we get there," said Dad. "That's a promise! We don't have time, right now. We've got a plane to catch."

"It'll be all right," whispered the Afterthought. "Dad'll take care of us."

I wished I could have as much faith in Dad as my little sister did.

We parked the car in the long-stay car park. I wondered what was going to happen to it, but Dad said his friend who owned the flat would come and get it.

"All taken care of! Don't worry. Now, Sammie, sweetheart, listen to me! About the kitten." I could see the Afterthought stiffen. I thought, so much for her faith in Dad. "You cannot take him over to France. OK? Just can't be done! So be a good girl, and let me have him—" Dad reached out his hands for the box. The Afterthought, immediately, backed away. "Come on, come on! Don't be silly," said Dad. "I haven't got time for all this! Give me the box."

"No!" The Afterthought shot round the other side of the car. "I'm not going without Titch!"

"I told you," said Dad. "There's no way you can bring him. We haven't made arrangements – we haven't even got a proper carrying cage."

"Then I'm not going!"

"Oh, for crying out loud!" Dad raced round the car and made a grab for the box. "Why you couldn't just have left him in the flat—"

"I'm not leaving him anywhere! I'm not leaving him!"

"Dad, you can't just *dump* him," I said.

"I'm not going to dump him, for God's sake! We'll leave him in the car. He'll be picked up in a couple of hours."

Dad made another lunge. The Afterthought scuttled for safety behind me.

"It's no use," I said. "She won't go without him."

"Oh, now, Stephanie, don't you start! You know perfectly well they won't let a cat on the plane."

It seemed to me that Dad should have thought of that before.

"Maybe you'd better go without us," I said.

"Don't be ridiculous! How can I go without you? I can't just go off and leave you here!"

"No, and I'm not just going off and leaving Titch here!" cried the Afterthought.

"*Samantha*—" Dad made one last snatch at the box. This time, he managed to get his hands on it. He wrenched – and the box fell to the ground. Titch let out a piteous wail.

"There, now! Leave him," said Dad. "Stephanie, open that car door and put him back in. And you!" He seized

353

the Afterthought by the arm. "Get a move on! We don't have all day."

That was Dad's BIG mistake. The Afterthought did as she always did in moments of crisis: she went into overdrive. Her piercing shrieks rang through the car park. "The screaming hab dabs" was what Mum used to call it. The Afterthought was an expert. When she was little she used to make a habit of it. She specially liked to do it in places where there were crowds of people, such as shopping malls – and car parks. Mum was the only one who could handle her when she got like that. Dad had never been able to cope. Dad was one of those people, he always turned his back on trouble. Which was what he did now.

"Oh, for God's sake!" he shouted.

Next thing I knew, he was striding off across the car park with his caseful of money, leaving me and the Afterthought on our own, with Titch.

Dad's voice came bellowing back to us: "Just don't say I didn't try!"

ten

ALL THE TIME the Afterthought was screaming, people were stopping to stare at us. *What is the matter with that child? Why is she making all that noise?* But the minute Dad walked away and the Afterthought calmed down, they all immediately went back to doing their own thing. It was like suddenly we weren't there. We stood by the car, with me clutching Titch, and no one took the slightest notice of us. I'm not sure what I would have expected, but I think perhaps I might have expected someone to ask us if we were OK, or something. Maybe they thought Dad would be coming back for us. It's what I thought, just at first. I really couldn't believe that he would just walk off and leave us.

I balanced Titch on the wing of the car, 'cos his carry box was quite heavy, and told the Afterthought that we would wait where we were.

"I'm not leaving Titch!" said the Afterthought.

I quickly reassured her before she could get herself all worked up again. I had this idea that Dad would come back and say he'd made arrangements for Titch to come with us. Or, alternatively, he would say that we had better all go back to the flat and we would catch another flight in a day or so, *after* he'd made arrangements for Titch to come with us. But he didn't. He didn't do either of those things. We waited and waited, and he never came. The Afterthought slid her hand into mine.

"What are we going to do?" She tugged at me. "*Stephanee! What are we going to do?*"

I thought, this is how it was at the beginning, when we arrived in London and Dad wasn't there. It had been up to me, then, to get us safely on the train for Brighton. Now it seemed it was up to me again – except that this time we didn't have any train tickets, and we didn't have any money, and it wasn't any use the Afterthought asking me what we were going to do because I didn't know!

"I want Mum," said the Afterthought. "Stephanie, I want Mum!"

I wanted Mum, too. I wanted her more than I'd ever wanted anything in the whole of my life!

"Ring her!" said the Afterthought. "Ring her, Steph!"

"What if she's still in Spain?"

"She can't be!"

But she could be. If what Dad had said was true – if Mum really *had* decided to make a new life for herself—

"*Stephanee!*"

"Yes, all right, all right!" I said. "I'll try." And then I remembered. "We haven't got any money!"

"We don't need money," said the Afterthought. "We can reverse the charges. *Please*, Steph! It's what Mum would tell us to do."

"But what if—" I was about to say, what if Mum wasn't there? But I looked down at the Afterthought's face, all puckered up with anxiety, and I sniffed and wiped my eyes on the back of my hand, and did my best to pull myself together. My little sister was relying on me. So was Titch. They were both waiting for me to do something.

"OK!" I picked up the carry box. "Let's go and find a phone."

"You have to dial the operator," said the Afterthought.

I said, "Yes, I know."

"And then they ask the person you're ringing if they'll pay for the call, and—"

"Yes," I said, "I *know.* Bring the bags!"

I tried not to think what we would do if Mum wasn't there. We would have to ring Gran, or Auntie Jenny. But

Gran was old, and in a home, and Auntie Jenny and Mum weren't the hugest of friends. Not since Auntie Jenny had said Dad was a con man, and Mum had taken exception. But we would have to ring someone! Or go to the police.

The police would want to know what had happened. We would have to tell them everything, and that meant Dad would get into trouble. They might even arrest him. I wondered how I felt about that, and decided that I simply didn't care. Dad deserved to be arrested! Abandoning the Afterthought was the meanest thing he had ever done. I didn't mind so much for myself – well, I pretended I didn't – but the Afterthought was his number one fan. She had always stuck up for him and taken his side. She had trusted him, and he had let her down, just like he had let Mum down. Just like he always let everyone down.

If Mum is not there, I thought, I am *definitely* going to the police.

I said this to the Afterthought, expecting her to scream, "Stephanie, no!" But she just nodded and said, "OK."

"We'll try Mum first," I said.

"Yes," said the Afterthought. "Try Mum first."

We found a phone and I dialled the operator and told her the number, and then I looked at the Afterthought and crossed my fingers, and she crossed hers, on both hands, and together we held our breath. And then Mum's voice came on the line!

"Stephanie?" she shrieked. "Is that you? Is Sam with you? Are you all right? Where are you? Where have you been? I've been going frantic!"

I said that the Afterthought was with me and that we were at Luton Airport. Mum's voice rose to a screech.

"Luton Airport? What are you doing at Luton Airport?"

"Dad was going to take us to France," I said, "but we—"

"*France?*" screamed Mum.

"Yes, but we – we decided we didn't want to go with him, and the Afterthought threw one of her tantrums and Dad got scared and now he's gone off and we're stuck here and – oh, Mum! Can we come home?"

"Can you come home? Oh, God, Stephie, of course you can come home! What do you think? I've been waiting here for you! I've been having nightmares, I've been ringing and ringing… get yourselves back here immediately!"

"We can't, we haven't any money," I wailed.

"He's left you without *money*? Oh, for God's sake! I'll wring that man's neck! All right, listen to me. I want you to go *at once* and find a Help desk. Can you do that? Are you inside the actual airport? OK! Go to the nearest Help desk and explain that you're stranded. Right? Tell them that your mum is on her way to pick you up. I'll be there as soon as I can! In the meantime, just sit tight. Don't move, don't talk to anyone. Just wait there for me. You got that?"

I said, "Yes, Mum."

"And if by any chance your dad comes back—"

"I don't think he will," I said.

"If he *does*," said Mum, "and tries to take you anywhere, on no account are you to go with him! Scream the place down, if necessary, but *don't let him take you anywhere.* Promise me, Stephanie!"

I promised, I gave her my solemn word, but Mum still wasn't satisfied. She seemed to think Dad might come waltzing back and carry us off. She told me yet again that we must sit tight and not move, and not go anywhere with anyone, and especially not with Dad.

"I mean it! Don't even go and have a cup of tea with him! Promise me!"

"Mum," I said, "I promise!"

"I shan't know a moment's peace till I have you back! These last forty-eight hours have been the worst of my entire life!"

She was back again, doing her old mumsy thing, and I was just so relieved!

"Mum's coming to fetch us," I said to the Afterthought. "She'll be here as soon as she can."

It was such a weight off my mind, knowing that Mum was on her way and that she hadn't washed her hands of us. It meant we could both stop being frightened for the first time since Dad had told us about the bad guys and whisked us off to our prison cell. I realised, now, that I *had* been frightened, even though I'd kept telling myself that it was OK because we were with Dad. It hadn't been OK at all!

The Afterthought, I must say, has the most amazing powers of recuperation. As soon as she had assured herself that Mum really did want us – "Really, *really*?" – she lost her puckered little anxious frown and went straight back to being her normal bumptious self. Quite extraordinary! She seemed to have totally forgotten that only a few minutes ago she had been clinging to me and whimpering.

The people at the airport, the ones who looked after us until Mum came, thought she was hilarious. She had them in stitches, telling them all about Titch and the things he got up to, imitating his tinny little voice, imitating the way he washed himself, the way he clapped his paws together as he jumped into the air, the way he rubbed himself round you. I suppose she was quite funny, but I am used to her being funny so I just sat back and let her get on with it. I was mainly just happy that I didn't have to be in charge any more.

They looked after us really well, the airport people. They fed us and bought us magazines and even gave us a little saucer of milk for Titch. The Afterthought was worried about him being shut up for so long, so a lady said to let him out and she would guard the door so he couldn't escape. Then the Afterthought started worrying in case he wanted to go to the toilet, so this same kind lady shredded a newspaper into a filing tray and told the Afterthought to put him in there. Titch thought it was great fun. He didn't go to the toilet, but he scattered a lot of newspaper!

In spite of everyone being so nice to us, and the Afterthought showing off like crazy, I couldn't wait to be back with Mum. The moment when I saw her coming towards us was THE VERY BEST MOMENT OF MY ENTIRE LIFE. The Afterthought shrieked, "Mum!" and hurled herself at her. I suddenly felt a bit shy, which I suppose sounds rather silly. I mean, how can you be shy with your own mum? But I am not as madly outgoing as the Afterthought. Then Mum cried, "Stephie!" and held out her arms and I just *fell* into them.

"Oh, God! I've been so worried about you!" Mum hugged us both like she wasn't ever going to let us go again. "What happened to your phone? Did you forget to re-charge it?"

I told her how I had run out of credit and how I couldn't get topped up because of Dad being scared the bad guys might trace any calls that I made. The Afterthought told her about being locked up in one room for five days and having to go to the toilet in a bucket. Mum listened in growing horror as we poured it all out, every last detail.

"Your dad told you *what*?" she said.

"He told us you didn't want us any more. He said that's what you'd said."

"No way!" cried Mum. "All I said was it was his turn to shoulder the burden. But I didn't mean permanently! I just needed a bit of a break."

"He said he'd asked you if it was OK if we went to live in France, and you'd said it was."

"Nothing of the kind!" Mum sounded really angry; almost more angry than I'd ever heard her. Angrier, even, than when she threw the frying pan. "He never said anything about France! A day trip; that was all he ever mentioned. Nothing about you going to live with him! That is total fantasy! He knew perfectly well I would never have agreed."

So Dad had actually lied to us. Probably about other things, as well.

"He wouldn't let me ring you," I said.

"Of course he wouldn't! He knew I'd go straight to the police." Mum raked her fingers through her hair. "Girls, I am so sorry! This is all my fault. I should never have let you go!"

"You needed a break," I said. "We were so mean to you!"

"You were a bit tiresome," agreed Mum. "But you had every right to be! Parents behaving badly... your dad and I were a real disaster area."

"It was Dad," said the Afterthought, "not you!"

"Oh, Sammie!" Mum hugged her. "That's a sweet thing to say! Does it mean you're not cross with me any more!"

"I won't ever be cross with you again!" said the Afterthought, wrapping both arms round Mum's neck.

"You'd better not make promises you can't keep," said Mum. "And by the way," she said, as I picked up Titch in his carry box, "what is that?"

The Afterthought said, "It's Titch! He's my kitten."

"Dad let her have it," I said. "She pestered him until he gave way."

"Hmph!" said Mum.

"Mum, I can keep him, can't I?" The Afterthought unwrapped herself and peered anxiously into Mum's face. "*Please,* Mum! Say that I can!"

"I suppose you'll have to," said Mum, "now that you've got him. I just hope he gets on with—" She stopped.

"With who?" I said.

"I'll tell you later. Oh, dear!" Mum gave an odd little laugh, which sounded more like she was about to burst into tears. "This is terrible! I'm in such a state I'd probably say yes to anything."

"It's 'cos of Titch we didn't go to France," said the Afterthought.

"Not *just* because of Titch," I said, quickly.

"Yes, it was! 'Cos Dad wouldn't let us take him."

"You mean, if you could have taken Titch, you would have gone quite willingly?" said Mum.

"No!" I kicked out, crossly, at the Afterthought.

Stupid insensitive child! "We thought we *had* to go. We didn't want to! But Dad said you were going to make a new life for yourself."

"*That man,*" said Mum. And then she stopped and bit her lip, because I think maybe she had been on the point of saying something really bad. About Dad, I mean. In some ways, in spite of everything, I don't think Mum has ever quite learnt to stop loving him.

"Let's go home," she said.

Home! That sounded so good. But there was something that was niggling at me. Something Mum had said. In the end, I just had to ask her.

"Mum, you know what you said just now?" I said. "About Titch getting on with—" I waved a hand. "Whoever."

"Yes," said Mum.

"You didn't mean… Romy, did you?"

"*Romy?*" The Afterthought bawled it at about a thousand decibels. "You're not going to *marry* him?"

"What if she was?" I said. "We wouldn't mind, Mum! Honest." Not even if he did have ginger hairs up his nose. I wouldn't ever begrudge Mum anything, ever again!

"Mum, *are* you?" said the Afterthought.

"Well, I have no plans right at this moment," said Mum. "But I'll certainly bear it in mind… it's always nice to have your approval!"

There was a pause.

"But if you didn't mean Romy—" I said.

"Which I didn't," said Mum.

What *did* she mean? She wouldn't tell us! It wasn't till we got home that we discovered Mum's secret.

"There you are," said Mum. "What you were clamouring for... I think I must be going soft in the head."

She'd got us a kitten! A dear little stripey one, even tinier than Titch.

"I booked him before I went away," said Mum. "He'd just been born. He was going to be your coming-home present."

"Can't he still be?" begged the Afterthought. "Can't we have two?"

"Oh, have as many as you like!" said Mum. "I told you, I'm so relieved to have you back safe and sound I'd say yes to almost anything... just make the most of it, because I can assure you it won't last! Yes, yes, you can have two! One each. It might stop you quarrelling!"

It didn't, of course. I don't think anyone could live with the Afterthought and not quarrel. She can be just *so annoying*! But most of the time, these days, we are good friends, and at least we don't quarrel with Mum. Certainly not like we used to. Mum still won't let me

read *Babe*, or stay out till midnight, or go to wild parties, and I still have occasional spats with her on the subject of clothes (*inappropriate*) or boyfriends (*unsuitable*), and the Afterthought still throws the odd screaming fit or goes into the sulks. But on the whole we would rather make Mum happy than have her mad at us, and one thing the Afterthought *never* does any more is use Dad as an argument. I can't remember the last time I heard her shout that "Dad would let me!" She now says that she hates Dad and doesn't ever want to see him again. Mum has tried to get her to be less extreme.

"What your dad did was criminally irresponsible, and it's certainly very difficult to forgive him for it. I'm not sure that I shall ever be able to. Not completely. But for all that, he's not basically a bad person. Just a weak one. He does love you both, very much, in his own way."

But with the Afterthought it is all or nothing. She says she doesn't care. "Titch would have *died* if we'd done what he said!"

It is quite true. We heard later that Dad's friend never did go back to collect the car. Poor Titch could have starved, or suffocated, before anyone found him.

We called the little stripey one Tiger. Tiger and Titch! They play together all the time, and sleep in each other's arms. Titch belongs to the Afterthought and Tiger belongs to me, but I think they love us both equally.

We had a postcard from Dad the other day. He's not in Nice any more – if he ever was. He's in South America. I can't imagine what he's doing there; he doesn't say. He just sends his love and promises that he will "be in touch". The Afterthought says "Not with me, he won't!" She says if ever she picked up the telephone and it was Dad, she would slam the receiver down. She was always willing to forgive him everything, until that moment at the airport. Dad really blew it. Mum says, "Well! That's your dad for you."

I don't know what I would do if he rang; I think I would talk to him. But I don't know what I'd say! I'm sure one day he'll turn up on the doorstep, trying to make like nothing ever happened. Because, as Mum says, that's Dad for you.

I still have my passion flower that he got for me. My beautiful tattoo has worn off, but I shall keep my passion flower for ever. It will always remind me of Dad.

Pumpkin Pie

JEAN URE

Illustrated by Karen Donnelly

.for all Pumpkins, everywhere

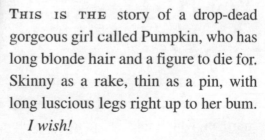

THIS **IS THE** story of a drop-dead gorgeous girl called Pumpkin, who has long blonde hair and a figure to die for. Skinny as a rake, thin as a pin, with long luscious legs right up to her bum. *I wish!*

It is my sister Petal who has long luscious legs and a figure to die for. I am Pumpkin, and I am plump. Dad, trying to make me feel better, says that I am cuddly. Some people (trying to make me feel worse) say that I am *fat*. I am not fat! But I did go through a phase of thinking I was and hating myself for it.

I am the middle one of three. There is my sister Petal (drop-dead gorgeous), whose real name is Louise and who is two years older than I am. And then there is Philip, known as Pip, who is two years younger. So you see I really am stuck in the middle. An uncomfortable position! Well, I think it is. Pip, being the youngest, and a

boy, is spoilt rotten. (Mum would deny this, but it is true. She is the one who does the spoiling!) Petal, on the other hand, being the oldest, is treated practically as an adult and allowed to do just whatever she wants.

At the time I am writing about, when I got all fussed and bothered thinking I was fat, my sister Petal was fourteen, which may seem a big age when you are only, say, six or seven, but is nowhere near as grown up as she liked to make out. She was still only in Year 9. My Auntie Megan, who is a teacher, says that Year 9s are the pits.

"Think they know everything, and know absolutely nothing!"

Petal was certainly convinced that she knew everything, especially about boys. To hear her talk, you'd think she was the world's authority. She was boy mad.

What do I mean, *was*? She still is! She's worse than ever! I suppose it is hard to avoid it when you are so drop-dead gorgeous. Petal has only to widen her eyes, which are quite wide enough to begin with, and every boy on the block comes running. She ought by rights to be a dumb blonde airhead. I mean if there was any justice in the world, that is what she would be. But it is one of life's great unfairnesses that some people have brains as well as bodies. That's Petal for you. She is not a boffin, like Pip, but she can pass all her exams OK, no trouble at all, without doing so much as a single stroke of work, or so it seems to me. Well, I mean, the amount of socialising she does, she wouldn't have time to do any work. Even in Year 9 she was busy buzzing about all over the place. This is what I'm saying: she's the oldest, so she could get away with it. Nobody ever bothered to check where she was or who she was with.

Actually, I suppose, really and truly, nobody ever bothered to check a whole lot of things about any of us. About Petal and her boyfriends, me and my fatness, Pip and his secret worries. This is probably what comes of having a dad who is (in his words, not mine!) "just a slob", and a mum who is a high flyer.

It was Dad who stayed home to look after us when we were little, while Mum clawed her way up the career ladder. It was what they both wanted. Dad enjoyed being a househusband; Mum enjoyed going out to work. She's into real estate (I always think that sounds more impressive than *estate agent*) and she pushes herself really hard. Some days we hardly used to see her. It was always Dad who sent us off to school and was there for us when we came home at teatime. It was Dad who played with us and read to us and tucked us up in bed. I think he made a good job of it, even though he calls himself a slob. By this he means that he is lazy, and perhaps there may be just a little bit of truth in it. It is certainly true that he always considered it far more important to stop and have a cuddle, or play a game, or go up the park, than to do any housework. But that was OK, because so did we!

Mum used to despair that "the place is a pigsty!" Well, it wasn't very tidy, and the washing-up didn't always get done, and sometimes you could write your name in the dust, but we didn't mind. We looked on it as one big playground. Poor Mum! She really likes everything to be neat and clean. And *ordered*. Dad has other priorities. His one big passion is food. Unfortunately, it is a passion which I share...

Petal is lucky: food leaves her completely cold. She can exist quite happily on a glass of milk and a lettuce leaf. She is a vegetarian and won't eat anything that has a face. Which, according to Petal, even includes humble creatures such as prawns. I know that prawns have whiskers. But *faces*???

"They are alive," says Petal. "They don't want to be eaten any more than you do."

In spite of her obsession with boys – and clothes, and make-up – I suppose she is really quite high-principled.

Pip is just downright picky. Where food is concerned, that is. He won't eat skin, he won't eat fat, he won't eat eggs if they're runny (he won't eat eggs if they're hard), he won't eat Indian, he won't eat Chinese, he won't eat cheese and he won't eat "anything red". For example, tomatoes, radishes, beetroot. Red peppers. Certain types of cabbage. Actually, *any* type of cabbage. Oh, and he absolutely loathes cauliflower, mushrooms, Brussel sprouts and broccoli. It doesn't really leave very much for him to eat. He is Dad's worst nightmare.

Now, me, I am Dad's dream come true. I would eat anything he put in front of me. And oh, boy! When he was at home, did he ever put a lot! It really pleased him to see me pile into great mounds of spaghetti or macaroni cheese.

"That's my girl!" he'd go. "That's my Pumpkin!"

When Pip started school full time, Dad went to work as a chef in a local pizza parlour, *Pizza Romana*, only we all know it as Giorgio's, because Giorgio is the man who owns it. He is a friend of Dad's and that is how Dad got the job. It means he has to work in the evenings, and quite often Mum does, too, so we are frequently left to our own devices. But it doesn't stop Dad trying to pile up my plate! He brings home these enormous great pizzas, which Pip won't eat (on account of the cheese) and Petal just picks at (on account of her sparrow-like appetite) so that I am expected to finish them off. If I don't, Dad is disappointed.

"What's all this?" he would cry, opening the fridge and seeing half a pizza still sitting there. "Come along, Pumpkin! Don't let me down!"

Pumpkin is Dad's pet name for me. Pumpkin, or Pumpkin Pie. My real name is Jenny. Jenny Josephine Penny. Dad calls us his three Ps: Petal, Pip and Pumpkin. I don't know how Petal became Petal; probably because she is so beautiful, like a flower. Pip is short for Pipsqueak. Meaning (I think) something little. Pumpkin, I am afraid to say, rather speaks for itself.

It didn't bother me so much being called Pumpkin when I was little, but it is not such fun when you are twelve years old. It is not dignified. It brings to mind a great round orange thing. Mum says it is a term of endearment and nothing whatsoever to do with great round orange things. Huh! I wonder how she would like it?

At school, thank goodness, I am usually just Jenny, or Jen. Nobody knows that at home I am Pumpkin. Only my best friend, Saffy, and she would never tell. We are hugely loyal to each other. Saffy is the only person in the entire world that I would tell my secrets to, because I know she can be trusted and would never betray me. Needless to say, I would never betray her, either, except maybe under torture, as I am not very brave. If people started pulling out my toenails with red hot pincers, or trying to drown me in buckets of water, I have this horrid feeling that I might perhaps talk. But not otherwise! Like the time in Juniors when she confided to me this big fear she had that she was not normal. She'd heard her mum telling someone how she'd been born in an incubator. Saffy, that is.

"I think I may have developed in a test tube... I could be an alien life form!"

Well, we were only nine; what did we know? Poor Saffy was convinced she was going to start sprouting wings or turning green. Later on, of course, she discovered that she had been born too early and had been *put* in an incubator, so then she stopped worrying about being an alien and got a bit boastful.

"I was a premature baby!"

Like it was something clever. If ever she starts to get above herself I remind her of the time she thought she was an alien, but I have never told a living soul about it and I *never will*. Her secret is safe with me! Because that is how it is with me and Saffy.

Maybe because of being premature, Saffy is incredibly dainty. She is not terribly pretty, as her nose is a bit pointy and her mouth is rather on the small side, but she is very sweet and delicate-looking. She has green eyes, like a cat – she really ought to be called Emerald, not Sapphire! – and feathery red-gold hair. Oh, and she has freckles, which she hates, but which personally I think are really cool. I would like to have freckles! I once tried painting some on but a rather horrible boy in our class yelled "Spotty!" at me, so I didn't do it any more.

Alone of all us three pennies, I take after Dad. Mum is slim and graceful: Dad is *tubby*. He is also a bit thin on top, which I am not! I have fair hair, like Petal – quite thick. But whereas Petal's is thick and *straight*, mine unfortunately is thick and curly. Ugh! I hate curls. Another thing I once tried, I spread my hair on the ironing board and ironed it, to get the kinks out, but instead I just went and frizzed it up into a mad mess like a Brillo pad. I didn't try that again! Saffy suggested I should hang heavy weights off it, which seemed like it might work. So I collected up all these big stones from the garden and spent hours in my bedroom sewing little sacks for the stones to go in, I even stitched ribbons on to them – pink, 'cos I wanted them to look nice in case anyone saw me – and I tied them on to my hair and went to bed all clunking and clanking in the hope that I would wake up in the morning with my hair as blissfully straight as Petal's.

383

Well. Huh! What a brilliant idea *that* turned out to be. First off, I had to sleep on my front with my nose pressed into the pillow, as a result of which I nearly suffocated. Second, every time I moved a stone would go clonk! into my face. Third, I woke up with a headache; and fourth, it had *no effect whatsoever* on my hair. All that hard work and suffering for absolutely nothing!

I should have learnt my lesson. I should have learnt that it is foolish and futile to put yourself through agonies of pain in a vain attempt to be beautiful. But of course I didn't. Saffy says, "Does one ever?" I would like to think so. I would like to think you reach a stage where you are content to be just the way you are, without all this stress about freckles and hair and body shape; but somehow, watching Mum put on her make-up every morning, watching her carefully select what clothes to wear (like when she has a client she specially wants to impress) Somehow I doubt it. I feel that we are doomed to hanker after unattainable perfection. Until, in the end, we get old and past it, which surely must be a great comfort?

Although in my plumpness I take after Dad, I think that in many other ways I take after Mum. I am for instance quite ambitious. Far more so than Petal, though not as much as my little boffin brother, who will probably end up as a nuclear physicist or at the very least a brain surgeon. But I wouldn't mind being a high flyer, like Mum – if only I could make up my mind what to fly at. Sometimes I think one thing, sometimes another. Over the years I have been going to be: a tour guide (because I would like to travel); an air hostess (for the same reason); something in the army (ditto); a children's nanny (I would go to America!); or a car mechanic.

It is so difficult to decide. I once tried speaking to Dad about it, because I did think, at the age of twelve, I ought to be making plans. Dad said, "Rubbish! You're far too young to bother your head about that sort of thing. Just take life as it comes, that's my motto."

"But I want to know what to *aim* at," I said.

Dad suggested that maybe I could follow in his footsteps and be a chef. He was all eager for me to start straight away. I know he would like nothing better than to teach me how to cook, but I feel I am already into food quite enough as it is. I don't need encouragement! I've seen Dad in the kitchen. I've seen the way he picks at things. He just can't resist nibbling! Sometimes when he cooks Sunday lunch Mum tells one of us to go and stand over him while he is dishing up.

"Otherwise we'll be lucky if there's anything left!"

She is only partly joking. Dad did once demolish practically a whole plateful of roast potatoes before they could reach the table. He doesn't mean to; he does it without realising. I can understand how it happens, because I would be the same unless I exercised the most enormous willpower. I think food is such a comfort!

I could see that Dad was a bit upset when I showed so little enthusiasm for the idea of becoming a chef. He said, "Don't let me down, Plumpkin! Us foodies have got to stick together."

I thought, *Plumpkin*? I looked at Dad, reproachfully, wondering whether I had heard him right. You couldn't go round calling people Plumpkin! It was like calling them fatty, or baldy, or midget. It wasn't PC. It was insulting!

"Eh? Plumpkin?"

He'd said it again! My own dad!

"It's up to us," said Dad, "to keep the flag flying. Beachballs versus stick insects! There's nothing to be ashamed of, you know, in having a healthy appetite."

Saffy has a healthy appetite. She eats just about anything and everything and never even puts on a gram. Life is very unfair, I sometimes think.

I managed to get Mum by herself one day, for about two seconds, and said, straight out, "Mum, do you think I'm fat?"

She was whizzing to and fro at the time, getting ready for work.

"Fat?" she cried, over her shoulder, as she flew past. "Of course you're not fat!"

"I feel fat," I said.

"Well, you're not," said Mum, snatching up a pile of papers. "Don't be so silly!" She crammed the papers into her briefcase. "I don't want you starting on that," she said.

"But Dad called me Plumpkin," I wailed.

"Oh, poppet!" Mum paused just long enough to give me a quick hug before racing across the room to grab her mobile. "He doesn't mean anything by it! It's just a term of endearment."

"He wouldn't say it to Petal," I said.

"No, well, Petal doesn't eat enough to keep a flea alive. You have more sense – and I love you just the way you are!"

"*Fat*," I muttered.

"Puppy fat. There's nothing wrong with that. You take after your dad – and I love him just the way he is, as well!"

With that she was gone, whirling off in a cloud of scent, briefcase bulging, mobile in her hand. That's my mum! A real high flyer. It is next to impossible to have a proper heart-to-heart with her as she is always in such a mad rush; but it would have been nice to talk just a little bit more.

It was definitely round about then that I started on all my fretting and fussing on the subject of fat.

two

BEFORE GOING ANY further I think I should describe what was a typical day in the Penny household.

Typical Day

8am. In the kitchen. Mum standing by the table, blowing on her nails. (She has just painted them with bright red varnish.) Mum is wearing her smart grey office suit, very chic and pinstriped. She looks like a high-powered business executive.

Petal bursts through the door in her usual mad rush. She is no good at getting up in the morning, probably because she hardly ever goes to bed before midnight.

(As I said before, she is allowed to get away with anything. I wouldn't be!)

Petal looks sensational even in our dire school uniform of grolly green skirt and sweater. The skirt is *pleated*. Yuck yuck yuck! But Petal has customised it; in other words, rolled the waistband over so that the skirt barely covers her bottom. Her tiny bottom. And nobody says a thing! Mum is too busy blowing on her nails and Dad wouldn't notice if we all dressed up in bin bags. But wait till she gets to school and Mrs Jacklin sees her.  Then she'll catch it! But not, of course, before all the boys have had a good look...

Mrs Jacklin, by the way, is our head teacher and a real dragon when it comes to dress code. Skirts down to the knee. *No jewellery. No stack heels. No fancy hairstyles.* It makes life very difficult for a girl like Petal. It doesn't bother me so much.

I am sitting at the table trying to finish off my maths homework, which I should have done last night only I didn't because I forgot – a thing that seems to happen rather frequently with me and maths homework. I, too, am wearing our dire school uniform but looking nothing like Petal does. For a start, there is just no way I could roll the waistband of my skirt over. I wouldn't be able to do it up! There is a hole in my tights (grolly green, to go with the rest of the foul get-up) and I suddenly see that I have dribbled food down the front of my sweater. From the looks of it, it is sauce from yesterday's spaghetti. Ugh! Why am I so messy?

It is because I take after Dad. He is also messy. We are both slobs!

Make a mental note to change my ways. Do not wish to be a slob for the rest of my life. Begin by going over to the sink and pawing at spaghetti marks with dish cloth. Have to push past Pip to get there. Pip is down on his hands and knees, packing his school bag. He is a compulsive packer. He puts things in and takes them out and puts them back in a different order. Everything has to be *just right*.

Query: at the age of ten, what does he have to pack??? When I was ten I just went off with my fluffy froggy pencil case and my lunch box and my teddy bear mascot. Pip lugs a whole library around with him.

"Don't tread on my things!" he yells, as I cram past him on my way back from the sink.

Pip is wearing *his* school uniform of white shirt and grey trousers. He looks like any other small boy. Perhaps a bit more intense and serious, being such a boffin, though I am not sure he is quite the genius that Mum makes him out to be. Although I don't know! He could be. My brother the genius...

What with Pip being so brainy, and Petal being so gorgeous, I sometimes wonder what it leaves for me. Maybe I shall have to cultivate a nice nature – like Dad. Dad never snaps or snarls. He never loses his temper. He's never mean. He's over at the stove right now, all bundled up in his blue woolly dressing gown, fixing a breakfast which only two of us will eat. ie, him and me!

From the way he's stirring it, I would guess that he's doing porridge. Dad's a great one for porridge. He makes it very rich and creamy and serves it up with milk and sugar. Yum yum! I love Dad's porridge. Mum won't eat it because she's in too much of a hurry. She'll just have black coffee. Petal won't eat it because she can't be bothered. She'll probably have a glass of milk and a banana. Pip, needless to say, won't touch it. He says it's all grey and slimy and reminds him of snot. Dad still tries to tempt him. I don't know why he bothers; Pip's a lost cause. Foodwise, that is. All he ever wants is two slices of toast, *lightly browned* with the crusts cut off (he won't eat crusts) and smeared with marge. Butter makes him sick; and marmalade, of course, being orange, is a shade of red and therefore taboo.

Dad and I finish off the porridge between us, sharing the cream from the top of the milk. We're still eating when Mum yells at Pip that it's time to go. She drops him off at school every morning; me and Petal have to take the bus. We don't really mind. It gives Petal the opportunity to show off her legs before Mrs Jacklin gets hold of her, and it gives me the chance to finish off my maths homework. Even, if I'm lucky, to pick someone's brains. Esther McGuffin, for instance, who gets on two stops before us and truly *is* a genius. She is very good-natured and never minds if I copy. The way I see it, it is not proper cheating as I always make sure to copy some of it wrong and have never ever got more than a C+. (On the days I don't copy I mostly get a D.)

At the school gates I meet up with Saffy. We're in Year 7. Bottom of the pile. Petal flashes past us, showing all of her legs, and most of her bum, in a crowd of Year 9s. Year 9s are incredibly arrogant! I can see why Auntie Megan doesn't care for them.

On a typical school day, I would say that nothing very much occurs. Of interest, that is. It just jogs on, in the same old way. One time, I remember, a girl in our class, Annie Goldstone, went and fainted in morning assembly and had to be carried out. That caused some excitement. Oh, and another time a boy called Nathan Corrie, also in our class, fell through the roof of the science lab right on top of Mr Gifford, one of our science teachers. Then there was Sophie Sutton, and her nosebleed. She bled buckets! All over her desk, all over the floor. But these sort of events are very few and far between. They don't happen every day, or even, alas, every week. Mostly it is just the daily slog. The best you can hope for is Nathan Corrie being told to leave the room. But that is no big deal!

In spite of all this, me and Saffy do quite like school. We are neither of us specially brilliant at anything, and we are not the type of people to be chosen first for games teams or voted form captain or asked to join the Inner Circle, but we bumble along quite happily in our own way.

The Inner Circle is a gang of four girls, led by Dani Morris, who consider themselves to be the crème de la crème (as Auntie Megan would say). They are the ones who get invited to all the parties. The ones who decide what is in and what is out. Like for instance when they came to school wearing ribbed tights and all the rest of us had to start wearing ribbed tights, 'cos otherwise we would have been just too uncool for words, until

suddenly, without any warning, they went back to ordinary ones again and threw us into confusion.

I personally wouldn't want to be a member of the Inner Circle with the eyes of all the world upon me. I would be too self-conscious!

"We will just be *us*," says Saffy.

Really, what else can you be? It is no use thinking you can turn yourself into someone completely different. I know, because I have tried it. Lots of times! These are just some of the things I have attempted to be:

Bright and breezy, exuding confidence from every pore. "Hey! Wow! Way to go!"

Pathetic. Utterly pathetic.

Loud and laddish. Smutty jokes and long snorty cackles at anything even faintly suggestive.

Total disaster. I boil up like a beetroot even just thinking of it.

Creepy crawly. In other words, humble.

Even worse. I just *oozed* humility. All I can say is *YUCK*.

Eager beaver sports freak. Madly playing football in the playground every break. Dragging myself to school at half-past seven to practise netball in the freezing cold.

Bore bore BORE! I quickly gave up on that one. It wouldn't have worked anyway.

None of them worked. None of these things that I have tried. When I thought I was being bright and breezy, I just came across as obnoxious so that people kept saying things like, "Who do you think you are, all of a sudden?" They don't say that to Dani Morris, and she is just about as obnoxious as can be. But she can get away with it, and I can't!

This is the point that I am making. Like when I went through my oozy phase. All I did was just smile at Kevin Williams and he instantly stretched his lips into this hideous grimace and made his eyes go crossed. Why did he do it???

He wouldn't have done it to Petal! If Petal had smiled at him, he would most likely have gone to jelly. But Kevin Williams is a friend of Nathan Corrie, so I should have known better. Nathan Corrie behaves like something that has just crawled out of the primeval slime.

However. To return to this typical day that I am talking about. Here are me and Saffy, sat together in our little cosy corner at the back of the class, and there at the front is Ms Glazer, our maths teacher. She's collecting up our maths homework from yesterday and handing back the stuff we did last week. She's given me a D+. Not bad! I mean, considering I did it all on my own. At least it's better than D-, but Ms Glazer doesn't seem to see it that way. At the bottom, in fierce red ink, she's written: *Jenny, I really would like there to be some improvement during the course of this term.* D+ is an improvement! What's she going on about? I happen to have this mental block, where figures just don't mean anything to me. Sometimes I seriously think that an essential part of my brain is missing. I have tried putting this point of view to Ms Glazer, but all she says in reply is, "Nonsense! There is nothing whatsoever wrong with your brain. Application is what is lacking."

Dad is the only one who ever sympathises with me. Mum, in her ruthless high-flying way, agrees with Ms Glazer.

"Anyone can do anything if they just set their mind to it."

That is RUBBISH. Can a one-legged man run a mile in a minute? I think not! (I wish I had thought to say this to Mum. I'd like to know how she would have wriggled out of *that*.)

To make up for my D+ in maths, I get an A in biology. It's for my drawing of the rabbit's reproductive system. I am rather proud of my rabbit's reproductive system. I have filled in all the organs in different colours – bright reds and greens and purples – so that it looks like one of those modern paintings that make people like Dad go, "Call that art?" I try showing it to Saffy but she takes one look and shrieks, "That's disgusting! Take it away!" She says it makes her feel sick. She says anything to do with reproduction makes her feel sick. She is a very sensitive sort of person.

All through the lesson I keep shooting little glances at my brilliant artwork. It occurs to me that the rabbit's reproductive system, in colour, would make a fascinating and appropriate design for certain types of garment. Those smock things, for instance, that people wear when they are pregnant. It would be a fashion statement!

I get quite excited by this and wonder if perhaps I should go to art school and become a famous clothes designer. Why not? I can do it! Already I have visions of being interviewed on television.

"Jenny Jo Penny, the fashion designer..."

I would put in the Jo, being my middle name, as I think Jenny Penny is just too naff for words. There would be the Jenny Jo Penny collection and all the big Hollywood stars would come to me for their outfits. I would be a designer label! And I wouldn't ever use fur or animal skin. I would be known for not using it.

"Jenny Jo Penny, the animal-friendly fashion designer..."

Hurrah! I've found something to aim at.

But wait! The last lesson of the day is art, with Mr Pickering. We are doing still life, and Mr Pickering has tastefully arranged a few bits of fruit for us to draw. In my new artistic mode I decide that just copying is not very imaginative. I mean if you just want to copy you might as well use a camera. A true artist will *interpret*. So what I do, I ever so slightly alter the shape of things and then splosh on the brightest colours I can find. Blue, orange, purple, like I did with the rabbit stuff. These will be my trademark!

I'm sitting there, waiting for Mr Pickering to come and comment, and feeling distinctly pleased with myself, when Saffy leans over to have a look. She gives this loud squawk and shrieks, "Ugh! It looks like—"

I am not going to say what she thinks it looks like. It is too vulgar. I am surprised that she knows about such things, although she does have two brothers, both older than she is, which perhaps would account for it. All the same, it was quite uncalled for. (Especially as it made me go all hot and red.)

What Mr Pickering says is not so vulgar, but it is certainly what I would call *deflating*. I am not going to repeat it. It makes me instantly droop and give up all ideas about going to art school. It is terrible to have so little confidence! But between them, Saffy and Mr Pickering have utterly demolished me.

Get home from school to find the house empty. Mum and Petal not yet back, Dad has gone off to pick up Pip. Help myself to some cold pasta and slump in front of the television till Dad and Pip arrive. Dad at once bustles out to the kitchen to prepare some food, while Pip settles down to his homework. I hardly had any homework when I was ten, but Pip has stacks of it. This is because he goes to this special school that Mum and Dad *pay* for, and where they are all expected to work like crazy and pass exams so that they can win scholarships to even more special schools and pass more exams and go to university and become nuclear physicists. Or whatever. Me and Petal just used to go up the road to the local Juniors. Nobody cared whether we passed our exams and became nuclear physicists. But Mum says Pip is gifted and it would be a crime not to encourage him. She is probably right. I am not complaining, since I don't seem to be gifted in any way whatsoever. Not even artistically, in spite of getting an A for my rabbit's reproductive system.

At five o'clock Dad goes off to Giorgio's for the evening, leaving a big bowl of macaroni cheese for us to dig into. I help myself to a sizeable dollop and go back to the television. Pip is still doing his homework. Petal comes waltzing in, snatches a mouthful of macaroni cheese and rushes upstairs to her bedroom, where she spends most of the evening telephoning her friends. Every half hour or so she wafts back down to grab an apple or a glass of milk. I hear her discussing some party that she is going to at the weekend. Her main concern seems to be whether a certain boy is likely to be there, and if so, who will he be there *with*?

"Please not that awful tart from Year 10!"

If it's the awful tart from Year 10, Petal will just *die*. Why, is what I want to know? But it is no use asking her. She has already gone wailing back up the stairs.

"What will I do? What will I do?"

Fascinating stuff! I sometimes think that Petal and I inhabit different worlds.

We all do actually. Me and Petal and Pip. There's Pip obsessed with work, and Petal obsessed with boys, and me very soon to become obsessed with fat. We never talk about our obsessions. We never really talk about anything. We are part of the same family and live under the same roof and I think we all love one another; but we never actually *communicate*.

Mum gets in at quarter to nine. She gives me and Pip a quick peck on the cheek – "All right, poppets? Everything OK?" – pours herself a glass of wine and disappears upstairs to soak in the bath. Pip packs up his homework, makes himself a lettuce sandwich and takes himself off to bed. Just like that! Without being told. It doesn't strike me as quite normal, for a ten year old, but that is Pip for you. He has the weight of the world on his shoulders.

Obviously nobody is going to eat Dad's macaroni cheese, so I decide I'd better polish it off to stop Dad from being upset. I then finish off my homework, watch a bit more telly, eat a bag of crisps and go upstairs.

At eleven o'clock Dad comes home from work and calls out to see if anyone's awake and wants a nightcap. I am, and I do! So Dad makes two mugs of foaming hot chocolate and we drink them together, with Dad sitting on the edge of my bed. I love these private moments that I have with Dad! I tell him all about school, about my A for biology and my D+ for maths, and Dad tells me all about Giorgio's, about the customers who've been in and the food that he's cooked. The only thing that slightly spoils it is when he says goodnight. He says, "Night night, Plumpkin! Sleep tight."

He seems to be calling me Plumpkin all the time now. I pull up the duvet and fall asleep, only to dream, for some reason, of whales. Big beached blubbery whales. I wonder what Petal dreams of? Boys, probably.

That was how it was when I was twelve. I'm fourteen now, but nothing very much has changed. Dad still cooks, Mum is still high-powered, Petal still casts her spell over the male population, Pip still does oceans of homework. The only thing is, I no longer dream about whales. That has got to be an improvement!

This is how it came about.

three

IT WAS SAFFY who suggested we should go to acting classes. I was quite surprised as she had never shown any inclination that way. Just the opposite! Once at infant school she was chosen to be an angel in the nativity play, a sweet little red-headed, pointy-nosed angel, all dressed up in a white nightie with a halo on her head and dear little wings sprouting out of her back. Guess what? She tripped over her nightie, forgot her line – she only had the one – and ran off the stage, blubbing. Oh, dear! It is something she will never manage to live down. She gets quite huffy about it.

"I was *six*," she says, if ever I chance, just casually, to bring it into the conversation. Which I only do if I feel for some reason she needs putting in her place.

When she is in a *really* huffy mood she will waspishly remind me that I didn't get chosen to be anything at all, let alone an angel, which you would have thought I might have done, having fair hair and blue eyes and looking, if I may say so, far more angelic than Saffy. In my opinion, she would have been better cast as a sheep. (Then she wouldn't have had a nightie to trip over, ha ha!)

The only reason I didn't get chosen was that I caught chicken pox. If I hadn't had chicken pox, I bet I'd have been an angel all right! And I bet I wouldn't have tripped over my nightie and forgotten my line, either. Saffy has absolutely no right to crow. It is hardly a person's fault if a person gets struck down by illness.

I have said this to her many times, but all she says in reply is, "You *picked* yourself."

What she means is, I scratched my spots. She says that is why I wasn't chosen.

"It was a nativity play, not a horror show!"

It's true I did make a bit of a mess of myself. Petal,

who had chicken pox at the same time as me, didn't even scrape off one tiny little crust. Even at the age of eight, Petal obviously knew the value of a smooth, unblemished skin. But it is all vanity! What do I care? In any case, as Saffy always hastens to assure me – feeling guilty, no doubt, at her cruel jibe – "It hardly shows at all these days. Honestly! Just one little dent in the middle of your chin... it's really cute!"

Huh! It doesn't alter the fact that she had her chance as an angel and she *muffed* it. It is no use getting ratty with me! What I didn't understand was why she should want to go to acting classes, all of a sudden.

I put this to her, and earnestly Saffy explained it wasn't so much the acting she was interested in, though she reckoned by now she could manage to say the odd line or two without bursting into tears. What it was, she said, was *boys*.

"Ah," I said. "Aha!"

"Precisely," said Saffy.

She giggled, and so did I.

"You think it would be a good way to meet them?"

"I do," said Saffy.

In that case, I was all for it! Meeting boys, in that second term of Year 7, had become very important, not to say crucial. We had to meet boys! There were lots of boys in our class at school, of course, but we had already met them. We met them every day, and we didn't think much of them. Well, I mean! Kevin Williams and Nathan Corrie. Pur-lease! Not that they were all primeval swamp creatures, but even those that hadn't crawled out of the mud seemed to come from distant planets. Trying to suss them out was like trying to fathom the workings of an alien mind. Were they plant life? Or were they animal? They probably thought the same about us. But you have to get to grips with them sooner or later because otherwise, for goodness' sake, the human race would just die out!

I didn't say this to Saffy, knowing her sensitivity on certain subjects. eg, the rabbit's reproductive system. I just agreed with her that meeting boys was an essential part of our education, and one which at the moment was being sadly neglected.

"I don't know how Petal got going," I said. "She just seemed to do it automatically."

Saffy said that Petal was a natural.

"People like you and me have to work at it."

"And you honestly truly think," I said, "that drama school would be a good place to start?"

Saffy said yes, it would be brilliant! She sounded really keen. At drama school, she said, we would meet boys who were creative and sensitive, and gorgeous with it. All the things that the swamp creatures weren't. It's true! You look at a boy like Nathan Corrie and you think, "Is this life as we know it?"

The thought of meeting boys who were both creative *and* sensitive *and* gorgeous seemed almost too good to be true.

"Do they really exist?" I said.

"Of course they do!" said Saffy. She said that you had to be all of those things if you wanted to be an actor. You couldn't have actors that were goofy or geeky or just plain boring.

"Or even just plain," I said. And then immediately thought of at least a dozen that were all of those things. I reeled off a list to Saffy.

"What about that one that looks like a frog? That one that was on the other day. And that one that's all drippy, the one in *Scene Stealing*, that you said you couldn't stand. You said it was insulting they ever let him on the screen. And that other one, that Jason person, the one in—"

"Yeah, yeah, yeah!" said Saffy. "But there's far more

who are gorgeous. I mean—" She gave this little nervous trill. Nervous because she knew perfectly well she was being self-indulgent. "Look at Brad!"

By Brad she meant Brad Pitt. (Famous American movie star, in case anyone has been hiding in a hole for the past ten years.) Don't ask me what Brad Pitt had to do with it. Just *don't ask*. Saffy brings Brad Pitt into everything. She can't help it, poor dear, she is infatuated. I somewhat sternly pointed out (being cruel to be kind) that Brad Pitt is not exactly a *boy*, in fact he is probably old enough to be her grandfather. Well, father. I might just as well not have bothered! Saffy simply smiled this soppy smile and loftily informed me that she preferred "the mature man".

"Well, you're not very likely to meet any mature men at drama classes," I said. "Not when they're advertised for 12 to 16 year olds!"

"That's all right," said Saffy, still in these lofty tones. "If I can't have Brad—"

"Which you can't," I said.

"I know I can't!" snapped Saffy. "I just said that, didn't I? He's married!"

"On the other hand," I said, trying to be helpful, "he's bound to get divorced. Movie stars always do. If you wait around long enough—"

"Oh!" She clasped her hands. "Do you think so?" Heavens! She was taking me seriously. Her cheeks had now turned bright pink.

"Well, no," I said. "I don't, actually. By the time you're old enough, he'll be practically decrepit."

Her face fell, and I immediately felt that I had been mean, turning her daydreams into a joke. It's not kind to trample on people's daydreams. Specially not when it's your best friend. But Saffy is actually quite realistic and never stays crushed for long. She is a whole lot tougher than she looks!

"Well, anyway," she said, "as I was saying, if I can't have Brad I'll make do with someone else. Just in the mean time. To practise on."

"While you're waiting," I said.

"Yes." She giggled. "As long as they're not geeky!"

"Or swamp creatures."

"Or aliens."

But they wouldn't be. She promised me! They would be creative and sensitive and hunky. She said we must enrol straight away.

"We've already missed the first two weeks of term. They'll all be taken!"

I said, "Who will?"

"All the gorgeous guys!"

410

"Oh. Right!" An idea suddenly struck me. If all the guys were going to be gorgeous, wouldn't all the girls be gorgeous, too? I had visions of finding myself among a dozen different versions of Petal. What a nightmare!

I put this to Saffy, but she reassured me. She said that loads of quite ordinary-looking girls (such as for instance her and me) fancied themselves as actresses, but the only boys who went to drama classes were the creative, sensitive, and divinely beautiful ones.

"If they're not creative and sensitive they go and play with their computers. And if they are creative and sensitive, but not very beautiful—"

I waited.

"They go and do something else," said Saffy.

"Like what?" I said.

"Oh! I don't know." She waved a hand. Saffy can never be bothered with mere detail. She is quite an impatient sort of person. "Probably go and write poetry, or something."

I thought about the boys in our class. Writing poetry was not an activity I associated with any of them. Ethan Cole had once written a limerick that started "There was a young girl called Jan", but none of it had scanned and it hadn't made any sort of sense and what was more it had been downright rude. That was the only sort of poetry that the boys in our class understood. How could you have a class with *fourteen boys* and every single one an alien?

I said to Saffy that if I could meet a boy that wrote poetry I wouldn't mind if he wasn't beautiful, just the fact that he wrote poetry would be enough, but Saffy told me that that made me sound desperate.

"Why settle for a creative geek when you could have a creative hunk? Ask your mum and dad as soon as you get home. Tell them your entire future is at stake! You don't have to mention boys. Just say that having drama classes will give you poise and – and confidence and – and will be good for your self-esteem."

"All right," I said.

I asked Dad the minute he got back from picking up Pip from school. I followed him round the kitchen as he chopped and sliced and tossed things into pans.

"Dad," I said.

"Yes? Out of the way, there's a good girl!"

I hastily skipped round the other side of the table. Dad hates to be crowded when he's in the kitchen. Mum says he's a bit of a prima donna.

"Do you think I could go to acting classes?" I said.

Dad said, "What sort of acting classes? Hand me the salt, would you?"

"*Acting* classes," I said. "*Drama*. At a *drama* school."

"Pepper!"

"It would give me poise," I said.

"Poise, eh? Taste this!" Dad thrust a spoon in my face. "How is it? Not too hot?"

"It's scrummy," I said. "The thing is, if I went to acting classes—"

"Bit more salt, I reckon."

"It would give me confidence, Dad!"

"Didn't know you lacked it," said Dad.

"I do," I said. "That's why I want to go. So could I, Dad? *Please*?"

"It's not up to me," said Dad. "Ask your mum."

I should have known! It's what he always says. Dad and me are really great mates, and he is wonderful for having cuddles with, but whenever it's anything serious he always, *always* says ask your mum. It's like Mum is the career woman, she is the big breadwinner, so she has to make all the decisions.

Well, of course, Mum didn't get in till late, and as usual she was worn to a frazzle and just wanted to go and soak in the bath.

"Darling, I'm exhausted!" she said. "It's been the most ghastly day. Let's talk at the weekend. We'll sit down and have a long chat, I promise."

"But, Mum," I said, "I need to talk *now*." Saffy would be cross if I didn't have an answer for her. She wanted us to be enrolled by the weekend. "All it is," I said, "I just want to know if I could go to drama classes."

It is easy to see how Mum has got ahead in business. In spite of being exhausted, she immediately wanted all the details, such as where, and who with, and how much.

Fortunately Saffy can be quite efficient when she puts her mind to it. She had told me where to find the advert in the Yellow Pages, plus she had written down all the things that Mum would want to know.

"It's right near where Saffy lives," I said. "I could go back with her after school on Fridays, and I thought perhaps you could come and pick me up afterwards. Maybe. I mean, if you weren't too busy. If you didn't have to work late. And then on Saturdays—"

"We could manage Saturdays between us," said Mum. "If you've really set your heart on it."

One of the *best* things about my mum is, when you do get to talk to her she doesn't keep you on tenterhooks while she hums and hahs and thinks things over. She makes up her mind right there and then. It's something I really like about her. Especially when she makes up her mind the way I want her to! Though considering Pip has his own computer and about nine million computer games, and Petal has her own TV and her own CD player, and I don't have any of these things (mainly because I don't particularly want them) Mum probably thought that a few drama classes weren't so very much to ask. She is quite fair, on the whole, except for spoiling Pip rotten on account of him being the youngest. And of course a boy. I really do think boys get treated better than girls! Petal doesn't necessarily agree. She says that if Mum spoils Pip, then Dad spoils me. But he only spoils me with food. He'd spoil Petal with food if she'd let him, but she won't, so she only has herself to blame.

Anyway, Mum said that on Friday she would leave work early and come with me so that I could get myself enrolled. When she said that, I just nearly burst at the seams! I thought that for Mum to actually come with me was worth far more than if she'd bought me a dozen computers or TV sets. Mum works so hard and such long hours, she almost never gets to do anything with us. I couldn't resist a bit of boasting, on the phone to Saffy.

"Mum is going to come with me," I said.

"Yes, well, she'd have to," said Saffy. "Mine's coming, too. You have to have your parents' permission."

I couldn't really expect Saffy to understand how momentous it was, Mum leaving work early just for me. Saffy's mum only works part-time, and then all she does is answer someone's telephone.

She's not high-powered like my mum! She is very nice, though. The sort of mum you read about in books. The sort that cooks and sews and all that stuff. Kind of... old-fashioned. Though I don't think Saffy sees it that way. She thinks it's quite normal to have a mum who's there in the morning when she leaves for school and there again in the afternoon when she gets back. She once told me that she found it a bit peculiar, me having a dad who stayed home to look after us.

"I wouldn't like that," she said.

When I asked her why not she couldn't really explain except to say that it wasn't natural. I said, "What do you mean, not natural?" Sounding, probably, a bit defensive. I mean, this was my mum and dad we were talking about! So then she wittered on about cavemen. How it was the cave*men* who went out and clubbed animals to death and dragged their carcasses back, while the cave*women* stayed in their caves doing the dusting and sweeping and making up beds.

She has some very odd ideas! That was back in the Stone Age. Does she think we haven't progressed?

As well as having odd ideas, I have to admit that Saffy does also have some good ones. Such as her brilliant plan for us to meet boys! As we got nearer to Friday, I found that I was growing quite excited. Partly it was the prospect of the gorgeous guys, but partly it was this feeling that I might be discovered. As a star, I mean! In spite of not being as show-offy as some people I could name, I have always had this secret belief that I could act far better than, for instance, an up-front in-your-face kind of person such as Dani Morris, who you can just bet your life will always be chosen for lead parts. I have simmered for *years* about Saffy being an angel and me not being anything. Even if I did have chicken pox and picked my spots. It wasn't as bad as all that! And anyway, what about make-up?

In case anyone is thinking ho, ho, you can't have plump angels, I would just beg to differ. I have seen plump angels! You only have to look at old paintings. There are loads of them. Plump angels, I mean. I would say that in those days you had more plump angels than you had thin ones. *But when did you ever see an angel with red hair?* I think that is a bit more to the point!

Not that I have anything against red hair, and certainly nothing against Saffy. It was just all this simmering that I'd been doing. Now at last I was coming to the boil! I saw myself on stage, acting a scene with one of the gorgeous guys. Holding hands... *kissing*. All the other gorge guys, who up until that point would not have looked twice at me, would suddenly be fancying  me like crazy, thinking this girl is magnetic, this girl is just so-o-o sexy! And all the rest of them, all those cool kids that would have sneered when they first saw me – *oh, she is no competition! She is a nobody* – they would be, like, gobsmacked, wondering how come they could have got it so wrong. Even Saffy would be sitting there with her eyes on stalks. That's my friend Jenny? Jenny that I've known since Infants? That wasn't even cast as an angel?

Way to go!

The drama classes were held every Friday after school and every Saturday afternoon. Four hours a week! It sounds like a lot, but when you are doing something you enjoy it is truly amazing how quickly time passes. As opposed to how *s-l-o-w-l-y* it passes when it is something you positively loathe, such as maths, for example. Well, in my case when it is maths. I dare say there are some people, with the right sort of brains, that derive great pleasure from the subject.

Possibly not everyone would think it such fun to get up in front of other people and act out your deepest emotions, or do things which make you look foolish, but it is far more fun, to my way of thinking, than right-angled triangles or stupid problems about men filling baths with water. I was so pleased that Saffy had made us enrol! Why hadn't I thought of it? Saffy only wanted to meet boys; the acting bit was just an excuse. She didn't really care whether she was any good or not. I was the one with serious ambitions!

To be honest, I thought at first that I was going to be disappointed. It wasn't a bit how I'd expected it to be! I'd pictured a real school with a proper theatre and a dance studio, but all it was, was this shabby old house at the end of Saffy's road. The paintwork was all peeling, and the window sills were crumbling. Outside there was a sign that said **AMBROSE ACADEMY** in faded blue letters. The lady who ran it, Mrs Ambrose, was pretty faded, too. She had long white hair done in plaits on top of her head and looked even older than my grans.

I stared in dismay as me and Mum walked through the door that first Friday. I didn't mean to be rude, but how could this decrepit person be a drama teacher? I remember that I looked at Saffy and pulled a face, but Saffy just mouthed the one word: boys! It was all she cared about.

Mum obviously wasn't too impressed because when she came to fetch me, later that evening, she said, "Pumpkin, I'm sure there must be better places than this! Why don't we have a look round?"

I shrieked, "Mum, no!"

After only two hours, I was hooked. In spite of being so ancient, and having white hair, Mrs Ambrose was a true inspiration. She had this really *deep* voice, very commanding, and when she moved about the room it was like she was a ship on the sea, ploughing through the waves. She was strict, too! She didn't make you take auditions because she said that "drama is for everyone," but she did expect you to work. She said, "Some of you may go on to become professionals. Some of you are just here for fun. But even fun has to be taken seriously! Work hard and play hard and we can all enjoy ourselves." I think it came as a bit of a shock to Saffy, who'd probably imagined she was just going to slouch around ogling boys.

For the first half hour we did warm-ups. Physical ones, and ones for the voice.

Ay ee oo ah oo ee ay

MmmmmmmAhmmmmmmmEemmmmmmmEeeeeee

Sproo sprow spraw sprah spray spree

Saffy said afterwards that she found it a bit boring. I didn't! Mrs Ambrose said that I had a good strong voice and good breath control, and I could feel myself glowing. It is nice to be good at things! Saffy, on the other hand, was told that her voice was too tight and too squeaky and that she needed to loosen up, and she was given some special voice exercises to help her. I could see that Saffy wasn't too pleased, but as I pointed out to her, when she was moaning on about it, "There is no such thing as a free lunch."

"Meaning what?" said Saffy.

"Meaning," I said, "that if you want to meet boys you've got to work at it. You," I reminded her, "were the one that said so!"

"Huh!" said Saffy. And then, in pleading tones, she said, "I haven't really got a squeaky voice, have I?"

What could I say? Mrs Ambrose spoke the truth!

"This is so humiliating," wailed Saffy.

To comfort her, I said that it wasn't nearly so humiliating as turning right when you should have turned left, which was what happened to me while we were doing our warm-ups. I crashed slap, bang into this girl next to me.

She gave me such a glare! I have never been the athletic type, which was what made it so pathetic when I tried to join in with the sporty set. Mrs Ambrose said that I must work on my co-ordination, and the girl I crashed into muttered, "Yeah, and work on something else, as well!" eyeing me  sourly as she did so. I wasn't sure what she meant by this cryptic remark, so I decided to ignore it. I'd already said that I was sorry. What more did she want?

Everyone except me and Saffy was wearing black tights and black sweats, with *Ambrose Academy* printed on them. It was a sort of unofficial uniform, and I was already looking forward to wearing it on Saturday. Black is so flattering to the fuller figure. Saffy doesn't have a fuller figure, in fact she doesn't really have a figure at all, but she was looking forward to it because she thinks it is a mature sort of colour. Saffy is really anxious to be mature! (In case she happens to bump into Brad while he is between wives, I guess.)

After we'd finished voice exercises we all settled down to work on this soap that we were creating. The title, which was *Sob Story*, had already been decided on before me and Saffy enrolled. It was about three girls who were trying to make it as an all-girl band. One of the boys was their manager, and another was a record producer, and one was a DJ. All the rest were friends and neighbours. Saffy and me had to invent characters for ourselves. Saffy decided that she would be "someone from America".

"Doing what?" said the girl I'd crashed into.

"Just visiting," said Saffy.

"Why?" said the girl.

"Why not?" said Saffy.

Angrily, the girl said, "It doesn't play any part in the storyline!"

"How do you know?" said Saffy.

Well, of course, she didn't. She subsided, muttering. I felt quite proud of Saffy! She is not a person who will let herself be pushed around.

"What about you?" said the girl, looking at me like I was a drip on the end of someone's nose.

I said that I was going to be an old person. Mrs Ambrose cried, "Good! That's good! Someone brave enough to do a bit of real acting."

The girl gave me this *look*. I could tell already that she didn't like me. As a rule I am such a creepy crawly that it really upsets me if I feel I am not liked. I want to be liked by everyone! But you can't be; not if you have any sort of personality, which I think I *do* have. When I can get it sorted out! When I stop trying to be all these other things. But anyway, for once in my life it didn't really bother me. I was having too good a time being this old person! I made up a name for myself, Mrs Fuzzle, and I went round complaining about pop music being just a horrible noise, and not like it was when when I was young.

I based it on one of my grans! Dad's mum, who is nearly seventy and says that nothing is the same as it used to be. (Mum's mum is younger and more with it.) Dad's mum doesn't grouch; she isn't one of those nasty cross old people. But my one was! Mrs Fuzzle. She spoke all the time in this whiny kind of voice.

"You kids today... no manners! No consideration for the old folk. It wasn't like this when I was young. When I was young we had respect. We had proper music, too! Not all this head-banging muck."

I found myself wandering into every scene, doing my complaining. I even managed to get into the recording studio! It wasn't exactly what I'd had in mind. I wasn't acting scenes of mad passion with a gorgeous guy, and people going ooh and aah and being gobsmacked. But everyone laughed, and the boy playing the record producer couldn't speak for corpsing!

"You were showing off," said Saffy, when we met up next day.

I didn't mean to show off. I am not a showing-off kind of person! I'd never realised before that I could make people laugh. Even Saffy agreed that it had been funny.

"But not very glam," she said.

She pointed out that next term, when we were going to record *Sob Story* on video, I would have to dress up as an old woman and paint wrinkles on my face. I hadn't thought of that!

"It's all right," said Saffy. "It just means you're a *character* actress."

But I didn't want to be a character actress! I wanted to be beautiful and attract boys! For a while I was crestfallen, thinking that I had made a big mistake. Everyone else was going to be cool and funky, and I was going to be an aged old hag with wrinkles! And then I had this bright idea.

"I know!" I said. "I'll do a transformation scene!"

Saffy blinked and said, "What?"

"At the end... like in pantomime! I'll have this mask and I'll tear it off, and I'll jump out of my coat and I'll be the good fairy with a magic wand that makes everyone's wishes come true!"

Saffy looked at me with what I felt was new respect. "That," she said, "is just brilliant!"

I thought it was, too. I thought, I've got what it takes! It is very important to have what it takes. You can't get anywhere if you haven't got it. But I had! I was going places. I had discovered my vocation!

"You've got to admit," said Saffy, "that it was a good idea of mine, wasn't it?"

"It was my idea!" I said.

"No, you twonk!" She gave me a companionable biff on the arm. "Going to drama school."

"Oh! That," I said. "Yes." I beamed at her. "It was one of the best ideas you've ever had!"

four

It was just *so good* to have found something I could do, other than drawing pictures of the rabbit's reproductive system (which now seemed rather gross). I could act! I could make people laugh! I had a good strong voice! I had good breath control! It made me feel all bubbly and enthusiastic, so much so that I actually started doing voice exercises every evening in my bedroom.

Ay ee oo ah oo ee ay
Mummy mummy mummy mummy
MmmmmAH! MmmmmmAY! MmmmmmEE!

Then there were the little stories, about Witty Kitty McQuitty, and Carlotta's Past, and Cook with her pudding basins. They were all for different vowel sounds, and I practised them like crazy.

Witty Kitty McQuitty was a natty secretary to Sir Willy Gatty mmmmmAH! MmmmmmAY! MmmmmmEE!

One day I opened my bedroom door to find Pip crouching there with his ear to the keyhole. Well, it obviously *had* been to the keyhole. You could tell.

"What do you want?" I said.

Pip said, "Who were you talking to?"

I said, "What business is it of yours? Can't a person have a private conversation in this house?"

Pip said it hadn't sounded like a conversation. "Sounded more like a cow farting."

Greatly annoyed, I said, "When did you ever hear a cow fart?"

"Just now," said Pip. "In your bedroom!"

"You shouldn't have been listening!" I screeched.

"Couldn't help it," said Pip, "the racket you were making."

He then galloped off downstairs going "Moo! Moo! Fart!" and making silly waggling motions with his fingers.

"Moron!" I shouted; but he just stuck out his tongue and fled along the hall.

I thought to myself that considering he was supposed

to be some kind of genius, his behaviour could be quite extraordinarily childish. But then, of course, he *was* only ten years old. I think sometimes we tended to forget that. It is probably quite normal, at ten years old, to be stupid and annoying. I just didn't want him being stupid and annoying about my voice exercises!

I was really determined to take this thing seriously. The acting, I mean. At the back of my mind I was already thinking that maybe, when I left school, I could go to a proper drama academy. One of the big ones, up in London! They'd just had the film awards on television and I'd seen myself, in a few years' time, stepping on stage to collect my Oscar for Best Actress.

The self that I saw was tall and willowy, verree sexy, wearing this slinky designer dress. Black with silver sequins, and a slit down the side. The dress would not only show a lot of leg, but a lot of everything else, as well, because by then I would have a figure worth flaunting. ie, *thin*. This was my daydream! But it was precious, and it was fragile, and I didn't need my little genius brother shattering it for me.

I hugged my daydream all to myself. I didn't even tell Saffy! I knew she wouldn't laugh, as we are never unkind to each other; but I had this feeling that beneath the polite exterior she would probably be going, "Yeah yeah yeah!" just as I do when she starts on about Brad. I do it to humour her. But that is different. Saffy must know, deep down inside herself, that her feelings for Brad are just fantasy. This was my whole future!

I remembered how Saffy herself had said this, when she was instructing me what to say to Mum. "Tell her your entire future is at stake." A premonition! I thought that when I was famous I would have a lot to thank Saffy for, and I immediately added an extra bit to my Best Actress scene.

In the new, extended version I didn't just waft on to stage in my slinky black dress to collect my award, I actually gave an acceptance speech in which I graciously referred to "My best friend, Saffy." Saffy would be there, in the audience. She would blush and clasp her hands to her cheeks as the camera zoomed in on her. She would be looking very chic but not too beautiful. Afterwards, I would invite her to join my party for a celebratory dinner in a posh restaurant, one where all the stars went. Maybe Brad would be there! He would walk past our table and catch sight of me and do this huge double-take and go, "Jen! Baby! Congratulations!" Then he would give me a big kiss on my cheek. And I would be very cool and laid back and say, "Brad, I'd like you to meet my friend Saffy. Saffy, I'm sure you recognise Brad Pitt?" And he would take her hand and say, "Hi there, Saffy!" and she would just nearly die.

Oh, it was such a beautiful dream! Far more exciting than any of my others. I simply couldn't *imagine* what had ever made me think I would like to be a car mechanic! It is without doubt an extremely useful occupation but I don't think anyone could call it glamorous and I have never heard of any Best Car Mechanic Awards, though of course there may be, there may even be Oscars, only it is not done on television and you would probably not get many of the mechanics wearing slinky black dresses and showing their legs. But it is a nice thought!

Not many of the boys at the Academy looked like they would ever become car mechanics. I don't think I am being unfair to car mechanics when I say that on the whole you don't expect them to be especially sensitive and creative sort of people. Then again, of course, I could be wrong. Just because a person likes to lie upside down beneath cars and stick his head into their engines, and get covered all over in oily black gunge, doesn't necessarily mean they are not sensitive. Or creative. I am sure you can be very creative inside a car engine. It is just a different sort of creative. That is all.

One thing Saffy was right about, we didn't have any boys like Nathan Corrie. Thank goodness! They weren't all gorgeous, but at least they all came from this planet. One or two of them were actually quite geeky, not to mention goofy, and even what I would call plain. But they weren't boring! What I mean is, they had *personality*. Plus they could talk about stuff other than football or computers. You could have real proper conversations with them, like discussing what you had just done in class or a new scene you'd worked out for *Sob Story*. I really enjoyed doing that! I'd never thought of boys as being people you had conversations with.

Some of them were quite funny. The boys, I mean. There was this one boy, Robert Phillips, who couldn't pronounce his Rs and had to keep reciting *Round the ragged rocks the ragged rascal ran*. It always came out as "Wound the wagged wocks," which drove Mrs Ambrose to despair. On the other hand, she said there was quite a demand, these days, for "upper class English twits" in Hollywood movies, so maybe he could turn his speech impediment to good use.

I personally found it quite difficult to picture Robert as a movie star, but Saffy, in her wise way, said that stranger things had happened. I was just glad that I didn't have any kind of speech impediment. Mrs Ambrose said the only sound I had to work on was the "oo" sound and she told me to practise "the moon in June" and *mmmmmOO*. I made sure only to do it when Pip was downstairs and safely out of earshot!

Another boy who was a bit geeky was Ben Azariah. He had a head like a turnip! His hair grew *upwards*, to a point. He did this thing of twizzling it with his finger which made us all laugh! In spite of being geeky, he was totally brilliant as a mimic. He could take off Ant and Dec really well. He could also do this famous footballer that I won't name in case it might count as libel, plus loads others, who I also won't name, because I mean you just never know. Celebs can be really touchy. Mum says they will sue you at the drop of a hat. I wouldn't want that!

Another person Ben could do was Mrs Ambrose. He had us all in stitches being her.

"Robert, my *deah* boy! You really must learn to pronounce your Rs!"

I certainly couldn't imagine Ben being a big

Hollywood star, but I could easily see him having his own TV show. Saffy agreed. She added that when people were a bit odd-looking, they often turned to humour. She said, "It's a defence mechanism."

I found this rather worrying and immediately rushed home to examine myself in the mirror and see if I was funny-looking, and if that was why I had chosen to play an old person in *Sob Story*, so that I could make people laugh and they would stop noticing how weird I was.

But I thought on the whole I was OK. I didn't have a head like a turnip, my hair didn't grow to a point. I even thought, secretly – I mean, trying to pretend to myself that I wasn't thinking it, as it seemed rather vain – that I had nice eyes. They are bright blue, like Petal's. Dani Morris once asked me if I wore coloured contact lenses, because she said you couldn't have eyes that were as blue as that, it wasn't natural. Well, it is, and I do! So sucks to Dani Morris.

All the same, I was glad that I'd hit on the transformation scene. Under my baggy old lady coat I intended to wear something really sensational. I hadn't yet decided what, since it was still a long way off, but even when I had I was going to keep it a secret so that everyone would be taken by surprise and go "Ooooh!"

There were two people I specially wanted to go "Ooooh". Both of them were boys. Surprise, surprise! There was Gareth Hartley, who was the one that had corpsed when I wandered into the recording studio doing my complaining, and there was Mark Nelson, who played the DJ. Both were truly cool! Everything that Saffy had promised. Creative and sensitive and *seriously gorgeous*.

Mark was like the big star. He had once been in a movie and had had real lines to say! Everyone fancied him like crazy. Even Saffy said that he was "lip-smacking" (what kind of disgusting expression is that?). She said that she would actually be prepared to accept him as a substitute while she was waiting for Brad to get divorced. But "Some hopes!" she added.

I told her that she could always dream, though as she was already dreaming about Brad I thought perhaps I could be the one to dream about Mark. I knew it was a dream that couldn't ever really come true. Gorgeous guys, especially when they are nearly seventeen, don't very often fall for plump twelve year olds, even if the plump twelve year olds do have bright blue eyes. Maybe when I'd taken the world by storm doing my transformation scene... Well, anyway. We would see!

In the mean time, there was always Gareth. He wasn't quite as gorgeous as Mark, but on the other hand he was only fourteen, so I thought perhaps I might stand a bit more of a chance. Saffy said he wasn't really mature enough for her, but that he would do "if all else failed." She had some nerve!

One thing she'd been wrong about, and that was the girls. She'd promised me they wouldn't all be gorgeous, and it was true they weren't *all*, but lots of them were! Even the ones that weren't were just so-o-o cool. And guess what? They were all thin! Thin as pins. All except for Connie Foster, who was little and bouncy and could walk on her hands and do the splits and pick up her leg and pull it straight up into the air, as far as her head. I would love to be able to do that! If I could do that I would be doing it all the time, just to show off. The only reason I don't show off is that I have nothing to show off about. What I mean is, it is not a *virtue*.

Connie was the same age as me and Saffy and really nice. I'm not just saying that because she was the only person who wasn't thin, but because she was sweet and giggly, and *she* didn't show off, either. Not like some of them! Angie Moon, for example. She was the most horrible show-off. She had this habit of twinkling, by which I mean she would suddenly open her eyes very wide and stretch her lips into this great mindless grimace with her top teeth showing. I think it was supposed to be a smile. She did it whenever a boy happened to look at  her, and especially Mark or Gareth. Me and Saffy thought it was pathetic. Saffy started calling her Little Miss Twinkle, which soon got shortened to just Twinkle, or Twink. She never understood why we called her that! She probably thought it was a compliment, as she had a very high opinion of herself.

Another girl who thought she was the cat's whiskers was Zoë Davidson. She was the one I crashed into when I got my left muddled up with my right and turned the wrong way. She had an even higher opinion of herself than Twinkle. This wasn't because she was specially gorgeous, it was because she'd been on television and had recently done a commercial for something-or-other,

I have forgotten what as thankfully I never saw it. Saffy did. She said it was nauseating.

"Vomit-making! Pukey! *Yuck*!"

Even though Zoë wasn't one of the gorgeous ones, I suppose she was sort of cheeky-looking. She had what Mrs Ambrose called "a televisual face". The sort of face that can be filmed from almost any angle.

"Either the camera likes you or it doesn't."

That was what *she* said. Zoë. Talk about loving yourself! She really reckoned she was some kind of star. Not that she was the only one who'd been on the telly or appeared in commercials. Several of the kids had. Mark had even been in the West End! But he didn't boast about it. Zoë just really fancied herself. Everyone said she was going to go places; even Saffy. Saffy said, "She's the sort that does."

She said that you had to be a bit big-headed and pushy and think a lot of yourself, because if you didn't think a lot of yourself then who else would?

I wondered if this was true. If so, I found it rather depressing. More than anything else in the world I wanted to have loads of confidence; but I didn't want to be big-headed and pushy! Did this mean I wouldn't ever get anywhere? I asked Saffy and she said it depended where I wanted to get. She said, "I expect you could probably get somewhere if you just wanted to do something ordinary, like working in a shop. But not if you wanted to be a big movie star."

My face must have fallen, because she then added comfortingly that that was all right because I didn't want to be a big movie star, did I?

"It's not what we came for," she said. "You know what we came for!" And she pulled a face and jerked her head and rolled her eyes in the direction of a group of boys on the opposite side of the street. (We were on our way to Friday classes at the time.) "*That's* what we came for... right?"

I said, "Right. But I wouldn't actually mind being a movie star!"

It just, like, blurted out before I could stop it. I thought for a dreadful moment that Saffy was going to laugh, but she is my friend and we always take each other seriously. After all, I had taken her seriously when she once confided in me that she thought she would like to be a missionary and go round converting people. Which was really quite funny considering she was the one who was sent out of an RE class for having an unseemly fit of the giggles at what Miss Cooper called "a totally inappropriate moment". (She has now decided that it is wrong to try and convert people as she feels they are probably quite happy left as they are. And, in any case, she is an atheist.)

"Do you think I'm being stupid?" I said.

Saffy said that it was never stupid to be ambitious and want to get on in life.

"Yes, but do you think I stand any chance?" I said.

Bracingly Saffy said that everybody stood a chance.

"It depends how determined you are."

"I'm very determined," I said. I was. I really was! I could see a whole glorious future unfolding before me.

"Well, this is what's important," said Saffy. "Knowing what you want and going for it."

"Even though I don't have much confidence?" I said.

Saffy told me that I had got to get confidence. She said there was no reason why I shouldn't have it.

"You know you can speak OK, Mrs A's always holding you up as an example. And you do have confidence when you get up and act."

I said, "It's different when you're acting. You're being someone else."

"But what about when you have to go for auditions?" said Saffy.

We'd been learning about auditions just recently from Mrs Ambrose. How to prepare ourselves, and what to wear, and stuff like that.

"You've got to have confidence being *you*," said Saffy. "I can't think why you don't! I would if I were you."

"It's all right for you," I said. "You're thin!"

"Yes," said Saffy, "but you're pretty."

I felt my face turn bright pink. It was the nicest thing she'd ever said to me! I felt quite touched and immediately began trying to think of something I could say to her in return.

"I'd rather be skinny like you," I said.

"Then you wouldn't have boobs," said Saffy. "You have to have boobs to be a movie star." She sighed. "I don't suppose I'll ever have any."

It's true that her mum hasn't; not to speak of. But Petal has, and she is skinny! I said this to Saffy, but she said that Petal was slim, not skinny. She said the two were not the same.

"Skinny is thin and scrawny; slim is when you've got some shape."

"Like Twinkle," I said. I think you have to be honest about these things. I didn't like her very much, but she did have a figure to die for.

"Yes," said Saffy, "but that's *all* she's got. She can't act to save her life!"

"She's been in a commercial," I said.

"Well, you know why," said Saffy. "It's 'cos she's pushy! Her and Zoë. They're both the same. It doesn't mean they can *act*."

Now that she mentioned it, I knew that she was right. About them being pushy, I mean. They were always elbowing and shoving, to get themselves up front.

Saffy said, "You gotta face it, babe! It's the way it's done."

I looked at her, doubtfully. I'm not a very shoving sort of person. I wanted to be discovered – but not by pushing myself forward! I wanted someone to come along and simply stare right through the likes of Zoë and Twink.

"Who is that girl at the back?" they would say. "The one with those startling blue eyes?"

Everyone would turn and stare. Mrs Ambrose would say, "That's Jenny... one of our little stars."

And I would be told to come out to the front and I would be signed up right there and then for this big part on telly, and Zoë and Twink would gnash their teeth and feel utterly humiliated. Ho ho!

"Babe, you gotta get real," said Saffy, in this accent she fondly believes is American. "It's no use hiding your light under a flowerpot, or whatever it is. You gotta, like, go up to people and say, *I'm Jenny Penny! Take notice of me!*"

"Just like that?" I said, alarmed.

"Well, not in so many words," said Saffy. "But you can't let people like that stupid Twinkle elbow you out the way! Just remember, you're as good as she is any day."

I thought to myself that Saffy can sometimes be so wise, and so clever. I *was* as good as Twinkle! Twinkle couldn't act to save her life. The only way she'd got to be a member of the all-girl band in *Sob Story* was by pushing and shoving. She couldn't sing, she couldn't dance, she couldn't even speak properly. She had this silly little girly voice, all high-pitched and tinny.

Zoë couldn't really sing, either, but she was one of those people, when she was on stage you found yourself having to look at her even if you didn't specially want to. I certainly didn't want to! Not after the way she'd been so horrid when I'd accidentally bumped into her. She'd gone on being horrid, for days afterwards. She kept saying things like, "Ever had a ten-ton trailer crash into you?" and "Keep away from me, Elephant!" So you can see that I had absolutely *no* reason to watch her, yet in spite of that I couldn't seem to help it. Which meant, I suppose, that she had got "what it takes".

But so had Mark and Gareth, and they didn't push and shove! Gareth was quite up-front, but he never *bulldozed*. And Mark was cool as could be! He had this very quiet sort of confidence, which I really envied. I thought that I would try to have a quiet confidence, too. I thought it might be easier than pushing and shoving. So when we all lined up that evening for our workout, I very firmly – but *quietly* – positioned myself at the front and waited to see what would happen.

Like normally, not being a show-offy kind of person, as I think I have said before, I would hide away at the back along with Saffy and Ben and a tall gangly girl called Portia, who was really sweet and tried *so* hard but just could never get anything right. Zoë always referred to her as Stilts, because of her legs being so long. I was Elephant, Portia was Stilts, and Saffy was Beetroot Bonce (on account of her red hair). Me and Saffy had racked our brains trying to think of a rude nickname for Zoë but hadn't yet come up with anything.

So, anyway, there I was, minding my own business, quietly doing stretchy exercises while waiting for class to begin, and guess what happens? Zoë comes waltzing up and rudely plants herself *directly in front of me*. Next thing I know, Little Miss Twinkle has joined her. And before I can say anything, such as "Excuse *me*!" or "Do you mind?" the door has opened and the boys have come in and Gareth and a couple of others have tacked themselves next to Zoë and Twinkle, so that now *they're* the front row and I'm pushed into the background. I mean, it wasn't Gareth's fault. He didn't know that Zoë had deliberately usurped me. When Mrs Ambrose arrived she told everyone to "Move back! You're too far out!" Zoë immediately sprang backwards, managing to tread on my toe as she did so. She said, "Oops! Sorry, Elephant, didn't know you were there." *That girl!* Is it any wonder she got on our nerves?

Saffy, of course, had seen what was happening. Saffy is very sharp. She doesn't miss much! She rang me later, when Mum had come to collect me and I was back home.

"You see what I mean?" she said. "You see what I mean about pushing and shoving? You gotta get your act together, babe!"

I said that I would try, but that it was very difficult when we were, like, the new girls on the block and Zoë and Twinkle had been there practically for ever.

"You think that would stop *them*?" said Saffy.

I had to admit that it probably wouldn't, and I humbly promised Saffy that in future I would stand up for myself. I knew she only had my best interests at heart. All the same, she is the most terrible bully!

five

ONE FRIDAY, MRS Ambrose told us that an old pupil of the school, Deirdre Dobson, was going to come in the next day and talk to us about acting and maybe even watch a class. I was so excited! A lot of people hadn't heard of Deirdre Dobson, but I had because I had *met* her. It was a long time ago, when I was quite young, but I could still remember this lovely lady with the jet black hair and silver rings. She came into my mum's office when for some reason I was there, and she actually talked to Mum about this house she was thinking of buying. Mum told me afterwards, "That was Deirdre Dobson!" Then when she got home she told Dad about it.

"Guess who came into the office today? Deirdre Dobson!"

Then she rang up both my grans and one of my aunties and told them about it, too, so I knew that Deirdre Dobson had to be somebody famous. Mum was always talking about "the time I sold a house to Deirdre Dobson", though it was a year or two before I realised that this famous person was an actress on television. She was in a soap called *Screamers*, which I was too young ever to have watched. It had finished about four years ago, which was why most of the kids had never heard of her. They were well impressed when I said that I had actually met her! Zoë immediately said that *she* had met Tom Cruise, but we had all heard about Zoë meeting Tom Cruise about a million times, and anyway she hadn't met him, she'd merely seen him at a distance.

"What's she like?" said Twinkle.

I said that I remembered her as being very slim and beautiful with dark black hair. Zoë sniffed and said, "She's probably an old bag by now. *I've* never heard of her."

"Just shows the depths of *your* ignorance," said Saffy; not that Saffy had ever heard of her, either.

I told Mum about it when she came to pick me up after class. Mum said, "Oh! Tell her that your mum once sold her a house. Ask her if she's still living there... Clonmore Gardens. Mind, it was a few years ago. She probably won't remember."

446

"I met her," I said, "didn't I?"

"Yes, you did," said Mum. "You were sitting on my desk, playing with the paper clips... very unprofessional! Miss Dobson said what lovely blue eyes you had."

"*Did* she?" I squirmed with a sort of pleasurable embarrassment. "Was she nice?"

"She was all right," said Mum. "I always find actors a bit gushy."

But she had said how lovely my eyes were! I wondered if she would remember, and whether I would be brave enough to remind her. I don't mean about my eyes, but about my sitting on Mum's desk playing with the paper clips, and Mum selling her a house. Saturday morning I rang Saffy to ask her advice.

"Do you think I ought to remind her, or would that be too pushy?"

Saffy screamed, "Jenn*ee*! It isn't possible to be too pushy... not if you want to get somewhere. How many times do I have to tell you?"

She said that if I didn't go and introduce myself to Miss Dobson she would disown me.

"All right," I said. "I'll do it!"

"You'd better," said Saffy. "'Cos I will disown you... I mean it!"

Miss Dobson was there, talking to Mrs Ambrose, when we arrived for class. I very shyly smiled at her as I came in, but she gave no sign of recognising me. But then of course she must have met thousands of people since seeing me on Mum's desk, and probably some of them would have had blue eyes like mine. And in any case I had done quite a lot of growing up since then.

Miss Dobson had done some growing up, too. She wasn't anywhere near as slender as I remembered, but her hair was still jet black, in fact it was even blacker than ever, and she still wore her lovely silver rings on every finger and was still quite glamorous. I was so glad she wasn't an old bag! If she had been, Zoë would have crowed like crazy.

Mrs Ambrose told us how Miss Dobson had been one of her very first pupils, way back when.

"Many years ago, when I was young. Because even I was young once," said Mrs Ambrose. We all laughed, politely, but Miss Dobson just gave this rather small tight smile. I thought perhaps she wasn't too happy at Mrs Ambrose saying how she had been a pupil "many years ago". Probably she would rather we thought it was just a short while back.

"Now, what I propose," said Mrs Ambrose, "I propose we show Miss Dobson how we do our warm-up exercises, and after that she's very kindly agreed to give us a talk, all about her experiences as an actor. So!" She clapped her hands. "Shall we get started?"

We headed off across the studio. I deliberately moved at a tortoise-like pace, thinking to myself that if I got there *last*, I would in fact be at the front. Only it didn't work out that way. The minute I stopped, Zoë and Twinkle, *in unison*, rudely elbowed their way past me and took up their usual prominent positions where they could be sure of being seen. Everyone else then shuffled forward to join them, with the result that I ended up – also as usual – at the back. Saffy poked me in the ribs and hissed, "*Push!*" But I couldn't. It was too late, it would have looked too obvious. I didn't want to be obvious.

It was probably just as well since I was so shaky with nerves I would most likely have done something stupid like turning the wrong way and bumping into Zoë all over again. At least at the back if I turned the wrong way it wouldn't be so noticeable. Actually, I didn't, but the point is I *could* have done. Being me. I thought that when it came to voice exercises I would be all right. Then I would be noticed, even at the back! But we didn't ever get to voice exercises because Mrs Ambrose said that now Miss Dobson was going to talk to us, and we all had to sit on the floor and listen.

I was disappointed at not being able to show how well I could do *hoo hoh haw* and *sproo spray spree*, but I did find the talk interesting. She told us all about being a pupil with Mrs Ambrose and how she had gone on to a full-time drama school when she was seventeen. She told us about "early struggles" and "bad times" when she had had to do all kinds of different jobs, such as for example being a waitress and scrubbing floors, to earn a living. She told us how her big break had come when she was chosen to play a part in *Screamers*. She had been in it for ten years. *Ten years!* A sort of gasp went up. Ten years was almost as long as some of us had lived!

Finally, she told us that the acting profession was the finest profession in the world, but that you had to be tough if you wanted to survive. Mrs Ambrose said, "Hear, hear! I second that," and Saffy poked me in the ribs, *again*, and hissed, "See?"

To end up we had a question and answer session when lots of people wanted to know how to get into drama school full time and which drama school to try for, and Zoë told everybody how she'd already been in two commercials and a television show, and Saffy kept

poking and poking until I
thought I would scream. I
hissed, *"Stop it!"* and she hissed,
"Say something!" and I
hissed, *"Not yet!"* I didn't
want to do it in
front of everyone.
After all, it was personal.

I waited till the session had finished and
Mark had said thank you on behalf of all of us and Miss
Dobson was putting her coat on. Then I scuttled across
the room – propelled by a particularly vicious jab from
Saffy – and breathlessly, before I could get cold feet,
gabbled, "Miss Dobson, my name's Jenny Penny and my
mum helped you buy your house in Clonmore Gardens!"

There was a pause, then she looked at me, sort of...
not in the least bit interested, and said, "Really? That
must have been a while ago."

"I was six," I said. "I was sitting on my mum's desk
and you said hallo to me."

"I'm afraid I have no memory of it," said Miss Dobson.
"I've lived in so many different places since then."

"Oh. Mum wanted to know if you were still there," I said.

"No," said Miss Dobson. "I'm not!"

I could see that she wanted to leave, but now that I'd
started I just didn't seem able to stop.

"I really enjoyed your talk," I said.

"Good," said Miss Dobson. "That's good."

"You told us so many interesting things!"

"Well, you know... one doesn't like to be boring."

"Oh, you weren't *boring*," I assured her. "It was just, like, incredibly fascinating! To hear all about when you were young, and – and being out of work and everything."

Miss Dobson gave another of her tight little smiles.

"Honestly," I said, "I found it truly inspiring!"

"I'm glad to hear that," said Miss Dobson. "Now, if you'll excuse me—"

She opened the door, and I raced round in front of her.

"I know it was a very long time ago and things have changed, like you said how you got a grant to go to drama school and these days you probably couldn't, but—" I beamed up at her. "It's what I want to do! More than anything... I want to be an actress!"

"You do?" said Miss Dobson.

I nodded rapturously. I had done it! I had talked to her! Saffy would be so pleased with me.

"You want to be an actress?" Miss Dobson was eyeing me up and down, as if weighing my chances. "Well, my dear, the best advice I can give you," she said, "is to shed some of that excess baggage you're carrying."

A terrible hush fell over the room. Everyone just, like, froze. Including me. Normally if I am embarrassed I will go all hot and red, but this time I did the exact opposite. I went very cold and could feel my cheeks turn white and fungussy. At the same time I broke out into a sweat. It was like someone had just punched me in the stomach. I couldn't believe that Miss Dobson would say such a thing!

Mrs Ambrose was the only person who hadn't heard. She'd gone into the small room next to the studio and now came beaming back, all unaware, carrying this huge bouquet of flowers.

"Jenny!" she said. "Give these to Miss Dobson with one of your very best curtseys!"

If I could have guessed, just ten minutes earlier, that I would be the one chosen out of all the class to present Miss Dobson with her bouquet, I would have been so excited. I would have been so proud! *Me*, of all people! But I knew that Mrs Ambrose had only picked me because I happened to be standing there, not because I was special. I wobbled down into a curtsey, on legs that had gone all weak and bendy, and thrust the bouquet upwards while keeping my eyes glued to the floor. I then overbalanced and sat down, with a thump, on my bottom.

Nobody laughed. Mrs Ambrose said, "Well! That

wasn't the most gracious of presentations, but never mind. These things happen."

She then said that she was going to escort Miss Dobson to her car.

"When I get back we'll just run the first few scenes of *Sob Story*."

The minute the door closed, everyone came flocking round me. It was terrible. They were all so nice!

"She didn't have to say that," said Mark. "That was a rotten thing to say."

"It was really mean!" said Connie.

"Even if it's true," agreed Twinkle. "She still shouldn't have said it."

"What d'you mean?" Saffy rounded on her. "*Even if it's true?*"

"Well—" Twinkle fluffed and huffed and looked a bit embarrassed.

"Jenny isn't *fat*," said Saffy.

"No, she's not," said Portia. Portia is thin as a piece of string. I'm sure she did think I was fat, really; she was just trying to make me feel better.

Gareth said that the whole conversation was becoming fattist. He said there were loads of fat actresses.

"*And* actors," said Ben.

"Yes, but it's worse for women," said Twinkle.

Saffy said, "Why?"

"It just is."

"It is!" Zoë did a little skinny twirl. "It's far worse. It's so unfair!"

"You could always do voice-overs," said Robert.

"Or radio," said Twinkle. "It wouldn't matter what you looked like on radio."

"Of course, you know why she said it?" said Zoë.

I said, "W-why?" Thinking that Zoë, in her mean way, would say something horrid such as, "Because it's the truth, Elephant!" But she didn't. She said, "'Cos she was feeling ratty!" Zoë twirled, triumphantly. "'Cos she used to be somebody and now she isn't and nobody's heard of her!"

Everyone nodded and went "Yeah! Right!" They were all on my side, even the Terrible Two, and I suppose that did help a little bit, but it couldn't stop me feeling utterly downcast and dejected. I thought, this is what happens when I try to have confidence. I wished so much that I had never spoken to Miss Dobson!

I went back afterwards for tea with Saffy. I told her that I wished I'd never gone and introduced myself.

"You mustn't let it get to you," urged Saffy.

"But she said I was fat!"

"She didn't, actually," said Saffy.

"She said excess baggage! It means the same thing. It means I'm *fat*."

"Jen, you're not!" said Saffy.

"I'm not thin," I said.

"So what?" said Saffy. "Who says you have to be thin to be an actress?"

I challenged her. I said, "Tell me one that isn't! A *young* one."

She couldn't, of course. Because I just bet there aren't any! I defy anyone to make a Top Ten of Fat Actresses Under the Age of Thirty.

"Well, anyway," said Saffy, "she had some nerve! She's not exactly a skeleton."

"She's not under thirty," I said.

"No, more like fifty," said Saffy.

She was still thinner than I was.

Mum called round at seven o'clock to fetch me. She said, "We're all going up the road to have a pizza. How was Miss Dobson? Did you talk to her?"

I said, "Mm," hoping Mum wouldn't want to pursue the subject. But naturally she did.

"Is she still living in Clonmore Gardens? Did she remember meeting you? What was she like? What did you talk about?"

I heaved a sigh. I said, "She doesn't live there any more and she didn't really remember but we didn't have time to talk very much, and I'm not sure that I feel like a pizza."

"Oh? That's unlike you," said Mum. "Well, you don't have to have a pizza! You can have whatever you want. You can have pasta, you can—"

"Not sure I feel like anything," I said.

But by the time we'd collected Petal and Pip and walked up the road to Giorgio's, I'd changed my mind. I not only had a pizza, one of Dad's specials, I also had garlic bread with cheese on top and a *big* helping of tiramisu. Food can be a real comfort when you're feeling low.

Unfortunately, lovely though it is at the time, food isn't what you would call a *permanent* source of comfort. It doesn't really last very long. It's all right while you're actually eating it and thinking to yourself, "Yum yum!" and not caring about the rest of the world and what you might look like; but then after a bit it starts to go down, and you go down as well. Sometimes you are in such despair that you have to go and eat even more food to bring yourself back up again, which was why I went and raided the fridge the minute we got back home. But *that* didn't help, because I just went straight up to my bedroom and burst into tears.

I forced myself to look in the mirror, the full-length one on the inside of my wardrobe door, and I just HATED what I saw. This great fat... *pumpkin.* All round and bloated. How could I ever think of being an actress?

How could I ever take my clothes off in front of a camera? How could I dance? Who was going to pay money to go and watch a great fat thing flolloping about? Ugh! I wouldn't!

As a rule when I am down I do my best to bounce back up, and usually I succeed. Maybe it is one of the advantages of being plump: you can bounce in a way that thin people can't. Well, that is my theory.

This time it took me the whole of Sunday before I managed to bounce. I ate eggs, mushrooms-and-tomatoes *and* cereal *and* toast-and-marmalade for breakfast, a big helping of lasagne and an even bigger helping of chocolate pudding for lunch, buttered crumpets and lemon meringue pie for tea and pistachio ice cream for supper, after which I felt a bit better. I decided that I would just *show* that Deirdre Dobson!

I told Saffy at break on Monday, and Saffy said it was good that I was thinking positively. She said Deirdre Dobson deserved to be shown.

"Stinky old bag!"

I said she wasn't an old bag *yet*, but I thought she probably would be in a few years' time.

"Yes, and by then," said Saffy, "you'll be a big star! You'll be on the way up, and she'll be on the way down!"

I immediately had a mental picture of a ladder, with me – slim as a pin, and dressed to kill – zooming up to the top, and Deirdre Dobson – all saggy and baggy and fat – on the great slide to the bottom. I was heading for the bright lights: *she* was going to the trash heap. We would pass each other and I would smile, ever so graciously, and wave.

"I shan't gloat," I said to Saffy, "because that would be demeaning."

"But you could remind her," said Saffy. "You know, just casually. You could say, *Who's the fat one now, then?*"

We giggled.

"She might even beg to be in one of your movies," said Saffy. "Would you let her?"

"I might," I said, "if she humbled herself."

"You could say, *Oh, yes, there is a part here for an old fat bag...* that's how it would appear in the cast list," said Saffy. "Old Fat Bag!"

We had a lot of fun, inventing parts that Deirdre Dobson could play in my movies. Old Fat Bag, Toothless Hag, Wizened Granny, Fat Woman in Bikini. I felt good. I felt strong. I would show her!

I ate a plate of chips and a doughnut at lunchtime to keep up the good feelings, and a packet of crisps during afternoon break. Dad had left ravioli and Black Forest gateau – one of my favourites! – for dinner, and I ate quite a lot of that because Petal only wanted salad and Pip won't eat ravioli on account of the sauce being red, so he just had a tin of sardines, which he disgustingly ate straight out of the tin, then went rushing off to do his homework.

Round about nine o'clock I had a bit of a sinking feeling and nibbled some biscuits, but by the time I went to bed I was feeling really miserable. I do try very hard not to be oversensitive, like there's this girl at school, Winona Pye (I know she can't help her name) who just starts crying at the least little thing. I find that quite annoying. But it is horrid to be told that you are fat! Especially in front of all your classmates. It is really hurtful. I don't care how much people go on about not being ashamed of your body, and saying how we can't all look like fashion models, and that in any case why should we want to? They can go on all they like, it's still horrid! 'Cos the truth is that nobody, practically, I shouldn't think, actually *enjoys* being fat.

That was the night I made my big decision: from now on I was going to stop behaving like the human equivalent of a dustbin. I was going to slim!

six

ALL THIS HAPPENED at the end of term. I made up my mind that when we went back after the break I would be slim as a pin. Well, perhaps not quite that slim. If I starved for an entire month I didn't think, probably, that I could get to be *that* slim. Maybe as slim as a darning needle. But at least a size smaller than I was now! All my clothes would be loose, so that I would have to buy a whole load of new ones. That was OK. I would ask Dad if I could take my savings money out of the building society, and Dad, in his Daddish way, would say, "Oh, you don't want to do that! You can go into Marshall's and use the store card."

I wouldn't ask Mum because Mum was harder than Dad. She was more likely to say that I didn't need new clothes, I'd just had new clothes. Which was true! We'd gone into Marshall's just before Christmas. Only then I'd been *plump* and now I was going to be *thin*. Now I could enjoy the experience! I would choose all the tightest, brightest, funkiest clothes that I could find. I would wear crop tops! I would wear skirts that showed my knickers! I would wear everything that I'd never been able to wear before.

Well, that was the theory. Unfortunately, when you have spent twelve years of your life as a human dustbin, it is not very easy to break the habit. Being holiday time just made it worse! I didn't even have Saffy to help me, because she was away for two weeks visiting her gran. I went out a few times with a girl from our class at school called Ro Sullivan, who lives just a couple of streets away, but we are not all that close and it wasn't like being with Saffy. I couldn't tell Ro about my struggles!

Mostly I just stayed home and practised voice exercises and dreamt about how it would be when I was thin. Petal was out every day, screaming round town with her friends, and Pip spent most of the time at his computer club or round at his friend Daniel's, which meant that I was on my own with Dad. A fatal combination! For a would-be thin person, that is. Dad's day is punctuated at regular intervals by what he calls "snackypoos". Like every two hours he would cheerily sing out, "Pumpkin! Time for snackypoos!"

At first I tried to resist.

"I'm not hungry!" I would nobly cry (while in fact being *starving,* having done my best not to eat any breakfast).

Alternatively, "I'm too busy!" "I'm working!" "I haven't got time!"

But Dad is not someone who will take no for an answer. Not where food is concerned. He'd knock on my bedroom door  and when I opened it he'd be there, beaming, with a plate of macaroons that he'd just made, or a wodge of gorgeous sticky chocolate cake. I can't resist chocolate cake! Even more, I can't resist it when I know he's done it specially for me.

"Done it specially for you! Special treatie. Don't let me down!"

Before I knew it, we'd be cosily perched on the bed together, eating yummy chocolate cake. Two hours later it would be lunchtime. Then another snackypoo. Then teatime at about half-past three, then dinner at five, before Dad left for work. Maybe even supper if I was still awake when he came back. We were fellow foodies! It was Us against Them. (Mum and Petal and Pip.) How could I disappoint him? If I went over to the other side, it would leave Dad on his own! How many times had he said to me "It's me and you, Pumpkin! Got to keep the flag flying."

Not that I can blame it all on Dad. I mean, he was just as used to me being a human waste disposal unit as I was. He wasn't to know that I'd become sickened by the sight of my own body. I did sort of try, in a half-hearted way, to tell him. One evening when Petal was out smooching with her latest boyfriend and Pip was round at Daniel's, and Dad and me were tucking into spaghetti bolognese together, I was overcome by this sudden burst of willpower and pushed my plate away from me. Dad was immediately concerned.

"What's the matter? Aren't you feeling well?"

He knew it wasn't his cooking. So it had to be me! I muttered that I was getting fat. Dad said, "Fat? Rubbish! Well-covered."

I said, "But I don't want to be well-covered!"

"Now, Pumpkin, don't be like that," said Dad. "You'll have me worried. We don't want any of that anorexic nonsense!"

I said, "It's not nonsense. This stuff is *fattening*."

"It's good for you," said Dad.

"It's not good to be fat," I said.

"You are *not fat*," said Dad. "You're my little plump Pumpkin and just the way you ought to be. You take after your dad, there's nothing you can do about it. Now eat your spaghetti and don't upset me!"

I didn't have to buy any new clothes. I didn't even have to take in any waistbands. I still couldn't roll them over, like Petal. I didn't dare step on the scales. By the time I went back to drama classes I was even plumper than I'd been before. I looked at all those cool thin people that first Friday of the new term and I hated myself worse than ever. I hated myself so much that I almost couldn't bear to change into my leotard and tights ready for our work-out session. I didn't want to be seen! I had a spare tyre, I wobbled when I walked. I felt like running away and hiding!

I really thought that I would have to tell Saffy I was going to give up. I would tell her that I wasn't going to come to classes any more. I would say that I was bored or that I wanted to do something else. Something such as... cooking. At cookery classes there would surely be other fatties; I wouldn't feel so grotesque.

Saturday morning I did this really cowardly thing: I rang Saffy and said that I wouldn't be going to class that afternoon as I wasn't feeling well. Saffy wailed at me.

"Jenn*ee*! You can't miss class!"

I wasn't brave enough to tell her that I wasn't ever going back to classes ever again. I just mumbled that I felt sick.

"I'd only throw up over everyone."

Saffy giggled and said that that was all right. "Just so long as you don't do it over me!"

She did her best to make me change my mind, but I wouldn't. I couldn't face it! Instead, I spent the day comfort eating. I had lots of snackypoos up in my room, where no one could see me. Dad has to work on a Saturday, so I snacked by myself. It wasn't as much fun, because snacking by yourself makes you feel really guilty, but I just had this great need. Every half hour or so I'd make these little furtive dashes downstairs to raid the fridge and go galloping back up with a chunk of pizza or a cream slice hidden under my sweater.

Mum was out, showing someone round a house, and Pip was shut away in his room. He always seemed to be shut in his room these days. I tried asking him once, what he did in there. I said, "I suppose you're playing with your computer?" He gave me this look of anguished scorn and said, "I don't *play*, I *work*." I said, "What, all the time?" "I have to!" said Pip. It really wasn't natural; not for a ten year old. But what could I do? I had far too much on my mind to worry about Pip and his sad way of life.

Then there was Petal, running all about the place like a mad woman with her moby clamped to her ear, screaming at people.

"Don't tell me! Just don't tell me! I don't want to

know!" Followed almost immediately by, "What, what? Tell me!"

I put it down to boyfriend trouble. Everything with Petal comes back to boyfriends. No big deal. She'll get over it.

While I'm furtively helping myself to some lemon meringue pie from the fridge, Petal suddenly appears in the doorway, pale and distraught, looking like the mask of tragedy (as opposed to the mask of comedy) and I almost say "What's wrong?" but in the end I don't because I have enough problems of my own without frazzling my brain over hers. In any case, what problems can you possibly have when you're as thin and as pretty as she is? It's sheer self-indulgence. I'm the one with problems!

467

We pass each other several times as Petal distractedly rushes to and fro and I creep in and out of the kitchen on my secret missions, but we never exchange any words. Petal never asks me *why* I keep racing up and down the stairs, and in and out the kitchen. I never ask her *why* she looks like the end of the world is about to come upon us. And neither of us spares a thought for our little genius brother, behind his bedroom door. We are all locked into our separate lives.

When Mum got back at lunchtime she was expecting to take me to drama classes, as usual. I couldn't very well tell her that I was feeling sick or she'd have started fussing – well, no, actually she wouldn't, Mum is not the sort of person to fuss. But she might have made me eat something really boring when we went up to Giorgio's for a meal later on. Something like a boiled egg, for instance. Or just a plate of soup and nothing else. I didn't want that! So I just said that I didn't think I could be bothered with drama any more, and Mum said that was a pity as I'd seemed to be enjoying it, but she didn't press me. She didn't even point out that she and Dad had paid for a term's classes and would have wasted their money.

But I think she was quite pleased that she didn't have to fetch and carry because she said, "Well, if you're sure... I might as well pop back to the office for a couple of hours. I've got some stuff I need to clear up. Will you be all right here by yourself?"

I told her that I would, and she went off quite happily, leaving Pip in his bedroom and me in mine and Petal still clamped to her moby. Whatever Petal's (purely imaginary) problems were she obviously got the better of them because when I crept downstairs for my next bout of comfort eating I found her all dressed up and about to leave the house. I heard her cooing, in syrupy tones, into her moby, that she was "on her wayeee!" She would never speak like that to any of her girlfriends so I guessed she was off to make it up with her latest gorgeous guy and do whatever it was they did together. Smooch and slurp round the shopping centre, guzzle each other's lips in the back row of the cinema. Disgusting, really. But nowhere near as disgusting as me, with all my flab and my wobbly thighs. I thought self-pityingly that I was probably just jealous, because what boy would ever want to smooch and slurp with a great fat pumpkin?

I expect by now you will be thinking to yourself, what is the matter with this girl? Why doesn't she just stop shovelling food down her throat if it bothers her so much, being fat? All I can say is this: it is easier said than done. For starters, you don't always notice that you're getting fat until it's too late. You've already got there! You can see these huge unsightly bulges ballooning out all over, out of your waistband, out of your sleeves, and it is so utterly depressing that the only thing to bring you any solace is... FOOD. But not just any food! Not fruit or muesli bars or sticks of raw carrot. Fruit and muesli bars and raw carrot don't bring any solace at all. It has to be chips or crisps or slices of pizza. Cheesecake or chocolate or Black Forest gateau. So you eat because you hate yourself and then you hate yourself even more so then you have to eat even more, and you just get fatter and fatter and fatter.

Well, that is what *can* happen. It is what probably would have happened if Saffy hadn't rung me at five o'clock that evening, when she got back from class.

"Hey! Jen!" she cried. "Guess what?"

I said, "What?" Thinking rather meanly to myself that if it was something nice for Saffy then I didn't want to hear about it. I was that low.

"Are you sitting down?" said Saffy.

"No," I said. "I'm standing up. Why?"

"'Cos I don't want you throwing a wobbly! Just make sure you're holding on to something... D'you remember that person that came in? That publishing person? Last term?"

I said, "Mm."

"D'you remember she was looking for faces? For this book they were doing?"

I said, "Mm," thinking *please don't say they've chosen Saffy! PLEASE!* I know it was horrid of me, but that is the way it gets you when you are depressed.

470

"Well." Saffy paused. (Dramatic effect. We'd practised it on Friday.) "She wants *you*!"

I said, "M-me?"

"Yes! You!"

I said, "W-what for?"

"To be this girl on the cover of the book! It's called *Here Comes Ellen* and you're going to be Ellen!"

I gulped. I couldn't believe it! I just couldn't believe that anyone would want *me*.

"H-how do you know?" I said.

"'Cos Mrs Ambrose asked me where you were. She wanted to tell you... they want to take your photo! She's going to ring," said Saffy, "and talk to your mum." She added that the Terrible Two had gone "green as gooseberries" when they heard.

"They really thought it was going to be one of them!"

I'd have thought so, too. Anyone would have thought so! Who'd want me rather than Twinkle or Zoë?

"Your face will be all over," said Saffy. "You'll be famous!"

I zoomed up out of my depression so fast it was like a space rocket taking off. One minute I was practically grovelling on the ground, the next it was like zing, zap, pow! Up to the ceiling!

I told Mum about it as soon as she got in. I told Petal and Pip. I told Dad when we went up to Giorgio's. Dad told Giorgio and Giorgio made this big announcement in the middle of the restaurant! Lots of the customers were regulars, who knew us. They all wrote down the name of the book and promised to buy it when it was published.

Next day, Dad rang up both my grans and told them, and then he told my aunties and uncles, and then he rushed round to tell the next-door neighbours. He was so proud! I think he told almost the whole road. Even Mum was excited. She said she was going to tell everyone at the office.

"I'll get them all to buy copies!"

Everyone was going to buy copies. Even people at school. I wouldn't have said anything to people at school as it would have sounded too much like boasting, but Saffy insisted. She said, "Jen, you're a *star*. You're going to be famous!"

She told Dani Morris and Sophie Sutton. She told Ro Sullivan. She even told our class teacher, Mrs Carlisle, who said, "Oh! We'll have to make sure we get copies for the school library." Soon it seemed that everybody knew. I was a celeb!

On Friday when I went back to class – I didn't care so much now about being plump. Not now that I'd been chosen for a book jacket! – a photographer came to take pictures of me. The lady from the publishers was with him. She told me that Ellen was "very lovable and cuddly and *pretty*. You're exactly right!"

I knew I mustn't let it go to my head, because I really despise people who gloat and smirk and think they're better than anyone else, but it was hard not to be just a little bit exultant as I was led away to have my photo taken. The look on Zoë's face! You could tell that she was thinking, "Why her? Why not me?"

And it wasn't just honour and glory! They were going to *pay* me for it. It was my first professional engagement! Saffy said that I was "on the way". She said, "Sucks to Deirdre Dobson! Sour old bag. I told you she was talking rubbish!"

Now that I wasn't depressed any more, I didn't have to comfort eat. But now that I'd been chosen for a book jacket I decided that I didn't have to go on any stupid diet, either. I wasn't fat! I was cuddly. And *pretty*. Just like Ellen! So I stopped raiding the fridge but I went on having snackypoos with Dad and generally mopping up all the stuff that other people didn't want, and I sort of closed my eyes to the spare tyre and the wobbly thighs. You can do this, if you really try. I mean, you don't *have* to keep looking at yourself in the mirror. Not the whole of yourself. You can just concentrate on selected bits and forget about the rest. Which is what I learnt to do.

And then one day, a few weeks later, a padded envelope came through the letter box. It was addressed to me, and inside was an early copy of *Here Comes Ellen*. And there was my face on the front of it! Mum and Dad, and even Petal, said that it was lovely. And it was quite nice, though it wasn't the nicest one they'd taken. It was a bit... well! A bit sort of... not very bright-looking. At least, that's the way it seemed to me. Mum and Dad said "Nonsense!" but Petal, after studying the picture from all angles, said she could see what I meant.

"Like she's one slice short of a sandwich."

Mum said, "Petal! Don't be so unkind."

"She said it first," said Petal. "I'm only agreeing with her!"

I raced upstairs to my bedroom and settled down to read about this girl Ellen. This girl that was so lovable and cuddly and *pretty*. I discovered that Ellen was a Fat Girl. She was also a Slow Girl. A girl with learning difficulties. A girl that's bullied and jeered at. A figure of fun!

That was why I'd been chosen. Because I was *fat*. And when the book was published and was in the shops everyone, but everyone, would be rushing out to buy it, and people like my grans would be feeling just *so* sorry for me, poor little Jenny! What a horrid thing to do to her! Whereas people like Zoë and Twink and Dani Morris would be laughing themselves silly.

I didn't finish reading the book. I couldn't bear to. Saffy told me ages later that in fact Ellen turned out to be a heroine, but it still didn't stop her being *fat*. I didn't want to know! I got half way through and then hid the hateful thing at the back of a cupboard. If Mum or Dad asked me about it, I would say I'd lent it to someone and they'd lost it. I didn't want them reading it! I didn't want anyone reading it.

You might think that at this point, being such a pathetic sort of person, I would have instantly fallen into another depression and rushed downstairs to fetch myself a snackypoo. But I didn't! I am not always pathetic. Sometimes I bounce. I get defiant. I think to myself that I will show them!

That is what I thought that evening in my bedroom. I made a vow: by the end of term, when we filmed *Sob Story* and I did my transformation scene, I was no longer going to be a fat girl. I was going to be a thin girl!

This time, *I meant it*.

seven

THIS IS WHEN I became obsessed. It is very easy to become obsessed. It is a question of focusing all your energies on just one thing and sticking to it. The thing that I was focusing on was the size of my body. Big fat bloated pumpkin! The fat was going to *go*.

I didn't tell anyone; not even Saffy. It was a matter of pride. I didn't want people knowing how much I cared. It was too pathetic! When I got thin, I wanted them to think it was just something that had happened quite naturally, all on its own, without any help from me.

"Jen!" they would go. "You've lost weight!"

And I would go, "Really? I hadn't noticed."

Like just so-o-o cool. I would be able to be cool once I was thin. It's difficult to be cool when you're fat. It's difficult to be *anything* when you're fat. You can't wear groovy gear. You can't ever look good. You just go round hating yourself and trying not to catch sight of your reflection in shop windows. It does terrible things to your confidence. Well, you just don't really have any.

But that was all going to change! I started counting calories. I read the information on the backs of packets.

Per pie... 350 calories.

BAD.

Per half can... 210 calories.

BAD.

Per slice... 400 calories.

Bad, bad, VERY BAD!

I soon discovered that there was almost nothing in the house that I could safely consume. I looked up pizza and pasta and chocolate fudge cake in a book that I bought called *Calorie Counter*. They were all *bad*. Chocolate fudge cake was deadly! In fact, most of my favourite foods fell into the same category.

B.A.D.

FATTENING!

All the nicest foods are. It is a sad fact of life.

So far as I could, I simply stopped eating. I weighed myself on the bathroom scales every morning when I got up and every night before I went to bed. It became a sort of ritual. My life revolved around the bathroom scales! If I found that I'd put on even so much as .1 of a kilo, it nagged at me all day, it kept me awake all night. Even if I just stayed the same, it threw me into total despair. Usually, for some weird reason, I weighed less in the morning than I did in the evening. I couldn't understand that, when all I'd done all night was sleep. How could you lose weight just sleeping? I thought that if I could stay in bed for a whole month without eating I would be thin as a thread without any trouble at

all! But even Mum would notice if I took to my bed. She didn't notice me not eating because she either wasn't there or was in too much of a rush.

Dad was my really *big* problem. Pip and Petal were like Mum, too bound up in their own affairs. Just as my life revolved round the bathroom scales, Pip's revolved round homework and his computer, Petal's revolved round boyfriends. They wouldn't notice if I lived on nothing but air and water.

But Dad would! Dad has eyes like a hawk where food is concerned. So what I had to do, I had to devise strategies. Being on a really determined slimming spree can make you very cunning. I would let Dad pile my plate as usual, then suddenly discover, at breakfast for example, that I was wearing the wrong shoes, or the wrong top, and go racing upstairs to change – *carrying my plate with me*. I would then dump the whole lot down the loo.

Or another strategy I had, I would pick and poke at my food, pretending to be eating it, then as soon as Dad left the kitchen I would dive across to the sink and scrape everything into the rubbish bin – being careful to cover it up with tea leaves or orange peel or whatever happened to be in the rubbish bin to start with. I told you I was cunning!

Once or twice, when I couldn't think of an excuse for going upstairs and Dad didn't leave the kitchen, I actually picked up my plate and wandered out into the garden with it. There's lots of porridge and pizza and ravioli hidden behind the bushes in our garden.

I did sometimes think of all those starving people around the globe and feel a twinge of guilt, but I comforted myself with the thought that if I wasn't chucking the stuff behind the rose bushes or dumping it down the loo, I would be eating it myself, so it still wouldn't get to the people who needed it. Such – alas! – is the way of the world. Too much food in one place, and not enough in another. You would think by now we could have arranged things a bit better. I, for instance, would have been only too happy to save up a week's supply and take it along to a central collecting point for redistribution. Far better than throwing it behind the rose bushes.

Fortunately, from my point of view, neither Mum nor Dad is into gardening, so they never came across the little festering piles of food. Probably the foxes mopped it up. Or the hedgehogs, or the squirrels. Or even next door's cat. But that was OK. If the starving people couldn't have it, I'd rather it went to the animals.

Weekends were the worst time. At weekends we always went up to Giorgio's and I couldn't very well keep rushing off to the loo with platefuls of pasta in the middle of a crowded restaurant. I thought even Mum might notice if I did that. One time when the weather was warm we sat at a table outside, on the pavement, and I toyed with the idea of upending my plate into a potted something-or-other, some kind of leafy thing, that stood nearby, but at the last minute I chickened out.

All I could do was try ordering the least fattening things I could find, but most of the stuff on Giorgio's menu is smothered in oil or butter or rich creamy sauce – *bad, bad, TRIPLE bad*! – and even if I just asked for soup and a sorbet the waiter would come beaming up with a dish of tiramisu or cheesecake, "with the chef's compliments". Mum would say, "Go on! Eat it. You've hardly touched a thing," and I knew if I sent it back Dad himself would come out and demand in hurt tones to know what was wrong. It was no use offering it to Mum because she would already have ordered her favourite, which was apple pie and cream, and it goes without saying that Petal wouldn't help me out.

"Ugh! I don't want it," she'd say, giving one of her little shudders.

So then I'd try Pip, but he'd just push it right back at me like it was something repulsive. Cold sick, or nose droppings. If Pip had a pudding it was always ice cream. *Green* ice cream. He says that white tastes like cardboard, and pink, of course, is too close to red. Likewise chocolate. I sometimes wonder if Pip is quite normal, but maybe geniuses aren't.

Mostly, at Giorgio's, I had to eat what I had always eaten, for fear of drawing attention to myself. I didn't want Mum to suss what was going on. I knew she would immediately think "Anorexia!" because that is what they always think. It is the modern bogey word for mums.

When we got back from Giorgio's I would always feel very ill and bloated. It was truly disgusting, eating so much! I knew I had to offload it, so I would wait until Mum was relaxing in front of the television then I would shut myself in the loo and stick my fingers down my throat and bring everything up. Not very nice, but it had to be done. In any case, I remembered reading somewhere how Princess Di had done the same thing. If she could do it, so could I! It had obviously worked for her, she had always looked so beautiful. I thought that I would give anything to look like Princess Di!

As well as jumping on and off the scales twice a day, I also took to measuring myself, specially round my waist and hips. I measured once when I got up, *before* I weighed myself; and once when I went to bed, *after* I'd weighed myself. This is what you do when you get obsessed. If I could have measured and weighed during the day as well, I would have done! I did at weekends. At weekends I practically lived on the scales.

At school I didn't really eat at all; it was easier there. I still had to go into the dining hall, but nobody checked what you had on your tray. I would just take a bit of salad and a yoghurt, and sit there nibbling at it while Saffy, as usual, tucked into chips and doughnuts and various other assorted goodies. *Baddies!* Saffy could eat an elephant and still look like a stick insect. Life is just not fair.

But then, whoever said it was? Certainly not me!

One lunchtime, when I was cutting up a lettuce leaf, Saffy said, "*Jen*! You're not *slimming*, are you?"

The way she said it, you'd have thought I was planning to rob a bank or mug a little kid for his mobile phone. I felt my face surge into the red zone. Slimming! Why did it sound so shameful? I might have known that Saffy would notice. We always notice things about each other. It's what comes of being so close.

"*Are* you?" she said. All grim and accusing.

I said, "Yes, I am, as a matter of fact."

"But why?" said Saffy.

Did she really need to ask? I would have thought it was obvious.

"I'm fat," I said. We were sitting by ourselves at the far end of a table so nobody could hear us. I wouldn't have said it otherwise. I would have been too ashamed.

"Jenny, are you mad?" shrieked Saffy.

Everyone turned to look, and I went, "Shh!"

"Well, but really," she hissed, "we've already been through this! You are *not fat*!"

"Look," I said, "it's my body. I ought to know whether it's fat or not."

"You're just being silly and oversensitive," said Saffy.

I muttered, "You'd be silly and oversensitive if you looked like me."

"I wouldn't mind looking like you," said Saffy.

I said, "Oh, no?"

"No! If you want to know the truth, I'd give anything to have hair like yours."

It is true that my hair is quite thick, while Saffy's is rather straggly. And her nose is decidedly pointy, and she is definitely not pretty. But she is *thin*.

"Honestly," said Saffy, "you're not fat, Jen! Really!"

"So what would you call it?" I said.

"I'd say you were... chubby."

"*Chubby?*"

"Cuddly!"

"Cuddly," I said, "is just another way of saying *fat*."

"Oh! Well." Saffy pushed her plate away from her. She had eaten chips and lentil bake. My stomach cried out in protest, and I rammed a lettuce leaf down my throat to keep it quiet. "If that's the way you want to think of yourself," said Saffy.

She sounded like she was just about fed up with me. Desperately, I said, "Saf, I *am* fat! I've got to do something about it."

"I thought we'd already been through all this?" said Saffy. "They'd hardly have chosen you for a book jacket if you were fat!"

So then I told her. I told her how lovable cuddly Ellen was a Fat Girl, and how I'd hidden the book at the back of my cupboard and didn't want anyone to read it.

That shook her, I could tell. I mean, that anyone could be so horrid! They had *tricked* me. Good as.

Then Saffy said slowly, "She may be fat in the book, but they wouldn't actually put anyone fat on the cover. Not *really* fat. That's why they chose you, because you're *not* really fat. You're cuddly!"

Saffy is such a good friend. She was really trying to cheer me up.

"With you on the cover," she said, "I should think it would go like hot cakes! Everyone will buy it!"

She wasn't to know that was just about the worst thing she could have said. I didn't want everyone to buy it! I didn't want anyone to buy it. I said this to Saffy. I said, "It's going to be published next week. It'll be in all the book shops. I just can't bear it!"

Our town has rather a lot of bookshops. There's Smith's, for a start. That's in the shopping centre. Then there is Ottakar's on the top floor, and Books Etc. in the High Street, and a tiny little place tucked away down the hill. Just imagine if they all had the book!

"Do your mum and dad know you're slimming?" said Saffy.

I said, "No! And you're not to tell them."

"I bet they wouldn't approve," said Saffy. "Specially your dad."

"It's nothing to do with them," I said. "It's my body!"

Saffy promised not to tell, but I could see she was dubious about the whole enterprise.

"So long as you don't overdo it," she said. "You know what happened to Pauline Pretty."

Pauline Pretty was a girl in Year 10 who'd faded away to practically nothing before anyone realised what was happening. There'd been an announcement last term in assembly, saying that she'd died. We'd all been shocked, even people such as me and Saffy who hadn't even known who she was. It was just the thought of someone our age, *dying*. But Pauline Pretty had had anorexia. She had been sick. I wasn't sick! I just wanted to get thin.

I said as much to Saffy and she said, "But then you won't be you!" I thought to myself that if being me meant being fat, then I didn't want to be me. I wanted to be someone different! Only I didn't say this to Saffy as I didn't want her to lecture me. Next week that hateful book would be in the bookshops and I needed Saffy to help me go round and hide it, because this was what I had decided to do. I couldn't stop it being sold in other places, but I was determined it wasn't going to be sold in my home town!

The following Saturday we met up in the shopping centre to go on a *Here Comes Ellen* hunt. We went all round the bookshops, starting with Smith's. The tiny little tucked-away place didn't have it, but all the others did. Ottakar's actually had it on a table! In full view of everyone!

"Oh, Jen, I don't know what you're going on about," said Saffy. "It looks brilliant! Why don't we just leave it?"

I said, "No! I don't want anyone buying it."

So when nobody was looking we took the books off the table and scattered them round the shelves, putting them behind other books that were face out. We did the same in Books Etc. and in Smith's. In Smith's the book *itself* was face out, and that was really frightening because loads of people go into Smith's. I mean, people that want other things, like CDs and stationery, and I had visions of them strolling past the book section and suddenly catching sight of my face staring at them from the cover and going, "Oh! That's that girl whose dad works in Giorgio's!" or "Oh, that's that girl that goes to my school!" So I took some of the books that were next to it and turned *them* face out and stuck *Ellen* behind them and hoped she would stay there, hidden from view, until she grew old and musty and the shop sent her back where she came from. And serve her right!

Saffy wondered about the poor author. She said how upset she would be when nobody bought any of her books, but I said that I didn't care.

"It was mean of them not to tell me!"

"Well, anyway, it's probably selling like mad everywhere else," said Saffy.

I know Saffy means well, but there are times when she can be just *so* tactless.

eight

LOSING WEIGHT IS a bit like saving money: it is very difficult to get going. You find that you are making all kinds of excuses such as, "I'll just finish this last packet of Maltesers, I'll just wait till my birthday, I'll just wait till after the weekend." etc. and so forth. And then, sometimes, you never get started at all, which was what had happened to me when I first decided to slim. I put it off so long, and had so many snackypoos and bars of chocolate, that in the end it didn't seem worth the effort. But once you *do* manage to get started it's like your life becomes ruled by it. You can't imagine living any other way. It gets so it's impossible to stop. Both with losing weight and with saving money.

Like there was this one time I remember, in Year 6, when I desperately, desperately wanted a personal organiser like a girl in my class had got. I didn't know what I was going to do with it; I just knew that I had to have one! Dad would have let me, but Mum as usual was more stern. She said I'd just spent all my Christmas money on what she called "useless rubbish" (meaning bangles and earrings and sparkly hair clips, which may be useless rubbish to Mum but certainly isn't to me!) and if I wanted a personal organiser as badly as all that I could save up for it. I wailed that it would take me ages.

"I'll be dead by the time I've saved up that much!"

So then Mum relented and said all right, if I could manage to save half she and Dad would come up with the other half. So I started to save, just little bits to begin with like the odd 20p, because I don't have very much pocket money, well I don't think I do, and I kept it in a jam jar with a plastic lid so that I could see how quickly it was mounting up. At first it didn't seem to mount up at all, but then one day I suddenly noticed that the jam jar was almost quarter full, and I took out the money and counted it and it came to nearly £6. Six pounds that I had saved almost without realising it!

That was when it got a grip and I started to save in real earnest. I saved every penny that I could! I even picked up 1p pieces that people had dropped in the street. When the first jam jar was full, I started on a second one. By the time the second one was full I'd saved my half of the money and could have had my organiser any time I wanted, but now I didn't want one. Well, I did, but I wanted the money more. I didn't want to *do* anything with the money; I just wanted to see it mounting up. I had become a money junkie! I was a secret hoarder!

I might have been hoarding to this day if something hadn't happened to break the cycle. It was only a little something, but that is often all it takes. Quite suddenly, for no reason, the whole of Year 6 went mad on body tattoos – the sort you stick on. If you didn't walk round covered in them, you just weren't cool. I begged Saffy to give me some of hers, but she wouldn't. She said I'd become as mean as could be and could go out and buy some of my own. So I did, and that was the beginning of the end. We went to visit my auntie and uncle and they took us to the shopping centre at Brent Cross and I saw these really *superior* tattoos in a shop and I just couldn't resist them, even though they were expensive.

I knew if I went to school with tattoos like that I'd be the coolest person there. I spent the whole of my pocket money on body tattoos! And that was that. Once I'd broken the habit, I couldn't get back into it again. I didn't even get the personal organiser; I just frittered the money away on more of what Mum called "rubbish".

So this is how it was with me and slimming, except that instead of money mounting up, it was kilos going *down*. I bought a red felt tip, a fine liner, and used it to mark the tape measure. Every time I measured myself, I made a little mark. At first, just as with the money in the jam jar, nothing very much seemed to be happening and it would have been all too easy to be discouraged, except that this time I was *determined*. And then, suddenly, the red mark moved! In the right direction, I hasten to add. Week by week, it kept on moving. Just a millimetre at a time, to begin with, then one Saturday a whole half centimetre! I could hardly contain myself! I immediately tried on every single skirt and pair of jeans in my wardrobe and discovered to my joy that some of them that I'd had difficulty fitting into now did up quite easily. It was working! I was getting thin!

There came a day when I actually had to use a safety pin to take in the waistband of my school skirt and pull in the belt on my jeans really tight to stop them slipping down. It just felt *so good*. Zoë looked at me in the changing room one Friday, as we were getting into our leotards. She did this double take and said, "Hey! Eleflump!" which was what she had taken to calling me. "Are you on a diet, or something?"

As carelessly as I could I said, "Me? No! Why?" Hoping and praying that Saffy wouldn't give me away.

"You look like you are," said Zoë.

"Yes. You do!" Twinkle was now gazing at me. "You look sort of... thinner."

"Really?" I said. Yawn yawn.

"You used to *bulge*," said Twinkle. "You used to look like a big hovercraft." And she puffed out her cheeks and went waddling across the room with her feet splayed and her bottom stuck in the air and her arms held out like panniers.

"Flomp flomp flomp," went Zoë, joining in.

Such sweet girls. I *don't* think.

"You do look as if you've lost weight," said Portia.

I was pleased, of course, but also a bit embarrassed. I wanted people to notice – but I didn't want them remarking on it! Saffy was really good. She could easily have betrayed me, but she didn't. When Portia turned to her and said, "Don't you think she looks as if she's lost weight?" Saffy just said, "I suppose she does. I hadn't really thought about it." But next day, when we went back to her place after class, she read me this mumsy-type lecture, all about how I'd lost as much weight as I needed and how I'd got to start eating properly.

"I can say this," she said, "'cos you're my friend. If you carry on not eating you'll get ill. You'll get hag-like. You'll end up like Pauline Pretty!"

What did she mean, I would end up like Pauline Pretty? How dare she say such a thing! I wasn't anorexic. I could stop any time I wanted, just like that! I said so to Saffy. I told her that I could stop *any time I wanted*.

"So when are you going to?" said Saffy.

I said, "As soon as I've reached my target weight."

"Which is what?"

Blusteringly I said, "Well! Whatever I decide."

I couldn't give her an exact weight because I didn't have one. I didn't have a target weight! I just had this fixed idea that I would go on slimming until I could finally look in the mirror and like what I saw. It wasn't a question of weight. It was a question of how I looked.

"I wish we'd never started drama classes if this is what it's done to you!" cried Saffy.

I said, "It was you that wanted to. Don't blame me!"

"I'm not blaming you," said Saffy.

"Sounds like you are."

"I'm not, but ever since that stupid woman came you've got all miserable and cranky and obsessed with yourself!"

"I'm just thinking of my future," I said. "If you don't mind! I'm just exercising a bit of *willpower*. You'd think," I said, "being my *friend*, you'd want to help me. Not go nagging on at me the whole time!"

Saffy pursed her lips, making them go into a narrow line. "What about your mum and dad?" she said.

I said, "What about them?"

"What do they say?"

"They don't say anything. *They* don't nag!"

The truth was that Mum and Dad still hadn't noticed. I was being that cunning! Plus Dad isn't the most observant of people, except when it's food. Plus Mum was always working. But I was developing new strategies all the time. I'd not only learnt how to avoid eating but when I was at home I'd deliberately wear clothes that made me look the same plump Pumpkin that I'd always been. I'd wear long baggy T-shirts over big saggy jeans, and when I dressed for school I'd wear my blouse outside my skirt. As soon as I left the house I'd tuck it back in and pin up the waistband. I didn't want to go out and buy new clothes until I'd reached my target body image.

That's what I was calling it. *Target body image*. I think I knew, deep down, that Saffy was right. I had to have some aim in view; I couldn't just keep slimming indefinitely. It was a question of knowing when to stop. And the answer to that was... when I was thin as a pin!

Sometimes on a Sunday me and Dad and Pip, and Petal if she doesn't have anything else to do, go and visit my gran. That is, Dad's mum. (The one I sort of based my old cranky person on for *Sob Story*, though as I believe I said before, my gran isn't really cranky. She just reckons that life is not as good now as it used to be when she was young.) Mum doesn't very often come with us when we visit as she and Gran don't get on awfully well, mainly because Gran thinks a mother's place is in the home. She thinks it is terrible that it was Dad who looked after us while Mum went out to work. So Mum usually stays behind while the rest of us go off, which is just as well for me since otherwise, on this particular occasion that we went to visit, I might have been found out!

Gran has very sharp eyes for an old lady; she notices things. She noticed *immediately* that I wasn't looking as gross as I had been.

"Jenny," she said. "Have you lost weight?"

Fortunately, although we were all together in the kitchen, Dad was busy checking the contents of Gran's cupboard – he always checks the cupboard, to make sure she's properly stocked up with food – and when

Dad is counting tins of baked beans or jars of marmalade the rest of the world simply passes him by. If Mum had been there, she would have pounced! Even Petal might have looked twice, but she'd gone to spend the day with Helen Bickerstaff, one of her friends from school, and Pip didn't because what did he care if I'd lost weight?

"Well," said Gran. Like in these accusing tones. "*Have* you?"

I said, "I wish!" Flapping my hands in my T-shirt.

Gran said, "What do you mean, *you wish*? What kind of foolish talk is that?"

"Gran! Everybody wants to be slim," I said.

"Well, everybody shouldn't," said Gran. "Everybody should have a bit more sense. We're human beings, not stick insects!"

Dad then turned round from the cupboards to ask why Gran didn't have any pasta in stock, and the talk swung off in another direction, but I noticed Gran looking at me every now and again with narrowed eyes so I made sure to really *glut* when it came to teatime. I knew I'd have to pay for it later, but the last thing I wanted was Gran going and putting ideas into Dad's head. As we left she said in a loud voice, as she kissed me goodbye, "And no more of that *I wish* nonsense, thank you very much!" This time, Dad heard.

"What was that about?" he said.

I was about to say "Nothing," in a vague and meaningless kind of way, when Pip had to go and pipe up.

"She wants to be slim!"

I could willingly have strangled him. But Dad just said, "Oh! Is that all?" Obviously not taking it seriously. Phew! Relief. It did set me thinking, though. I thought, what is the point of losing all this weight if I still have to go round pretending to be fat in front of Mum and Dad? I decided that as soon as I had reached my target body image I would REVEAL ALL. By then I wouldn't need to diet any more, so it wouldn't matter what they said. After all, not even Dad could *force* me to eat pizzas and pasta and Black Forest gateau.

One Saturday – the Saturday after our visit to Gran – Mrs Ambrose announced that we were going to do some improvisation. She said that we could improvise on our own or with a partner, whichever we preferred, and the theme was to be "travelling".

She said, "You might be on a bus or a train... you might be walking, driving a car... riding a horse. You might be on a plane, you might be at an airport. Anything that takes your fancy! All go away and think about it, then we'll see what you've come up with."

Normally, me and Saffy would have been partners, but today, for some reason, she didn't seem to want to work with me. She teamed up with Portia instead. I thought, *Huh! See if I care*. I'd do it by myself.

I was just going off into a corner to think of something when Ben Azariah (whose hair grew to a point like a turnip) poked me in the ribs and said,

AMBROSE

"Hey, Jenny! Want to do it together?"

I frowned. I'd had this feeling, just recently, that Ben was getting a bit interested in me. Last term I might have been flattered. I mean, what with being so fat and not having much confidence. But I wasn't fat any more! I wasn't yet *thin*, but at least I wasn't bursting out of my clothes. I felt that now I could pick and choose. And I wasn't going to choose a geeky turnip head!

"No," I said. "I don't think so."

Ben's face fell. Just for a moment I felt sorry for him and wished I'd been nicer, but then I hardened my heart. People like Zoë and Twinkle didn't worry about being nice. It didn't bother them if they hurt someone's feelings. And *they* didn't get partnered by geeky turnip heads. Zoë had gone into a huddle with Gareth. Now if *he* had asked me...

"I thought we could do something funny," said Ben.

I didn't want to do anything funny! I was sick of being a figure of fun. I wanted to be a figure of romance!

"Sorry," I said. "I've got other ideas."

I swished off towards my chosen corner. Ben came scuttling after me. Some people just won't take no for an answer.

"It doesn't have to be funny," he said. "It can be anything you like!"

Not with a turnip head. How could you be romantic with a boy whose hair grew to a point? It looked ridiculous! Why didn't he have it cut?

"I want to do something by myself," I said.

I worked out this scene where I was on the Eurostar, travelling to Paris to meet my boyfriend. I was on my mobile, talking to him. Talking the language of love. When all of a sudden—

"We're going to crash!"

It was just so dramatic, and so sad. I really didn't know what people found to laugh at. There is nothing remotely amusing about a train crash.

Mrs Ambrose (mopping her eyes) said, "Jenny, I'm sorry! That was such a good idea. You weren't quite able to carry it off... but it was a brave attempt. Well done!"

Saffy said later the reason people had laughed was that one minute I'd sounded "all syrupy and slurpy" and then it was "Help, help! We're going to die!"

I said, "You must have a very warped sense of humour if you think that's funny."

"It was you that was funny," said Saffy.

Angrily I said, "You're sick! You know that? You are *sick*!"

"You're the one that's sick," said Saffy.

We parted on very bad terms. I didn't like quarrelling with Saffy, but just lately she had been really starting to annoy me. What had come over her? Why did she have to be so picky all the time?

I decided that I would ignore Saffy and concentrate on what I was going to wear for my transformation scene. Everyone knew that I was going to do a transformation scene, because I had introduced it at the last rehearsal; but nobody knew what I was going to wear! Neither did I. *Yet.*

I lay awake in bed that night, mentally trying on everything in my wardrobe and rejecting it all as too big,

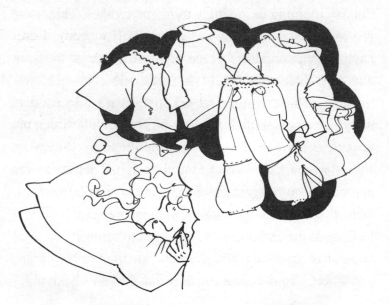

too baggy, too boring. I'd got to look glam! But not what Mum would call "tarted up". I wasn't aiming for a fairy-at-the-top-of-the-Christmas-tree effect. I wanted to look more natural and casual, like I hadn't made any special kind of effort; but at the same time I wanted everyone to think "*Wow*." A difficult combination!

I knew what I was going to wear as an old lady: an ancient raincoat of Mum's that came down to my feet, with a scarf tied under the chin and a pair of joke specs with a long rubbery nose that had what looked like a dribble at the end. Truly disgusting! I'd found the specs in the Party Shop last time I'd gone to the shopping centre with Saffy.

The old lady gear was easy. But I spent the whole of Sunday morning desperately trying on clothes. They were just as baggy and boring as I'd feared! How could I ever have worn such stuff? Huge pairs of elephant trousers, and tops like tents. Ugh! It made me feel sick, just thinking of how I used to be. I still wasn't thin enough, nowhere near. I could still pinch bits of flesh between my fingers, and my thighs still went flomp! like jellies when I sat down. I had a good long way to go before I even approached my target body image, but at least I could now walk down the street without feeling that everyone was looking at me and going, "That is some fat girl!"

In the end, squashed away at the back of the wardrobe, I found a denim skirt that I hadn't been able

to get into for absolutely ages.
I'd forgotten all about it. I pulled
it out and put it on, and oh, joy!
It fitted me. It was quite groovy,
I could see why I'd bought it. It
had little embroidered stars on
the pockets and a zip with a red tassel. And it was *short*!
Really no more than a strip, which if I'd worn it a few
months ago – if I could have got into it – would have
been positively indecent. I mean, who wants to see huge
jellyfish thighs slapping and banging against each other?
No wonder I'd hidden it at the back of the wardrobe!

What I needed now was a hot top to go with it, and
maybe a pair of boots. I decided to ask Dad. Not Mum!
I can wheedle almost anything out of Dad if I put my
mind to it. I waited till I came home from school on
Monday, when I could be sure of having him to myself.
Dad was making a cheese sauce to go with some
macaroni. He was eager for me to try it, so I obediently
took a spoonful over to the sink and said, "Yum yum!
That's good!" at the same time frantically running the
tap and washing the sauce down the plug hole, because
cheese is *extremely* fattening.

"Dad, do you think I could have a new top and a pair
of boots?" I said. "I need them, Dad! It's for this show
we're doing. We're going to film it on Saturday, and I've
got nothing to wear!"

That was all the wheedling I needed to do. Dad was so taken up with his sauce that I think he would have said yes to anything. He told me to go ahead and buy whatever I needed.

"When do you want it?"

I said, "Tomorrow?"

"I'll come and pick you up after school," said Dad.

I was so grateful that I gave him a big hug and took another spoonful of sauce to dump in the sink.

"Is it OK?" said Dad.

"Scrummy!" I said.

I knew that it had to be, because Dad's sauces always are; and in any case some had touched my lips so that I'd been *almost* tempted to eat it. But I knew that I mustn't! Just one mouthful would be enough to set me right back. It had to be all or nothing – which was what I explained to Saffy when I invited her to join me on my shopping trip and she started on at me yet again about not eating.

"I don't know how your mum and dad let you get away with it. My mum would go spare if I stopped eating!"

"Look, just *shut up*," I said. I'd invited her to come with us 'cos I thought she'd enjoy it, helping me choose what to buy. Now she was going and ruining it all! "Don't keep on," I said. "It's very bad manners." I mean, for goodness' sake! She was my *guest*.

Dad took us to Marshall's and sat himself down in a

chair while me and Saffy roamed about, examining stuff. I could buy anything I wanted! Skinny rib, halter neck. Anything! With Saffy's help I finally got a blue T-shirt with writing on it (*Funky Babe*, in gold letters) plus a pair of blue denim boots with zips and high heels. I thought that Mum's raincoat would cover the heels so that no one would know I was wearing funky footgear and not old lady shoes. I swore Saffy to silence.

"You're not to tell anyone! It's got to be a surprise."

Saffy said, "Yeah. OK." and waved a hand like all of a sudden she was bored.

"Now what's the matter?" I said.

"You!" said Saffy. "Always giving orders. You're so *bossy*."

Well! Bossy is just about the last thing I am. I said, "Look who's talking! I'm not the one that's been going on."

At that point we left the changing room area and found ourselves back out in the open. Just as well, or we might seriously have fallen out. With Dad there we couldn't very well go on slinging accusations at each other so we both simmered down and tried to make like there was nothing wrong. Dad wanted to take us upstairs to the restaurant to have tea. Once I would have thought this was a brilliant idea, since Marshall's is famous for its cream cakes and squidgy buns. Once I would have guzzled a whole plateful of them. Today I was thrown into panic at the mere thought of it.

"Don't you think we ought to get home?" I said.

"No, I think we ought to go and have some tea," said Dad.

"But Saffy's got to get home!" I said. "Her mum will be wondering where she is."

"No, she won't," said Saffy. "I rang her."

"So what do you reckon?" said Dad. Talking to Saffy. Not *me*. "Do you reckon we ought to go and have some tea?"

"Yes, please!" beamed Saffy.

Oh! She was *such* a traitor. I glared at her all the way up in the lift, but she resolutely took no notice and chattered brightly to Dad about absolutely nothing.

"Now, what shall we have?" said Dad, rubbing

his hands in delighted anticipation as he studied the menu, which I am here to tell you is a total nightmare of carbohydrates and calories. "Mm... raspberry pavlova! How about that?"

Dad had raspberry pavlova, Saffy had fudge cake, I had the plainest thing I could find, which was a packet of boring biscuits. But even boring biscuits are fattening! If I'd been on my own with Dad I could have slid them off the table, one by one, and hidden them in my school bag. I couldn't do that with Saffy there; she watched me the whole time. Well, actually, she watched the biscuits. She got, like, fixated on them. I just had this feeling that if I tried anything she would tell on me. So I had to force myself to eat them. It nearly made me gag! There is nothing worse than having to eat when you don't want to.

But anyway, ho ho to Saffy! The minute I got home I did my usual trick. I raced upstairs to the lavatory and stuck my fingers down my throat. I was distinctly annoyed with Saffy, though, because it is not at all pleasant sticking your fingers down your throat. For one thing it makes your throat sore, and for another it makes your stomach muscles ache with all the heaving and straining you have to do. But I couldn't afford to put on weight. I had to be thin for my transformation scene!

nine

Saturday came. And I was so excited! We all were, but me, I think, more than anyone. I put on my transformation outfit before leaving home, with Mum's raincoat over the top. I wanted it to stay a secret right until the very end! While everyone else was changing, I sat in a corner, huddled in my raincoat with all the buttons done up. People kept tweaking at it and going, "Come on! Let's see what you're wearing!" but I wouldn't let them.

"I bet *she* knows," said Twinkle, pointing at Saffy. "Tell, tell! What's she got on?"

"My lips are sealed," said Saffy, zipping a finger across her mouth.

One girl, Mitch Bosworth, even crawled on her hands and knees and tried to see underneath! The boys were nowhere near as interested. In fact, they didn't really seem to care what I had on underneath Mum's raincoat. I thought that was good, because then it would really come as a surprise.

Filming was due to start at two o'clock. I had always thought that making films was a very slo-o-o-w and laborious process. I'd read somewhere that it could take an entire day just to shoot one tiny little scene, but we filmed the whole of *Sob Story* in one afternoon. I suppose it wasn't quite the same as real movie-making. Two students came in from the local art college with a video camera and we just had one final run-through and then it was, like, *go for it*!

We did have one or two stops and starts. That silly girl Mitch Bosworth, for instance, got the giggles, and Saffy went and forgot her lines. Her *own* lines, that she had made up. She just, like, froze, and this trapped expression appeared on her face. It wasn't quite as bad as the angel disaster back in Juniors, when she had to be led off stage, sobbing; but I did think it went to show that she was not cut out to be an actress.

Zoë, on the other hand, far from forgetting her lines actually went and added to them! She launched into this mad speech that she had *never* done before. It went on and on, going absolutely nowhere, saying absolutely nothing, and the rest of us just standing around with our mouths sagging open, wondering what to do. It was Mark who saved the day. He just suddenly cut in over the top of her, and that shut her up. If it hadn't been for him, she might have gone rambling on for ever, and all the things that were supposed to happen – all the things that we had so carefully rehearsed – would no longer have made any sense. Mark pulled it all together again, and I thought that showed that he was a true pro. Whereas Zoë was nothing more than a silly selfish show-off, with no control over her own mouth.

I would like to report that I *rose to the occasion*, as the saying goes. I would like to tell how I rushed in to the rescue, and came to Mark's support as he struggled to get us back on track; but I didn't! I wasn't a true pro. I just stood around with the rest of them, gaping, and not knowing what to do. I felt like running at Zoë and strangling her, but in fact I took root, like a pot plant, and did nothing at all. I was just so worried that she might ruin my transformation scene! That was all I cared about. I had long since lost any interest in being a crotchety old woman who went round complaining. I didn't care if it did make people laugh. I didn't want people to laugh! I wanted them to gasp and go *wow*! I wanted to be glamorous! I wanted Gorgeous Gareth to be gobsmacked! I wanted Beautiful Mark to take notice of me... which I suppose must mean that I am no more cut out to be an actress than Saffy. *Sigh.*

Thanks to Mark and his quick thinking, we were able to move on. We got to the end. My big moment... ba-boom! Gasp. Wow!!!

Nobody actually did gasp or go "wow!" because by now they were all expecting it, and in any case it would have been unprofessional, but Zoë came up to me in the changing room afterwards and said, "Groovy gear, Granny!" Portia said I looked fab, and Mitch Bosworth told me that "That was a really neat idea... like  something out of panto." Only that stupid Twinkle had to go and upset me. She poked me in the ribs and said, "Come on, you can tell us now! You *have* been slimming, haven't you? Was it because of the book?"

Acting as hard as I could go, I said, "What book?" Like very cool and sophisticated.

"You know!" said Twink. "The one you were on the cover of... the one about the fat girl."

Oh! I was so hoping they wouldn't have seen it. But I might have known they would. I had to pretend not to care. I mean, there is such a thing as pride. (I may have said this before.) I gushed, "That photo was just so *awful*. They padded it out!"

"They what?" said Zoë.

"Padded it! You know, like they take away people's lines and wrinkles and double chins? They padded it out to make me look fat."

"How do they do that?" said Mitch.

I said, "I don't know *how* they do it, but that's what they did. And it looked so horrible!"

"I thought it looked like you," said Twinkle.

"Oh, thank you very much!" I said.

"So is that when you started slimming?" said Connie.

"I didn't!" I said. "It just happened!"

Saffy made this noise in the back of her throat. There was a pause.

"Well, anyway," said Portia, "you look fab in that gear!"

"If you could just manage to lose another few kilos," said Mitch, "you'd almost l—"

"*Don't!*" That was Saffy, suddenly coming to life. "Just stop encouraging her! She's lost as much as she needs to."

I wondered what Saffy's problem was. Could she be jealous? She'd always been the thin one! I'd been the fat one. Maybe she didn't like me being thin? How utterly pathetic!

I decided yet again that I would take no notice of Saffy. We were having a party to celebrate the end of term – and the end of filming – and I was going to enjoy myself! I went marching out of the changing room with Connnie and Portia, leaving Saffy on her own. I didn't think I liked her any more. She was jealous and mean and spiteful! She was trying to ruin my little moment of success. Just because she had gone and forgotten her lines!

The party was totally brilliant, in spite of Saffy skulking around like a big black cloud. I refused to let her spoil things. She was being mean as could be, and I wondered why I'd ever become friends with her.

As soon as we'd changed we all sat down to watch the video. I sat in the middle of the front row, next to Gareth! Saffy sat way back, where in my opinion she belonged. After all, she was little more than a glorified extra. She'd never bothered to develop her part. She'd never become a real character; just someone who occasionally spoke in a (very bad) American accent, saying things which she fondly believed to be American, such as "Gee" and "Shucks" and "Hot damn!" If she hadn't turned up, nobody would have missed her. Whereas if I hadn't turned up, we wouldn't have had a proper ending. So I deserved to sit in front, in the middle, next to gorgeous Gareth. It was like I'd earned the right. I wasn't a nobody any more. I was SOMEONE!

The video lasted three-quarters of an hour. The biggest parts were played by Zoë and Twinkle, and Mark and Gareth, but I was the next biggest! If it hadn't been for the cast being listed in alphabetical order, I would definitely have been number 5. It quite annoyed me that simply because of her surname beginning with B, Saffy was number 2. She didn't deserve it!

When we got to the transformation scene I held my breath thinking, "Please don't let me look fat!"

Well! I didn't look *too* fat. Some people might have said I didn't look fat at all, but once you start slimming you set these very high standards for yourself and know that you can't stop until you have shed every single gram of excess weight. I still had a long way to go. But maybe not everyone agreed with me because guess what? They all applauded!

It was Gareth who started it. When I threw off my old lady raincoat he cried, "Way to go!" and burst into loud clapping, and everyone joined in. Except, probably, Saffy. I bet *she* didn't. I bet she just sat there, all sour and scowling. But who cared about her?

For the party we had loads of nibbles. The two students from the art college stayed on and acted as DJs, and we all danced, including Mrs Ambrose. Even though she was old she could still move! It made me realise that when she was young she must have been really good. It made me think about being old, and how horrid it must be; but I only thought about it for a few seconds as Gareth asked me to dance. He danced with me and with Zoë, but not with anyone else. I didn't dance with anyone else, either. It was Gareth or nobody! I knew that Ben would have liked to dance with me. I could see him, out of the corner of my eye, hovering and quivering, but I kept pretending not to notice. If he wanted someone to dance with, he could dance with Saffy. Not me!

It was really difficult to avoid picking at the nibbles as everyone kept getting into little huddles round the table and people would have noticed if I hadn't eaten anything. Plus I didn't want to give that spiteful Saffy any chance to start up. So I picked and nibbled along with everyone else, thinking to myself that I would do my usual thing. Stick my fingers down my throat before I went to bed. I couldn't afford to start putting on weight again!

Mum came at eight o'clock to pick me up.

"How did it go?" she said. "Where's Saffy?"

We usually gave Saffy a lift, because although she lives in the same road it is quite a long walk.

"Where is she?" said Mum. "Isn't she coming with us?"

"I think she's going with someone else," I said.

"Oh. Well! All right." Mum sounded a bit surprised. She is used to me and Saffy going round like we are stuck together with Super Glue. "You're sure you don't want to wait for her?"

"No," I said. "Let's go! Oh, I must just say goodbye to Gareth."

He was standing with Zoë on the front steps. I sidled over and said, "Byee!" Gareth said, "Bye, Jen," and flapped a hand. Zoë looked at me as if I were dog dirt. She said, "See ya, Granny!" Jealous cow. She was as bad as Saffy.

As always on a Saturday, me and Mum, and Pip and Petal, went up to Giorgio's for dinner. I said that I had already eaten hugely at the party, but then Dad came out with a big plate of something creamy and gluggy that he had just invented.

"Pumpkin Pavlova!"

He said that he had made it specially for me, and he sat himself down at the table and insisted that I try some.

"Just a mouthful!"

Dad's mouthfuls are like elephant bites. Eeeenormous!

"Come on," he said. "Open up!"

Everyone in the restaurant was looking, and laughing, and I just didn't know how I could get out of it. I couldn't create a scene in the restaurant! Plus Dad had made it specially. So I reluctantly opened my mouth and let him spoon in the lovely disgusting gooey concoction, and oh, it was so scrummy! Before I knew it I'd let him feed me the whole plateful. Well, Mum tried a bit, but Petal and Pip turned their noses up and Dad knew better than to push them. I was the foodie!

The minute I'd eaten it, the very *minute* I'd eaten it, I felt myself balloon. I actually felt myself getting fat. I could have wept! How could I be so lacking in self-control? So *stupid*? All my hard work, ruined, in one mad moment of gluttony. I wanted to go running off to the loo right there and then, and stick my fingers down my throat, but it is too horrid in Giorgio's loo. I mean, it is quite clean – I *think*. But it is tiny and dark, like a cell. The floor is concrete and the walls are whitewashed, and the thought of kneeling down with my head in a toilet bowl where strangers had done things – ugh! I couldn't. I would have to wait, in my fatness, until I got home.

But then we stayed late at the restaurant because some people came in that Mum knew and they sat down at the table next to us and Mum started talking, and then Giorgio came over and *he* started talking, and by the time we arrived home I was just so tired!

Once I could have stayed up all night, practically, but these days I was almost never awake when Dad got back from work. I even, sometimes, felt myself falling asleep at school. And not just in maths classes! I'd even nodded off in the middle of English, while we were reading *Jane Eyre*.

There are those who might say that *Jane Eyre* is quite a boring book, being so long and so old-fashioned, but I don't think so. I was enjoying it! I hadn't wanted to go to sleep; it was just this thing that happened. It kept happening. It happened that night, when we got back from Giorgio's.

I thought, I'll just get undressed and lie down for a bit, and wait till Mum's watching telly, then I would go to the loo and offload all the foul fattening food that I had shovelled into myself. Instead, I fell asleep! When I woke up next morning, it was too late. The foul fattening food had all been digested and gone into my system. I heaved and heaved, but nothing came. And then Petal banged on the door and yelled, "What are you doing in there? I'm bursting!" and I had to give up.

I managed not to eat any breakfast, because Mum and Dad were having their Sunday morning lie-in, and Petal was getting ready to go somewhere, and I thought that Pip wouldn't notice if I shrank to a shadow. He probably wouldn't notice if we all shrank to shadows. The only thing he would notice would be if his computer blew up.

After not eating breakfast I scooted upstairs to the bathroom to weigh myself. *Disaster! Of cosmic proportions.* I had put on half a kilo! It depressed me so much I nearly went straight back downstairs to raid the fridge. I just managed to stop myself in time. I made this vow that I would starve for the whole of the rest of the week. I had to be strong-minded!

It is actually very boring, starving yourself. It is all right while you are obsessed, as every meal you don't eat is like a big victory. You feel all the fat dropping off and it gives you a tremendous sense of achievement. But you only need one little setback, like eating nibbles at the party, all those crisps and sausage rolls, and then gorging on Dad's new creation, and instead of being obsessed and triumphant you are simply struggling, every minute of the day, to resist the temptation of FOOD. All the joy goes out of life. Instead of looking forward (like normal people) to meal times and wondering what goodies you will eat, or gloating (like obsessive dieting people) over all the goodies you are *not* going to eat, you are just left with this grey boredom and mental torment. It is no fun at all. It is miserable!

To make matters worse, Saffy and me didn't seem to be on speaking terms. It was the last week of term, so school was quite relaxed. Normally, we would have enjoyed ourselves, but we were just too busy trying never to be in the same space. If Saffy sat at the back of the class, I would sit at the front. If she went out at breaktime, I would stay in. All week long we managed to avoid each other, but then on Friday we had this terrific bust-up. We were going out through the school gates.

I was on my own: Saffy was on her own. We had to walk up the same bit of road to the same bus stop and catch the same bus. Before I could stop myself I had blurted out, "Look, what exactly is your problem?"

Saffy tossed her head and said, "I don't have any

problem! You're the one with the problem. Going round starving yourself!"

"I happen to be on a *diet*," I said.

"Call that a diet?" said Saffy. "More like a death wish!"

I told her that she was obviously jealous, because of me being one of the stars of *Sob Story* and her going and forgetting her lines. Not that I actually said the word "star"; that would have been too vulgar. Too like Zoë. I think what I probably said was "one of the leads". I can't be sure, because at the time I was just so monstrously angry. Saffy was angry, too. She told me that I had become totally self-obsessed.

"All you ever think about is *you*." And then she said that I had made a complete idiot of myself at the party on Saturday. "Smooching up to Gareth like that! Going all goo-goo eyed. It was pathetic!"

I said, "I knew you were jealous!"

"Jealous of what?" screeched Saffy. All shrill and squeaky. She'd never done anything about her voice.

"Jealous of me and Gareth," I said.

Saffy made a scoffing noise. She said, "What's to be jealous of?"

"Because he danced with me," I said.

"Oh! Big deal," said Saffy. "Why should I care if he danced with you?"

I said, "Because he's one of the coolest boys there and *everyone* would like to dance with him!"

"Who says?" said Saffy.

"Well, if you'd rather dance with old Turnip Head," I said. "It seems a bit odd, considering you were the one that said we were going to drama school specially to meet gorgeous guys and the only one you can get is a turnip head!"

Saffy turned bright scarlet. She said, "Ever since you started on this stupid weight thing you've got meaner and meaner! You were as hateful as could be to poor Ben the other day. You really upset him!"

I said, "When did I upset him?"

"When he wanted you to be his partner and you wouldn't!"

I said, "No, because I wanted to do my own thing!"

"You wanted to show off," said Saffy crushingly. "And you just made yourself look stupid anyway. Utterly *pathetic*!"

We quarrelled all the way to the bus stop. We quarrelled while we waited for the bus. When the bus came, I went inside, Saffy went on top. When Saffy got out, four stops later, she didn't even look at me. She'd already told me, "I never want to speak to you again!" To which I had retorted, "Just as well, 'cos I don't want to speak to you!"

We had been best friends since the age of six. Now we hated each other.

These things happen.

ten

NOW IT'S FRIDAY evening. I'm up in my bedroom, having a fit of the glooms. I've quarrelled with Saffy and I'm utterly, totally depressed. I shouldn't be. I've lost all that weight and I've been a success and I've danced with gorgeous Gareth. But I am! I am just so-o-o depressed.

I haven't only quarrelled with Saffy, I've quarrelled with Mum and Dad as well. Quarrelling with Mum is not that unusual, but quarrelling with Dad is practically unheard of. Dad just isn't a quarrelling kind of person.

It was this afternoon when I quarrelled with Mum. I got home early from school (because of breaking up) to find that Mum was already here. Surprise, surprise!

When is Mum ever at home when I get back from school? I made the mistake of saying so. I said, "Surprise, surprise! Has the bottom dropped out of the housing market?"

I thought that was quite clever, actually. It was meant to be *funny*, but I think it must have come out as a bit – well, sarcastic maybe. I was still seething about Saffy and was just in this really vile mood.

Mum snapped, "I can do without that tone of voice, thank you very much!" I guess she was in a bit of a mood, too. She'd raced back home, all in a lather, to pick up some papers she needed. She said, "Some of us round here have appointments to keep!" pushing rudely past me as she did so. I said, "Well, gosh, don't let me stop you."

"Jenny, I'm warning you," said Mum. She paused at the door to point a threatening finger at me. "I've had just about enough of you recently. You'd better mend your manners, my girl, or you'll find yourself in trouble!"

With that she was gone, leaving me standing there, speechless. What had I done to deserve such treatment? Dad then came bowling in, wanting to know what was going on.

"Who's having a go at who?"

I said, "*She* is."

"She?" said Dad. "Are you referring to your mother?"

"Oh!" I said. "Is that who it was? I thought it was some stranger come into the house!"

"What exactly do you mean by that?" said Dad.

"That woman that was yelling at me," I said. "*My mother*. I didn't recognise her! Does she live here?"

Well! That was when Dad blew up. Unlike most chefs, who are extremely temperamental and will run at you with murder in their hearts and a carving knife in their hands on the least provocation, Dad is really a very amiable, easygoing person. But there is one thing he will not tolerate, and that is any criticism of Mum. He told me how Mum had worked her fingers to the bone, providing for us all, and said if I couldn't keep a civil tongue in my head I could go to my room. So I came up here and have been here ever since.

It's now six o'clock and Dad has gone off to work. Mum isn't yet back, Petal (I think) is in her room, Pip (I think) is in his room. I, of course, am in my room. Brooding and resentful. Why does everything always, *always* seem to go wrong for me? Why can't I be like Petal and Pip? Nothing ever goes wrong for them. Petal is beautiful, Petal is slim: Petal is popular, Petal has boyfriends. Pip is a genius; Mum spoils him. He's her favourite, without any doubt.

I am consumed with self-pity, and with vengeful envy of them both. My sister and my little brother. I think that Petal is probably slapping on the lip gloss, getting ready to go out with her latest gorge male, while the boy genius will be on his computer, lost somewhere out in cyberspace, doing whatever it is that techno freaks do. Not a cloud on either of their horizons!

I decide to go to the bathroom and weigh myself. I haven't done it for at least an hour. As I open my bedroom door I hear the sound of weeping. It's Petal! She's crumpled in a heap at the top of the stairs,  dramatically clutching her mobile phone to her bosom and sobbing her heart out. I cry, "Petal! What's wrong?" I drop to my knees beside her and she raises a tear-stained face and wails, "My life is over!"

I say, "Why? What's happened?"

She sobs that it's Andy (her latest gorge male). "He's going with another girl!"

I feel like pointing out that Andy is not the only gorge male in the world, that he is not the first gorge male she has been out with (I should think he must be at least number 3, or even 4) and that with her looks she can pick up another one "just like that!" But I don't, because I realise that at this moment in time it will be of no comfort. There can never be another male as gorge as Andy. If he has deserted Petal for someone else, then that is it. THE END. Life has nothing more to offer. All I can do is commiserate.

"Oh, Petal," I go, "I'm so sorry!"

Petal immediately bursts into renewed sobbing and begins to rock to and fro. While she is rocking, the door of Pip's bedroom is thrown open and Pip rushes out. He doesn't even look at me and Petal. He dives into the bathroom, and I hear a crash as the door of the bathroom cabinet flies back and bounces off the bathroom wall. Pip then reappears, with something in his hand. It looks like a bottle of aspirin. It *is* a bottle of aspirin!

"Pip," I say, "what are you doing?"

He looks at me, wild-eyed. He says that he is going to put himself out of his misery. He has tried smothering himself with a pillow, and now he is going to swallow aspirin.

"Go away, Pumpkin!" He pushes me to one side and makes a dive for his bedroom. "You can't stop me!"

But I can. I do! I grab hold of him and scream, "Are you out of your mind?"

Pip says no, he's not out
of his mind, he's a *failure*.
He is no longer top of his
class. He has come second.
Second! Shock, horror! The
shame of it is more than he
can bear. He is going to
take aspirin and put an end
to it all.

"Get out of my way! I'm serious!"

I'm serious, too. I can't believe it! A ten-year-old boy, wanting to put an end to it all? This is madness! Are we all neurotic wrecks in this family?

By now, Petal has come to her senses and taken note of what's happening. Between us, we march Pip into his bedroom and sit him down on his bed, one of us on either side. Sternly, Petal says, "What is this all about?"

Pip says again that he has lost first place (to a boy called Fur Ball Donnegan, or at least that is what it sounds like) and that his life is at an end. I say, "That makes three of us."

"You as well?" cries Petal. "What's your problem?"

What *is* my problem? I think about it. It's not just that I've fallen out with my best friend and got into trouble with Mum and Dad. I hate, hate, *hate* quarrelling with Saffy, I'm none too keen on having Mum get mad at me, and it's perfectly horrid to have upset Dad; but those are only symptoms. The real problem is that *I am not happy*.

I wonder to myself, was I happy before? When I was fat? A happy fatty! I think that on the whole I was. I was happy in my fatness! I wasn't happy in my thinness. I spent every waking hour worrying about food and whether I was eating too much. My life had become bounded by food! My stomach kept rumbling, I was permanently starving. I weighed myself up to a dozen times a day. My throat was sore from having fingers stuffed down it. My ribs ached from all the heaving I'd done. I was tired and cross and crotchety. I was *miserable*. But I did so want to be thin! I wanted to have cheekbones. And hip bones, and thigh bones, and just *bones*, generally.

Petal, meanwhile, is still waiting for an answer to her question: what is my problem? I give a deep sigh and say, "I thought being thin would make me happy!"

"Ye-e-e-es..." Petal considers me, her head to one side. "You *are* thin! You've lost weight!"

"That's because she hasn't been eating," said Pip.

What??? That shakes me! I wouldn't have thought he'd notice. Can it be that Pip sees more than we realise?

"When she does eat," he tells Petal, "she goes and sicks it up again. She's got that bullimer thing."

"That what?" says Petal.

"He means bulimia," I say. "Like Princess Di. It's what she had. But I haven't! I only sick up when I've been on a binge."

"That's what people do when they've got bullimer," says Pip.

How does he know???

"Pump, this is terrible!" cries Petal. "You could die!"

"Let's all die together," says Pip.

Petal rounds on him. Her tears, miraculously, have quite disappeared.

"We'll do no such thing!" she tells Pip. "Give me those aspirin!" She snatches them from him. "What's the matter with this family?"

In tones of morbid satisfaction I say, "We're dysfunctional."

"Well, it's got to stop," says Petal. "If Mum and Dad aren't around to keep an eye on us we'll just have to keep an eye on ourselves. In future, we'll all watch out for one another!"

And for starters she reads Pip this long lecture about exams not being the be-all and end-all, and how coming second in a class of twenty-two is hardly what any sane person would consider a disaster.

"Most people would think they'd done *well*!"

She says that Pip has had too many pressures put on him.

"The family isn't going to collapse if you only come second instead of top! You've got to stop trying to be a genius all the time and start behaving like a normal boy!"

Then she gets going on me. "From now on you are going to eat *properly*. Do you understand? You are not going to go on binges and then sick up. You are not going to go on binges *full stop*. When Dad pushes stuff at you, you just say *no*."

I wail that this is easier said than done. "He gets so upset!"

"So he gets upset! So what? It's better than you having *bulimia*!"

I admit that it is, but am doubtful whether I will have sufficient willpower to resist the temptation. Petal assures me that either she or Pip will always be there to watch over me. I say, "But you can't *always* be there!"

"We can for the holidays," said Petal. "By the time we go back to school you'll have developed all new habits and will be safe to be left on your own."

She gives me her promise. So does Pip. I begin to feel a bit more optimistic. I almost begin to feel *happy*. It is good to have a brother and sister to look after you! I tell Pip that in return me and Petal will help him behave more like a normal ten year old and less like a poor little boy genius with the weight of the world on his shoulders. And then I say, "But what about you?" looking rather hard at Petal.

Petal says I don't have to worry about her.

"I'll be so busy watching out for you and Pip I won't have time to think about myself. In any case," she adds, "I'm through with boys."

Oh, ho ho! She needn't think I believe *that*. Not for one moment!

When Mum gets home, about an hour later, we're all sitting in a row on the sofa, watching telly. A thing we

never do! Not all in a row. But it's like we suddenly have this need to stay close. Mum is in one of her brisk moods. I mean, brisker-even-than-usual moods. She cries, "Come on, you lot! Have you eaten? Let's go up the road, I can't be bothered to cook."

When does she ever? Cook, I mean.

"Well, come on!" Mum snaps off the television. She doesn't bother asking us what we're watching, or whether we want to go on watching. We probably don't – I'm not even sure we know what channel we're on. But that is Mum for you.

She hustles us out of the house. I exchange nervous glances with Petal. Well, my glance is nervous; Petal's is reassuring. She clamps her arm through mine and hisses, "Stand firm. We're with you!"

One of the waiters, Angelo (who is rather divine and has a bit of a thing about Petal) shows us to our usual table, the big round one in the corner. He then rushes off to the kitchen, where we hear him calling out to Dad.

"Eh! Franco!" (Dad's name in Italian.) "Your *famiglia* is here!"

Dad bustles out to see us, in his chef's apron and hat. Beaming, he says that he has just prepared some fresh pasta. One of his specials. I gulp. I adore Dad's pastas! Petal squeezes my hand.

"We'll just have salads," she says.

"What?" Dad looks from me to Petal in bewilderment. Obviously can't believe he's heard right. "Pumpkin's not having salad!"

"She is," says Petal. "We both are."

"Rubbish!" says Dad. "You can eat like a rabbit if you want. I'm not having Pumpkin infected by the bug!"

Earnestly, I say that it's not a bug. "It's healthy eating!"

It's a bit of a feeble protest, but I can't leave it all to Petal. Pip obviously feels the same, because he pipes up in support.

"Give us salad! We want salad!" And then he adds, "*Green.*"

"Green for him, mixed for us," says Petal.

Poor Dad is looking more and more confused. Even Mum seems to realise that something isn't quite as it should be. Little Podgy Plumpkin eating *salad*? Since when?

"Now, look," says Dad, "this is ridiculous! You can't just eat a few lettuce leaves, young lady. You'll have a nice plate of pasta, with salad on the side. Right?" And he turns away, as if the matter is now settled. Which, if it had been me on my own, with Petal making eyes at the waiters and Pip solving puzzles in his head, it probably would have been. I would never find the strength to hold out against Dad! But Petal has a lot of what I would call *backbone*. She definitely has a stubborn streak. Luckily for me!

"Dad," she says, "we're having salads. We don't want pasta."

Mum suddenly wakes up and rushes in to Dad's support. "Pasta's good for you!"

"Now and again," says Petal. "Not every day. Not in the quantities Dad dishes it up!"

"Not with that horrid red sauce," says Pip. "Ugh! *Glug*."

Not really very helpful, but at least he is trying.

"Maybe tomorrow," says Petal. "Tomorrow she can have pasta... but just a *small* helping."

Oh, dear! It is so embarrassing. I feel that everyone in the restaurant is watching us, waiting to see what will happen.

Somewhat crossly, Mum says to Petal, "You've become very bossy all of a sudden!"

"One of us has to be," says Petal.

Dad now decides that the time has come to make a stand.

"See here," he says, "I won't have you bullying your sister! You keep your food fads to yourself. Plumpkin's got more sense. She's a foodie, aren't you, poppet? Same as her dad!"

"Not any more," says Petal.

"No!" Pip bangs triumphantly on the table with the salt cellar. "Not any more! This is the start of a new regime!" He uses words like that. I suppose it's what comes of being a boy genius. "We're in charge now!"

"That's *right*," says Petal. "We've taken over."

"Taken over what?" says Mum.

"Well, Pump's intake, for one thing," says Petal. "We're monitoring it."

"What for?" Mum now seems every bit as bewildered as Dad. "She's not fat! In fact—" She narrows her eyes, studying me across the table. It's like she's seeing me for the first time. I want to dive beneath the red check tablecloth and hide. I feel like some kind of exhibit. "Have you lost weight?" says Mum.

Petal rolls her eyes. I mean, she hadn't noticed either, until today, but then she is only my sister. Pip, growing excited, bangs again with the salt cellar and cries, "Hooray! Mum gets a gold star!"

By now, you can see that both Mum·and Dad are

completely at a loss. They haven't the faintest idea what's going on! Petal, taking pity on them, says kindly that there's no need for them to worry.

"Just leave it to us. We're quite capable of looking after ourselves."

There's a silence; then Dad shakes his head, as if it's all just got too much, and goes trundling back to the kitchen to prepare one plate of pasta and three salads. Poor Dad! He can't work out what's hit him.

"There you are," says Petal. She nods at me, and pats my hand. "That was quite painless, wasn't it?"

Pip yells, "Kids unite!" and beats a tattoo with his knife and fork. Almost like a normal ten year old! Maybe there is hope for us all.

Mum is still studying me with this puzzled expression on her face, like she's trying to decide whether I've always looked like I do now, or whether her eyes are deceiving her.

"I hope you're not getting anorexic," she says.

"Mum, she is not getting anorexic," says Petal. "She *might* have been – but we've put a stop to it. Now she's going to eat sensibly. Aren't you?"

I nod, meekly.

"We're going to help her," says Petal.

Mum says, "But—" And then she stops, puts both hands on top of her head and closes her eyes. "All right," she says. "We're obviously going to have to talk."

"We can," says Petal, "if you like. There are certainly things to talk about."

"That," says Mum, "is becoming painfully clear."

Poor Mum! I've never seen her so... chastened, I think, is the word. Like when someone tells you off and you know that you've deserved it. Not that anyone has told Mum off! But she seems to be having guilt feelings, as if maybe she hasn't been a proper mum. I feel like telling her that it's not her fault. I like having a mum who's a high flyer! I'm proud of her! She can't be expected to go out every day doing an important job like hers *and* take notice of all the little banal things going on around her. How was she to know I wasn't eating properly? Or that Petal was tearing herself to pieces over ratlike Andy, and Pip wearing his brain to a frazzle?

Petal, kindly, says, "Don't worry! It'll all get sorted out."

Mum just gives her this look. The sort of look I imagine a plant might give before you brutally wrench it out of the earth.

"I don't know," she says, wearily. "I just don't know!"

It's Dad who brings out our salads. (Angelo's standing at the kitchen door, grinning.) Being Dad, of course, he can't just do plain *salad*. On mine and Petal's he's added new potatoes, hard-boiled eggs, slices of salami (on mine, not Petal's) and a sprinkling of parmesan. Humbly he asks if that is all right.

"Everything except the salami," says Petal. "She can't have that."

Dad opens his mouth to protest, but Petal cuts firmly over the top of him.

"You don't want to eat *animal*," she says. "Do you?"

I don't particularly want to eat animals; but I do like salami!

"*Do* you?" says Petal.

I go, "W—"

"Apart from anything else," says my remorseless sister, "such as for instance being disgusting and cruel and utterly repulsive, it is *chock full of fat*."

Pip goes, "Ugh!"

"Yes. Ugh!" says Petal.

Very meekly, Dad removes the salami from my plate and puts it into his mouth. Someone in the restaurant starts a round of applause. Angelo, over by the kitchen door, thrusts a clenched fist into the air. We watch, as Dad chews and swallows.

"Is that better?" he says.

"Yes! Thank you." Petal gives him one of her dazzling smiles (the ones she uses to get gorge males). "That is *healthy*!"

In weak tones, quite unlike her normal up-front self, Mum says, "Why do I get the feeling we're being ganged up against?"

"Because you are!" squeals Pip. "We're the Gang of Three and we are **YEW**nited!"

It's funny, we've never been that close, the three of us. We've all tended to do our own thing, go our separate ways. Now, suddenly, we're like a proper family. We're all going to pull together! It makes me feel warm and safe. I'm so glad I have a brother and sister! I haven't always been. There have been times when I would cheerfully have drowned them both in buckets of water. I expect there may be more times like that in the future. But just right now, I love them both to bits!

finale

WELL, I SUPPOSE really that I have reached the end, at least of this particular bit of my life. My struggle with fat!

The struggle goes on, except that I am not obsessed any more. I am trying very hard to *eat sensibly*. I am determined not to go back to being the human equivalent of a dustbin, and even Dad is beginning to accept that he cannot pile up my plate the way he used to.

We had this long, long talk, Mum and Dad, me and Petal and Pip. Mum said, "I have been such a bad mother!" Dad said, "No, I have!" which made us laugh. Mum then said, in all seriousness, that perhaps she should give up her job; at which we all shouted, "Mum! *No!*" Dad said maybe he should be the one to give up, but Mum said that wouldn't be fair. She said he'd already done his stint as a househusband. In the end we unanimously decided to continue just as we were, except that from now on we were all going to sit down, once a week, as a family, and *share*.

I must say that it has worked quite well. We all gather round the table and say what we've been doing. We "air our grievances" and ask if anyone has got any problems they want to discuss. We tell all the good things that have happened, and the bad things, too. I know more about Mum and Dad, and about Pip and Petal, than I ever did before!

Pip still works really hard, but I think, now, it's because he likes to rather than because he's under pressure. Petal still obsesses over boys; I can't see that ever changing! But just recently she seems to have settled down a bit. She's been going with the same one for almost three months, which is practically a record! I expect sooner or later they will break up, and then we shall have tears, and marathon wailing sessions on her moby, but at least she will be able to tell us about it and we can all sympathise.

As for me... it has not been easy, learning to eat properly. But everyone has helped, and I think that I can *almost* trust myself. I fear that I shall never be thin as a pin; I just don't seem to be made that way. I am doing my best to be happy with my body, because after all it is the only one I am ever likely to have. Not that it stops me yearning! I would still rather be slim, slender and stick-like than pudgy, podgy and plump. I would think almost anyone would. I don't care what people say! But you can't always be how you would like to be, and I have come to the conclusion that there is simply no point in making yourself miserable over it.

I once read that inside every fat person there is a thin person waiting to get out. But the way I see it, inside every short person there is probably a tall person. And everyone with thin hair would probably die to have thick hair. And those with long droopy faces would just love to have round cheeky faces. And those that are plain would give anything to be beautiful. But that is the way it goes.

As I said at the beginning, dream on!

Actually, I don't think I did say it, but I could have done. I could have said a lot of things, only it is a bit late now. I have told my story and it is time to finish.

Oh, I made up with Saffy, by the way. I couldn't stand not being friends with her! She said that she couldn't stand not being friends with me. I apologised for being so mean and cranky, Saffy apologised for not being more understanding. Now we are closer than ever!

We still go to drama classes because we really do enjoy them. We are working on a musical this term. I have discovered that I can sing! We are still in search of those hunky, sensitive boys... we still live in hope, though Mark has left to go to a full-time drama school in London and gorgeous Gareth has moved away. Boo hoo! Little Miss Twinkle and Zoë are still with us. *Unfortunately*. But they don't bug me any more, even though Zoë has taken to calling me Heffelump. I have learnt to ignore her. I just rise above it! A couple of new boys have started taking classes, and we think, me and Saffy, that they may turn out to be quite promising...

but actually, at the moment, I am sort of going out with Ben. He may look like a turnip, but he makes me laugh! We have lots of fun together.

I have decided, however, that I don't want a career in the movies after all. I don't think I am really cut out for it; I am not show-offy enough. What I am considering at the moment is entering one of the *caring* professions. Helping people. Saving the rainforests. That sort of thing. I think it is ignoble to just aim for fame or money. Of course, I may change my mind about this. I have changed it several times in the past! But those are my feelings at this moment in time.

Oh, and hey! Guess what? They have done another *Ellen* book and I am on the cover again! I'm dead proud of it. As soon as it hits the shops I'm going to be out there, making sure it can be seen. If that author doesn't end up rich as rich can be, it certainly won't be my fault!